3/7

The
Best People
in the World

The
Best People
in the World

a novel

JUSTIN TUSSING

HarperCollins*Publishers*

HarperCollins books may be purchased for educational, business, or sales promotional use. For information, please write: Special Markets Department, HarperCollins Publishers, 10 East 53rd Street, New York, NY 10022.

FIRST EDITION

Designed by Laura Kaeppel

Printed on acid-free paper

Section titles are taken from Dorothy Van Ghent's essay "On Don Quixote," which appears in her book *The English Novel: Form and Function*, Harper & Row, 1953.

Grateful acknowledgment is made to the editors of the *New Yorker*, where a part of this book appeared in slightly different form.

Library of Congress Cataloging-in-Publication Data
   Tussing, Justin.
      The best people in the world : a novel / Justin Tussing.—1st ed.
       p. cm.
     I. Title
   PS3620.U86B47 2006
   813'.6—dc22   2005046064

ISBN-10: 0-06-081533-7

ISBN-13: 978-0-06-081533-2

06 07 08 09 10 ❖/RRD 10 9 8 7 6 5 4 3 2 1

For my parents

The
Best People
in the World

The Highway

TWO MEN

*T*hey had a tiny rental car and accordion-style foldout maps.

They reached the house of the girl who cried glass tears. This was in Brazil. The cardinal met them in a dirt-floored front room. He had shaky, liver-spotted hands. He unfolded a handkerchief to show them the colorless gems. The older of the two men tucked the handkerchief into the breast pocket of his suit. He kissed the cardinal's hand. Where was the girl? She was resting in a back bedroom. They asked if they could see her.

She owned a plain, suffering face. Mirthless. Was she a virgin? the younger man asked. Unquestionably. And who had discovered the tears? The girl's mother. The men looked around. She was easy to spot, black brocade dress, wooden crucifix around her neck. The rosary would be somewhere nearby. There, on top of the dresser. Where was the husband? At work? Yes. The older man got down on his knees at the bedside of the girl.

"Have you had any visions?" he asked her.

There was a subtle shift. Yes, she'd had visions.

He asked her to tell him what she'd seen.

"She's been visited by the Holy Virgin twice," said the cardinal.

The older man raised a hand and the cardinal took a step backward.

"Twice, the Blessed Virgin," said the girl.

"Allow me," said the older man. He reached up and touched her eyes. Beside her tear ducts he found knots of hard scar tissue.

He leaned over and kissed her on her forehead. He stood up. "Please," he said, "I must be alone with the girl." The mother lingered, but when the younger man took her arm, she submitted. The older man shut the door so he was alone with the girl. He went back to her bedside. He stroked her arm.

"Do you know why I'm here?"

"You're here to see the miracle."

He nodded his head. "Please," he said. He got himself a chair and set it beside her. "When you are ready."

The girl watched him for an instant. Then, almost imperceptibly, her lids descended. It appeared as though she were having a dream. Her eyeballs traced shapes on the backs of her eyelids. A dew of sweat bloomed on the pale hairs of the girl's upper lip. Then an indelicate lump appeared in the corner of her right eye. With his thumbnail the older man coaxed it out, a piece of glass, as large as a kernel of corn.

"Thank you," said the man. "Can you do it again?"

It took a few minutes, but soon another piece of glass appeared. The old man gently harvested it.

The girl's scalp was damp. It shone beneath her hair.

"Can you do that a third time?"

The girl nodded her head. She bit her lip. It took a very long time. Snot ran from her nose. But, eventually, a third piece of glass was produced.

"Extraordinary," said the man. He handed the girl her tears. "You can put them back now."

She shook her head.

"Your mother put them in for you?"

The girl gave him the smallest signal. It was enough.

He made the cross on her forehead.

When he left the room, the girl was soaking herself with tears.

The two men got back in their car, the younger man behind the wheel.

"I had hope at first," said the younger man.

"Her face was much more convincing than the tears," said the older man. "It was not easy for me to dismiss it. It would be a great burden to be a saint. But what we thought we saw was just the shape of her shame." He rolled the window down, took the handkerchief from his pocket, and shook it outside the car.

They continued toward the capital.

I

1972

I looked up and saw my father standing at the foot of my bed. "Get up," said Fran. "Rise and shine." He went to the window and lifted the shade. He had a fragile-looking nose, which was my nose. "Do you have to wear your bangs so long?" Fran asked.

I walked over to the dresser, where the clothes I'd set out the night before waited on the red enamel top.

"Now we're talking," said Fran. "Now we're making some progress."

"Are you going to do this every day?" I asked.

"*Every* day? Come on. Be fair."

I got my clothes on.

Fran said, "Say good-bye to your mother."

I poked my head in their darkened bedroom. Mary turned toward me, but couldn't force her eyes to open. "Have fun," she said.

"I wish I was still mowing lawns," I said.

Fran wouldn't permit me to duck into the bathroom. They had a bathroom where we were headed.

A moment later I found myself behind the wheel of my father's cornmeal yellow Buick. It was important I know how to drive when tired, Fran believed. I backed us down the driveway and into the road. "You didn't look first," said Fran. He was right. "Well, forget it.

Look next time." Fran didn't want the little things to impede the larger mission. He was in the process of introducing me to something momentous. The driving lesson was distinct from the mission. This was a Monday morning late in June. We were on our way to work. Having just completed my sophomore year of high school, I was to begin training for a summer job as a subsystem technician at Western Kentucky State Power. Fran worked as an operations comptroller at the plant. Neither of us had a clue what a subsystem technician did. What we knew was that I would be compensated at a rate slightly below what I had received the summer before. But mowing lawns was not a job. Getting a tan was not a job. Being somewhere on time, doing what was expected of you, not loafing, that was a job.

"Remember," said Fran, "a job is a privilege, not a right. You have to show up every day and do your best and not settle for good enough. Good enough is a trap."

Fran would make the same before dawn drive through seventeen more summers, but never again with me. And then one morning he wouldn't get up and I would drive all day, arriving just after dusk, to find Mary shivering on the front steps. She would ask me if I remembered the summer Fran and I went to work together.

"Are you jazzed?" asked Fran.

I said, "I'm jazzed."

"Yeah, you are."

A rabbit dashed across the road. Fran grabbed my arm to ensure I stayed my course. Somehow the animal avoided being killed. Paducah, Kentucky, had a rabbit problem. It was sort of picturesque, brown bunnies huddling beneath each shrub. But they also injected a sense of the tragic into the everyday. You were constantly coming across their flattened corpses, crows nagging at the broken bodies. The summer before, I had run over a nest of baby bunnies with a mower. It was completely depressing. Fran insisted the floodwall made the rabbit problem worse.

People were always finding fault with the Army Corps of Engineers. Like how our river town didn't have a river view anymore. The wall was so monotonous, it was almost Soviet. But the thing that really drove people crazy was that the Ohio River neglected to test it. The wall stood poised, an army without an opposition.

Fran had me turn onto Pemberton Street, which passed through the Pemberton Street Sally Port—"sally port" was the name the engineers gave to the gaps in the wall; if the river ever came up, reinforced steel plates could be slid into the gaps and the town made watertight. Outside of town I had to pay attention because Pemberton ran on top of a levee. Tire scars in the slope marked where daydreamers had left the road.

Fran was looking toward the river. "Pull over," he said.

It was mostly scrubland; huddled stands of cottonwood and ash made islands on the floodplain.

"You see that?" He rolled his window down so I could follow his pointing finger.

In the middle of acres of nowhere bottomland stood a little shack, an outpost in the slough grass. It was a wonder he saw the place at all. The harder you looked at it, the less evident it became. Like a shadow, it was more about its edges than its substance.

"The king of the river rats is back," said Fran.

A river rat was an expression used to denote a person with low prospects. There were river-rat neighborhoods and river-rat taverns. If someone annoyed him, Fran might say, "You know, that river rat so-and-so."

But I'd never heard of the king of the river rats. I thought maybe Fran was pulling my leg.

"That's how I think of him—Shiloh Tanager."

I didn't know Shiloh, but I knew about him. Supposedly, as a baby, he'd been abandoned on the limestone steps of the police station. He'd run away from orphanages and foster parents and everybody else. People claimed he could make a radio from a battery and a twist of wire. He'd been in knife fights and shovel fights. Using block and tackle, he recovered a Civil War cannon from the river's muddy banks. The public schools served as a reliquary for stories about Shiloh Tanager. He had been known to ride railcars, associate with criminals, elude the police. But it had been a couple of years since anyone had seen him. Some people said he was dead. There was a persistent rumor about some kid who knew some kid who had come across his stinking bones.

"How do you know it's his place?"

Fran turned to me. "Can you think of someone else who'd want to live out here?"

From our perspective it was impossible to know if anyone was living there at all.

"Anyway, it's about dead smack center where his old place used to be," said Fran. "Time's up. We can't spend the day gawking. We're workingmen."

I steered the car back onto the road. "I hope I like my job," I said. Fran didn't have anything to add.

In the distance I could make out the solitary smokestack of the power plant. A red strobe warded off airplanes.

2

Sump

Formerly I'd considered electricity an essentially noble force. As a subsystems technician I learned it was inseparable from the diesel stink of the frontloaders racing to relocate mountains of coal, from the buzzing of the transformers, from the turbine's pervasive whirr.

For the protection of the workers all catwalks and access tunnels were shielded with a pliable steel mesh. In the building's lower levels a constant humidity was quickly turning the mesh into rust. Orange-red dust settled on everything; if I brushed against a handrail, it painted a mark on the chambray jumpsuits the plant provided me with. The other thing the plant provided were rubber gauntlet gloves. The gloves were supposed to prevent you from inadvertently becoming an electrical pathway, but everyone wore them looped over the belt of their jumpsuits.

There were twenty-six critical measurements I needed to record hourly on a clipboard. Another dozen non-critical indicators needed to be confirmed at the beginning and end of every shift. The route I followed had been carefully calibrated to eat up exactly one hour. But I discovered that by jogging, I could take all my measurements in under forty minutes, leaving twenty minutes unaccounted for.

Off the main service passage, down three stairs and through a heavy door, I discovered a sunken room. In the center of the room, three identical motors lined up, side by side, beside a low guardrail. On the other side of the guardrail, the floor fell away. The motors looked like cattle coming to a trough to drink. From each engine a single pipe descended into the darkness. This was the sump room. Between my rounds, I would lie down amid the machines and take a catnap. I would prop my feet on the rail and close my eyes. The vegetable heat of the place and the dull humming of the machinery lulled me to sleep. When I woke up I'd jog about the building taking another set of readings. Sometimes I'd sleep for fifteen minutes and sometimes I'd drop off for an hour. And, because it was the design of things that each technician worked independently of every other, there wasn't much chance that someone would stumble across me.

Of course, I started thinking about girls. Living in close quarters with my parents and Pawpaw, there wasn't much use dwelling on girls, but here I was unobserved. And since I had already made peace with sleeping on the job, it wasn't a big step to more unprofessional behavior.

Western Kentucky State Power wanted me to walk the corridors, double-check my readings, and keep my eyes open. I was supposed to keep to my assigned area and keep my hands off things unless they were things that I was supposed to put my hands on. This was for my safety. And there I was leaning against the railing with my eyes closed and sometimes my knees would buckle and, for a moment, it would seem like I was going to pitch forward into that black pit.

On a blistering day in August, as Fran piloted us across the levee, he said, "Don't be embarrassed, but you're going to have to start using some sort of deodorant." He turned his head toward me.

Something in his voice told me he'd been putting off this conversation for a while.

"A spray or a stick. Not the roll on. They pull the hairs."

I blushed with the shame that came from smelling bad and from all the time I'd been spending in the sump room.

"It comes in different scents, pine, mint, forest, ocean, musk. Just pick something out. It doesn't matter which. Or have your mother choose. She can probably tell you what smells best from a woman's point of view."

I was relieved when he finally stopped talking.

"And don't think you can start skipping showers. It's no substitute for soap and water."

After all the time I spent in the sump room meditating on girls, I started to believe in the existence of real girls. Since they weren't going to show up at my parents' house, I thought I'd go looking for them. Every chance I got I'd wander down to the brick plaza in front of town hall. The place was practically designed for girls, with rose-bushes and hydrangeas and birds singing in trees that looked like lollipops. There were benches everywhere, but hardly ever any people. The floodwall prevented the pleasant breezes that kicked off the river and which had been the town's birthright. Since you couldn't watch the river anymore, the only thing to look at was the vintage Mercury patrol car parked directly across from the police station. The hulking cruiser crouched over the bricks, all gleaming chrome and bottomless black paint.

On an overcast August day, I watched dark polka dots appear on the bricks. The rain wasn't enough to send me home. When someone finally appeared, it was a guy. I watched his hunched figure cutting across the plaza. Tucked beneath one arm he carried an object wrapped in a bedsheet and secured with a length of twine. His head was bent over, maybe to keep the rain off his face. I expected him to pass me by, like everyone else, the pigeon feeders and the kids on bicycles and these women with their babies in strollers who would give me a wide berth. Instead of walking past, this guy stopped in front of me and stared, as if we had some history and he was only waiting for me to realize it. I didn't feel like meeting his eyes. Instead I looked at his shoes. They were the weirdest shoes I'd ever seen; they looked as though he'd stolen them from a museum. They appeared to be made of straw. Maybe he'd made them himself.

He asked a question. "Are you thinking about turning yourself in?"

"Into what?"

He jabbed his thumb over his shoulder, toward the police station.

"What would I turn myself in for?"

The stranger took his place beside me. He spread his arms, resting them on the back of the bench.

I leaned forward, then left and right, as though I expected someone.

"I like to keep an eye on them," offered the stranger.

"You like to keep your eyes on who?"

"The Man."

"What's wrong with your shoes?" I asked.

He looked down at his feet. "There's nothing wrong with them; they're huaraches."

"Huaraches?"

"Mexican Indians make them. Theirs is the oldest civilization in North America."

The stranger had a chubby face.

"They look crazy," I said.

"Are you a philosopher?"

"Am *I* a philosopher?"

"That's what I'm asking you." Pink wrinkles lined his forehead. I saw that what I'd thought of as a tan was, instead, a layer of dirt.

"I'm a student."

"What do you study?"

"I don't study anything. I'm in high school."

"Classic."

"I have to go," I said. I stood up and turned toward the police station; it seemed less likely that he would bother me if I headed that way.

"Hey," he said. He reached out his hand so we could shake.

Behind his squinted, fleshy lids, his eyes were a fragile blue.

He refused to let go of my hand. "Do you know who I am?"

I looked at him hard, but, instead of figuring out who he was, I was trying to tell him who I was—namely, not the kind of person he wanted to mess with. I shook my head.

He turned his palm up. "Think for a second?" His thumb prevented me from retrieving my hand.

"Are you a musician?" He looked like he could own a guitar.

He shook his head. His hair was curly and burned butter brown. "I don't know."

He pointed a forefinger at my head and cocked the thumb. "Bang."

"What's that mean?"

"Kill the cop in your head."

"Okay," I said.

He let go of my hand. "You into transcendental meditation?"

I had no idea how to answer. I started to walk away.

"Do you believe in the existence of superintelligent agents of progress?"

"Do you?" I asked.

His hands flew apart, as though I'd asked him to weigh two equal things.

I'd gone about ten yards when something dawned on me. I turned around. My inquisitor had poked a finger inside his shoe and was scratching his instep.

"You're Shiloh Tanager."

The stranger perked up. "In the flesh."

I felt like the detective who triumphantly announces that he's alone with the killer.

"You going to tell me your name?"

I shook my head.

"What were you doing down here anyway? Someone stand you up?"

"I just came here to think."

"Any luck?"

There was nothing hostile in the way he asked his questions. He sounded like someone who'd engaged hundreds of strangers in pointless, circling conversations. I felt like I was doing a poor job of holding up my end of things.

"Fran and I noticed your house was standing again, but we didn't know if you were living there."

"Who's Fran?"

"Fran's my father." I walked about halfway back to where he sat.

Shiloh reached up to scratch the crown of his head. Next he scratched the back of his arms. It occurred to me that he might have fleas.

"Is Fran a cop?"

"He works at Western Kentucky State Power."

"You think he'd let me poke around that place? I could cause some honest trouble in a joint like that."

I said, "It'd be pretty hard to mess things up. Everything is automated."

"What do you imagine would happen if I sprinkled iron filings on the right spot?"

"Probably nothing."

"WHAMM-O! Blackout. The whole state goes dark."

"I don't think iron filings would do that. Besides, they'd just call one of the other power stations and someone would flip a switch and that would be it."

"Has your dad ever let you inside the plant?"

"I work there."

"Then I've got a question for you. Does nepotism ensure society or undermine it?"

I just looked at him.

"You know what nepotism is, right? People giving jobs to their relatives. That's nepotism."

I was pretty certain I hated him. "People thought you were dead."

"No, I wasn't dead. I was traveling." Either a raindrop fell on his face or he winked at me.

But who would return to a falling-down shed on the bank of a boring river?

"Abracadabra," he said.

"What does that mean?"

He looked up at the sky. "Time for me to disappear."

*   *   *

I couldn't remember to look when I backed down the driveway. Fran expected I'd kill the paperboy or some insomniac. Sometimes, cruising along the levee, we'd see light leaking through the wall of Shiloh's house, like light leaks through your hand if you cup the end of a flashlight. Then we arrived at the plant, where Fran and I went our separate ways.

On my last day, all of the people I hadn't gotten to know crowded into the break room to help eat a cake that smelled like electricity. Someone took a photo of me standing next to Fran. I got the feeling everyone else was as bored as me.

Driving home, Fran started talking very enthusiastically about the significance of school. "Are you going to tear it up this year?" he asked. He kept saying "tear it up" like it was some code we'd agreed on. I felt myself falling for it a little bit. "Yeah, I do think I'm going to tear it up." "That's the spirit. Take no prisoners," he said. I said, "I'm going to show them who's boss."

We were talking like that when we got home. Mary thought we were a couple of lunatics.

3
The Laser Age

These days high schools look like pastel-hued laboratories. Sunshine pours down through skylights while vents in the walls pump in ionized air. At the back of the room you find a newspaper archive or else a place where the kids watch through a Plexiglas window as bees secrete royal jelly. There's no sense of curriculum. Everyone is too busy building their résumés. Instead of study halls the students hold internships. The teachers don't teach—they just sit at the front of the class and laugh at the jokes the kids make. If the kids ask a question, then the teacher responds with another question.

In 1972 my peers and I climbed the cast-concrete stairs to Annex 5—"annex" was the word the school district used for the plain, white trailers stranded on the blacktop. On a humid September

morning, thirty-five of us, heat anesthetized and yawny, busied ourselves scratching our names into the desktops with house keys and
pen knives and the resilient points of our ballpoint pens. Someone
had drawn a pair of boobs on the ceiling with the soot from a lighter.

"Mahey, why are you so pale? You look like a troglodyte." Ray
Moschi's vocabulary was all science fiction. He filled graph-paper
notebooks with sketches of rocket prototypes and babes with swords.

I was supposed to say, "Because I was under your mother all
summer." Instead I said, "I was making electricity."

"So was I," said Moschi, "with your mother." He stood up and
pumped his hips. Then, pretending his dick was a stick shift, he raced
around the desks, changing gears. *"Vroom vroom vrooooooom vrooooomm."*

The door snapped open and a confused-looking girl came in. She
wore a brown tweed skirt, a gauzy shawl folded across her shoulders.
She carried too many books and the wrong sort of bag. We recognized her as a stranger.

"How'd you find this place?" she asked.

While Moschi continued abusing his gearbox, the girl made the
really unexplainable mistake of choosing the wrong desk. Some of us
considered correcting her, while the rest of us reached the obvious
conclusion. Moschi was going up and down the aisles making burn-
out sounds. She asked him his name.

Moschi's face lit up; he put his dick into reverse and sidled up
beside her. "Raymond," he said, which was not how any of us thought
of him.

At the dawn of a new school year you were allowed to pretend
that you were not yourself. Something might have happened over the
summer. You hoped that you had become smarter or more attractive.
It was a small hope, but it was significant. It wasn't a secret. Your
mother took you out and bought you a new outfit so that the teachers
wouldn't recognize that familiar disappointment you'd been the year
before. But we were juniors now. We were running out of time for
reinvention. No one really expected our caterpillar selves to emerge as
butterflies. We were all second-tier students. That was why we'd been
enrolled in the History of Technology instead of Ancient History.

HisTech owed its origin to an often-observed phenomenon: those same students who struggle with the standard curriculum have no trouble reboring V-8 engines.

The girl opened one of her notebooks and turned a page. "Raymond Moschi," she said, making a mark in her book. "Do me a favor, Raymond. Race back to the office and see if you can find us some chalk and an eraser."

The class burst apart like thunder, our delight reverberating inside the melamine walls.

The teacher made a show of placing her shawl over the chair back, organizing her desk, slotting folders into desk drawers, sharpening pencils, all the while not looking at us looking at her. When Ray came back with the chalk and eraser, she sent him out for a fan. Then she walked to the front and wrote her name on the chalkboard. I wrote "Alice Lowe" on the palm of my hand. Miss Lowe looked at me, looked at my hand, and told me to add "notebook" so I'd remember to get one.

Miss Lowe stood before the class, our book propped against her hip, or she sat on her desk and placed the book beside her—tucking her wheat gold hair behind her ear whenever it fell across her face. Right off the bat we knew nothing, but she taught us how things put into our brains could be retrieved with some degree of reliability.

Everything we took out of the class was a testament to her will. She wasn't a graceful teacher; her lessons didn't unfold before us. She taught like someone might dig a ditch. She spaded the soil of our ignorance and pitched it out. There was something single-minded about it. She would pause to dab at her forehead with a blue bandanna. I'd never known a woman to perspire so much. We had no idea she'd just earned her teaching certificate.

Miss Lowe asked us to interpret, infer, and extrapolate. She encouraged us to deduce. She reminded us to consider the big picture. She said we should remember that everything inside the book is just a depiction of everything outside the book. What did that mean?

Well, she said, what is the significance of the wall that rings this town? Significance? What does it tell you? That the river would flood sometimes. Yes, that the river would flood sometimes. Not recently, added Chrissy Ledew. Chrissy liked to sit at the back of the class and read magazines like *Hair Today!* and *Bangs.*

I wanted to reinvent myself as a student, not for me, or for Fran and Mary, but because of this woman with her thick fingers and too-small nose. I was trying to harness my powers of perception. And so I looked at what was close at hand. The covers of each of my textbooks depicted a variation on the same theme—a laser being pulled apart by a prism or rebounding within the edges of the book. A bigger picture of the world took form in my head. I asked Miss Lowe, "Right now, is this the Laser Age?"

"Is what the Laser Age?"

"This," I said. "Now."

She handed the question over to the class. "Does anyone know the name for the present age?"

Someone said, "Stadium-Rock-and-Roll Age."

"What about jet planes?" asked a classmate.

"Maybe the first thing we ought to do," said Miss Lowe, "is consider what stone, bronze, and iron have in common?"

"They're metal," came a voice from the back of the room.

All you need to know about that class is that not one of us had the confidence to question that statement.

"You make things out of them," I said.

"And what kinds of things?" prompted Miss Lowe.

The class raced to list all the many things that could be formed from stone, bronze, and iron.

"And what could you call those things?" Miss Lowe asked.

"Tools," said Ray Moschi.

"Right. So one thing to consider is what we make tools out of today."

"Steel," shouted one of the shop-class savants.

"It's the Nylon Age," said Chrissy.

Someone voiced the group's concern: "Is this a trick question?" We felt very vulnerable to trick questions.

"I don't see how," said Miss Lowe.

And then the bell shot us into the hall.

Later, Ray told Chrissy that she could be the queen of the Lumber Age, because she gave him a woody.

4
Flood

The congested halls between bells, the stoned kids, the bullies and the scared-o's, the kids from the marching band with their heavy plastic cases. The cymbal crash of locker doors and the zip spin of combination locks. Everywhere I turned, girls—in jersey dresses and faded dungarees. But they were the wrong girls somehow. We honed our peripheral vision out of necessity. We existed in a state of hyper-awareness and we had dull, thoughtless faces.

I stopped when I heard my name. People flowed around me. Miss Lowe stood at the threshold to the teachers' lounge. "Someone looks pensive," she said. She looked at me with an intensity that made me sick. Her pea-colored sweater, her suede boots, the point of her chin, her pale pink gums.

I wanted to appear as though I had a lot on my mind, but I was afraid I'd overdone it. I wanted to convey the impression of being thoughtful. I didn't want to look like one of those kids who moved their lips when they read.

"I was spacing out."

We were close enough that I could smell the banana in her shampoo.

She looked at me. I looked at my shoes. One of the laces had come undone. I knelt down. All of a sudden I was sprawled in the hall.

"Wipeout," someone said.

The other kids stepped over me. Girls in short denim skirts stepped over me. I was invisible to them.

Miss Lowe gave me her hand. She leaned back and pulled me to my feet.

"Thought I lost you for a second."

I couldn't make up my mind about the color of her eyes. I hung my head. "I was pushed."

"I'll bet it was an accident."

"I don't believe in accidents."

Already the current was abating; kids slipped through doors.

"No?"

Miss Lowe inspired me to have opinions. I said, "Some people see everything as an accident. They're always asking how this or that happened, and they always come up with the idea of an accident. My mother claims my father is accident prone, but nothing bad ever happens to him. Meanwhile, her first husband was killed when a type of deer they have in Germany jumped off an overpass and through the windshield of their car."

"How awful."

"If he'd swerved the deer could have killed my mother, then I wouldn't be here."

"Well," she said, like adults will when confronted by a kid's stupidity. But after a moment she added, "I'd miss you."

Miss Lowe, I thought, who have you mistaken me for? You are my teacher, but there is, also, some ambiguity. I hope that I have a tragic accident or that I do something foolishly brave to confirm what you are thinking. And I knew that there was no way that she was thinking what I was thinking. She had to have some higher purpose in mind. The three freckles on her neck formed a line that pointed to her collarbone.

"It would be a tragedy," I said. "I suppose."

In class she seemed so self-possessed, as if she had weighed and measured everything we might possibly say. But now a quick sound escaped her, a laugh. I don't know if I'd heard her laugh before. I wanted to hear that happy sound again. If she'd laughed when I'd fallen down, I could have fallen again, but she laughed at what I'd said and I was less certain of my ability to reproduce that.

"Then again, if I weren't alive my grandfather could stop sleeping on the porch and move into my room. Of course, he wouldn't be my grandfather, either."

One of the science teachers walked behind Miss Lowe to see which brainless fool she was talking to. He stopped to tap on the foggy glass of a terrarium. Then he let his eyes drift down Miss Lowe's back.

"Your grandfather sleeps on the porch?"

"He's an iconoclast. Which means . . . well, I guess you know what it means. He spent his life's savings trying to contact my grandmother."

"Where is she?"

"She's dead. He tried to contact her with a psychic."

The hall was empty, but for the two of us. I had to be somewhere, certainly.

Miss Lowe stepped toward me, pulling the door closed behind her. She reached out and brushed a fingernail across the shoulder of my shirt. "Dust," she said.

I said, "Miss Lowe, do you think that I could meet you some time at a neutral location?" I had to make it ridiculous to say it at all.

"By neutral, I presume you mean somewhere away from school."

"And, obviously, not a bar or a library, though a library would be pretty neutral for me."

"We couldn't talk in a library." She might have been looking at my lips.

"You would really meet me at a diner?"

She closed her eyes for a second. She seemed to be working out something complicated. Maybe she was thinking about aqueducts or Pythagoras. I was afraid she was going to say something, like, I'm very disappointed in you. Sometimes in class this look would come over her as if, despite our chirping questions and mouth breathing, she found herself alone in the room. Now her lips started to make this shape, this spreading, opening shape. She said, "Okay."

From my parents' house it was about a fifteen-minute walk to the river. If you knew where to look, you could find the old limestone footers that were all that was left of the bridge my grandfather had helped build.

I walked along the river's sun-cracked bank. Wavelets licked at the shore, at the junk that managed to climb out of the water. Pieces of nylon rope harnessed rafts of rotting saw grass. Everywhere you saw those white peas, like the eyes of poached fish, the broken Styrofoam from beer coolers, and those brittle life-preserver rings they sold in drugstores. The senseless meanderings of raccoons and birds were preserved in the mud like an ancient language. The water stunk, sometimes of sewage, sometimes of kerosene. The same stuff ran through the pipes in my parents' house. The greatest surprise in my life was coming across odorless water.

When I thought I'd gone far enough along the relatively clear and open riverbank, I stumbled my way through the brambles and saw grass, knowing full well I'd likely scare up yellow jackets and mud daubers and possibly cottonmouths.

The night before, we were gathered in the kitchen. Mary rolled chicken breasts in coconut flakes. As we watched, she plopped them into a pan of hot oil.

"I saw Shiloh finally," Fran said, walking over to tug on the refrigerator door. "He's put on some weight."

"When did he get back in town?" asked Mary. When the coconut turned brown, she fished the chicken pieces out of the oil. She set the meat on a wire rack to drain.

"Fran spotted his place this summer," I said.

"Where'd you see him?" asked Pawpaw.

"He was down by the plant."

"He was probably collecting parts for his paranoia boxes." Pawpaw raised his hands to indicate a shoebox-size device. "He claims they monitor a secret radio frequency our government plans to use in the event of a nuclear catastrophe."

Mary shivered. "They don't work do they?" She found doubt irresistible.

"Of course not," Fran said, reaching over to pat her forearm. "It's just a bunch of wire and a little blinking light. That's people for you. They don't know science from nonsense."

"I don't suppose anyone is going to get it in their heads to run him off again."

"People tried to run him off?" I asked.

"Some fools tried to burn his place down," said Pawpaw, "but the place wouldn't burn. It was too damp."

"While they were dicking around, he snuck up behind them with an axe handle." Fran nodded his head. "What they should have done is left it to the cops. They could bust him for vagrancy. That place of his is an illegal encampment."

"I'm not crazy about vagrancy laws," Pawpaw said.

"Your grandfather is an extremely moral person," Fran told me. "That's his privilege for surviving a war. He's got ideals. Most people only have principles."

"I just don't see how you can hold a person liable for their luck," explained Pawpaw.

I didn't understand how my parents could know so much about a ghost.

I was unsticking myself from the puckerbrush when I spotted the dark little home. It looked ancient and abandoned. The walls were swollen particle board, the roof, a sheet of tin held in place with round stones. Tufts of yellow insulation shivered to register a breeze. I saw a figure walk out, shirtless and wearing canvas pants. He looked like he'd just woken from a nap, sort of unsteady. The muscles of his shoulders were stacked like rocks, but he was soft around the middle. He walked about twenty feet from the house, stopped, tilted his head back, and pissed in the grass.

I turned around and started to pick my way back to the river.

"Hey," he called out to me.

I froze. If I'd run I don't think he could have done a thing about it.

"You found me," he said.

"I wasn't looking for you."

"Bullshit." It looked like someone had slapped his chest with a wide brush of black paint.

"You really live in there?" I asked, pointing at his house. The front door had scraped clear a half-moon of dark earth. The house was the losing turn in a game of pickup sticks.

"You want to see inside?"

I shook my head.

"Suit yourself."

He made a visor with his hand and scanned the panorama.

"You come all the way out here by yourself?"

I said, "It's a free world."

"Oh, man," he said, "I wish you hadn't told me. I wanted to be surprised when I found out."

There wasn't much out there to distract us from each other.

"Want to see something?"

I didn't give him an answer.

He ducked back inside his place. In the next moment he came out waving a long brass rod. An extension cord trailed from his other hand. He stabbed the rod into the ground, twisting it back and forth to force it deeper. A power cord extended from the top of the rod. He asked me to back up, then he plugged it in. Nothing happened.

"What's it supposed to do?" I asked.

"Give it a second."

I expected sparks to start leaping off the rod, or maybe it would melt.

Then, just a few inches from where the rod stuck into the earth, a worm came writhing to the surface. And then another and another.

"Cool, huh?" He seemed a little old for the expression. I suppose, like everything around us, he'd scavenged it from somewhere else.

When he unplugged the device, the worms retreated into the earth. "It makes a great Father's Day gift."

My eyes traced the extension cord back inside his place. "How'd you get electricity out here?" I knew he was stealing it. It wouldn't be difficult to tap into a streetlight or a telephone pole, but he'd still need half a mile of extension cords. It was hard to believe.

"I worked out a deal with someone who had access to spools of wire. You are aware that there's another economy, a gray market, that exists in response to the insidious capitalist markup?"

"So you basically stole it."

"I haven't stolen anything. They were compensated."

"What did you give them?"

"It just so happens I was able to pay in legal tender, which I had accumulated in exchange for other goods and services."

"Your paranoia boxes."

"Disaster scanners and worm prods, this and that." He coiled up the extension cord and pried the metal rod from the ground.

"Where did you go when you left here?"

"If you can find it on a map, chances are I've been there."

"And you came back here?" I asked.

The two of us looked at his bankrupt little house.

"I have to be somewhere, right?" said Shiloh. "The opposite of somewhere is nowhere and I'm not interested in being there."

"You mean dead?"

"What a strange bird you are, son of Fran."

I told him my first name.

"Thomas, I'm here to rebuild my heart."

I looked around us, at the silent river, the empty sky. What was wrong with me that drove people to talk like that?

"I should get going."

"You don't have to ask my permission. You can go whenever you want to. My foremost belief is that a person has the right to do as he or she feels.

"I wasn't asking your permission."

"And if you'd listened, you'd know I can't grant it to you anyway."

"I'm not the strange bird. You're the strange bird."

Shiloh put his hands over his chest. He staggered backward. "You got me," he said. "I'm wounded."

I was angry all of a sudden, for walking all the way out there, for his stupid answers, for this feeling inside my chest like an unreachable itch.

"Well, what is it?" asked Shiloh.

"What is *what*?" I shouted back.

"The thing driving you crazy."

* * *

I didn't see Miss Lowe for the two weeks between Christmas and New Year's. She'd told the class she'd be visiting her sister outside Chattanooga. I felt her absence acutely. I did stupid things like sniff soap at the pharmacy trying to determine the brand she used. Before the break everyone had given her presents—chocolate apples, winter gloves, a bootjack. I put a card on her desk that read, "Miss Lowe, You will be receiving a one-year subscription to *Popular Mechanics* magazine, Courtesy of the Mahey family. Merry Christmas!" Mary had bought subscriptions for all my teachers, at a discount, from someone at our church.

My pawpaw stayed on the screen porch, smoking cigarettes and growing thinner. He slept out there on a cot. He came inside for meals and, sometimes, to use the bathroom. The azalea bush beside the porch door showed signs of ammonia poisoning. He liked to lie in his cot, entertaining his thoughts. Most of his thoughts revolved around mornings he'd spent smoking in France when he was sixteen and seventeen. He could remember the faces of the people he knew then, their boy faces and girl faces, their sleeping and tortured and peaceful faces. Mostly he liked to think about the faces they made while they smoked, what he thought of as their true faces. Often when they weren't smoking, they were scared, but most of the time while they were smoking, it was beautiful. The cigarettes were free.

The army had trained him to set up and maintain telegraph wires. But when he'd arrived in France, he'd been put in charge of three dozen messenger pigeons. He wasn't supposed to feed the pigeons too much, but it was hard not to, because the pigeons would always eat. In general, recalled Pawpaw, it was a slow war.

He had been stationed near a small stone bridge. He liked to stand on the bridge, staring into the water, and smoke. He could see the mossy stones on the streambed.

I asked him once if he ever wanted to go back to that bridge.

He cocked his head. "Why would I want to do that?"

"You could see everything again?"

"And what do you think that would accomplish?"

"It might help you remember things."

"I remember things fine. I remember the cigarettes. I remember the egg pies." There was a farm just down the road and every morning the farmer's wife brought him and his buddy an egg pie.

"I just thought it might be cool if you got a chance to see those things again."

This was on one of those misty days when the water fills the screens so that every tiny opening offers a portrait of the outside world, perfect and upside down.

"The whole point of that war was to get your pawpaw off that bridge."

"How do you mean that was the *point* of the war?"

"Forget those supposed histories you find in books. I mean exactly what I said. The whole purpose of the Great War was to get me off that bridge."

"That's the craziest thing you've ever said."

"The crazy thing was that twenty million people died. Yet as soon as they sent home all of us guys who'd been standing on bridges, the war was over. Why couldn't they have done that first?"

"Do you think it's weird that when you came back here, your first job was building a bridge?"

"This is the great mystery of anyone's life, Thomas."

"What's the mystery?"

"Everything that you ever did or will do. How, looking back on it, you can almost detect an intelligent force leading you from one place to the next."

While they were building the floodwall, the Army Corps of Engineers erected a new bridge upriver, a terrifying modern arc. Then they jackhammered and dynamited the old bridge apart.

Except for an usher going over the carpet with an automatic broom, the movie theater was empty. It had a high tin ceiling. Off to the side, the snack bar was crammed into a little alcove. On three of the walls there were these weird mirrors that were crazed with veins of gold paint.

Miss Lowe came in wearing a boatneck sweater and a skirt like a Persian rug. The fabrics rubbing together generated so much static that, as she made her way to my booth, her hair levitated about her face. This, I imagined, was the kind of effect that would prevent a woman from wearing something a second time. I concluded she'd dressed just for me.

"You're here!" she said.

Outside of the classroom, her voice had a great capacity for warmth.

"In the flesh," I said.

The woman behind the grill circled words in a pulpy pamphlet and paid us no attention.

The second thing Miss Lowe said was, "I'm glad we did this." I'd planned to say something similar when we went our separate ways. I had no idea what I would say now.

"This place is great," she said, pulling her hair back from her face.

From beneath the table Miss Lowe's bare feet appeared. They found a spot beside me on the booth. Just as suddenly they darted away.

"Sorry," she said. "My manners are the pits."

I said, "I don't even have manners."

She reached across the table and poked my arm.

It's hard to remember if she acted the way I like people to act or if what I like in people is to be reminded of Alice.

"You've got green eyes," she said.

Nothing she might have said could have made me any happier.

"Well," said Miss Lowe, "aren't we a couple of cheap dates."

The last word just hung in the air.

"Can I see your necklace?" I asked her.

She pinched the chain and lifted it out of her shirt, a delicate cross with silver filigree.

"That's cool," I said.

Did I wear a cross?

I felt disappointed in myself; I didn't.

She dropped the cross back inside her shirt.

"Don't you love the idea of miracles?" said Miss Lowe.

"Any welcome event is a miracle, according to Pawpaw."

"So you believe in miracles, but not accidents?"

That was it.

Miss Lowe's feet reappeared on the cushion beside me. By Pawpaw's definition, a miracle.

"This was your idea," she reminded me. "Ask me more questions."

Her favorite color: yellow. Her favorite sport: waterskiing. On one arm she wore about a hundred silver hoops, while wrapped around the other wrist was a braided leather band. At that time jewelry still meant things to people. Pawpaw wore a gold wristwatch that his mother had given him. In addition to his wedding band, Fran wore a silver Timex with the watch face over the inside of his wrist because he was convinced that was the logical place to have it. Mary wore her wedding ring and clip-on earrings that left hollow spots on the lobes of her ears. The only jewelry I owned was an enamel pin from the Mexico City Olympics.

She turned things back toward me. "Can I ask you a question?"

I had allowed myself to slouch in my seat. When I tried to push myself up, my hand came down on Miss Lowe's ankle. I was amazed that my hand had achieved something I couldn't will.

I told her she could ask me anything.

"Thomas," she said, "what do you think about when you look at me?"

An honest answer was unthinkable. I said, "I'm probably just day-dreaming."

"And what are you daydreaming about?"

"I don't think I should say right now."

"I'm the worst teacher," she said.

I smiled at her.

"I really am," she said.

I think she might have meant it.

The woman behind the counter left her station to prop open the theater's red doors. Miss Lowe turned her face toward the mirrored wall, as an orchestra played a martial tune and couples emerged, blinking, into the bright lobby. I met her reflected gaze. We stayed like that for several uncomfortable moments.

I said, "You're the smartest person I know."

She turned to look at me head-on. "Thomas, do you have a girl-friend?"

I felt like I was leaking information. The longer we sat there, the greater the odds that I would be left without secrets or hope.

"Currently I have exactly zero girlfriends." It sounded stupid to say it that way, but I wanted there to be no ambiguity.

Back behind the counter, the woman poured popping corn into a hopper.

"I don't think I'm going to college," I said, though I hadn't given the matter any thought before.

The woman I'd been sitting with disappeared and a more familiar person took her place. "What do you think you're going to do?"

I said, "I'd prefer to learn things in a more realistic environment."

"Sure," she said, and something about her tone suggested that she didn't quite agree with me.

"Or maybe I'll travel."

Miss Lowe drew shapes on the Formica tabletop with her finger-tip. "Do you ever get lonely, Thomas?"

It was obvious she didn't know the first thing about me. My bed-room and my parents' shared a wall—only the dehumidifier in Mary's closet disguised our night sounds. Pawpaw's military background meant he didn't think twice about visiting me in the bathroom. How, in that house, could a person feel lonely? "Why?" I asked. "Do you?"

She drove a Plymouth Valiant, a schoolteacher's car, modest and neat and seven years old, with full-length chrome molding and Blue Dot whitewall tires. The paint, a sort of blooming algae.

I walked over to the passenger door.

She slotted the key in the lock. "You knew this was my car."

"You were walking toward it," I said.

"No," she said, opening the door. "You were in front of me."

Inside her car, the headliner cloth was coming unglued from the ceiling—it jiggled like the walls of a tent.

It was the emptiness of her car that bothered me. Then I noticed, dangling from the turn-signal indicator, a red ribbon, like you might win at a fair.

"What's that?" I asked.

She turned the ribbon in her hand. "I don't know."

She drove me to the lowest tier of River Park. We listened as the water slapped against the mud banks. I took casual, sidelong glances at her face. She had a high, blank forehead. I was singularly aware of her body, the radiating waves of heat that registered on my arms and neck. It was terrifying.

"Wouldn't you like to just float down that river?" said Miss Lowe.

It was as though she'd pulled the idea from some place deep inside me. I couldn't find the strength to speak with her.

A car crept toward us with just its parking lights on. They raked our car with a spotlight before driving off.

"Creeps," said Miss Lowe. She cranked her window down.

"That was the police," I said.

Miss Lowe turned in her seat. "You're right."

"I should probably get home," I said.

"Right," said Miss Lowe. "I'd better get you home."

In the month after Miss Lowe and I met in town, nothing passed between us but a sly look now and again. Her comments on my papers never revealed a hidden thought. We'd walked up to the edge of something and flinched.

Then warm rains melted Pennsylvania's snowpack, causing the Ohio to swell beyond its banks. It didn't matter that overhead we had clear skies and sunshine. Public Works employees scrambled about River Park, collecting anything that might be washed away—oil-drum ashcans, the sign reminding people to set their parking brakes on the boat ramp, the bases on the baseball field. They dogged down the sewer pipe overflows to prevent the rising river from following those passageways into town. Finally, the breaks in the flood wall, at North Main, Clairmont, and River Way, were sealed off with heavy steel plates. For the first time, the town was shut off from the river.

When the weather was fine, Baptist congregations gathered in the park, every Sunday, in white nightshirts and cassocks and dresses and trousers, to wade into that turbid muck and bathe in God's graces. Young families backed their station wagons to the water's edge to eat picnics on the ledges of their tailgates. But with the park under water, people returned to the downtown. They reclaimed the plaza for their shrieking kids and their yappy dogs. They gathered by the glass wall of City Hall's rotunda to look out over the flooded land. From that vantage, way in the distance, Shiloh's home looked like the pilothouse of a swamped ship. A driftwood boardwalk—damp planks sagging between sawhorses and cement blocks—connected his island to shore.

I felt something building in my heart. In the middle of the night, I sneaked out my bedroom window and across town to a squat, Federal-style building. I stood there, without a clue how to proceed, studying the iron stars that wept rust down the side of the brickwork. A window shuddered open. Miss Lowe leaned her head out, one hand on the sill, the other holding her hair back. After a moment she disappeared inside.

I heard a door open and then she came from around the side of the building. She wore cut-off jeans, a T-shirt and rubber flip-flops.

"We have to be like a couple of mice," she said, taking my hand.

The hallway was too narrow for us to walk side by side. I followed her up the linoleum-covered stairs. On the third floor she pushed through a door into a cramped room filled with milk-colored light.

"Well," she said, "take a look around."

The furniture, a sofa and an armchair, was cloaked with white sheets. On one wall, a free calendar from the hardware store hung by a thumbtack. A banker's gooseneck lamp rested on a card table piled high with books. A blocky school phonograph sat beneath it on the floor.

I said, "This is a nice place, Miss Lowe."

She wagged her finger in front of me. I understood.

"Alice," I said.

I wound up in the bathroom; it was like a bathroom on a train, the sink as small as a salad bowl.

"Are you looking for the bedroom?"

Twin bed. Rainbow sheets. On a bedside table a lamp with a red scarf draped over the shade.

We sat on the edge of the bed with our knees touching. Alice showed me a picture of her sister with some guy—the two of them were waving like they were going off to live on the sun.

"Okay," said Alice. "We need to have a conversation."

Yes, a conversation.

"First of all, are you here of your own accord?"

"Yes," I said, "I guess."

She said, "I'm not on the pill."

I was unprepared.

We went back into her kitchen to kiss. When things got too intense, she boiled water and introduced me to herbal tea. I was ready to swallow any bitter thing. In the drying rack beside the sink, I counted a single sponge, a single spoon, a single plate, a juice glass.

"Who's that ugly cuss?" my pawpaw asked, catching me as I checked my reflection in the bathroom mirror.

"Do I need to shave?"

He pinched my jaw in his bony fingers. He squinted at my bare cheeks. "A kitty cat could lick those off."

"They're beginning to come in."

He stood behind me so our heads were side by side in the mirror. "You know who used to look at himself all the time?"

"Who?"

"Robbie O'Dell."

Mary's first husband. All I knew about him, other than the accident, was that he'd worked as a commercial pilot. ("Your mother's friend flew planes," was how Fran put it.) They'd married straight out of high school. In a single year Mary and O'Dell lived in Texas, Montreal, and West Berlin. Then the accident and, as soon as she was released from the hospital, Mary moved back home. She married Fran on a rainy spring day, in a raw-wood gazebo in her parents' backyard. At his office Fran kept a favorite picture: my mother, in her wedding dress, leaning against him. Because the rain-soaked ground keeps wrenching her heels off, she is barefoot. Fran faces the camera, but his eyes aim up through his eyebrows, at the rain. Mary smiles, with her lips pulled back from her teeth, like she is about to bite into something.

I said, "No one ever told me that."

"You never met someone so in love with his own face."

Pawpaw's only vanity was his hair, which he washed with Ivory soap and combed with coal tar. Hooking his hand around my elbow, he pulled me out of the bathroom.

I was in the kitchen watching Mary debone a chicken. She slid the blade under the skin, making quick, jabbing cuts. When the phone rang Mary indicated it with the point of the greasy knife.

The person on the other end of the line gave me simple instructions.

"Well," said Mary, after I'd returned the handset to its cradle.

"I have to go out," I said. "That was a girl."

Mary dropped the knife in the sink. "It's a school night, you know." She caught me by the shoulder and poked at my bangs with her fingernails. "Comb your hair first."

I tried to appease her.

"Now you're making it worse."

Pawpaw came in from the porch, a cigarette pinched dead in his fingers.

"Ask your grandson what he's up to."

"I only came in to run interference for him." He maneuvered himself between me and Mary. "Scoot, kiddo."

It dawned on me, as I cut across the yard, that I was about to be dumped. Nothing else could demand such immediacy. I'd visited Alice's apartment six times. Twice she cooked me dinner. One time, when she was sick, we sat together on her little sofa. But she'd found the nerve and now it was up to me to put my head on the chopping block. It was sort of reassuring to be complicit. There was some honor to be mined. I jogged off, down the center of the street. I didn't get more than a few blocks before I was winded, but I didn't let it slow my pace.

Her schoolteacher car bore down on me. The jouncing suspension sent the headlights up and down, like the car was winking at me. She never slowed. At the last moment I had to dive for the curb.

There was a shrieking sound as she locked up the brakes. The car slid to a stop. I ran to the driver's door. She waved me to the other side. I ran around and got in.

"I can't believe this night," she said. She'd been crying.

She wore this short corduroy skirt. I had seen her wear it before with fuzzy tights, but her legs were bare now. And her naked legs and the fact that she'd been crying were like two voices competing for my attention.

She ran a stop sign and then another.

I asked her to let me drive.

It was very nice to steer Alice's car. The wheel was warm where her hands had been. I wanted to stop the car and look at her, but I didn't think she would tolerate such scrutiny. In order to make the town as big as it could be, I followed the roads that paralleled the floodwall. Some of the seams in the cement seeped black water. The diesel engines powering the bilge pumps made a wall of sound.

I wracked my mind for a place better than this. I could drive her to her sister's in Chattanooga. Her sister lived with a dentist, Alice had told the class. They had a huge stereo. Their refrigerator housed nothing but leftovers from their favorite restaurants. Right outside their back door was an artificial lake that had been optimized for waterskiing. Taking Alice there might demonstrate my selfless heart. But I didn't want to stand beside things I couldn't afford. I didn't want to be measured against something like that.

Alice lifted my right hand from the steering wheel and pressed it against her cheek. "Do I feel hot to you?"

I held my hand against her forehead, then touched my own forehead. Then I smelled my hand. "I can't tell."

"I took some aspirin earlier. I hoped it would make me tired."

I concentrated on driving in a soothing way.

"I love that car," Alice said as we drove past the police station. "It's like a big, black cat."

She left a space for me to speak. I studied the blank expanse of the floodwall, searching for the thing to say.

Alice leaned the side of her face against the window. And it seemed something stood between us, too, something as transparent and unyielding.

I wanted to forgive her for what she was about to do. I felt that big.

She said, "Stop the car."

The headlights reflected off a shallow puddle that hugged the base of the wall. Alice got out. She stuck her whole fist in her mouth, like a girl at a party trying to get attention.

Poking my head through her open door, I asked if she was okay.

She nodded and pushed her hand deeper into her mouth. Her eyes were bright. She coughed and coughed. Finally something came up.

I got out of the car and stood beside her.

There was a shiny mess on the pavement—saliva, bile, and small pieces of chalk.

"Is that all aspirin?"

She put her hand back in her mouth. She spit some more up. She wiped her eyes with her sleeve. Her hand looked boiled.

We could hear the river sliding past on the other side of the floodwall. We were underneath the water and dry.

Alice turned to look at me. "I received an upsetting phone call." Tendrils of hair glued themselves to the corner of her mouth.

Someone had died, I thought. That was it. Someone she loved maybe. She started shaking. I rubbed a palm against her spine.

"At some point he's just going to make up his mind and come down here." Alice had left her door ajar and the light inside the car tried to coax us back.

"An old boyfriend?" I asked.

"My ex-husband."

I don't remember saying anything, but Alice answered me nevertheless.

"Yes," she said.

It was an awful revelation, but at least she hadn't dumped me. And then I realized she might dump me still.

"He threatened me."

"How did he threaten you?" My voice was as empty as a parrot's.

"He occupies the moral high ground." She walked away from the car. If we walked far enough, we'd end up back where we started—the floodwall would see to that.

"Did you cheat on him?"

"He would have preferred that. No, I decided I'd had enough. We'd been together three years and I couldn't bear the idea of another day with him. While he was off at work, I loaded all my things in my car. I taped a note to the bathroom mirror. But when I went outside, he was there."

"You mean he was waiting for you?"

"He said he'd seen something in my eyes."

I was jealous of anyone who knew her well enough to interpret her veiled intentions.

"He demanded an explanation. I had my keys in my hand, Thomas. I couldn't wait to leave. He snatched the keys and crammed them in his mouth. I guess he tried to swallow them. They got caught. He started coughing. I went inside and called an ambulance. I waited by the front door. A pair of police cars rolled up. By then he was curled up in the yard. The officers made sure he was breathing. They were ready to stab his neck with their tracheotomy kits. Then an ambulance arrived and the paramedics loaded him in back."

I said, "I'm sorry."

"I did everything I could to make it work, Thomas. But I saved myself. I can be cruel when I need to be now; that's what I learned from him. I went inside the house and got the spare set of keys."

All along, in her empty apartment and her empty car, he had been the thing that was missing.

"Do you think he might show up?"

"I told him not to."

It was clear to me that that would not be sufficient. Given the choice between not seeing her and seeing her displeasure, there was no choice. I didn't know much about love, but I knew that.

Alice said, "I want to go someplace he can't find me." She turned the pockets of her skirt inside out.

"What are you looking for?" I asked.

She didn't seem to hear me.

After tucking her pockets back in, she reached over and took my hand. "Gum," she said.

"I'd protect you from him," I said.

"Maybe, you would."

I thought, I'll go with you, with nothing but the clothes on my back. Later you may run from me. If someone else is there to save you, it will fall on you to give that person some accounting of who I was. That will be your obligation. And though it's hardly possible, I would like to be that next person, too. I would like to save you over and over again. That's the type of life I wanted to lead when I was seventeen. We continued walking. Our shoulders bumped together. I lifted her hand and kissed it. "Do that again," she said. I kissed her hand again. It was a long walk back to the car.

5
Cause and Effect

One moment the midnight black cruiser sat there, in front of the police station, under the floodlights, bigger than itself. And the next moment there was just the empty space where everyone expected the car to be, the floodlights drowning themselves in the night sky. There were no witnesses to that crime. And when, a few minutes later, the cruiser was driven into the most unforgiving thing in town, there were no witnesses then either.

While, formerly, the condition of the car might have been described as flawless or cherry, the impact was sufficient to render the vehicle totaled. The object the car had been run into: a blank span of floodwall.

The collision precipitated a series of notable events:

1. The force of the car impacting the wall tripped a sensor,
2. Which caused a red bulb to go on in a control room.
3. Where a human monitor flipped a switch,

4. Triggering an automated warning system.

5. At which point the monitor picked up a telephone and called the public works department,

6. Who contacted one of their own,

7. Whose job it was to climb into the cab of the dump truck called "Little Dutch Boy" and head to the scene,

8. Just as the sirens were beginning to cycle up,

9. As people sat up in their beds, trying to comprehend what they were hearing,

10. Which sounded like a lovesick monster.

11. While I looked at Alice—in her tawny-colored bedroom—and said, "That's the flood warning."

12. As the dump-truck driver said, "That's the police car."

13. As Pawpaw stared into my empty bedroom and thought, Where's the boy off to?

14. While everywhere neighbors were concerned about neighbors, pounding on their doors, ushering them into the emergency. Not satisfied with a mere voice, they demanded to see faces, even when those faces didn't want to be seen because they had unexplainable company at an unexplainable hour.

15. As the dump-truck driver—in a moment of real insight—made sure no one was trapped inside the crumpled, black Mercury before entombing it under twenty cubic yards of sandbags.

16. As a procession of townspeople marched to high ground—which was how they thought of the cemetery,

17. Alice included—to wait among the tombstones.

18. Everyone except the dump-truck driver, who felt too heroic to huddle,

19. And I, though I had told Alice I'd meet her there, though my parents would expect me to meet them at the rendezvous point—which was my grandmother's headstone—I, feeling too guilty to be safe, made my way home.

All the while, presumably, the river was rushing into town, carving channels and pulling down street signs, a viscous black wave poised to break through my bedroom window and flush me into the night. I'd heard about these sorts of things, how a flood has a tendency to strip the clothes from the bodies of its victims. I'd be bobbing through the neighborhood and then what? Left high and dry, or swept back out to the river when the waters retreated. The siren went on and on, reminding me of what was coming. I was seventeen. I didn't head to the cemetery. Instead I went to my parents' empty home. Around Alice, I was constantly afraid of doing something stupid, but now, alone, I could relax. I thought about Alice and her body and what we were doing together, with the pleasure of stepping back from it. Even with my eyes open, I saw Alice's nakedness.

When, many hours later, I woke up, the yard was still grass and shrubs—not liquid. The green-yellow buds on the forsythia poised to open. Though the siren still pleaded for my attention, I had stopped hearing it. It was supposed to be a school morning, but the vacant neighborhood gave me the impression that I needn't worry about that. I got into the shower, and while I was in there the siren finally stopped sounding—I didn't notice when it stopped as much as I sensed that there was no longer a need to ignore it. By the time I was dressed, families had started returning to their houses. Children with drowsy heads marched beside overloaded strollers. Excitable dogs nipped at their leashes. I saw cats cradled in arms and in sewing baskets, a few birds in cages. Some folks carried family Bibles and examples of atrocious art. The women wore their necklaces stacked and rings on every finger. Everyone was conspicuous for those things they valued most. Then this strange parade was down to the stragglers.

I saw Mary and Pawpaw walking arm and arm up the sidewalk. I watched them talk, the turn of their heads as they acknowledged each other. I waited on the front steps. Pawpaw looked older than I'd ever seen before, the grizzled white stubble on his loose neck, his tentative steps. Fran must have gone to the plant.

"Hi," I said, offering neither alibi nor excuse.

Pawpaw reached down, covering the crown of my head with his hand, but didn't stop, went inside.

"Wait here," said Mary. "I'm going to help your pawpaw and then I'm coming right back."

It was almost a shame the wall hadn't come down, because if there had been some horrible accident, then they could have focused on that instead. I felt as though I had triggered the siren by climbing into Alice's bed.

A few minutes later Mary sat down beside me, took her shoes and socks off, and stretched her toes. No matter what she said, I would bear it. I'd never known her to be anything but fair.

"To wake up like that and find your son is not in his bed, I swear, Thomas, how do you think I felt? But at least you could have met us at the meet-up place. We all believed the stupid wall was coming down. You should have heard what those nitwits were saying. I've never known you to be selfish before. People asked me where you were. I told them that you were helping Fran. I lied because of you. Your mother is not a liar, Thomas, but you didn't leave me any choice."

The corners of her mouth were red and creased. I watched her cut the words from the cloth of her breath.

"Here's the deal, buster. You need to tell me where you were and who you were with so I can speak with her parents. And let me tell you, this is not something I look forward to. Believe me. But I won't have her parents calling me and me looking like some nincompoop with no idea where her son is."

But I couldn't give her Alice's name.

"The whole time, your poor grandfather kept looking for you. That he spent one second worrying about you makes me crazy. You didn't know there wasn't a flood. What did you plan on doing? Swimming?"

I wanted to suffer, too, and I wanted to be back in Alice's bed. And might Alice infer what my mother would demand? Had they seen each other? Had something slipped between them, and would Mary recognize it? I sat there, mute.

Mary sank her nails into my forearm. Frustration had led her to that point. I didn't even mind so much. Later it would be an embarrassment for her that I wore the marks. She went inside the house and shut me out. I climbed in through my bedroom window, bringing the day full circle.

A little while later Mary came to the door. There was a person on the telephone who wished to speak with me. Mary had undone the twist tie that held the cord together, enabling me to take the call in my room.

"I understand, you and your mother are having a misunderstanding." In the background I could hear the front loaders shuttling between the coal barge and the plant. "I'm pretty sure that's all it is. Your mother is definitely in your corner nine times out of ten. This, however, is one of those times when she is not one hundred percent in your corner and she called me because she is very upset to be in this position. Do you understand? She asked me if there's something she's not picking up on. It's important to her that she's being fair with you. What do I think? I think that, yes, she's being fair with you, but she also has never been a boy, right, so there are certain codes of, right, chivalry, basically, that we have to broach.

"Now apparently you don't want to give the name of this young girl who you were with. I understand it can be embarrassing, for one thing, to have your mother inquire into your personal habits. I can see your side of it and I can see your mother's side of it. It puts me in a sticky position. And, I don't try to misrepresent myself here. How can I, or your mother, guarantee that we're doing the right thing here? We have to go by feel. Well, in the same vein, I can't expect that you can undo some of your decisions. What I do expect is that you'll take responsibility, and not telling the girl's name is not taking responsibility. Not telling the girl's name is shirking responsibility. Are you listing to me, ace?"

I was listening to him.

"Right now your mother's upset and, obviously, you're upset. The thing you have to do is get past that and move toward making it less upsetting. And I'm saying this as your friend, right, not just your father."

"I really can't talk about it."

"Well, your mother isn't going to have much interest in talking with you until you do."

Who took the trouble to pilot the police cruiser past the fragile inconvenience of ornamental trees, flower boxes, and vacant benches? And after he had gone through that trouble, to point it at something as resilient as concrete? What sort of sense did that make? It made no sense. So who had the opportunity? When the chief of police drove the car at the head of the River Parade, no one asked him about opportunity. Presumably he had as much opportunity every other day of the year.

And what about the dump-truck driver? Some people found it a bit too convenient how the driver was cast as a heroic figure. They saw evidence in the dump-truck driver's behavior to justify their suspicions. On the night in question, and under highly trying circumstances, he, a municipal worker, did a job exactly as had been expected of him. Come to think of it, hadn't he been a bit of a striver, a Johnny-come-lately?

No one, not the police (who were waiting for the river to recede before they could remove the sandbags and give the car a thorough once-over), or the John Birch Society (who'd offered a cash reward for the opportunity to interrogate the vandal), or the court of public opinion, for that matter, was able to get to the bottom of these questions. And though Mary and I weren't talking, I heard her say something that put the situation in sharper focus. Pawpaw had voiced his respect for such a clear message against the police department, or, as he put it, "those uniformed thugs."

"Wait," said Mary. "You think someone was trying to get back at the police?"

"They totaled the damn car," Pawpaw reminded her.

"Sure," said Mary, "the car was ruined, but what makes you think that was the intention? The car getting ruined was just incidental. Don't you see? They weren't trying to destroy the car. They were trying to let the river in."

*   *   *

For the next couple of days, Alice flat out ignored me. If I lingered after the bell, she walked out. When I raised my hand to ask a question, she called on someone else. She allowed Ray to eat up half an hour of class explaining his feelings about the origin of Atlantis. I called her, but she never answered her phone.

So I showed up at her place unannounced on a Sunday afternoon. She threw the door open. "It's you," she said, as though she was used to having all sorts of visitors. She was wearing a blue dress that tied around her waist. She looked as if she'd just gotten back from church.

If she just wanted me to feel bad, there wasn't much point in giving her the satisfaction. I turned around.

"Wait," she said. "You have to explain to me where you went after you left here."

I told her I went home.

"That's the stupidest thing I've ever heard."

I couldn't offer a defense.

"I was worried about you," said Alice.

"I wasn't actually in any danger."

"But you didn't know that at the time."

It wasn't clear if she was ever going to let me into her apartment again.

"My parents keep asking where I was."

"You can tell them if you want. After this term is over, I'm going to take a break from teaching. I already turned in my resignation. A teacher needs to show better judgment than her students."

We might have stayed like that, standing across from each other in a doorway, but I stepped toward her and kissed her lower lip. "Well," she said as she closed the door behind us.

Tucked neatly beside her sofa, I saw a red toolbox and a stack of men's clothing.

Alice said, "I had a revelation."

The clothes—though they looked dirty—had been ordered in fastidious piles.

"What kind of revelation?" I asked.

"Well," said Alice, "I haven't been sleeping well. The reason for this, I think, is that I'm nervous about living alone. I don't like noises in the middle of the night. Ideally I'd like to get a dog."

Of course, those weren't a dog's clothes.

"At the same time, I don't want a dog. So what I decided was that I needed a roommate."

"Oh," I said.

"And guess what, I went out and found one."

I looked at the guy shirts and the guy pants. "What's her name?"

Alice came over and gave me a hug. "Nothing is going to change between us," she said.

"What's your roommate's name?"

"His name," said Alice, not spitefully, but clearly, "is Shiloh Tanager."

6

House Guest

Three days before, Alice had carried a stack of papers down to the little brick plaza across from city hall. She wanted to take advantage of the weather to do some outdoor grading. People came and went. She could hear the river sweeping past.

Shiloh took a spot at the opposite end of her bench. He seemed preoccupied, watching passersby. He reached a hand up, threaded it inside the neck of his shirt, and massaged his left shoulder. Turning toward Alice, he assessed the pile of papers. Somewhere in the pile was an essay I'd written on vaulted ceilings.

"You're a teacher?"

Alice nodded.

"Reading. Riting. Rithmetic. Which are you?"

"I teach history."

"I'm a student of history," said Shiloh. "Social theory, Judeo-Christian democracy, capitalistic monotheism. I'm interested in non-discriminatory political fabrics."

"Where do you study?"

He stuck a finger out, as though ringing a doorbell.

She didn't comprehend his gesture.

He jabbed his finger twice more.

"You got me."

"On the shores of the Ohio River."

"Cincinnati?"

He shook his head, pleased.

"Pittsburgh?"

"I was homeschooled," he said.

"Oh."

"In my own home." But, again, he'd failed to convey his message. "By myself."

"That's ambitious," said Alice.

A flattened smile found its way onto his face. He kneaded his shoulder again. "You know anything about shots?"

Somewhere Alice had picked up one of those apologetic shrugs.

"They gave me tetanus at the clinic."

"A tetanus shot?"

He rolled the cuffs of his pants up, revealing shins crossed with black scabs and red welts.

"Ouch," said Alice.

"I woke up in the middle of the night to see that water coming up. The stove shorted out. POP! Blue sparks. I didn't know if the TV had gone yet. So I waited while the water came up. I didn't want to step in at the same moment the TV went. ZAP! Killed by television. It was coming up five inches an hour. I waited till I couldn't wait any longer and I floated out of there."

"You floated out of your house?"

"Like a water bug. I had a duffel bag under each arm."

"I hope your house is okay."

Shiloh made a chopping motion with his hand, a gesture that divorced himself from the house. Maybe there had never been a house, he seemed to indicate.

"I was fortunate to have had an awful childhood," said Shiloh. "Short of everything else, it's probably the best way to teach a person optimism." He rapped on the bench with a knuckle.

"What made it awful?" asked Alice.

"My hateful father, of course!"

"Ah," said Alice. A perfect puckered sound.

"A scoundrel. A family man. A millionaire. A poet. That's my father. You won't hear me say his name. All I have to do is open my mouth and there'd be a Cadillac full of lawyers waiting to drag me off to court."

The name Shiloh Tanager meant nothing to Alice. She had never seen his damp little home or one of his paranoia boxes. It also seemed to Alice that she'd never spoken to a person less interested in her. For some reason she found this reassuring.

Alice showed me the growing evidence that she'd picked the perfect roommate. Here was the door that no longer squeaked, the window that slid in its sash. Gone was the wiggly chair, the sink's drip. All of a sudden the light came on when she opened the refrigerator and the milk didn't freeze when it got pushed against the back wall. Dishes left in the sink miraculously put themselves away. But for the toolbox and stack of clothes beside the sofa, he was like the cobbler's elves.

She kept waiting to thank him, but their paths never seemed to cross. She couldn't just leave a note. A note suggested that she didn't want to see him. And while she didn't necessarily want to see him, she didn't need it to be so established. Her invitation had been an invitation to compromise, but where was the compromise? She was supposed to be doing him a favor, not the other way around. This wasn't what she'd expected.

One night she decided to wait up for him. That would allow them to put things in perspective. It would establish some boundaries. He couldn't just come and go as he pleased, like some wild animal. She would express her gratitude and then they would straighten this stuff out. Midnight came and went. At three in the morning, he still hadn't returned. How had this happened? Just when she'd gotten over worrying about herself, she had to worry for everyone else. Maybe teaching wasn't the best fit for her. She worried for all of her students. Parents' night had been a disaster as she found herself worrying about these sad, hopeful parents. And grading. Grading was really the worst of it. If she gave the students the grade they had earned, it just confirmed their deepest fears, but if she didn't, if she gave them the grade that they hoped for, well, it wasn't realistic. And eventually all of these grades were compiled and then the report cards had to go out and those poor parents and their poor student children. She'd tried to express this to her sister when they got together over her Christmas break, but her sister wouldn't hear any of it. "Fuck your brains out," had been her advice. Her younger sister. Which was absolutely no surprise at all. The dentist had a brother in Florida, and if Alice only said the word, then the brother would hop in his plane and fly up and show her a good time. The brother had built the plane in his garage.

She turned the lights off, but she couldn't go to bed. Had she invited this stranger into her home only so that she could worry about him? That took the cake. But in the next moment, she heard footsteps coming up the stairs and she waited in the darkened living room as the door opened. Shiloh slipped inside, made his way across the darkened room to the reading lamp, which he snapped on— hadn't she broken the bulb off inside the socket? How does a person learn to fix things like that?

Shiloh saw Alice sitting on the sofa.

"You want me to boil you some water or something?" He gave her just a fleeting look and he was in the kitchen putting the kettle on.

"That would be nice." She looked at her watch. It was a quarter till four. "I was waiting up for you," she said.

"Oh," he said. There were a couple of cups in the sink and he quickly washed them. He came back in, drying his hands on a dishtowel. "You're upset about something."

"I'm not upset. I just don't understand where a person can go, in this town, at four in the morning."

He went back into the kitchen and grabbed a butter knife. Holding it in front of her face, he turned the blade so she saw her reflection. Her eyes were red rimmed, her lashes clumped together.

"I wanted to thank you for fixing the toaster," she said, emotion choking her throat.

"All I did was clean it," he said.

"Well, it doesn't make that burning smell anymore." She stood up suddenly, disappointed in herself.

"I'll be out of your hair in a couple of weeks."

"Oh," said Alice. "Are you building another house?"

"I'm returning somewhere."

"I'm prying."

"Not at all. The water coming up sent me a message. I used to be very absorbed in myself, but now I'm very absorbed outside myself."

She found herself nodding.

"You're a really great roommate," said Alice.

"I ought to be," said Shiloh. "I'm an anarchist."

"You're an anarchist?" repeated Alice.

Shiloh was all too glad to explain. "Anarchists make the best roommates. Socialists are shit. They'll rob you blind."

Alice went to her room and shut the door. She heard him get up and, for a moment, she was afraid that he'd misunderstood her. She was afraid he might knock on her door, or, worse, just come in. She felt stupid. She followed his footsteps into the kitchen. He turned the burner off. Then he returned to the living room—she would have sworn she heard him shuffling something, a soft cardboard sound, a deck of cards, maybe.

It was like what, these days, is called an intervention. I'd been in my room daydreaming when Mary and Fran came in. They stood there, between me and the door, sort of looking and not looking at the window.

"Basically," said Fran, "your mother and I are very patient people. But for some reason you seem bent on discovering the limits of our patience. Let me tell you that we have more patience than you do. Knowing how you spend your time is basically a right we have."

Mary addressed me. "It might not make sense to you, but, as your parents, we need you to tell us who you've been spending time with."

"Here's the deal," said Fran. "Your mother and I have to meet this person, so you're going to invite your little friend over for dinner."

"We're not offering you a choice," said Mary.

"It's Shiloh Tanager," I announced.

"He's kidding. You're kidding, right? The river rat?" Fran leaned over and butted his head against the doorjamb.

Mary called my bluff. "Just find out what night would be good for him."

What, I wanted to know, were they thinking?

"I doubt he'll come."

"You still need to ask him."

Alice and I sat down with Shiloh and explained the situation to him.

He said, "I can't remember the last time I was invited to eat with regular people."

"Does that mean you'd actually consider coming?" I asked.

"I'm definitely coming."

"They're very nice," said Alice. "His mother is very sharp." And then, to me, "That was my impression at parents' night."

I said, "It would probably be best if you cut your hair."

"My hair?"

"Fran has said some unfavorable things about men with long hair."

"Do I know Fran?"

"Fran is his father."

Shiloh considered this for a moment. "And do I have opinions about how Fran deports himself?"

"You've said that the people who work at the power plant are fascists," Alice reminded him.

"Well, that's a figure of speech."

"You're not going to do anything about your hair?" I asked.

"We'll get him cleaned up," said Alice.

Shiloh looked at her, looked at me, nodded his head, a deal.

Fran put on the three-piece, gray, pinstriped suit that he wore to weddings or when he had to fire someone. He had on a purple rep tie and oxblood shoes and he looked like a greater version of himself.

Mary wore a starched brown dress that made her hair look colorless. My pawpaw had on a yellow corduroy smoking jacket over a pajama top shirt and green civvies. Fran and Mary wanted me to change, to play the part of their son. I disappointed them by refusing to wear my only suit. Instead Fran tied a tie under the collar of a buttoned-up tennis shirt. We scurried around straightening up.

I felt dread.

Pawpaw went out to the back porch to smoke.

I asked Mary what she planned on saying to Shiloh, but she disappeared into the bathroom and left me with Fran.

"Your friend's late," was what my father said to me.

I opened the refrigerator door and stared at all the food.

"He probably doesn't own a watch," added Fran.

Mary came down. She wore lipstick and she had changed into a shimmery green blouse. "Don't stand there like an Eskimo."

I closed the refrigerator.

The back door opened and Pawpaw shuffled in with Shiloh.

I watched Fran as he made sense of the stranger who'd appeared in his house.

He stuck his hand out like he was drawing a pistol. "Shiloh, I take it."

Shiloh had shaved his beard. He had a baby face. He shook hands with Fran and Mary.

"You surprised us," said Mary.

"We expected you'd come to the front door," said Fran.

"I try not to do things like everybody else."

"Welcome," said Mary.

"Yes," said Fran.

Shiloh pulled a knapsack off his shoulder. He rummaged through the bag.

"You lose something?" asked Mary.

"Wait," said Shiloh. "Are either of you drinkers?"

"I wouldn't say either of us is a drinker," said Fran, who had opened the oven and was prodding a casserole with a fork.

"On special occasions," said Mary.

"Well," said Shiloh. "An associate of mine laid this on me." From inside the backpack he produced a bottle of wine.

"Look at that," said Mary, "wine."

"I guess it's from Italy," said Shiloh.

"Thomas's grandfather has been to Italy," said Fran.

"That's right," said Mary.

"Are you from there, or were you traveling?" asked Shiloh.

"Those my only choices?" asked Pawpaw, heading for the living room.

"You're not still staying by the river, are you?" asked Fran.

"I found a situation in town. My old place has a problem with humidity."

"He means it's underwater," I said.

"I think that's awful," said Mary.

"There are worse things." He pulled a corkscrew out of his knapsack and opened the bottle. He poured glasses for my parents and Pawpaw.

"You're not going to have some?" asked Mary.

He shook his head. He carried the glass out to Pawpaw and took a spot beside him on the sofa. With his bent legs and bug eyes, he looked like a frog. "I didn't expect you'd get dressed up for me."

"Well," said Mary, pushing me before her. She didn't finish her sentence.

There were mud stains on the cuffs of Shiloh's pants and cockleburs sticking to his straw shoes. But somehow, maybe by coming in the back door, Shiloh had managed to make an end run around my parents' defenses. My parents were treating a stranger like a friend. They were doing it for me.

Fran and Mary drank their wine. Pawpaw chased his with blackberry brandy in a cordial glass. Shiloh and I had tap water. At one point, as the conversation was flowing back and forth, he winked at me. It happened so fast, I couldn't be sure I'd seen him do it. What did it mean?

Shiloh told an off-color story about a parrot that was liberated from a brothel and then took up roost across from a church. Mary laughed so hard that she covered her mouth to hide her bridgework. I'd never known these lighthearted people.

And I had no idea that Shiloh would want my parents to like him. He seemed almost desperate to please them. Out of the blue he said, "What's Thomas told you about his love life?"

"We know he's got his eyes on someone," volunteered my mother.

"She's a class act," said Shiloh. "It'll be educational to find out whether she sees him as grade-A material."

Pawpaw came to my defense. "If Thomas has the good sense to remain quiet on the subject, I don't see how spilling the beans makes you his pal."

"I'm not telling any secrets," said Shiloh.

Pawpaw said, "I'm not so old that I need people telling me what I've heard."

Mary patted Shiloh's arm. "I shouldn't have been prying." She turned to me. "Sorry."

I told her there was no harm.

"He's afraid we'd embarrass him," said Mary. "He doesn't think she'd like us."

"Sure she likes you," said Shiloh.

"Wait," said Mary. "Have I met her?" She looked at me, confused.

"From what Thomas has told her about you, she thinks she'd like you."

"I'm going to have a cigarette," said Pawpaw. He got up from the table and headed out the back door.

Fran said, "How old are you, Shiloh?"

"You don't have to answer," said Mary.

Shiloh shook his head. "I don't actually know my birthday. I have, basically, an educated idea of about when it was."

Mary bit her lip.

"What, thirty-five?" asked Fran

"I don't like to get caught up with a number," said Shiloh.

"It's not a number," said Fran. "It's your age."

We could hear Pawpaw carrying the food into the dining room.

Mary said, "I'm afraid my husband and I are typical nosy parents."

"Let me tell you," said Shiloh, "nosy parents beats no parents."

Mary did the most amazing thing. She got up from her seat and went over and gave Shiloh a little hug. He tried to pass me a look, but he didn't seem to have control over his face. "Mrs. Mahey," he said, "please don't touch me."

"How presumptuous of me, honey. I'm sorry." She dashed into the kitchen.

I'd never seen a person eat so much at one sitting. He just kept shoveling it in. When it was clear that the casserole wouldn't withstand his assault, Mary ducked into the kitchen. She returned a few minutes later with a pork chop still sizzling on a plate, a lump of applesauce collapsing on top. Shiloh reduced it to a Y-shaped bone.

After ice cream the five of us found chairs in the living room. In no time Pawpaw fell asleep. Fran and Mary were talking in low, happy voices. Shiloh held out, for our inspection, the wine's cork and Pawpaw's Zippo lighter.

"I'm going to show you a magic trick," said Shiloh.

Mary honked with excitement. "Fun," she said.

With the lighter Shiloh blackened one end of the cork. Then he asked Mary to extend both her hands. She showed him her palms. He weighed her hands, had her make fists. Did she believe in magic? Her eyes got wide. She did. He had me hold my mother's hands as we sat there in the living room. I jiggled Mary's hands. They were tiny things, as frightened as a toad.

"You're squeezing too hard, honey."

I apologized.

Shiloh asked me which hand felt more relaxed. The left hand? Fine. I could let go of her right hand. He touched the burned cork to the back of her left hand. It left a dark, silvery mark. He wanted me to rub the mark away. Gently, he said. Mary thanked him. I stroked the spot with my thumb. "There. It's going," said Shiloh. "It's almost gone. A little harder. Be sure it didn't just move onto your thumb, Thomas." There was a little color on my thumb. He asked me to rub a bit more.

"Voilà."

Mary looked at Shiloh, expectant.

He held his left hand out in front of us and showed us his palm. There, in the center, was a faint mark.

"Cute," said Mary.

Shiloh shook his head gravely. "Thomas, would you mind checking your hand?"

Somehow the dot had moved onto my hand.

Mary squealed. "I love it!"

"Very clever," I said.

"Magic," said Shiloh. "Now, Mary, let's see your hand."

Of course there was a spot there, too.

"Fantastic," said Mary.

Fran showed us his unblemished palms. "That's an old trick," he said.

Mary turned around and swatted Fran on his thigh.

"Count yourself lucky," Shiloh said, speaking to me. "I'd give anything to know just one of my parents."

Mary leaned over and bumped her shoulder against mine.

Outside, a car crept along the street. It had to be Alice.

Shiloh stood up. "Thank you for your hospitality, but I think I'd better be going."

"Oh," said Mary, pronouncing her disappointment. She grabbed Pawpaw's chair and gave it a little shake.

"All good things must come to an end," said my grandfather. He shielded his eyes from the light in the room.

I fetched Shiloh's knapsack from the kitchen.

Mary and Fran walked him to the door.

"You get to see the front door," said Mary.

"Right," said Shiloh.

"Not the back door," said Fran.

"Got it."

And he was gone.

Fran and Pawpaw went to bed. I cleaned the kitchen while Mary kept me company.

"Shiloh has sort of an aristocratic face, don't you think?" She got up to pour herself a glass of milk. "I don't know what came over me when I tried to embrace him. Your father thought I'd lost my mind."

"You just caught him by surprise."

"Imagine not knowing how to dress for dinner."

Fresh smoke leaked in from outside. Pawpaw was having a night-cap cigarette.

Mary handed me her empty glass.

Once it was loaded I flipped the dishwasher on. I sponged down the counter and rinsed the sink. As soon as Mary went to bed, I was going to sneak off to Alice's.

Mary kissed me on my cheek. "Tell Shiloh I said he's welcome anytime."

But Shiloh didn't visit again. For his next trick, he made me disappear.

7
Away

Shiloh gave me a promise. "You're going to thank me for this, Thomas. You get into a car expecting it to take you somewhere physical, but when you travel, you bring more than just your body."

He watched me stow my luggage, such as it was, in the two-wheeled fiberglass trailer he'd bolted to the rear of Alice's car—the trailer looked like one of those Styrofoam boxes fast-food places used for hamburgers. I had two hundred dollars in my wallet, another four wadded in my shoe. I'd never carried so much money in all my life. I felt both rich and stingy.

Shiloh pulled a pair of cheap-looking sunglasses from a paper bag; the lenses were heavily mirrored at the tops and bottoms but had a stripe across the middle where the mirroring had been worn away. He put these on. "Say hello to the rest of your life. Here's Alice."

She was pulling half a dozen grocery bags out of her building. I went to help her. The bags contained kitchen stuff: pots, pans, a cookie sheet, plastic bowls, a set of measuring cups, a stack of dishes.

She must have just stepped out of the shower; her eyelashes held the tiniest globules of water. Alice's eyes were a compromise between gold and green. The faintest crow's feet made her appear a little dour. The only explanation I can give for those wrinkles is that she smiled with all her face. She was twenty-five. She wrapped her arms around my waist and kissed my neck. I saw where the bandanna she wore was soaked through. The blunt ends of her hair, dripping onto the collar of her blouse, rendered the fabric translucent. Her hair looked almost black while it held water, but it dried yellow blond, like pine wood. She used to keep it shoulder length, but in the spirit of change, she had allowed Shiloh to cut it above her nape. Her complexion was particularly fair, but the skin those shears exposed was buttermilk. I hooked my thumbs beneath her earlobes and bent her head back. I kissed her on the lips and on the point of her chin.

"Let's go," she said.

And while Shiloh found room for these last, last things (he packed them on either side of himself for the sake of symmetry and because he didn't expect he'd have a need to get out of the car in a hurry), Alice got the car started, selected a gear, eased out the clutch.

The dappled light scrolled across the windshield.

Shiloh slapped his hands on the back of my seat. "Wait and see. You get into a car expecting the scenery is going to be the only thing to change. Watch out. Watch out!" A rabbit darted across the road. "We'll become better people with every mile."

I hadn't worked out anything to say, and the moment felt so full I just wanted to keep it inside me. At the first stoplight I was almost overcome with emotions. I needed to shout or for someone to hit me. I faked a yawn in order to relieve some of the pressure inside my chest. The light went to green. Alice got us on the elevated highway and then we were on that vertiginous bridge and the town was behind us. There was a hiccup at the top when the car crested and got light on its suspension. The Ohio beneath us, as still as a line on a map. One thing we couldn't see was Shiloh's crooked shed. Had it washed away or was that single room intact but inundated, like the chamber of a heart?

"I predict," said Shiloh, "we will never need return to that damp town." He reached his arm past my head and stuck his hand out the window.

"Don't do that," said Alice.

"What did you do?" Every breath was holding on and letting go.

"A gesture."

"I can't believe it," said Alice.

She was correct. Each moment was unprecedented. At some point Mary, Fran, and Pawpaw would come to a similar conclusion. And years later, when I had even less of an idea of what I'd done, Fran would ask me if it hadn't been that stupid job that I was running from.

We weren't in the car ten minutes when Shiloh said, "A generation ago, your average person died less than fifteen miles from where he was born."

I asked Alice the name of the mountains around us.

They didn't have names. They were hills.

Gaps in the interstate system meant that for every ten miles of highway, we spent a mile creeping through some perfectly forgettable town. It rendered the whole idea of escape anticlimactic.

Three hours into the future, we were exhausted and just a hundred miles from where we'd started. We stopped for gas. I bought cheese sandwiches. Alice asked me to drive. The sandwiches were damp inside their plastic wrap. We tossed them out the window. Alice fell asleep. The car converted fuel into miles. Shiloh sat up high in the backseat; whenever I checked the rearview mirror, his face was right where my eyes wanted to be. I trained myself to use the side mirror, but the moment I forgot, his face perked up.

His mouth made word shapes.

"What?"

"How do you feel?"

"Great."

"We're on our way."

On either side of the road, chicken farms stretched as far as you could see, low aluminum barns. Downy feathers carpeted the road. The turbulence from the car snatched the feathers into the air.

That afternoon, the road amazed us by passing over the Ohio again. The river had turned steely, and narrow. We wouldn't have recognized it except for a sign. This bridge was an unremarkable cantilevered cement span, and crossing it seemed less an event, just as the river seemed less of a thing.

Alice woke up and moaned. She'd slept in such a way that the right side of her face was sunburned. She commandeered the mirror in order to study her face.

"Tell me the truth," she asked, "how noticeable is it?"

I turned from the road to face her. Her lips took on a vulnerable shape.

"It's fine."

"There," Shiloh said, pointing to a billboard that was being pulled down by vines. A place to spend the night.

Tiny white cabins were scattered among gnarled trees. A hand-lettered sign, "Pool," pointed around the back. I gave a man twenty dollars for a key.

Inside, there was just one big room. The bathroom and shower stall were hidden behind a kitchenette. The ceiling was open beamed and the rafters painted white. Organdy curtains in the windows. "God," Alice pronounced from the bathroom. When she came out her face was buttered with Noxzema. She slumped into a chair.

Shiloh and I decided to visit the pool.

It wasn't a swimming pool, but a diving pool, straight sided and as deep as a well. There was a springboard with handrails and a wheel underneath so you could adjust the board's fulcrum. The water was green. Shiloh and I entertained ourselves with jackknives, cannon balls, suicides, and sailor dives. When we got tired of pulling ourselves out of the water, we stretched out on the cement apron and let the heat rise through our skin.

Excitement pulsed through me, like money I needed to spend.

Later the three of us sat on the cabin's lumpy mattress and referred to a map. Assuming we got on the road at a decent hour, we were guaranteed to reach New York before noon. And what, Alice wanted to know, did New York have to do with Vermont? Shiloh had a friend he needed to see. This friend knew people in Vermont. He would help us find our way.

Alice asked what the chances were we'd be in Vermont tomorrow night. That, Shiloh said, was not a matter of chance, but a statement of fact.

I took my shoes off and slid my legs beneath the sheets. Alice did the same. Shiloh told us he'd sleep in the car. Could he borrow the bedspread? He rubbed it against his face. He wanted us to know it was too scratchy, too dirty, too thin. He was on a talking jag. He started a story about a guy who might have been him, who got so cold he broke into a pigeon coop and stuffed the birds inside his pants. He was still in the room when I fell asleep.

I was the last up in the morning. I heard Alice stumble into the shower stall. I put my shoes on and walked outside, into the gentlest storm I'd ever known. The rain sifted down. I went over to the car to check on Shiloh. I could see him propped up in the backseat, but when I opened the door, he wasn't there, just a pile of his clothes.

Something shifted in my peripheral vision and I turned to see Shiloh wend his way through the stunted trees.

"What've you got?"

He placed six tiny apples on the roof of the car. With the rain it was dim beneath the trees. The apples were as dark as plums.

Alice had finished her shower. Whenever she stepped between the window and the table lamp, I saw her silhouette.

Another moment passed.

"Have you ever seen rain like this?" I asked.

"Many times."

"I hope Alice comes out soon."

"That's the spirit."

I turned to look at Shiloh. He was using a fingernail to scrape a stain from the front of his shirt. "You'll get a kick out of New York," said Shiloh.

"What are these people like?" I asked.

"For a certain period of time, they were the best people in the world."

When Alice came out of the cabin, the rain had stopped. She asked to drive. We piled into the car. Shiloh leaned his body forward so his chin rested on the seat back. In a voice that seemed full of regret, he said, "I promised myself I wouldn't go back there."

Inching through the orchard there were just the dark trees around us and the woolly clouds above.

Alice asked him why.

"I told you already," said Shiloh. "I got my heart broken. Heading back I'm bound to see things that will bring that into focus."

Alice got us onto the highway.

"It's no big deal," said Shiloh. "We'd never get anywhere trying to avoid my past."

There was a horn blast and then a car pulled abreast of us. I thought for a second it might be Alice's ex-husband. But it was only an angry man in a blue Cadillac. He gave us the finger before motoring on. I guess Alice had drifted out of her lane.

"This morning I almost forgot the name of this guy we have to see," said Shiloh. "I remember all these details about him. His shoes are fourteens, for instance. He's not a forgettable cowboy. It was as if some part of me didn't want to carry his name. Can you believe that?"

"But you remember it now," I said.

"Thomas, how many people have you met in your life? Now of those people, how many can you greet with their name? If energy can neither be created or destroyed, what goes on when we forget someone's name?"

It was about that time that the road came around a bend and we saw a whole town contained in a valley. A millworks bordered one side of a shallow river. Every window of the building had been broken out. There was no way for us to know if it had happened all at once or if it had taken years of hail and rocks and bullets.

Shiloh had something else to add. "What sort of responsibility do you have to those people, people you loved even?" He spit the sentences out as though they were poison. We were taking him to his heartbreak.

Alice turned toward me and rolled her eyes.

"His name is Parker," said Shiloh. "What he and I have in common is this other man. And this guy, this other guy, what made him most special was, he forgot no one. I'd give anything to talk with him."

"I wouldn't mind meeting a man like that," said Alice.

"Did I say *man*? I should have said boy."

"Look," I said. Next to the highway a huge billboard welcomed us to New Jersey. The signs said "Philipsburg." "Newark." "Jersey City." I saw a finger of land bristling with buildings. Alice reached to touch the windshield and I extrapolated a line from this. There in the water, the Statue of Liberty.

"Not like the brazen giant of Greek fame," Shiloh sang, "with conquering limbs astride from land to land; here at our sea-washed, sunset gates shall stand a mighty woman with a torch, whose flame is the imprisoned lightning, and her name Mother of Exiles."

And then the road came to something that looked like a pair of gargantuan drainpipes set into a wall of cement. The Holland Tunnel. What did we do? We drove underneath a river.

Shiloh didn't know the names of half the places we raced past. We saw bright sculptures like the skeletons of dinosaurs. Parks and squares and narrow streets. The Italian consulate was somewhere. John Lennon lived somewhere. There was this really cool toy store somewhere and a place where a person could buy two-dollar boots and a place where you could get an egg sandwich for twenty-five cents and had we ever had an egg cream or a real bagel or, shit, tried Oriental food? The streets were greasy. Loose trash was piled at the curb. We followed those fissured avenues up the island. Take a look at all these people. They were all living together, well, not together, but near each other. He had Alice zigzagging around. She'd never been here either. Had we ever played handball? Had we ever listened to opera? That was the opera house or the symphony. See? Central

Park. There's a zoo inside it and murderers. He pointed out the Metropolitan Museum of Art, the public library, and other grand things meant to commemorate a race of fantastic geniuses who had lived and died there, and ages ago. And had we heard of Washington Square Park? A person could buy anything there. Anything. He told us the city is made up of one-quarter immigrants, one-quarter intellectuals, one-quarter working stiffs, and one-quarter of the richest, most beautiful people and they all get along, and even if you live there, you can't tell them apart.

Beneath Shiloh's voice there were car horns and sirens and there were radios playing in the cars around us and kids beating on plastic tubs and kettle drums. In the middle of an intersection, a woman balanced on one leg playing a violin.

I looked over at Alice.

Alice's shoulders were all hunched up. She seemed to be suffering some sort of attack. "Do we have some sort of destination in mind?" she asked.

"We are headed," said Shiloh, "to an area of great hope."

He directed Alice to a place where the street names were numbers you could count on your fingers and avenues were just letters of the alphabet. We'd reached the heart of the city, or so it seemed.

Some of the buildings were missing corners. Some had windows created with sledgehammers. I kept expecting some type of transformation in the landscape. The bombed-out ruin we moved through wasn't landscape but destination. Every block had a thin dog with gummy eyes and a crooked tail. People scooted down sidewalks with nervous, bouncy steps. Everything was veneered with spray paint. Guarding the windows were wooden grates, metal bars, vinyl sheeting, and grilles from cars. Alleys were stuffed with mattress coils and trash cans. Shiloh explained that society's future was being forged in this sacred neighborhood.

Shiloh asked Alice to slow down. While the landmarks were coming back to him, he was used to negotiating the area on foot.

We saw a man in track shorts sleeping beneath a card table. Later I watched a pair of twins, middle-aged women in sky blue pantsuits and matching heels, hobble across a vacant lot toward something we thought might be a revival tent.

Finally, Shiloh had us let him out at a convenience store. The clerk eyeballed us through three-inch glass. Shiloh and the man had a conversation.

I wondered how a place could get so torn up without making the national news.

I said, "I don't think I will ever fall asleep on the island of Manhattan."

Alice said, "People can get used to anything."

I said, "That's a great disappointment."

Shiloh exited the store. He opened my door and got in beside me. His fingers massaged the dash. "He's moved, apparently."

"There are only nomads in the desert," said Alice. Then, as if the mention of a desert jogged her memory, she spread another coat of Noxzema on her face.

"I could show you where we used to live, but you guys probably don't want to wander through a bunch of empty buildings." He paused here, either to give us the chance to argue with him or so he could savor his defeat. He gave a little wave to the man in the store.

"I'm sorry," I said.

"Tell me how to get out of this city," said Alice.

"Whoa," said Shiloh. "I know where he went."

So we headed back up the island. Alice drove just on the acceptable side of recklessly. We headed up past Yankee Stadium where the dragon's teeth of flying pennants made me think of the Colisseum in Rome, and what a wonder that must have been while it was intact. I said, "Alice, doesn't that remind you of the Colisseum?" Shiloh said, "That's the spirit."

All at once we arrived in a neighborhood indistinguishable from the one we'd left. The question, it seemed: did Shiloh's friends seek destruction or cause it?

Shiloh gave me an encouraging slap on the leg. "Let's hit the pavement."

Alice found a parking space big enough that she could pull straight in.

Up on a stoop a woman dumped a saucepan of water on a toddler's head. They studied us as we stretched and twisted on the sidewalk. We probably looked as though we intended to perform an athletic feat. Shiloh popped the hood and wrenched some plastic part off the engine, putting it in his pocket. He dropped the hood and gave a signal that meant Alice and I should follow him.

I said good-bye to the car. I feared our circumstances might shortly dictate that I do something heroic or humiliating to ensure my safety. My heart beat, and only for me. Some of the streets were flooded with sunlight and others with shadow, and I didn't know, when the time came, which I would run to.

Shiloh pointed to the soaped windows of a storefront. Getting right up to the glass, we could see through to a room littered with broken floor tiles and skeins of gray lint. Limp rubber hoses hung from the walls. In the entranceway next to the laundromat, a narrow staircase led to a fire door.

We stood on the sidewalk and wondered what to do. We watched a boy on a bicycle tow a girl on roller skates. The girl wore tiny shorts; her knees touched, but not her thighs. She took a hand off the tow rope to give us a quick wave.

"Well?" Alice asked.

"This is the place," said Shiloh, "or it's someplace else." He held the door for us. I led the way. Alice followed, her hands on my hips either to guide me or to use me as a shield. If I paused, her hands urged me on.

The fire door was heavy and red and opened out. A man sitting on the floor just inside struggled to find his feet. He was high on some drug. His eyes and the rest of his face couldn't agree on which emotion to display. He was one person impersonating a throng.

Alice and I said, "Hey."

Shiloh peeked around us to check the guy out. "This could be the place."

"I shouldn't have let you in." The sleeper searched his pockets for something.

"It's okay," said Shiloh. "We're here for Parker."

Alice studied a hallway of doors.

"You're not looking for me?"

I shook my head.

"Fifth floor."

"That'd be the roof," said Shiloh.

"You'll see."

At the end of the hallway, we found another stairwell. I smelled bleach everywhere, but I didn't see anything that looked like it had been cleaned. When we reached the landing on the fourth floor, we found a ladder lashed to a trapdoor in the ceiling. Shiloh climbed up first, then Alice, then me. It was an ordinary roof with tarred machinery and bird shit and copper flashing tarnished green. Where a taller building abutted one side of the roof, something had made a great hole through the masonry. We walked through the hole into an abandoned bedroom.

"Recognize anything yet?" Alice asked.

A door opened and a girl walked in. A baby was held against the girl's shirt in a blanket sling. The girl could have been my age.

"Shiloh," said my friend, extending his hand.

"We don't sweat names here," said the girl. She looked down at the baby and kissed it on its head. Someone had tied the baby's hair into wispy braids.

"Where is here, exactly?" asked Alice.

The girl smiled. "This is Eden. Some people call it Eden East because of the other Eden, but they're not related. They call the other Eden 'Left Eden' because it's in California, on the left coast, and because of what it means. Eden East doesn't mean anything."

"We're looking for Parker," said Shiloh.

"You and everyone else."

"He and I are old friends," bragged Shiloh.

"Parker's sure got a lot of friends," observed the girl. She sighed. "My friend was supposed to be getting diapers."

We followed the girl into a dim hallway. Scraps of clothes littered the floor. She led us past open doors connected to empty rooms. A dog barked in a high, yappy voice. Pigeons slept on empty window-sills. Stepping through a pair of French doors, we found ourselves in front of a waiting elevator. Above us pebbly glass vaulted into a sky-light. We got inside the elevator. The girl pulled down a safety gate. We could hear children playing. Somewhere a man counted by fives. The acoustics of the building were such that the elevator acted like a tin-can telephone. The cage descended past empty halls and dark doorways.

The cage shuddered when we'd reached the end of the line.

"We're at least two levels underground," said Alice.

"Did you count? Because you shouldn't have counted. I should have said something." The girl sounded disappointed in herself.

Shiloh said, "It's okay. I've been here before."

The girl threw open the gate. She hit a switch and a grid of in-candescent bulbs came popping on. The lights were protected by wire cages and mounted at regular intervals across the ceiling. It was a tremendous room, two parallel planes connecting in the distance, a vast hole in space.

We all said, "Wow!"

"Maybe you were thinking of somewhere else," said the girl.

I watched the baby struggle to burrow toward a darker part of the girl's chest. The girl motioned for us to step out of the elevator. She had us wait there. Her sneakers squeaked on the clean cement as she minced across the open room. She disappeared behind a column and we didn't see her for a while.

"A lot can happen in a year's time," said Shiloh.

Listening as the elevator pulled voices out of the air like some per-fect radio, I had this irrational fear that I might overhear my own voice.

We heard footsteps long before we saw the people approaching.

That the girl wasn't carrying the baby anymore depressed me more than the stocky guy with the prospector's beard who accompanied her. Under all that hair I could make out a chin and a mouth, but nothing that might be called an expression. He looked younger than Shiloh. He might have been some freaknik farmer, except for his boots, not just any GI lace ups, but kangaroo-leather jump boots. It was no secret that some of those guys had come back high-strung. The longer I looked at him, the more convinced I was that he was the genuine article.

"Your friend?" Alice asked.

"I don't know," said Shiloh, who slouched his shoulders and tried to make himself look small.

The man stopped a few feet in front of us and spread his feet. His teeth peeked through his beard.

"I'll be fucked," said the stranger. "An honest-to-goodness ghost."

Shiloh stuck out his hand. "Hi, Parker."

Instead of shaking hands Parker stepped forward and wrapped Shiloh in his arms. They thumped each other on the back.

The girl's look told us that she considered this reunion an immense waste of her time.

Parker released Shiloh, then took a step back in order to consider Alice.

"I'll call you Venus," he told her.

"Alice," said Alice.

"Venus," said Parker, nodding.

"Give me a break," said Alice.

"And this is Thomas," said Shiloh. "He's a genius."

I don't know where that came from, but it had an effect on Parker. He had to look at me all over again.

"What sort of genius are you, kid?" Parker put his arm around the unimpressed girl.

"He's crafty," said Shiloh.

I had no idea what he was talking about. I didn't like meeting people in a place so hidden from the world. And I never expected Shiloh to know a guy like Parker.

Parker said, "I'm glad you made it."

"It took us a while to find you," said Shiloh.

"I'm keeping a low profile, but it hasn't stopped people from finding me."

"Yeah," said Shiloh.

Parker arched his eyebrows. All these thin lines, like paper cuts, showed on his forehead. "I mean lots of people."

Parker solicited ohs from Alice and me.

"Everything's still cool, I hope," said Shiloh.

The girl rolled her eyes, as though we were withholding her oxygen.

"Are things cool? Things are decidedly uncool. Choices have to be made. But you know what I say? Tomorrow isn't supposed to look like today."

"Tell him why we're here," said Alice.

"The thing is," said Shiloh, "we're actually on our way to Vermont."

Something passed across Parker's eyes. He turned toward the girl. "Why don't you go find your sister."

She walked off. When she was out of earshot, Parker turned back to us. He broke into a gigantic smile. "Now that's smart. I wouldn't mind getting back to the basics myself. Things are falling apart around here. I don't mind telling you, my popularity isn't what it once was."

Parker produced a pack of cigarettes from out of a jacket pocket. He lit one, took two puffs, and tossed it on the floor, ground it out under the toe of his boot. In the distance a single bulb inside a single cage flickered on and off.

"Maybe you're here to save me? I don't know."

At the moment it seemed unlikely that we would be capable of rescuing ourselves.

"Can you believe I'm going back to Vermont?" asked Shiloh.

"Lots of folks have been heading up that way," said Parker. "There's a new element. If I were you, I'd steer clear of them."

"What do you mean by 'element'?" asked Alice.

"He means people," said Shiloh.

"I understand that," said Alice. "I didn't think he was talking about carbon or salt. What sort of people?"

"You want an accounting?" asked Parker. "How about pushers, dopers, AWOL deserters, bail jumpers, along with every other type of conflict avoider you can imagine. Choose your friends wisely."

"You don't need to plant ideas in their heads," said Shiloh.

"How's it feel to be back at the scene of the crime?" asked Parker.

"Please," said Shiloh, his voice sounding tiny all of a sudden.

Parker said, "The last time we saw each other, you had some choice words for me."

"As you'll recall, I was out of my mind."

Parker wrapped Shiloh in another bear hug. He said, "I accept your apology." Then he kissed Shiloh smack on the lips.

I felt completely trapped. When the elevator cage lurched up the shaft, I felt even worse.

Parker said, "I'm touched that you'd bring your little friends by on your way up north."

"I thought maybe you'd have an idea what's going on up there," said Shiloh. "I thought you could get us pointed in a general direction." When he reached the end of this appeal, Shiloh turned to Alice and gave her a look like: see how reasonable I can be?

Parker said, "I know people who can help you get settled. They're God's children. They're doing very positive things. They take in stray cats and runaways. It's all part of their faith. They can look after you while you get your feet under you. They're into charity cases."

"We can pay our own way," said Alice.

"Oh, man, don't bring up money. Trust me, whatever you've got isn't enough, and whatever you're trying to get rid of nobody wants. Money won't do you a bit of good. In about twenty years they're going to figure out how to make diamonds in the laboratory and then the whole structure of wealth will go right out the window. Farmers will always be able to feed their families and dentists will always have to stick their fingers into strangers' mouths."

"Her sister lives with a dentist," I said.

"You're a fount of knowledge," said Parker. "Get this, the place those people live was going to be one of those places like Disneyland."

"An amusement park?" I asked.

The guy turned toward me. "More historical, like a village. They were going to have rides eventually, only things didn't get to that stage. It was after that movie, that musical. The Japanese were crazy for it, but then they decided it was easier to walk away than see things through. They had all the money in the world, but they ran out of courage." He nudged Shiloh with his elbow.

"A Japanese musical?" Alice asked.

"No, the movie isn't Japanese. The family lives in this really old-world place. Well, things go wrong, the Nazis, and they're forced to climb these mountains."

"*The Sound of Music*?" I asked.

Parker leveled his finger at me. "Bingo."

"And these are friends of yours?" asked Alice.

"I trust them, if that's what you're asking. Take my word, this place will be perfect for you. Just give me a couple of hours to beat the bushes and I'll tell you exactly where you can find them."

Alice said she was worried about her car.

"That's no problem," said Parker. "I'll help you move the car somewhere safe. After that I'll make these inquiries. You'll be back on the road first thing in the morning."

Alice glared at Shiloh.

"I told them we wouldn't have to stay in the city." Shiloh sounded unconvinced.

"There you have it for best-laid plans."

Parker led us across the vast room to something like a stamped steel pulpit. He had us mount the platform. There was a little console with a slot for a key. He pushed a button and the platform started inching upward. The ceiling yawned open and we passed through another dark floor. A siren cycled a few times before the ceiling parted again and we saw clouds. The lift delivered us to the sidewalk. All around us loomed the familiar ruined buildings.

It was a relief to be out from under all that cement and gravity. I didn't know if I could submit to it again.

We found the car. Shiloh replaced the part he'd carried with us, one of the battery cables.

We piled in. Parker told Alice where to turn.

"How long have you been staying here?" Shiloh asked.

"A little while. A couple of months. They want me out, but no one has the stones to tell me to split." Then he said, "Ha! What did the girl tell you?" He looked at us expectantly.

Shiloh looked from Alice to me. "You know," he said.

"I run the place, basically," said Parker. "They're kids. It's a younger generation. They're idealists, I guess. They suffer from limited thinking."

He had Alice turn again.

"What are you doing these days?" Shiloh asked.

I didn't necessarily want to hear Parker's answer to the question. It was bad enough that we were going back inside that building.

"New things," said Parker. "Here we go."

Wedged between two basically intact buildings, a bulldozer hulked, its scarred blade rested on the pavement. We waited as Parker climbed over the steel blade and into the vehicle's cab. In a moment the diesel stack started to flutter. He gave us the high sign and the bulldozer crept out of its lair. Inside the alleyway there were motorcycles in different states of disrepair, cars on blocks and parts of cars on blocks, a yellow sports car and a blue van. With the bulldozer idling in the middle of the street, Alice parked the Plymouth at the head of the line. After he'd backed the bulldozer into place, Alice asked how she was going to get her car out. Parker said we shouldn't get ahead of ourselves. Shiloh asked Parker what he needed a bulldozer for.

"Have you ever had access to a bulldozer?" asked Parker.

Shiloh said he hadn't.

"Imagine you had a twelve-inch dick. Let me tell you, I'm going to hate to give it up."

It started to rain. Outside the laundromat, suds formed on the sidewalk.

Opening a door on the side of the building, Parker led us back into the maze. He led us up a flight of stairs, down a hallway choked with humming refrigerators, and into a large room where six floor-to-ceiling windows shared one terrible view. The room was crowded with defective furniture, as though the previous tenant had spent all his time trying and failing to invent the chair.

Parker told us to sit tight.

On what?

I propped a bench up with a stool while Alice wandered about trying to find something redeeming in the place. Shiloh just stretched out on the floor. He stared at the ceiling as if he could see stars.

"How'd you and Parker meet?" I asked.

Shiloh turned to look at me. "You're asking me about history," Shiloh said, "but from now on I only want to think about the future."

All at once we were starving. Shiloh and I retraced our route to the refrigerators. What we found inside didn't give us any hope, row upon row of brown plastic jugs, some empty, others full, dates written on white labels.

"Do you know what this is?" I asked.

"I have a hunch," said Shiloh. He picked a jug up and weighed it at the end of his arm. "I don't think we want to eat it."

We returned to the bleak room. Alice didn't say anything. She stared out the windows.

The girl came in carrying the baby. Something about her face made me sympathetic to sleep.

"Did you get the diapers?" I asked.

She held the baby away from her body, so its bowlegs dangled.

"This is a different girl," said Alice.

The girl took a spot on a filthy sofa and bounced the baby on her thigh. "This baby is crazy for jumping."

The three of us watched the baby, who looked, if not thrilled, at least content. Then the girl embraced the baby the way a girl will a doll or kittens, as though overcome with happiness, as though, in her exuberance, she might accidentally smother the child.

I wanted to say something to her.

She propped the baby up on the sofa. The baby toppled over and rubbed its mouth over the upholstery.

"Are you baby-sitting us?" Shiloh asked.

"No," said the girl. "I'm waiting with you."

Alice took a ten-dollar bill out of her front pocket and held it in the air. "If you get us some food, you can keep the change."

The girl took the money and left.

*   *   *

A little while later Shiloh said, "Do you think she's coming back?"

Alice asked, "You don't think she will?"

"I don't know," said Shiloh.

"I think she'll come back," I said.

Alice just groaned.

The girl marched in with two greasy bags containing a dozen beef tamales, a Styrofoam container of rice and beans, and a six-pack of orange soda—the most exotic meal I'd ever seen. The smell of the food drove me crazy. The spicy oil burned my lips. I sucked the rim of the can of too sweet soda. It was painful and wonderful. Perspiration evaporated from my forehead.

"What do you think of Parker?" the girl asked.

Shiloh said they were old friends.

"Did he ask if you were here to save him?"

"He said something," said Alice.

"He's like a broken record. He's not fooling anyone."

"What do you mean?" asked Shiloh.

"Every time someone shows up looking for him, he pretends it's some great mystery."

I said, "I hope we're not getting him in any trouble."

"Parker doesn't need anyone's help finding trouble." She smiled at me. "I've got to get this baby to bed. I'll show you where the bathroom is and then you can make yourselves comfortable."

The bathroom was across the hall. The toilet flushed with pails of rainwater. This struck me as a beautiful process, meditative and honest. Immediately I resolved that my life should be like this, a little more involved, a manageable struggle.

We whispered thanks to the girl—the baby had fallen asleep in her arms.

We went back to the room. We expected to be tired at any moment. Alice said spicy food always knocked her out. It turned out that the soda contained a lot of caffeine.

"We'll be away from here tomorrow," said Shiloh.

Alice said, "I can't tell you how much of a relief that will be."

*   *   *

In the morning a purple light cut across the room. I went to the bath-room, poured rainwater in the bowl.

I got turned around on my way back. Instead of returning directly to the room, I wound up in a dark hallway. Black plastic lined the floors. When a corridor intersected, filled with the light I'd woken to, I thought I'd rescued myself. I came to the room where we had stayed, but there was no furniture and no Alice. I tried to understand what had taken place. It was the time of day that proves conclusively how light can bend. Looking out the window I saw that the building wasn't a solid, blocky cube, but was composed of a series of linked towers. Insulated by a hundred yards of air, I spied a room, the twin to the one I was in. In that room I had a twin who approached the glass. It was Parker, peering down at the sidewalk, rubbing a spot on the glass with his finger. I couldn't believe I'd left Alice alone. I needed to get back to that room before he moved from the window.

I sprinted down the purple corridor, nearly losing my footing when I turned onto the slick plastic. I burst into a windowless room filled with racks of folding tables. Then I understood my mistake and found the right room. I was back before Alice had finished rubbing the sleep out of her eyes. Shiloh and Parker were eating egg sand-wiches. They had a coffee for Alice and a chocolate milk for me.

"You did right coming here," Parker said. Maybe Parker didn't have a lot of opportunities to give people good news, because he seemed to relish his station. He told us that he had managed to track down a few of his contacts, people who were not easy to find. He had an address for us and a set of directions. These people he was putting us in touch with were salt of the earth. They had a covenant with God that was equal parts Lutheranism and socialism. They believed they had the right to take from those who had more and lose to those who had less, and all the time they endeavored to remain very pleasant. All of this they claimed to have picked up from the Bible—technically, they were fundamentalists. They were smart, business savvy, just the type of people we needed to help us get set up. And if we didn't like their scene, we were free to move on. That was part of their faith, too.

"Welcome to the new radicalism," said Parker.

"You'll have to take us to our car," said Shiloh.

"You're in a rush all of a sudden?"

"I've been waiting for the next part of my life forever," said Shiloh.

"I like that," said Parker. "That touches me."

He led us out of that place and into the shadow-filled streets. There was a quietness in the air, like the fading echoes of raindrops. The oily pavement was beaded with dew. Parker fired up the bulldozer and eased it out. The three of us got in our car, Alice at the wheel. It started right up.

"Thank God," said Alice.

Parker tapped on Alice's window.

Alice rolled it down.

"Now you folks look after one another," said Parker.

Shiloh leaned forward from the backseat. "I see you still got that van," he said, pointing his thumb at a blue cargo van stashed in the alley.

Parker nodded.

Alice hit the gas. Her seven-year-old Plymouth, the three of us, all our things stored in the trailer, we left that place behind. Somehow Alice managed to find a thoroughfare with signs and options. She saw a sign that said "Upstate." The road curved, merged. We joined the traffic heading north.

"It's not a good thing to have so many visitors," said Shiloh, "especially when they're making drugs."

"They were making drugs there?" Alice asked.

Shiloh fell back in the seat. "You saw all the refrigerators."

"Why would they keep grass in refrigerators?" asked Alice.

"Who said anything about grass?"

Alice decided to pursue a different channel of inquiry. "What exactly did Parker do?"

"He's not guilty of half the things people blame him for."

"I've never met so many persecuted people," observed Alice.

"I'm not persecuted," said Shiloh. "I'm misunderstood."

Alice shook her head, as if to say, Let the record show I shook my head.

"Trust me," said Shiloh, "neither of you has a clue."

"What are you talking about?" I asked him.

"The problem is determining what It is."

"But you know what It is?"

"I have an opinion."

I made a gesture, like I was trying to draw this thing out of him.

"It's personal."

"What does Parker have to do with It?"

"Parker is like us."

"How is he like us?" Alice wanted to know.

"He's just like us. He's on the run."

8
Idyll

I wasn't on the run. Every moment with Alice I was home. Not getting into her car would have been running. I was certain of this.

I had dropped my things from the window of my boyhood room. A moment later I'd dropped myself. And I'd felt worse before I jumped than after.

Mary and her noble intentions, Fran's wounded empathy, were secure in their beds. I paused to gather up my things.

The rusty spring securing the screen door whined. Pawpaw eased himself down the steps and into the yard. From his outpost on the porch, he'd heard my escape.

"You're sure up early," was the first thing he said.

I didn't know who was being deceived. "I have to meet some friends," I said. It was about half-past five in the morning.

"I see," said Pawpaw. He patted his pants' pockets. "Let me walk you. I'll buy you breakfast."

"I don't want them to have to wait for me."

"I understand," he said, then, softer, he repeated himself, "I understand."

"I'm probably late already."

We waited at the corner while a milk truck rattled past.

He said something under his breath.

"What?" I asked him.

"A window makes a novel door."

I turned toward him. The muscles of his face were slack, as though they'd been severed from the bone. Still, I thought he'd live forever. I thought all of us would.

"I forgot my ciggies," Pawpaw said.

We'd come about five blocks.

"You want me to run and get them?"

"No. No." He wrapped me in his sinewy arms. "Your friends are waiting for you. Get going. Away."

Despite their size it took forever to get anywhere in those New England states. It never dawned on those people that a road might be made straight. We headed up one hill and down another. Western Massachusetts was just one green headache. Separating the towns were rivers a person could have waded across.

I'd been traveling for three days. As far as I could tell, we weren't heading toward anything at all. I was ready for the traveling to come to an end. I was ready to arrive.

Our shadow raced beside us. The silhouette of the car, as simple as a child's drawing, the little trailer keeping pace. In that spare illustration anyone could recognize a family on a trip. The curve of the windshield projected a faint prism's rainbow in the dust and gravel of the shoulder, and for a moment the rainbow centered so perfectly over my head that I couldn't help but take it as an omen. I didn't bother seeking a witness, since the phenomena depended as heavily on them as on me. To try and capture it would certainly dispel it. And when the trick ended, I didn't cheapen it by trying to reproduce it.

We made progress. At some unmarked point we slipped across a border. The trees flashed their silver leaves at us.

"Now that's Vermont," said Shiloh, pointing at a sway-backed barn.

"Completely Vermont," said Alice.

Some guy in a red truck all cankered with rust. "Mr. Vermont," I dubbed him.

"Exactly."

These small little calving sheds at the edges of the fields: Vermont. A boulder-choked stream and its chalky water: Vermont.

The directions Parker provided relied on landmarks rather than street names. We ticked off the duckweed-covered marsh, the mailbox mounted on a wagon wheel. Every indication was that we were on the right course. And the challenge of decoding this imperfect document distracted us from that central question: what were we going to do when we found this place? What were we supposed to do when the voyage stopped, when we arrived? We'd come this far out of faith in each other and in the process itself.

We came to the last line of instruction: *When you come to the land of tiny flags, you're there.*

We didn't anticipate anything other than being surprised.

Beside the road we saw a jumble of brightly painted rocks. A little ways on, a stack of I-beams rusted in the grass. Then Shiloh noticed how, through countless empty acres, color-coded tassels of survey stakes measured the wind. Alice lifted her foot off the gas. Tucked away on the hillside above us, half hidden from the road, a group of A-frame houses huddled together. From our vantage the sloping hill obscured the bases of the buildings. The pointed rooflines were as sharp as fence pickets. A dirt driveway led up toward the houses. By the side of the road, on a post, someone had built a mailbox to look like an A-frame house. The only markings on the mailbox were the initials DWG, which had been painted in white on the untreated wood.

"Drive already," said Shiloh.

And we started up the hill.

Compared to the scope of the surveyor's stakes, the four houses were humble. They were arranged around a small pond, like hours on a clock face. In the center of the pond, there was a little island and on the island an empty picnic table. I thought I saw a couple of heads bobbing in the water, but then we were behind the nearest house and

I lost sight of the water. A sun-faded coupe rested on cinder blocks, the only car we saw.

Alice parked beside the wreck. Clusters of paper birches dotted a recently mown pasture.

I turned toward Shiloh for a clue as to how we should proceed.

He had just opened his door when I heard someone shouting a warning to us. Through the dusty glass of the back window, I saw a woman running toward our car. She waved her hands above her head, but I was more impressed that she was naked.

Then there was a crashing sound, like someone hitting the car with a sledgehammer.

Shiloh slammed his door shut and practically climbed over the seat back.

"It's a goat," said Alice.

I saw the animal rise up on its hind legs and drive its bony skull into the quarter panel of the car. The sheet metal rang like a rotten bell.

The naked woman crouched behind the animal and wrapped it in her arms.

"He doesn't like people parking next to his car," she said by way of explanation. The animal struggled in her arms. It had yellow reptilian eyes.

Alice moved her car a safe distance away.

"I wonder if they're nudists," said Shiloh. "That would be like Parker, to neglect to mention something like that."

Alice gave Shiloh a humorless look.

We had gotten out of the car and were examining the damage when a man's voice called out to us.

"You're the refugees from New York, I take it."

When we turned around, his head eclipsed the noontime sun. He could have been seven feet tall. He had on tan logging boots and a black bikini. His body was completely hairless. Underneath the damp fabric, his unit looked like a baby's arm.

"Your goat attacked my car." Alice rubbed her hand over the dent.

"No," he said, "it is not my goat."

Squatting beside us, he reached a hand inside the wheel well. He used his hand like a mallet to pop the sheet metal back into place. The paint showed fine cracking, like spiderwebs.

I wanted him to put some pants on. He had this strange accent. Every word was a stone he dropped on our heads.

The goat had clambered onto the roof of its car. It looked immensely satisfied. I didn't see where the woman had gone.

"You are Parker's friends, yes?"

We introduced ourselves. The giant's name was Gregor. And the woman who had run out to help us? We could call her Magdalena.

"That's a beautiful name," said Alice. "Is she your wife?"

This put a smile on Gregor's face. "She is more my sister." Gregor seemed half asleep or maybe stoned. The way he spoke, I got the feeling that the voice inside his head wasn't speaking English.

"Is it just the two of you?" asked Shiloh. "We were under the impression that you had a thing going on here."

Gregor pointed straight up. "It's the middle of the day. The others are out working. I am here only to greet you. Follow me inside, you will find out why Magdalena is here."

With his booming voice it sounded almost like a threat. So when he swept his hand toward the nearest house, we stood fixed to our spot.

"She has made lunch," said Gregor.

We followed him on a path between two houses and up onto a deck. There were window boxes balanced on the railing and painted gingerbread running underneath the roof's gables. Finally we'd come upon some people interested in keeping up appearances.

The big man hustled us inside through a sliding glass door.

Inside we found bare framing and exposed wires. Rolls of insulation had been stapled in between the ribbing of the steep roof. Where we'd entered, the roofline was the ceiling, but at the back of the house an open staircase led up to a second-floor platform. The whole place smelled of pressure-treated wood and spoiled milk.

"This is cozy," said Shiloh.

Gregor seemed to take inordinate satisfaction from seeing our unfamiliar faces in his living room. He pointed at some chairs, indicating that we sit. In the darkest corner of the house, someone was shuffling dishes and pans.

He left the three of us alone while he went to see how things were proceeding in the kitchen.

"I hope he puts some pants on," I whispered.

"If they ran out of money," said Alice, "they didn't have much to begin with."

"These houses are amazingly efficient," said Shiloh. "The shape of the roof funnels the warm air upstairs."

"I'd need a bit more privacy than this," said Alice.

"No you wouldn't," said Shiloh.

"Well, I'd prefer it," she said, reaching over and placing her hand on my knee.

I imagined taking those back stairs with Alice.

Gregor returned with a plate in each hand and another balanced in the crook of his arm. He handed them to us. There was some brown meaty thing and mashed potatoes and carrots, and covering all of it a thick gravy. Our host returned to the kitchen. He came back with two more plates. Magdalena trailed behind him, carrying a tray of jelly jars and a pitcher of water. She had put on a sack dress. Her lips were drawn into this line, as if she didn't intend to speak. I was glad I hadn't gotten a better look at her before.

"What beats this?" Shiloh asked, scooping a pile of potatoes into his mouth.

Instead of eating, our hosts lowered their heads.

"Pardon me," Shiloh said, out of the corner of his mouth.

Gregor dismissed his apology. "Our Lord is certainly sympathetic to hunger."

Shiloh pointed his knife at the hunk of meat. "What are we having?"

"It's pheasant," said Gregor.

"Did you make all this, Magdalena?" asked Alice.

"I cooked it." The woman blushed. She whispered something in Gregor's ear.

"She can't remember your names," said Gregor.

"I don't think we told her," I said.

Gregor slapped his forehead. "I am no good at introducing people to people. My talent is introducing people to God."

"He turned God on his head," bragged Magdalena.

Shiloh shifted in his seat. For a moment I thought Shiloh might say that he had turned God on his head, too.

"People seek us out all the time," said Gregor. "They tell me where they've been and who they know. These are very persuasive people. But I turn them away. I turned away Bob Seger's brother, an ordained priest. He offered me ten thousand dollars just to live in one of these houses. What did I say?" He turned to Magdalena.

"You asked for fifty thousand," she said.

"This is true. Now did I want that money? No. It was a principle. He was only willing to part with what he could part with easily. Ten thousand to him was what? Ten dollars for you and me. He called me a Judas. Can you believe that?"

The three of us couldn't believe it.

"Even if he had paid, it would have been the greatest bargain of his life. He would have gotten a home, a family, a job, and a purpose. How many folks do you know who have those four things? But what is their purpose? Is it gaining access to paradise? Or is it gaining a headstone at Paradise Acres?"

"Are you saying that you can guarantee passage into heaven?"

When Alice asked this Magdalena perked up in her chair.

"I am not selling tickets for some elevator ride," said Gregor. "I introduce people to a pathway."

"Do you believe in saints?" asked Shiloh.

Gregor put his plate down and walked to the sliding glass door. "What is a saint?" He looked out at the property. "Most people think a saint is a person who performs miracles or acts of grace. How can they do this? I would like to think that there's a fragment of God inside them, a little crumb. Then the next question is, why does God put that crumb inside them? Perhaps there is a crumb of God inside all of us?" Now he turned around like an attorney addressing the jury. "Does it surprise you that some people believe I am a saint?"

"That's not what I meant," said Shiloh.

Gregor shrugged his huge shoulders. "Let's ask Mags what she thinks."

The woman sucked on her lower lip. "A lot of people are looking for answers. But what they should be looking for are better questions."

For some reason I found her logic very exciting. Like flushing the toilet with rainwater, it suggested that we were on the road to some higher understanding.

"If you ask me why," said Gregor, "I won't be able to explain myself, but I'd like for you to join us here, the three of you."

"You mean," said Shiloh, "we can just move into one of these houses?"

"Well," said Magdalena, "all the houses are occupied for the time being. But in the fall . . ."

"In the meantime," said Gregor, "you should come by, meet the family."

"We get together every Thursday to share a meal," said Magdalena. "Friends are always welcome to stop by."

"Once the crops are harvested," continued Gregor, "we're going to concentrate on improving the facilities, like more of these houses and possibly a barn. If we have time there are some other projects we might get around to. We have blueprints. You probably saw how things are already staked out."

"Parker said something about an amusement park," said Alice.

"The previous owners, that had been their intention," said Gregor. "I only wanted the land, but they made me take it all, lock, stock, and barrel. It worked out okay. Now we're a fully licensed educational nonprofit."

"Alice is an educator," said Shiloh.

"I was teaching at a high school," explained Alice.

Gregor was slapping his forehead again, but in a different way, as if he couldn't believe his good fortune. "Just the other day I was telling someone that the one thing we needed to find was an educator."

"For the babies," added Magdalena. On her calf she sported a tattoo of a mouse sitting on top of a wedge of Swiss cheese. The tattoo perplexed me.

Alice was trying to keep up with the conversation, but something held her up. "How do you run an educational nonprofit without any educators?"

"The licensing is just to establish a beneficial tax climate," answered Gregor. "What it means is that when you initiate, every cent goes back into the corporation. Uncle Sam gets nothing for his war machine."

"What do you mean 'initiate'?" asked Shiloh.

"I don't like the word either," said Magdalena, who started gathering our dirty dishes and carrying them to the back of the house.

"People in the family contribute labor and skill. That's the currency," said Gregor. "We plant crops together and tend to the fields, and when we sell our harvest the proceeds benefit everyone. But with new folks we can't just give you a house to live in and put food in your stomach. You haven't contributed any work yet. If we did that we'd be running a deficit. Would you want to involve yourselves with a group that ran a deficit? It wouldn't be healthy. Instead of thinking of the initiation as the cost of joining our community, consider it bail you're paying to skip out on your old lives."

"How much is the fee?" asked Shiloh.

"What's it worth to you to live here?"

Alice massaged her eyebrows with her fingertips.

Shiloh stared at his hands.

"Three hundred dollars," I said.

Gregor gave me an appraising look. "It doesn't really make sense for us to have this conversation before you've seen the whole community."

"Are there a lot of pheasants up here?" I asked.

"There are fewer every day," Gregor said, standing up.

Apparently lunch was over. Gregor and Magdalena walked us to our car. I thought I was watching the ripples where invisible fish disturbed the surface of the pond, but it was only rain. Magdalena wrapped me up in her arms and kissed both my cheeks.

Alice started the car and we limped away. "Where the hell do we go now?" she asked.

Shiloh and I were in no rush to answer her. If you pointed in a direction and then things didn't pan out, that might confirm that you were unlucky or undeserving of luck. Rather than try to shape our destiny, it seemed safer to let things run their course.

The car had baked in the sun and now it refused to cool down. The heat was something we hadn't expected. We couldn't help but marvel at how, like some dim-witted pet, it had followed us.

I'd been watching a bright band of light flashing through the trees and finally I got a good view of it. "There's a river over there," I said.

"Oh, man," said Shiloh, "you know what that is? That's Lake Champlain."

"Tell me how to get there," said Alice.

But we'd made our way onto some highway, and there were no exits.

When the lake disappeared behind a low hill, it drove us crazy. We were like the mind of a suicide who cannot be consoled, impatient even after the bullet is on its way.

And once again we spied the flashing water.

Shiloh took his shirt off and held it out the window. It was a white shirt. It streamed alongside us, as though we were surrendering to the state. He let it go and the shirt hung above the roadway for an instant before our wake tumbled it to the asphalt.

Shiloh tilted his head back and howled at the ceiling. He kissed my cheek and then he kissed Alice's. A flashing yellow light marked our exit.

Alice took the corner at a reckless speed. We were racing toward the water. Immediately she had to jump on the brakes. The tires made a plaintive protest. Behind us the trailer turned onto its roof and skidded across the asphalt. On either side of the road, Little League games were in progress. The street was filled with kids, some in uniforms, others straddling bicycles, lined up before an ice-cream truck parked alongside the road. Parents and grandparents crowded bleachers. Our unfortunate entrance turned them all against us.

Shiloh and I got out of the car. The little kids shook their heads at us. We rocked the trailer until we could get it back on its wheels. We clambered back into the car.

Everyone watched us creep away.

Shiloh slumped in the backseat and fooled with the hair on his chest. His eyes were this shade of blue-green, like seawater. They were his one exceptional feature. "We can live anywhere but here," he said.

When we reached the end of the street, Alice sighed. She may have been holding her breath. We came around a corner and the only thing between us and that wonderful, glimmery lake was a hamburger joint with a dirt parking lot and some redwood tables with umbrellas. Alice drove to the back of the lot. We piled out of the car and ran toward the water.

The surface of the lake shone like chrome. Shiloh yanked his pants down. He wasn't wearing any underwear. He hadn't taken his shoes off, and now his pants tangled around his ankles. He lost his balance and toppled to the ground. I watched Alice peel her pants over her hips and pull her blouse over her head. In orange panties and black bra she walked backward into the lake. I followed her in my briefs. Ridiculous Shiloh, his ape arms and skinny legs, his soft, furry face, he ran in after us.

"No matter what happens," I said, "it will be worth it just for this." I believed that.

Alice and I porpoised in the water, pulling our underwear down to moon our friend.

Alice and I invented a game where we took turns baptizing each other. The winner was the one who performed the act with the most grace and piety. We repeated this over and over.

"I feel so *clean*," said Shiloh. He used handfuls of mud to scour his chest and under his arms, until the skin glowed bright pink.

Alice took my hand and led me toward a clump of cattails. For whatever reason we were horny. The lake bottom became cold and muddy, but I followed her into the thick of the reeds. The sounds we made; the water's rhythmic slapping; our quick breathing; the dry stalks, all around us, rattled like bones.

9
Shiloh Takes a Stand

We ate dinner in a convenience-store parking lot. Maybe there were so many insects because so few lights competed for their attention. When we couldn't stand it a moment longer, we got back in the car. Alice drove a little farther, but her heart wasn't in it. She parked beside a clapboard church. "Sanctuary," said Shiloh. We were all too tired to talk. Shiloh carried a few blankets off into the woods. Alice and I managed to spoon in the narrow backseat. Maybe we were thinner than I remember. I know we couldn't stand to be apart.

The revolutionary, Shiloh explained the next day, can't afford to let the perceived stand in for the actual. He was driving. Perception is a tool of the establishment, he said. He asked Alice and me to vow not to take anything for granted. He turned to see that we understood.

"And how does a person know they are perceiving the real?" asked Alice.

They both sounded like maniacs to me.

"I'm just reminding you to keep twisting your antennae," said Shiloh. "The difference between what stands in for the world and the world itself is like the difference between a portrait of a loved one and their actual face."

If I'd asked him to list the top five things on his mind, I don't think driving would have made the list.

Had we noticed the mountains? Shiloh asked. Their evergreen crowns? They were telling us something about this world. Ravens, Shiloh explained, were like muscular crows that lived high up in that pure mountain air. Did we believe that? Did we believe that there were big crows living on top of the mountains? Ravens, said Shiloh. Ravens.

I wanted to be back at the lake.

We were on a paved road that adjoined a fenced-in pasture when Shiloh stopped the car. There wasn't much of a shoulder to pull onto. He stepped out of the car and walked over to the fence. Pulling the strands of wire apart, he entered a field with half a dozen Holsteins. The cows stopped their grazing to watch him approach.

"What's he doing now?" Alice asked.

I got out of the car.

"Which one's the bull?" I asked.

"I don't think there always is one," said Shiloh.

"What will you do if they decide to stampede?"

Alice came up beside me and leaned her head against my shoulder.

"What do you suppose this is about?" she asked me.

Shiloh turned around to smile at us. "Check out the grass."

Inside the enclosure everything had been nipped back, but where Alice and I were standing, it was vibrant and thick. I didn't think I'd ever seen healthier grass in all my life. It seemed a person might sustain themselves on the stuff.

One of the cows trotted over to investigate us. Its big wet eye lolled in the socket like one of those cheap key-ring compasses.

Alice wanted me to feed the cow.

I ripped up a handful of juicy stuff and reached over the top strand of the fence with it.

"Look," said Alice, "there are veins on its udders."

Shiloh came over and slapped the cow's flank. I expected some dramatic reaction. The cow meandered off.

"Well?" he asked.

"Wherever we're going, I hope we get there soon." Alice started toward the car.

"Do you see what I was talking about?" Shiloh asked. "About the way we perceive things and the way they really are?"

"You mean the grass," I said.

"I mean everything."

10

Procession

I was driving. Shiloh sulked in the backseat. Alice had relieved him of the keys after he had almost wrapped the car around a telephone pole, which, for no reason, had been planted dead center in the road. "I can't be held responsible for other people's thoughtlessness," he said in explanation. Now it was raining so hard that the wipers couldn't keep up. When I spotted a pair of gas pumps in front of a general store, I saw an excuse to get off the road for a moment.

It was a soaking rain, not exactly warm. I wished Alice and I were on our way to another cottage motel, and this time I wouldn't let myself fall victim to sleep; in one of those tiny rooms, we'd be alone with our happiness. I topped off the tank and stuck my head in the car to get the money from Alice—she insisted on buying all the gas, since it was her car, and neither Shiloh nor I was in any position to argue. Shiloh had made it clear that, while he didn't have a great deal of money, were we to put a value on his technical expertise, he would be a full partner.

"That was dumb," said Shiloh.

The rain drummed on the roof. "Huh."

"You probably got water in the tank." He mimed turning the ignition key. "Won't start."

I felt like a kid.

"Or you're driving along when she conks out on you."

Alice made no attempt to conceal the concern on her face.

Inside the store a middle-aged woman sitting behind the counter studied the cover of a book: *Contradance!* The cover was made up of diagrams of shoe prints. I asked if they sold a treatment for water in the gas tank.

She showed me two products. I asked for her suggestion. She pulled the more expensive of the two off the shelf. We walked back to the register.

When I returned outside the sky was unchanged, but the rain had stopped. I read the directions on the treatment and poured the bottle's contents into the tank.

Alice got out of the car and rested her arms on the roof. She tilted her head back and yawned. "What'd you get?"

I showed her.

We heard high, happy voices. Out on the road a pack of cyclists climbed the hill. Their tires hissed on the wet pavement. Some of them wore clear plastic jackets that slapped and cracked against the pull of the wind. They rolled past, a collective breathing.

Shiloh got out of the car, turned to watch the last of the cyclists disappear around the next corner. "We ought to get bikes." He turned back to us and smiled. He picked the package of gas treatment off the roof.

I didn't say anything.

"I hope you stole this stuff. Don't tell me you paid that price."

I picked a point on the horizon and let my eyes rest there.

"We could fill a bathtub with this gunk for about a quarter of what they charge."

Alice said, "Well, since we don't have a bathtub, I suppose Thomas made a wise choice."

I was grateful that she'd come to my defense.

The Plymouth shivered up the loose gravel of those washboard, nowhere roads. The roads I chose petered out in trenchlike ruts, at muddy stream crossings. We found little hollows with one-room schoolhouses and corrugated steel hutches. Cornfields extended into the narrow pie slices of land where two similar roads reached an agreement. We saw a young girl riding a chestnut horse in her underpants. A man, his car, and a long machine, alone in a clearing, split wood; the man fed the machine rounds of wood and the machine halved them. The land canted and tilted and fell away. I lost all faith in the here and there. The name of the countryside was déjà vu. The roads digressed. I drove too fast and nobody tried to stop me. I caught myself grinding my teeth. The road straightened out. I slowed us down. We saw a black car in the distance, but when we caught up, it was an ox. Loops of saliva were suspended from the animal's gums. In front of the ox, a small boy was occupied with pushing a stick through the gravel.

Shiloh said, "I wish I were that kid."

Alice waved to the boy.

"What could he be afraid of?" asked Shiloh.

We went over a hill. A paved two-laner bisected the road we'd been following. A green sign pointed to the right and said "Underhill." In that direction a few houses crowded each other. Beyond them I saw the makings of the town. The buildings had those facade fronts. That sealed the deal. I drove across the blacktop to see where the dirt road could take us. We started on a gentle climb. After a ways we reached an overlook. All around us the mountains were soft green humps. The road entered a forest. We kept heading up. We passed a series of emerald pastures. Tiny cabins hid among the trees. They excited us. I had a growing sense that we were getting close to whatever it was we'd come looking for.

A line of cars approached with their headlights on. In one of his outpourings of trivia, Shiloh had told us how Canadians kept their headlights on all day.

The obvious was invisible to me. I thought I was seeing a convoy of Quebecois.

"The last ride," said Shiloh.

I didn't get his point.

"Someone's off to see the old generals," he said.

They practically put me in the ditch.

Shiloh slugged me in the shoulder. "Get off the road, Thomas."

The hearse passed so close, I saw my reflection in the door. The procession continued, peppering our windshield with kicked-up stones. Bringing up the end of the cortege, a hay truck, kids in back tackling one another and throwing handfuls of the stuff into the air. The yellow straw drifted down around us.

"They're taking him to his low home," Shiloh said.

After the heavy dust settled, I eased us back onto the road. I was wary of stragglers. In places the road narrowed enough that meeting another car would have necessitated one of us backing up. We wound up a short hill before we came to a clearing. On the far side of the clearing, the road began to slope away. And there, way in the distance, we saw a body of water that looked to be a great river and, whether due to a general disorientation or an underlying belief in the mystical, nothing could convince us this was the same lake we'd camped beside the night before.

We hadn't expected that road to take us to any single place, but that it would connect us to other places. The funeral procession gave us hope. We thought we'd stumbled upon a shortcut through the mountains. The assumption was that roads didn't just head into the mountains, but through them. Sometimes, like a river, a road has a source.

We passed an Airstream trailer parked near the crown of the hill. The yard was overrun with tire tracks. The silver trailer looked almost medicinal, like some fantastic capsule. I slowed as we drew past. Inside a split-rail corral, a shaggy pony turned to watch its tail slap its back. Behind the trailer a pair of green lawn chairs were arranged side by side.

I drove on. The hump of the road became more pronounced, the gravel looser. We continued past pastures choked with brush. It seemed as if we'd reached a summit or crested a ridge. The trees pinched in on the road. The road passed over a culvert; a little stream gurgled and splashed. The trees began to thin and we came through on the other side. A couple of hundred yards farther, two crossed boards marked the place where the road dead-ended at a wall of trees. On the left side of the road, an empty field. On the other side, set back a ways, a house.

The Inn Where Strangers Meet

TWO MEN

*T*he two men had been in the room for a little more than an hour. The younger man was drinking ice water to pass the time. There were two double beds, and the older man was lying on top of the one closest to the door. There was a single fly in the room, but, for the moment, it was resting.

From time to time they heard people shuffle by in the corridor.

The older man got up and went into the bathroom. He washed his face in the sink. There was a soft knock on the bathroom door. "He's here," said the younger man.

The older man was meticulous about drying his hands. When he came out of the bathroom, there was another man in the room. The other man wore an overcoat, suit, and tie. He set a valise on the table.

"That is a very nice valise," said the older man.

"You mean the briefcase? Thank you. A gift from my wife."

The younger man nodded, as if to say they knew of wives.

"Excuse me," said the older man. He retrieved his briefcase from between the beds and carried it over to the other man. "I like that yours has the strap. See, mine has the locks, but I never got in the habit of using them. The strap seems more academic somehow."

The other man looked a bit perplexed. "Yours seems serviceable," he said.

"Indeed," said the older man, who now returned his briefcase to its place between the beds. "Yes."

"I believe you have something to show us," said the younger man.

The other man lifted two manila envelopes from the valise. Lengths of red string secured the envelopes. He opened the first and retrieved a piece of X-ray film.

The younger man pulled the curtains apart a few inches, then turned off the room lights.

"Do you need me to explain?" asked the other man.

The older man studied the film in front of the opening in the curtain. "He has suffered a broken scapula at some time."

"Let me see," said the other man. He traced a line. "I would have to check the patient's history."

"It's not important," said the older man. Shifting his finger to another region of the film, "It is this mass, then, that is at issue." He pointed to a fist-size opacity.

"Indeed. I took one look at it, and considering its location and his reporting symptoms, it appeared . . ."

"Calcification of the muscle."

"Of the heart muscle, yes. That was the diagnosis."

"How old?" asked the younger man.

"At the time of this first scan, the patient was twenty-eight."

The older man passed the film to his companion. "What was done for treatment?"

"The patient refused treatment."

"Was there a prognosis?"

"They were not very hopeful, a matter of months."

"And you have something else to show us, I think?"

The other man opened the second envelope and handed it to the older man.

"This was taken how much later?"

"About five months later."

The older man passed the film to the younger man.

"I've shown this to specialists," said the other man. "They can find no medical explanation for the transformation."

"And we are certain," asked the younger man, "that the X-rays are of the same individual?"

"There can be no doubt."

"Did the patient have any insight?" asked the older man.

"He said my client cured him."

"And is that the position of your client?"

"This is what he claims."

"And what would you like us to do?"

"Ideally," said the other man, "I would like you to make an appeal on his behalf."

"An appeal to whom?" asked the younger man.

"We could start with the governor. If his eminence would want to get involved . . ."

"What was your client convicted of?" asked the older man.

"They say he killed his wife."

"And what would he like us to argue in this appeal?"

"He wants the opportunity to do good and to share the word of God."

"That is very noble," said the older man.

The other man returned his envelopes to his briefcase.

"Tell your client he has nothing to worry about."

"You will take up his cause, then?"

"Rather I mean that God will not abandon him."

"I don't appreciate it when I think people are wasting my time."

"I'm sure you've been compensated," said the younger man, who walked to the door and held it open.

The other man exited the room.

The fly awoke and started to bump against the window. The older man walked to the window and let it out.

"Given the time," said the younger man, "I doubt there is much a clever man can't create."

"You believe he manufactured those X-rays?" asked the older man.

"Of course. Don't you?"

"It is immaterial. Instead I was thinking about his wife."

"You're wondering why he killed her."

"I am thinking about a wife giving her husband a briefcase. It is a very nice gift. I called it a valise, but he said briefcase. I don't know what is the difference."

"I think you were correct. Valise, I think, means the strap."

"'Valise' is a beautiful word."

It was the time of day when the two men were accustomed to taking walks. But the older man found a baseball game on the television and they sat on the edge of the mattress, watching until the final out.

I

The Place I Will Later Refer to
as the Place I Can't Return to

Two dormer windows faced the road, like eyes with arched brows. The front door, faded and red, looked almost festive, almost welcoming, but the rock slab that made up the front step had sunk so far below the threshold that a person would need to jump to get inside. There were two windows to the left of the front door and one to the right. This deviation from symmetry saved the house from plainness. Wild grass scratched at the clapboard. Mossy shingles scaled the roof. In the empty windows the palest pink curtains hung limp. Two stories high, bookended by stone chimneys, the roof bowed like a clothesline. In the shadow of the main building, a low wing extended—the eave sheltered a shallow porch, where a wood-slatted swing hung from chains. There were three closely spaced windows, and, furthest from the main building, a battered door. The lot sloped with the road. At the lowest corner a few feet of the foundation showed, stone and mortar. On the high side of the house, parallel tracks of bald earth, as hard as stone. The driveway ended at a pile of rotting boards, what could have been rabbit hutches or the remains of a garage.

Shiloh couldn't get the front door to open, so I climbed onto the porch and tried the door there. It didn't have a lock, just a great big spring to pull it shut. The three of us crowded into a room no bigger than a closet and baking hot. We would learn to call this the mudroom. The entrance to the kitchen was on our left. With both doors shut, the mudroom was the darkest room in the house, no windows and strips of wool felt tacked along the edge of the door. We identified a row of wooden pegs for hanging coats, a single peg at a child's height, a three-legged stool on its side. Alice pushed into the kitchen. She gasped when she saw the stove. It hulked against the far wall. The way the stovepipe ran straight down from the ceiling made it resemble, Shiloh pointed out, a beetle on a pin.

On the left were the three windows we had seen from the car and underneath them was an open space where a kitchen table would have to go. A person sitting there could watch anything passing on the road.

A deep, enamel sink was set in a plywood countertop bristling with splinters. Standing at the sink, I looked out a milky window, past a narrow meadow, and then, above that, to the wall of the forest. Grasshoppers were taking short flights in the high grass. The pantry shared a wall with the mudroom—the floor-to-ceiling shelving was laced with fine cobwebs. A small, square, four-paned window, dirtier even than the one over the sink, let in an imprecise light. Between the stove and the sink stood a narrow door. When Shiloh opened it he found a stairway as steep as a ladder, leading up.

Between the stove and where the table would go, an open doorway connected the kitchen to the rest of the house. This was something of an entrance hall. Set into the right wall was a shallow fireplace composed of whitewashed stone. To the left side was a hall closet and, past that, the front door was framed on either side by narrow windows of beveled glass. The door wasn't locked, but rusted shut. Shiloh kicked it free and threw it open. Fresh air pushed inside. A main staircase led up to a landing before turning back upon itself. Underneath the landing was another door.

A sort of half wall or partition framed the living room, which, if you came through the front door, would have been immediately on your left. Four windows and eggshell walls made the room seem large and airy. Lichen and water stains gave a greenish cast to the stones of the second fireplace. Compared to the compact opening of the fireplace in the hall, this gray mouth seemed grand.

Back in the front hall, we climbed the stairway. The stairs had a dark-stained newel post, handrail, and white banisters. The first room we came to upstairs was a bathroom. It had a sash window, a sink balanced on a chrome pedestal, and a tub, one of those high-walled beauties with claw and ball feet. Someone had left a tower of aeronautical trade magazines teetering by the toilet. Shiloh checked the dates. The most recent: April '72. Fifteen months between us and the anonymous reader. Alice opened a door beside the sink and found the linen closet; it was only about ten inches deep, more like a hollowed-out wall than a closet. Inside this we found a cloth bag full of mothballs and the largest cake of soap I'd ever seen. Shiloh didn't have any patience for the details. He went back into the hallway. A moment later we heard him say, "Mine." He'd chosen his bedroom. "Come right in," he said. It was just to the right of the bathroom. The chimney from the living-room fireplace ran up one wall of his room. The exposed rock varied from pale river stones to dark and jagged shards. He saw me covet the chimney. "First come, first served." A dormer window looked out behind the house at the empty meadow. Shiloh walked to the center of the room and indicated an imaginary bed. He got under imaginary covers and closed his eyes.

"Should we go see our room?" asked Alice.

Our room. And still the two dormer windows we had seen from the road were unaccounted for. I felt my blood flooding to my cheeks. Alice took me by the arm. I couldn't believe she and I would share a room, but the house had its own order that we had to conform to. Whatever I'd imagined when I'd climbed into the car . . . it hadn't been this.

There was no exposed stonework—a closet backed up against where that first chimney must have been. I went to a window and looked out across the road and the overgrown field. I could see that mysterious blue water. If that wasn't enough, in the corner of the room I saw a piece of furniture singular in size and appearance. I didn't know what to call it.

"It's a sleigh bed," said Alice. "It's a sleigh bed."

The sole purpose of the house might have been to shelter this one thing. Bas-relief faces adorned the headboard. Spiral spindles crowned the corners, like an animal's horns. In scale and stature its closest relative was the stove.

Shiloh came in to see what Alice was yelling about.

He couldn't hide his disappointment. He'd been too rash by half. Or maybe I mistook the expression that clouded his face. Maybe he didn't regret that we had the better room. Maybe he was seeing the shape of things to come.

"How does one go about squatting?" asked Alice.

This seemed to bring Shiloh around. "Well, the most important thing is that you believe in your hearts that you have as much right to the place as anyone else. Then you make yourself at home, no apologies."

2

Hopeful Commerce

The Sears store, as it turned out, was a catalog center. They had copies of the newest catalog, a counter, and some red phones that, if you picked them up, connected you to someone waiting to take your order. In search of more immediate gratification, we crossed the street to the Ben Franklin Five-and-Dime.

There was something inside us that allowed us to make impossible decisions. We were flesh spread thinly over a framework of desire. We weren't just buying clotheslines, washcloths, and dish soap—we were buying our future, and at bargain prices.

We bought candles and cloth napkins. We bought napkin rings. Alice bought an entire spool of sisal rope and a bag of wooden beads because she wanted to get into macramé. We loaded a shopping cart so full that the wheels seized and we had to drag it to the front of the store. Then Alice found the gardening section, a sort of satellite store. The walls and ceiling were translucent green plastic. Shiloh said he had the overwhelming sensation of being in the stomach of a green animal. We bought a shovel, fertilizer, Burpee's entire selection of garden vegetables, gardening gloves for Alice, a trowel, wire tomato trellises. We made sure that we had one of every device we didn't understand the use of and most of everything else. The cashier and a manager exchanged looks and then double-checked their accounting. We couldn't get rid of our money fast enough. The manager held the bills up to the light.

"Do we look like criminals?" Shiloh asked.

No one would say.

I felt loose in my bones.

We couldn't stop laughing as we crammed everything into the backseat. The three of us scrunched together up front. Shiloh convinced us that, if we so much as saw a pothole, the Plymouth's frame would crack. The light was fading fast in those forested corridors. Alice let out a sigh when we crested the final hill. I, too, had been secretly afraid we'd never find the place again. We carried our new things inside. That we'd forgotten food seemed a minor thing. But we hadn't forgotten food! Shiloh had a secret stash of Clark bars and One Hundred Grand bars and Bit-O-Honey. And we ate that crap until our teeth ached.

Across the lake the sun was sinking behind yet another ripple of mountains.

We still needed to unload the trailer.

Shiloh said, "I don't need any of the things in there."

Neither did Alice.

I decided to wear the same cruddy clothes tomorrow and the next day and the next.

Alice said, "I don't want to worry about what I wear. I want to be the kind of person who doesn't think about clothes at all."

So the three of us unhooked the trailer and towed it beside the house.

When it was time for bed, Alice and I undressed in our new

room. I looked at her naked body. She lay down on the bare bed and pulled me on top of her. Her wet mouth tried to eat my ear.

In the morning there was no sign of Shiloh or Alice's car, but a pile of furniture was gathering in the yard, two dressers, three kitchen chairs, a twin mattress, and a pair of skis. Our friend had discovered the dump.

A little before noon he came over the hill with an ancient refrigerator lashed to the roof. It had a handle like a slot machine.

"What good will that do without electricity?" asked Alice.

Shiloh said one word: "Wait."

Before anything could be brought inside, we needed to air it out; it had to lose the scent of being cast off and take on the scent of being saved. We took the dresser drawers out and let them warm in the sun.

3
All the Parts That Make the Whole

As far as Alice and I were concerned, beams, boards, windows, and doors made a house. Shiloh uncovered the mysteries. He opened a valve in the basement and there it was, water. But how, asked Alice, had he known which valve to open? How had he known it was shut? It was simple; if the water had been left on, then the pipes would have frozen over the winter. Simple. And another thing, did we understand that the water was flowing without a pump? Did we know what might cause that? He'd deduced that there was a spring-fed collection reservoir at some higher elevation, on the slope above the house, perhaps. We wanted to go see it. We couldn't just go see it; it would be underground; it would be below the frost line. And what was a frost line? Oh, man, said Shiloh.

With a claw hammer and lineman's pliers tucked inside the waistband of his pants, Shiloh climbed the utility pole. The possibility of seeing him electrocuted foremost in our minds, Alice and I had told him we preferred to live in darkness. There were principles involved, he explained. Did we know, on a basic level, what electricity represented? Work in a can. The juice ran through the wires whether he tapped it or not. If there were no hydroelectric dams or coal generators or nuclear reactors, only miles of wire, power would flow through them regardless. That can't be true, said Alice. It's a fact of magnetism, said Shiloh. It seemed that Alice had run into the limit on her education.

After a few minutes of tinkering, Shiloh climbed down the pole.

"You're a genius," she told him when he showed her hot water in the tub. "You're a genius," she said, and she pushed the two of us out the door. "Oh my God," she said. And we could hear her naked body slip into the water.

4

Housekeeping

According to the seed packages, we were late putting in the corn and peas. On the road to town, small plots already showed leafy green rows. Alice and I picked a flat area above the house that got lots of sun. We staked out the boundaries for an ambitious garden. The roots of the grass were so tightly packed that I took to sharpening the blade of the shovel with a file. Alice came behind me and broke the clods up with her toes. It was a tedious process. When the sun got too high, we'd wander off together. We had nothing but ourselves to distract us from the black earth. We wound up with a tiny garden. But who were we trying to impress? We decided to be satisfied. We buried all the seeds.

And Shiloh, our pole star, was nowhere to be seen. Gardening didn't interest him. He preferred small parts, springs, and gears. From the dump he'd rescued a mantel clock, a handsome thing made of shiny brass and tiny screws. Shiloh had illusions about getting it to run. He'd sit in the kitchen and inventory the parts. When a small assembly did some perfect thing, he'd call me inside to be his witness. "This we call a pinion gear," he would say. Or, when he found two initials engraved on the casing, "The clockmaker knows his work will survive him so he's left this message for you and me."

At the end of the day, Alice and I would lean against the house, watch the sun drop beyond the lake. Porcupines crossed the road above the house. Once or twice deer entered the meadow to graze. Their dun hides made them nearly invisible. It was easy to imagine that they were always out there watching us.

On a night when a full moon prevented me from sleeping, I listened to the porch swing creak. I put on some shorts and went down to see Shiloh.

"Hey," he said.

I sat beside him on the swing. The moon had a way of making the sky seem colder than it really was. It was a matter of acclimatizing yourself to it, or so Pawpaw claimed. He would sleep out on his porch late into the winter, sometimes not coming in even when the temperature dipped below freezing.

"You like tea?" Shiloh asked.

I did.

He had me wait while he went inside. When he came back he had two cups. He held something under my nose. Mint.

"It grows by the side of the house," he said. He crushed a few leaves between his fingers and dropped them in our cups.

I tasted the bitter tea and lemon and then the graininess of the sugar.

The two of us sat on the swing, not rocking because it made too much noise, just drinking our drinks, letting our eyes travel from the empty road to the empty field and up, to a night sky so poached by the moon that only the brightest stars were visible.

"I went to see Gregor yesterday."

Shiloh waited for me to respond.

I said, "Was the goat still there?"

"Of course," said Shiloh. He pushed his foot against the porch and the swing rocked a few feet. "They really want us to stop by for one of their dinners."

"Alice and I have been pretty busy here."

"Well, the food is free and I'd like to take another look at those houses. This place is going to be a brute to heat come winter."

"You think you're going to go?"

"They're trying to figure out a way to live in the world, Thomas. And it's a moral and sustainable way. I find that pretty encouraging. I won't mind seeing some new faces either, no offense."

"Alice found that initiation thing a bit much. She's not even sure Bob Seger has a brother."

"Can I offer you a piece of advice?"

I was all ears.

"Be her boyfriend, but don't be her boy."

"And who's her boy?"

"The same dope who buys her regiment."

"What regiment?" The only woman for me.

"All I want is for us to go over there and get a free meal. They invited all of us. Opening their homes up to strangers is a matter of decency to them. It's not based on religion. They recognize that people are basically good. It's something I believe in very deeply. It's why I'm an anarchist."

"Shiloh," I said, "what do you mean by anarchist?"

"I mean that I don't believe in hierarchies. I don't believe in power structures. I don't believe in people telling other people what they should do. People know what they should do, basically. It means I'm for people. People who are against people, those are the people I'm against."

The whole time he was speaking his voice sounded very optimistic, very positive, but I also had the sense that he weighed more than all of the stars we could see, that he had this astounding mass and maybe even his own gravity—I could feel myself getting pulled toward him.

"If we go over there, they aren't going to make us do anything?"

"No. They won't make you say an oath or something like that. It's just a picnic. I just felt like, since they invited us, we couldn't not stop by. I mean, I know Gregor's a bit of a windbag, but don't you think he means well? Maybe he's got an exaggerated sense of his own importance in the scheme of things, but who hasn't been guilty of that? Not me. Not Alice."

"What about her?"

"I'm not speaking badly of her, Thomas. We all have different ideas about how the world works. Is it significant that you and I are awake and she's asleep? I mean, if someone asked me that, I'd have to give it some hard thought. Maybe we're the same kind of people and she's something else. I'm not saying that for a fact—I'm just theorizing."

"She's just really tired."

"And then someone might say that you were with her all day long and yet you're not tired."

"I'll go. But I can't make Alice go if she doesn't want to."

"You have no idea what you can make her do."

I went back upstairs hoping what he'd said was true.

But before we left, Shiloh wanted us to participate in a ceremony. Each of us, in turn, got a hand massage while the others looked you in the eyes and said what they thought were your most admirable qualities.

I didn't see the point.

"The point," said Shiloh, "is to do it. And, after we've done it, well, maybe then we can find some point."

Alice thought it would be fun.

I had never done anything like it before, so I was the first recipient. Alice worried my hand, bending to kiss each finger. Shiloh ran his thumbs up and down meridians in my arm. I found it impossible to ignore their eyes.

Shiloh asked me if I was comfortable.

I asked him what he was doing. He said that by shunting the blood in my arm, he could cause me to experience whole-body sensations of heat and chill. And—whether it was his technique or the power of suggestion—I felt it.

"I never feel as though Thomas judges me," Alice began.

"He's a decent cook."

Alice credited me with a well-developed morality.

Shiloh insisted there was something special about the quality of attention I paid to things.

"Thomas never loses his temper."

"He has an elegance," said Shiloh.

"He's moral."

"And a good kind of cautious."

White teeth. An understanding of human nature. Attentive. Curious. A wonderful kisser. A confidant.

Their fingers kept reassuring me that this wasn't a trick.

Shiloh recognized in me a healthy suspicion of authority figures.

Alice trusted that I couldn't betray her.

I believed in the basic goodness of human beings. I was gentle. I valued personal integrity over societal conventions.

"I need him here," said Alice.

Shiloh dropped my hand. "My turn."

We switched spots. He flexed the muscles in his arm.

"Shiloh stands up for what he believes in."

I said, "He's self-reliant."

"People look up to him."

"He plans for the future."

"I've never seen him afraid."

What I hadn't imagined was what it was like to stare at the person you addressed. I saw in Shiloh an eagerness. "He understands the way machines work."

"He's direct."

"And funny."

"His voice is sexy."

I said, "Birds could nest in his sideburns."

"No one can keep a secret like Shiloh can."

"He's looking out for us."

Shiloh nodded, as if this was a burden that he accepted. He still held Alice's hand and so, rather than wait for him to move, I did.

"Well," said Shiloh, "I don't think it's a secret: if Alice isn't happy with the way things are going, she changes it."

"I've never seen her mad."

Alice frowned at me. "Start over."

"She's sexy when she's angry." I ran my fingernails under her shirt sleeve.

"She believes in the decency of people."

"Alice is generous."

"Changes don't frighten her."

"Every time I look at her, she's more beautiful."

"People know to trust her."

"She's easy." I paused. "To talk to."

"If there's a proper name for something, she always knows it."

"Alice has poise." Her eyes were much calmer than Shiloh's.

"She's selfless."

"We owe this house to her."

"You can't credit both of us for the house," said Shiloh.

"I didn't," still looking at Alice.

"She won't tolerate injustice," said Shiloh.

"Ms. Lowe is a teacher."

"When no one else would take me in, Alice offered her house."

"Apartment," Alice corrected.

"See?"

"The way she drives with both hands and never whistles."

Shiloh stood up. "We should get going, if we're going at all."

Alice turned her head a few degrees. "Of course we're going. I can't wait to see those maniacs."

"Well, don't call them maniacs."

"I was being facetious. You know what Thomas calls that place? The Sound of Music Commune." She leaned over and kissed me.

"Gregor calls it DWG," said Shiloh.

"What does that stand for?" asked Alice.

"Doing It with Goats," I said.

"Down with God," said Shiloh.

Alice furrowed her brow. "Seriously?"

"It's his whole philosophy." Shiloh didn't quite look like himself. He'd tucked a long-sleeved shirt into a pair of work pants.

"You would know," said Alice. "Thomas and I haven't been sneaking out to meet with these people."

"Of course not. You're only interested in each other. I'm tired of your whispered conversation, your conscientious sex. This house has never been emptier than with you two in it."

That last remark echoed.

"I'll just go alone," said Shiloh.

"Don't be such a martyr," said Alice.

Everything was a different color green. The grass. The leaves. The bark of the trees was a kind of green. The water of the lake was a green reflection. The green glow on our faces. The greening shadows.

And then we arrived.

A garland of white flowers, the long, wilted stems plaited, were draped over the mailbox. A dozen adults used a parachute to toss a child into the air. They stood in a circle; every time the child landed, they leaned back and launched the tiny body heavenward. We got out of the car. The projectile wore underpants and nothing else. Maybe she was four. Every time they shot her up, she released a breathless scream.

The three of us stood, conspicuous for the distance we maintained between ourselves and this spectacle. A huge pair of arms reached from behind to lasso us together.

"Hello. It is Gregor."

The group stopped firing the girl into the sky. She ran at Gregor, who set us free in order to snatch up the girl. He handed her to Alice.

"Sonya," he said, "is the next generation."

The girl hid her face in Alice's hair.

"Who's the shy one?" cooed Alice; her mincing fingers reduced the girl to jelly.

Shiloh said, "A kid would be lucky to be raised in a place like this. She doesn't have to wonder if she's appreciated."

"This makes me happy that you have come." It could embarrass you, the way Gregor had of pronouncing his thoughts. "I don't think you are eating well. Make sure Katie feeds you."

We didn't know who Katie was.

"Katie is Sonya's mother," said Shiloh.

"Who's your father?" Alice asked the girl.

But the girl didn't answer.

Gregor lifted the girl out of Alice's arms. He had business to attend to, but he promised that we would talk to him later. We were to make ourselves at home. He and the girl disappeared into his house.

Despite Shiloh's insistence that we'd been invited, I felt like an intruder.

"Did I say something wrong?" asked Alice.

Shiloh made an ambiguous gesture. Forget about it.

Magdalena came out of the house and made a beeline for us.

We each received a hug and a kiss on the cheek. I'd never had anyone do that to me before. I felt clumsy and dull.

"So you have done well, I think. You have a place you are staying."

"For the meantime," said Alice.

"She means we're squatting," said Shiloh.

"I know Gregor wants to help you find something more permanent. He loves all of you."

"Where's Gregor from?" Alice asked.

"Utah."

Shiloh nodded. More cars arrived and pickup trucks and camper vans. It was as if there was going to be a concert.

"But the accent?" Alice asked.

"English isn't his first language. His parents are missionaries. He was born in Chile. Actually, English was his fourth language."

"He speaks four languages?" I asked.

"He speaks seven, including two types of Chinese."

"Is everyone here tonight"—Alice searched for a word—"associated?"

"What a great word," said Magdalena. "Gregor is such an amazing judge of people. But, I mean, I don't know. Do you feel associated?"

Alice waved her hands as if to ward off a piece of cake.

"He is very special. He recognized how churches traditionally bring people to God and he devised a way to bring God to people. It's very revolutionary. I mean, he's made enemies."

"That will happen," said Shiloh.

"What sorts of enemies?" asked Alice.

"It's not really my place to say. I know Gregor looks forward to talking with you."

Two men came by carrying a long steel spit that was skewered through a whole pig. The animal had been cooked already and fat dripped off its shiny skin. Magdalena excused herself, then went trailing after the men.

We watched partygoers hug and kiss. With their short-sleeved shirts and their battered boots, the men seemed to have agreed to a uniform. And except for the little girl, everyone was older than me. We spotted four women sitting at a picnic table shucking peas; they wore peasant skirts and mood rings and one of the women had a fanciful design, like a tropical bird, that emerged from the corner of her eye, and each was so imminently pregnant that, seen together, it took on the aspect of spectacle.

Shiloh scraped his feet on the ground. He announced he was going to take a walk around. It wasn't an invitation. He wandered off.

People started to bring food out and set it on a few picnic tables. Alice and I got in line.

We piled our plates with fried chicken, lamb kebabs, curried rice, and pickled beans. There were punch bowls of lemonade and simmering teapots. Cider flowed from a spigot in a wooden cask. Alice and I found a place to sit by the edge of the pond. An older couple took up a place next to us.

"You have to wait," the woman informed us, a plain woman with unmanageable brown hair and a receding chin. She pointed her fork at the food to explain herself. The guy she was with leaned forward to give us a sympathetic smile.

"You live here?" I asked.

"We're sharing a place," the man answered, "until we can increase the family."

"Congratulations," said Alice. It was the perfect thing to say.

They introduced themselves. They were Pam and Don Fowler from Cleveland.

"We've just moved up here," Alice said.

"You're going to love it," Don assured us.

Alice asked how long they'd been here.

"May," Pam said.

"This spring," said Don.

We explained that we'd never been to one of these things before.

"You'll catch on quick," Pam promised; her smile displayed a perfect set of teeth.

"You have fantastic teeth," I said.

She clucked her tongue and spit them into her hand.

"I used to drink," Don said. "That's my cross to bear."

Pam pushed her teeth back into place.

There wasn't anything else for us to say. I searched and searched, but I didn't see Shiloh anywhere.

The crowd assumed an anxious silence. Alice tapped me on the shoulder.

In the center of the pond, a woman stalked about on the little island. Layers of colorful gauze, plum, mustard, pine, obscured all but her eyes. It appeared someone was putting on a play.

One of the pregnant women (it was impossible to differentiate one from another) walked to the edge of the water, then turned to face the audience: "We have all been stuck in the wilderness. Searching for answers and fellowship."

Out on the island the woman moved about wildly.

The orator continued, "We have wandered through that desert called loneliness."

On the island the costumed woman crawled on her knees like a legionnaire.

"Been pecked by those vultures that accompany failure."

The actress swung her arms to ward off invisible attackers.

All around the woman this amazing thing was happening where yellow lights sparked just above the grass, as ephemeral as paper embers. I thought it was part of the show until it dawned on me: fireflies.

"Some of us even lost faith."

Here the actress collapsed, as if her robes had been transmuted into stone.

"But in Jesus Christ we find strength to continue. To keep looking." The pregnant woman wandered off, her part apparently through.

Sonya walked through the crowd with a hurricane lantern. She stopped just before the water.

The actress sat up. She rolled her neck, gazed at Sonya, and, as if in disbelief, turned away. She stood, brushed her clothes, and looked back at the little girl with the lamp. "Who are you?" the actress asked, her voice almost too soft to carry across the water.

"This light will guide you home," said Sonya.

"Home? Do you know me?"

"I know you!" Sonya's voice pealed.

The actress unwound her veils.

"That's Sophie," said Don.

"She used to be on television," explained Pam.

Yards of gauze unrolled. I'd never seen a more beautiful person.

"Do you know me?" the actress asked again, directing the question at the rest of us.

"We know you," we responded.

Down at the bottom of the valley came the sound of a car or a boat. Closer by, a cricket made a racket.

Gregor strode through the pond to the island. The water only came up to the base of his ribs. He plucked the woman up and carried her to shore. He set her on the ground, and man, woman, and child stood there, a tableau.

"What you have witnessed," said the big man, "is a representation of the journey all of us have taken in order to reach this place. Maybe some of you are thinking that you've wound up at a pretty decent place. Well, I want you to consider that this place is not nearly as great as it would be to stand beside the Lord's throne in heaven. That's where I want this party to reconvene, in our due time, of course. The important thing to remember with a journey is that it's not where you start from but where you wind up that's important. If we could all join hands." He paused to give us a chance to form a chain of souls. "Okay, people, can we bow our heads? Let's pray for this place on earth, for the safety of our friends. May our crops grow in abundance, and let us continue to receive the graces of our Lord. Now, if we could all take a moment to remember what we have to be thankful for."

I was seventeen years old and already I had found the life I planned to lead. All we needed to do was stay in love and take care of the garden. I was thankful for Alice and Shiloh. And I hadn't forgotten my parents, my other family. Even if they didn't know where on God's green earth I was, I was still their son. Alice sat Indian style and her knees flapped up and down like wings.

5
Idyll

Apparently some of the people were nudists. The pond slowly filled with bodies. They had a beach ball that they batted around and around the island. The way they laughed and shrieked it seemed like the most fun in the world. Everyone seemed healthy and fresh. The pregnant women stalked around the yard, as if they were being led by their bellies. White chickens roosted in the low branches of a cedar tree.

A woman came over to give us a paper plate that held two wafers of honeycomb. It was another revelation. We could keep bees, I thought. Maybe that was where Shiloh had disappeared to. He was always looking for opportunities to learn about new things. He possessed a disciplined curiosity. For instance, he habitually asked people how they liked their cars. It wasn't that he'd consider buying a car; he just wanted to have an educated opinion. He was a big fan of Saabs— because the company also designed airplanes.

Alice and I were talking about the things we'd had to eat. Onion-mashed new potatoes and chicken ragout. Last year's apple cider. Alice buried her head in my neck and whispered one word: brownies. And did she want me to get these brownies? No. She needed me to get them.

I thought, I will feed her and when she is blind to eating, I could be her food. I checked the picnic tables for leftovers. Dogs were on their hind legs, whipping the platters with their tongues.

"Didn't get enough?" asked a woman's voice, the beauty from the play. She looked familiar, the way really attractive people look familiar.

When she shoved the dogs away from the table, they snapped at her, then sulked away with broken-looking necks. She showed me a cigarette. "You got fire?"

I didn't.

"What are you looking for?"

I told her about the brownies.

She motioned for me to follow her.

The only thing to differentiate one house from the next was the type of flowers planted in the window boxes. Gregor's house had yellow flowers. We walked past a house with pale blue flowers, past red geraniums, and then she led me up onto a porch with wilting orange petals that had turned black around the edges.

We passed through the sliding glass door. Sleeping bags had been spread across the floor, like an enormous patchwork quilt. Clothes hung from nails pounded into the rafters. The place resembled a stable more than a house. We pushed past sheet curtains and bead curtains, into the kitchen. There was a sink filled high with dishes and a camp stove on top of a card table. A bare bulb glared from a fixture on the wall. She plucked a match from out of an open box and got her cigarette going. In the rafters above our heads, a cat balanced on a beam and meowed down at us.

"I told Magdalena she's got to drown these cats while it's manageable. The whole place is going to sink under the weight of kitties, puppies, and bastard kids."

I noticed the teats on the cat. It was pregnant, apparently.

She exhaled a stream of smoke toward the cat's face.

"I enjoyed the play," I said.

She ashed the cigarette onto the card table. "That's very generous of you. I don't think it made any sense." She took a quick pull on the cigarette, then used it to draw circles above her head. "I mean, it makes sense for what it is, but what is it?"

"I thought it was sort of an allegory."

"Exactly," she said. "It's not a play. A play is something an audience watches to try and figure out what's going on on the stage. Whereas what we did, everyone tries to figure out what it means about them. The difference is in the audience." She dropped the cigarette in the sink. "I don't feel well," she said.

She said it so matter-of-factly that I almost didn't hear her. She reached out and grabbed my hand. Hers was damp and cool.

I followed her into a tiny room. There were clothes piled on the floor and on a dresser. She reached into a curtained closet and there was the sound of pipes shaking and then water. We were in a bathroom. The toilet had been hidden behind the door we'd come through.

She let go of my hand and then raised both of her arms straight above her head.

I was dumbfounded.

Grabbing her shirt by the hem, I lifted it over her head. She did a little shimmy and her skirt dropped to the floor. Her breasts were huge and soft. She bent over in front of me, so that her head and shoulders were inside the shower stall, but her ass and legs were there before me. She stretched onto her tiptoes. The water coursed down her body, soaking into the clothing on the floor.

Inside the shower stall she made a grunting sound.

I bolted from the room, through the living room choked with other people's things, and out onto the porch and fresh air and a retreating blue light.

Down by the pond's edge, Shiloh, Gregor, and Alice were turning in place, looking for something. I was that thing.

"No luck?" asked Alice.

"No luck."

This exchange seemed to bother Gregor. He frowned. "Why are you without luck?"

"I went looking for dessert."

"Oh," said the big man.

"Gregor has offered to give us a tour of the place," said Shiloh.

A dog loped by with a distended belly. The naked swimmers had left the water and now they'd become pale points scattered through the meadows.

The little girl wandered over to where we stood. She pretended to be preoccupied with a grass stain on her knee.

"Do we know that little wood fairy?" asked Alice.

"That's Sonya," answered Gregor. We all knew her name.

Sonya seized Alice's arm and demanded to know what fairies were. Gregor did a ridiculous impersonation of a fairy—he couldn't be cunning, quick, or lithe. Alice teased Gregor, saying that he could be an ogre. I suggested a troll. We told Sonya that only fairies could tickle trolls, but no matter how hard she tried, Gregor didn't even fake a giggle. Sonya looked frustrated. The little girl smelled bad, I realized. Granted, a lot of the adults smelled bad, too. For them it was a matter of choice, but with the girl it spoke to a lack of attention.

Alice asked Sonya if she had any siblings. The girl made a face to show she didn't understand the word. Brothers or sisters?

She held up one finger.

"That's right," said Gregor. "Sonya is the only one."

The girl held her arms out like wings and zoomed off.

"She's like Switzerland," said Shiloh, but he didn't explain what he meant.

Gregor started walking and the three of us fell in behind him.

"Magdalena told us you have enemies," said Alice.

The big man nodded. "If you propose to turn Christianity on its head, this is no wonder."

"What did you do?" I asked.

"I introduced gravity to God."

"How does one do that?" asked Alice.

Gregor hooked a finger under the chain around Alice's neck and raised the shiny piece of metal from between her breasts. "Why do you wear this cross?"

"It was a gift," said Alice.

"So I expect that it reminds you of a person, not God. This is only natural. Why I am hated is that I've proposed that we put people before God. In traditional models, God is above us, followed by kings and then clergy. At the base you have laypeople. Imagine a pyramid." Gregor reached his hands upward to trace the slanting walls. "All I did was propose that God can also be found at the bottom, too. If we fall, we fall toward God, rather than away from him. Adam and Eve were never closer to God than when he kicked them out of paradise. This is lost on some people. They find my ideas heretical, but heretics are often rescued by history."

We reached a clearing on the opposite side of the pond. Survey stakes marked a house-size square. Gregor had us stand where a front door might go and look out at the rest of the compound. The parachute was now being used to toss a woman into the air—each time she shot up, she clapped her hands over her head, and when she started to fall, she moved them to her dress which she modestly pinned to her thighs.

"Tell them what you told me about this place," said Shiloh.

"This is the place," said Gregor.

Shiloh scratched his head.

More than anything I wanted to get back to our own home. I didn't want to see the woman from the shower or the pregnant women or the honest-looking men in their work pants and boots. I belonged to Alice alone.

"I can't tell you what's right for you," said Gregor. "But I think you're right for us. Shiloh is a very resourceful person, and we need resourceful people. And Alice, as an educator, we could use your gifts to help us shape our next generations—of which Sonya is just the first. We're expecting to be blessed with more children at any moment. So you can understand where I'm coming from. The word I prefer is 'family.' This is an intentional family. We're self-governing, self-reliant, and self-centered. Now Thomas is uncomfortable because I haven't addressed him yet. He is thinking that he is, maybe, disposable. This is not how I see it. You think that I don't recognize your purpose. I've been watching you, Thomas. What you are is the glue holding these people together. I'm not even sure they realize it, but that's what you are. And as much as I want Alice to be here and Shiloh to be here, without you, if they came on their own, for example, I couldn't accept them. I'm not saying I would turn them away. I'm saying that they would be missing something important, and that something is you. That is the thing I want to say to all of you. And even if it's hard for you to scrape up what will probably cost you five or ten thousand dollars when things are all said and done, well, I think it's worthwhile for you to consider it. I think it's the future for both of us. I believe this and I am rarely wrong about matters like this. You can ask anyone, but especially the women. Women, Alice, are the most valuable members of a society. Women know about the future because they carry it inside them. And, Shiloh, when you look toward the future, can you imagine the sort of influence that you could have when you're acting as part of a society as opposed to acting at the periphery of a society?"

It was a tremendous relief to return to our stolen home.

Alice beat me upstairs. I found her naked on our bed, a yellow towel draped over her face. I lifted just the edge of the towel. No peeking, she said. While I removed my clothes, she scissored her arms and legs like she was making angels.

"What's with the towel?"

"This is how we use towels on our planet."

"On your head?"

"On our heads," she said; she laughed a little.

I touched her. Goose flesh on her chest and arms.

She held my hand to her breast.

A name I hadn't forgotten. He showed up one day, with his terrible van, the headlights set in their chrome dishes like dead eyes. I stood in the yard and watched it creeping down the hill. The van rolled to a stop just a few feet in front of me and we stared at each other through the windshield glass. He had a cigarette holder pinned in the corner of his mouth and he was wearing a leather stovepipe hat.

The door swung open and he stepped into our yard. "I told you we'd cross paths again. Where's your sweet la-de-da?"

There were black scabs on the knuckles of his hands.

"Oh," he said, "I almost forgot." He stretched himself over the seat and rooted around. He handed me a box wrapped with cotton string.

I peeked inside the box. Italian cookies.

"A little housewarming gift." He turned around in the driveway as if he expected people to sneak up behind him.

I asked how he'd found us.

A little bird told him.

"Tanager," I said, Shiloh's last name.

"That makes you the whiz kid."

"You're Parker."

He stuck his hand out.

He tried to force my hand to do something complicated. "That means we're pals. How old are you again?"

"Seventeen."

"With your face it doesn't matter."

His dark, curly hair bobbed before his green-brown eyes. He wore leather pants and was barefoot, great, big, filthy feet. He reached an arm into the van and mashed the horn.

"You folks have a nice place here," he said. He stared at the house. "Isn't this the nowherest corner of this world."

The front door jerked open. Shiloh came into the yard. They performed a more intricate variation of the handshake.

"I didn't know if you were coming," said Shiloh.

"I caught your lookout napping." He pointed his finger at my head.

"Thomas."

"That kid's face . . ."

"His face is fine."

"Says you."

Alice appeared at the mudroom door. She turned around and went back inside.

"So what's the good word?" asked Parker.

"We're getting along," said Shiloh.

"From the darkest soil spring the brightest flowers," said Parker. "That's Gerard Manley Hopkins, I think. I met up with Gregor and those freaks last night. We ate lamb. He's very sharp. You know his parents were missionaries. They disappeared in the Amazon. Sad. He wants me to find him a school bus. I felt very at ease. Good-looking chicks serving me food. I was starting to think he was on to something. I was stroking this one girl's hair. Then Gregor asks about our old friend. Can you believe that?"

"Asked about him how?"

"Had I seen him recently."

"What did you tell him?"

"I told him that I wasn't necessarily of the opinion that our old friend existed."

"Oh," said Shiloh.

"You're telling me. So he stared at me for about twenty minutes and the chick with the soft hair has to go do something by herself and pretty soon yours truly is back in his vehicle alone with his dreams. And then, in the middle of the night, the lamb doesn't agree with me so I have to go off into the bushes. So I'm squatting there, my hands clasped around the trunk of this tree. Well, I hadn't really checked out my surroundings. I look over and see a couple of folks standing waist deep in this pond and they're just watching me." He paused and looked from Shiloh to me. "I am not without a certain degree of pride, you understand." He reached into the van and pulled out a little hard-shelled overnight bag.

Alice and I sat at the kitchen table eating the stale cookies. Her favorites had a dab of peach preserves. I preferred the ones made of shredded coconut. We hadn't had sweets for a long time. They seemed frivolous.

It was just the two of us in the house. After Parker took a shower, he and Shiloh drove off in the van.

"Promise me," said Alice, "when Shiloh and I get into it over his friend, you will take my side."

"Of course I'll take your side. It's not even a contest."

"Yes it is."

The refrigerator made a sound like someone had slipped a baseball card between a bicycle's spokes. I went over and wedged a wooden spoon against the vibrating part.

6
Nighthawks

Alice stretched out beside me and so still she might have died in her sleep. I heard bodies come up stairs, the rusty sigh of a leaf-spring suspension, shuffling feet. I crept to the window. Parker had backed the van right up to the front door, neatly docking with the house. Something was being moved into the basement. They worked with whispered grunts. They were conscientious, reining in their voices to protect our sleep. I went back to bed and listened some more. I counted ten trips up the stairs, fifteen. The numbers didn't matter since I had no idea if they started working when I started counting or if I had joined them late. And, not knowing, I left them to their lifting. In the morning, the van was back in the driveway, red curtains pulled across the windows. The front hall swept, the house silent.

7
Apex

Alice wanted to get away, so we got in the car and drove. With the windows down, the air whipped Alice's hair about. I reached across and gathered it in my fist. The road we chose wound its way up a mountainside. At a dirt parking lot, tipped so precariously it seemed poised to slide away, the road came to an end. A man stooped beside a pickup, pulling cockleburs from a pair of Irish setters. He looked worse than exhausted. He scratched his chin and said something un-intelligible. I walked over to hear him better. He held a gadget to his Adam's apple and asked me, with a voice like a kazoo, "Picnic?" He'd had a tracheotomy. "Sightseeing," I said. Keeping my answer clipped was a sympathetic gesture. He straightened himself up. The dogs trembled with anticipation; they were full of this wonderful energy and they forfeited it to him. He opened the tailgate and flicked his hand. The dogs sprang into the bed.

Alice and I scrambled past dwarf pines that burst apart the seams of rocks, over mats of dense sedge. Before we reached the peak, we came upon a low foundation. Three flagstone stairs took us up to a little square of land, a place level and neat. There were six tombstones standing upright and three small ones on their backs. The gravestones were as slim as books. The names had been erased by rain. I'd heard that, over time, bodies will shift under the soil. I thought of all the bones knotted in a corner. Alice and I kept our voices close to us. Squirrels scratched through last year's leaves. I took Alice's hand and led her down the ringing steps. We followed the path, trusting it would take us where we wanted to go.

Broken stone crowned the top like a balding skull. Alice had never stood on top of a mountain. From that vantage point we could see the full 360 degrees. We took the opportunity to name all the mountains. Alice spotted the Giant's Brow and Mount Fantastic. The Bawdy Virgin's Knees. Nameless Hill. That sacred Indian holy land, Lumpofshit.

On the other side, for a couple of hundred feet, the mountain face was almost sheer. I watched Alice take a crow's hop and fire rocks out over the abyss. My heart seized every time she ran up to the edge.

By now someone has built a place on top of that mountain. They do that sort of thing. Some days it can take my entire life to keep me from driving up there and looking for that road.

8

Allegiance

Shiloh had left the door to his room open. I ducked my head in. He was stretched out on his mattress. He turned his head and looked at me.

"Come in," he said. He might have been addressing a cat, that's the kind of hope he had that I would obey.

Alice had gone down to the porch swing to write a postcard to her sister. They kept a labored correspondence, partly because her sister didn't approve of Alice's general delivery address. She and her sister were close, but in a strange, uncertain way. In her letters, Alice recommended her sister join a consciousness-raising group, not out of any conviction, but because she felt the need to argue for something. Whatever kind of parents they shared, Alice didn't say. She and her sister had both gotten far from home—that's all she thought I had to know.

I slipped inside Shiloh's room. Except for a dresser, there wasn't any furniture. A gooseneck desk lamp, a spiral notebook, some pens, and pocket change piled together by the head of the mattress. Shiloh propped himself up on his elbows and looked at me. His beard was coming in again, like a dark stain. A pair of canvas shoes, caked with pale mud, waited by the closet door.

"You're alone for once," he said.

I said, "Look who's talking."

He checked his bare wrist for the time. "Have a seat."

I plopped down on the floor. "You look tired."

"I was taking a catnap."

"You should get a chair in here."

"What would a chair do?"

There was a long pause while I tried to get more comfortable on the hard floor. Finally, I just said it. "What were you moving with Parker's van?"

"Moving?"

"You backed the van up against the front door." I did my best to look inscrutable.

"We needed to get some things inside."

I turned my head from side to side, his empty room. "You don't want to talk about it?"

"We were just doing fix-it-type chores. It's no big deal." He looked, even then, as though he might slip backward into sleep.

"I could carry stuff or whatever you need. Wouldn't that make more sense than having Parker do the work? At least I really live here."

"Trust me, you're doing a job already."

"You mean the garden?"

"You're keeping Alice out of our hair."

He read the look on my face and knew he'd made a mistake.

"That's just an expression," said Shiloh.

"Why do you need her out of your hair?"

"I really love Alice," said Shiloh. "I do. She's irrational sometimes. She's self-absorbed sometimes. She doesn't always take me seriously. These are her faults, basically. She also has many virtues, of which you are certainly aware. I'm not some idiot who thinks he can tell a guy what's wrong with his girlfriend and actually expect that the conversation is going to remain secret. That's what you expect when two adults have a conversation, but it's not what happens. So tell her what I said. Let her fume. Then remind her that it was my idea to come up here, that I found this place for us. Remind her who got the water running and the electricity. I would have been perfectly happy to come back here on my own. I was ready to do that. Maybe the problem is with me. I didn't have a family to coddle me or a fancy education. I have basically relied on my wits." He'd stood up and wandered over to the window. "I know Parker is not making things any easier. He can be an abrasive guy. Alice would be happy to boil him."

"So why do you let him stay?"

"Parker has nothing to do with you or Alice."

He had these neat stacks of rocks balanced on his windowsill. They looked like the cairns you see on mountaintops.

"Is he hiding from people?"

"Parker's sense of self-worth is completely out of scale with the evidence."

"You're talking in riddles."

"Believe me, Thomas, that's the best I can give you."

"Alice is going to want to know more."

"Parker is a nobody. And Alice can ask me any question she wants."

"Are you a nobody?"

"The only difference between me and Parker is that I know I'm a nobody." He slipped on his dusty sneakers. Our conversation was coming to a close.

"What should I tell Alice?"

"Tell her whatever you want. I've said all along that I'm going to take care of everyone. Nothing has changed. In a week or so Parker is going to leave. We might not see him after that. It would be great if everyone could keep cool until then, but I don't expect that's what's going to happen."

"Where will Parker go?"

"Parker will go wherever he thinks the action is."

Of course, if action had been his target all along, then his aim was off. Nothing happened here. The polar opposite of action was what we were all about. Instead of action we had habits. At some point habits became rituals. Alice and I had the bowls-of-cereal ritual. We had the sleeping-in-the-sunlight ritual. We had the ritual of being disappointed by what we found in the refrigerator. The ritual of being disappointed at discovering our savings were dwindling. We had sunset and twilight rituals. The closest thing to action was the ritual of shaking things up, the day we wore each other's clothes, the day we didn't leave bed.

But it didn't matter that I'd spoken with Shiloh. It didn't matter if I had tried to hide things from Alice. Shiloh and I had nothing to do with the problem. We were just some potential witnesses, biding our time.

Something in the atmosphere seized me. The reaction before the stimulus. Alice's voice reached us, a half-restrained shout, "Thomas."

I raced to her, Shiloh close on my heels.

Alice and Parker stood toe to toe at the top of the basement stairs.

"He doesn't want me in *my* basement," explained Alice.

No one had ever called for me before, not in such a way. By calling my name, Alice implied that I possessed some potential she wanted to harness. My muscles felt like hot grease.

A smile twisted on Parker's face. "I never said she couldn't go down there. There's a lot of stuff lying around, and if she doesn't pay attention she might get hurt, that's what I said."

Alice shot me an unambiguous look. "What sort of stuff?" I asked.

"Exactly," said Alice.

Shiloh acted as if he'd never seen a banister before in his life. Suddenly it was the most fascinating thing he'd ever run across.

"I don't get it," said Parker. "Shiloh tells me you wander around like some horny zombies, not paying him the least bit of attention, and all I get is people sticking their fingers up my nose. How would you like it if I followed after you while you were flower picking or what have you? It's a lack of respect, basically. I don't want to have to use the *f* word, but you act like a fucking fascist."

"How has it come to this?" asked Alice. "I let myself get baited into arguments with dropouts."

It was a poor choice of words on her part. I've never felt smaller.

Shiloh stepped around me on the stairs. "Parker doesn't mean unsafe. If anything it's safer down there. But with the tools laying around, you have to be careful where you step. I asked him to make sure that no one went down there before we got the mess cleaned up."

"We were just trying to be considerate," said Parker.

Outside, the weather underwent some subtle shift. A breeze lifted the curtains in the window frames.

I suggested that they give us a tour so that we'd know what to watch out for.

Sweeping his hand in a grand, welcoming gesture, Parker said, "Excellent idea."

The four of us descended into the basement. In the center of the room, construction materials had been piled beside a stone column. Three pallets rested on the dirt floor. Empty paper sacks were balled up on the ground. According to the block printing on the bags, at one time they'd contained cement. We saw two coils of garden hose, an immaculate green wheelbarrow, and the shovel.

"What's all this stuff for?" Alice asked.

Upon closer inspection, I saw that some of the bags had held sand.

Parker picked the shovel up and jabbed it at the column. Sharp pieces of mortar broke off. "Why do you think places like this get abandoned? No structural integrity."

"You stole all this stuff," Alice declared, grabbing the handle of the wheelbarrow.

"Prove it," said Parker.

The chalky dust coated my tongue.

"Whoa," said Shiloh. "Don't ask her to do that."

Parker studied Alice. "We found it along the side of the road."

Alice maintained her countenance.

"Are you going to let him lie to me?" she asked Shiloh.

"I'm telling you, it's not stolen," Parker insisted.

"It's stolen," said Shiloh.

"Thanks, friend," said Parker. "Remember, it takes little people to bring big men to their knees. I've known the sting of arrows."

"It was basically a matter of this stuff being overpriced," said Shiloh. "Just about anything in this society that might be used to construct a building, a house or a factory, has a surcharge built into it. The only way anyone can afford those things is by getting a regular job. And when everyone buys into this, we have what is called capitalism. That is why bags of sand and limestone dust go for a price that is not proportionate to their manufacturing cost."

Alice said, "I won't have people bringing stolen goods into my house."

"Listen to you. *Your* house. Let's take a trip to the freezer. Huh?" said Parker. "Cool out. This was a one-time deal. The house needed some work and I suggested we do it this way. I'm not used to being part of such a gentle cooperative. I'll make a pledge right now. No more thieving. I think that would be a good idea. What do you think?"

Shiloh looked relieved that his friend might have found an escape hatch. "I can live with that," he said.

"What about you, Alice, can you live with that?"

She stroked her hand over a bag of sand, like a favorite piece of furniture or a pet. "You make it sound like it's a compromise."

"He doesn't mean that," said Shiloh.

"We haven't asked Thomas what he thinks." Parker walked over and put his arm on my shoulder. "What do you make of your girlfriend's rules?"

Parker's attention made me feel less certain about myself. I wasn't ready for his scrutiny. He'd compliment the way I cracked an egg into a skillet, so the next time I cracked an egg, I found myself trying to recall how I had done it the time before. He made it his business to notice the things that nobody wanted noticed. It was Parker who'd asked me about my folks. What do you think they're doing right now? he'd asked. Do you wonder if they're pulling their hair out or celebrating? They let you call them by their first names, he said. Fran, right? Mary. They don't buy into that Mom and Dad business. I think that's a cop-out.

I wanted things back to the way they were before he'd arrived, or the way I'd imagined they were. We hadn't really been there that long.

That morning while I was washing dishes, Parker had started in on Pawpaw. He wanted me to know that he'd been close to one of his grandfathers, too. The two of them built model trains together.

"You know about model trains?" he asked.

"You mean did I ever play with them?"

"I know you haven't," he said. "You gave yourself away by saying 'play.' That was one of my grandfather's tests. If you liked trains you were okay in his book. Same thing with animals. You ever have a pet?"

"I had a fish."

"Did you love it?"

I said, "I'm not going to play your game."

"Everything is play with you. Huh?"

But it wasn't all play for me. Parker needed to learn that.

In the dim basement light, I looked him in the eye and said, "We still don't know why you're here."

"Didn't anyone tell you? I'm a saint."

"Cut it out," said Shiloh.

"I travel around doing good."

Shiloh said, "Shut up."

9
Postcoital

Just because I wasn't talking about my parents doesn't mean they weren't on my mind. I could still imagine the spaces they moved through. I carried them inside me. I knew what I had done. I really believed that I was in the process of doing something very important. And when I felt bad, I told myself I was being selfless. And when I felt good, I believed I was deserving. Sometimes I experienced a sensation like God's leaning over to whisper to me that I was his favorite. I found evidence in every moment.

Alice and I were having sex and we stopped. It was the middle of the night. Parker and Shiloh were working deep in the basement. We were having sex and we stopped. There was such a quiet to the house. The next moment the noises picked up in the basement, but our bodies had lost their temper and cooled.

I said, "Would you want to go for a walk tomorrow?"

"How long can their project go on?"

"Not too much longer, I don't think."

"Can I say something?"

"Sure."

"You won't like it."

I said, "Shoot from the hip." I was trying to teach myself to be cavalier.

"'Shoot from the hip.' That's not the way you talk. You've started to sound like him."

"That's not true."

"You don't even do it like yourself."

"Please take that back."

"I'm sorry."

"Just take it back."

"Where are you going?"

I had gotten up. "The bathroom."

"You never say mean things to me."

"I don't know."

"I'm horrible."

I washed my face in the basin. I felt a bit nauseous. I felt a bit out of myself. Alice came in and dried my face with a towel.

"My handsome man," she called me. "My gentle Thomas."

"I don't know why you said that."

"I don't know why either. It was a mistake."

"You just wanted to hurt my feelings."

She hung the towel on the towel bar and retreated from the room.

When I got back in bed, Alice kissed my chest about a hundred times. At first it made me really excited, then it made me tired. Her head kept bobbing and she made the smacking sound. She kissed each rib and my collarbone. She kissed my shoulders. She kissed my arms.

I asked her if this was some form of apology and she kissed my neck and my forehead and she kissed my closed eyes.

The next morning we slept in. The summer sun beat on the house. The rising heat made the meadow shimmer. At some point I noticed that all the houseflies had died. They were everywhere, on the windowsills, on the kitchen table, scattered like black currants across the floor. I got the broom and swept them into a pile. I opened the front door and sowed them in the grass. Parker's blue van hulked in the driveway.

I stared at the van. There was a nagging thought that I knew had something to do with Parker. I was reluctant to let myself think about him. I wandered out into the yard. The windows were all rolled up. The red curtains were drawn. I put my hand on the side of the van. My hand jumped back. The sheet metal was skillet hot. I said his name. I rapped a knuckle on the driver's-side door. The door was locked. I went to the passenger's door and then around to the back. Alice made her way across the yard.

I said his name a little louder. "Parker," I said, no longer a name, but a summons. "Parker!"

"He can't be in there," said Alice.

"I didn't see him inside the house."

Alice touched the side of the van. "I bet he's in Shiloh's room."

"Go check," I said.

From inside the house I could hear Alice yelling to Shiloh. It seemed that the crisis had migrated away from me and I was safe. I stood next to the blue van and felt the waves of heat radiating off it. Then they were coming across the lawn, Alice and Shiloh. He was barefoot and half asleep. Just as mellow as could be he walked over to the van and knocked on the quarter panel. He was only then arriving at a place we'd already left. He adapted quickly, rechecking the door handles, trying to stare through the curtains.

"Why does he lock the doors?" asked Alice.

"Is he in there?" I asked Shiloh.

Shiloh didn't know.

"Check the basement," said Alice.

I called his name as I went down the stairs. The center column was jacketed with new cement. The air was cool and humid. It was the only sane place to be, but Parker wasn't down there.

Outside, Shiloh had a wire coat hanger inserted between the window glass and the weather stripping; he yanked it now and then as if he was trying to snag a fish. Alice looked over her shoulder at me. Parker wasn't the type to go off for a walk. I went into the living room and grabbed the fire poker. As I headed across the lawn, I saw the small, square windows at the back of the van. I cocked the poker over my shoulder and swung it through.

Glass alone wasn't enough to stop the rod's momentum. I creased the window molding. The shock of those noises that accompany breaking glass and shaping metal sent Alice bolting into the road. Shiloh had his head tucked between his shoulders and his jaw set in a cower. He walked over to me like that, looking like a turtle.

"Put that thing down."

I dropped the poker.

"Shit." Shiloh pulled his T-shirt over his head.

"See if he's in there."

"That's what I'm doing." He used the shirt to brush the loose glass from the window frame. He reached a hand through and moved the curtain. He stepped aside so I might take a look.

There was just a plywood floor where the mattress should have been. I stood there in the stream of oven heat escaping through the hole where the window wasn't.

"You don't do that to someone's property," Shiloh said. His voice was low and full of regret.

I had tried to recast myself as a person who was capable of decisive action. And look where it had gotten me.

"Whoa," said Parker. He stood in the doorway in a T-shirt, Jockey underwear, and wool socks. He put a hand on the door frame and came down the flagstones and over to the van.

There wasn't anything any of us could think to say.

He joined us. He stuck his hand through the window, twirled it around, and withdrew it. Then he looked up.

Shiloh and I looked up too. There was the empty sky and the giant sun.

"I'll be double fucked. Which of you assholes did this?"

Alice put her hand over her mouth.

"I broke the window," said Shiloh. He picked up the fire poker. "With this," he said.

I felt a powerful love for Shiloh.

"Get on with the story."

"Thomas thought you were maybe trapped in there."

Parker reached through the broken window again to unlatch the lock. He swung open the butterfly doors to air the van out. Carefully he brushed away the glass that hung on the curtains and along the bumper. "What, that I was incapacitated?"

"The heat," I said.

Parker gave Shiloh a hard look. "I can't believe you're that stupid."

"They woke me up. I'd been sleeping," explained Shiloh. "I wasn't thinking straight."

"None of you was, I guess."

Alice had something she wanted to add. "Where were you?"

"I was just asleep." Parker started to gather shards of glass in his left hand.

"So you're sleeping in the house now?"

"Loverboy can tell you; if I'd slept in the van, I could be dead."

"I thought Thomas checked the basement."

"Did I say I was in the basement?"

"You're dressed like you were in the basement."

"That's right. I had no idea it got like this in Vermont."

Shiloh said, "It sure does."

"Did you check down there or not?" Alice asked me.

Everyone looked at me. "I did."

"On a bright day like this," said Parker, "your eyes probably couldn't adjust."

It was clear, suddenly, how my decisions were responsible for building this drama. I said, "I'll pay to fix the window."

Parker traced his finger over the empty window. "A hundred should do."

"Come on," said Shiloh.

"If he can't afford it, he shouldn't be encouraging people to damage other people's property."

"Haven't you two finished working down there?" Alice asked.

"Oh," said Shiloh. "Have we?"

"Just about," said Parker.

To Parker, I said, "The column looked finished to me."

"Suddenly he's an expert."

"We'll finish soon enough," said Shiloh.

"Where were you in the basement, exactly?" I asked.

"I was just lying down sleeping," Parker said. "Be careful where you step. The glass is everywhere."

"In the basement?" Alice asked.

"Right here. This glass." He held his hand up for her to see.

For a moment I thought Alice might help him pick up the glass. "I don't know," she said.

"What?" asked Shiloh.

"I think it may be time for Parker to move along."

Parker straightened up and looked from Alice to Shiloh to me. "You're pulling my leg."

Alice sucked in her breath, as if she meant to say something measured.

"Wait," said Parker. "You break into my van and then tell me it's time I packed my bags. Someone tell me what I'm missing. I wasn't doing anything but having nice dreams."

"The man was the victim of innocent circumstances," said Shiloh.

Alice looked to me. "Back me up, Thomas."

"Originally he was just going to be here for a few days."

"I've been here five days," said Parker.

"Five days," echoed Shiloh.

"You're all crackers." Snatching the fire poker out of Shiloh's hand, Parker touched it to my chest. "You owe me a hundred bucks."

"Don't threaten him," said Alice.

"I'll leave in two days," said Parker. "You can say bye-bye now because I'm going to stay out of your hair until then. I'm going to be a ghost." Still carrying the poker he stormed back inside the house.

Shiloh shook his head. "We damage his property and then have the nerve to ask him to leave."

"If you had told me he was sleeping in the basement, this wouldn't have happened."

"Why do you care where he sleeps?"

"Because he's a thief, for one thing."

"He's my guest."

"When we left New York, did you know Parker would come here to see us?" This was Alice's question.

Shiloh looked at me. He shook his head.

"Is that your answer?" Alice wanted to know. He refused to look at us. I felt as though I'd betrayed him.

A couple of hours later, I went down into the basement to apologize. Parker was on his mattress, in the best lit corner of the room, curled up on his side, and underneath a blanket. I hadn't really planned a particular thing to say, but hoped we might have a talk. It seemed to me that I was doing something honorable by ignoring his earlier threat. At the time, it made my blood cold, but now I felt an awed respect for his passions. Plus, if Shiloh had chosen us over him, didn't that make me at least his equal? I just stood there at the base of the stairs and watched him, considering how to proceed.

"I knew things would go down like this. It could only be postponed for so long. I thought if I stayed out of her eyesight we could have avoided this, but I didn't figure you'd try to rescue me either."

I had his money in my hand. The bills represented about half of the money I had left. I walked over and gave it to him.

He tucked them into his pocket. "It's a nice gesture."

"It's not a gesture."

"I mean the idea that you were trying to save me."

I was certain his mattress hadn't been where it was now. "This isn't where you were sleeping earlier."

He stuck a finger in his ear and wiggled it around. "You're right."

"Where were you?"

"I was underneath the stairs." He pointed beneath my feet.

"I guess I didn't look there."

"You must not have."

What made it worse was that I had thought that he and I were becoming friends. A couple of days before, we had actually engaged in a conversation. Alice was asleep on the living-room sofa and Shiloh was snoring in his room. It was the middle of the day, not oppressively hot yet, but getting there. I wasn't planning on doing anything, but sort of stewing in my freedom, listening to the chains squeak as I kicked myself back and forth on the porch swing. Parker came out the mudroom door. His hair was tousled and wet. He'd come from the bath. He considered himself a city person and bathing in a stream was too hillbilly for his tastes.

"What are you looking at?" he asked.

I hadn't been looking at anything in particular. I was just letting my eyes follow what caught their interest. "You know, you can see New York from here." I bent at the waist to illustrate. "That's it on the other side of the lake."

"Right there?" He leaned forward to see.

"Look familiar?"

"Funny. That's funny."

I knew he meant something else entirely.

"Tell me," he said, "what do you think about as you look out there?"

I didn't much want to talk about my family again.

"Let's try another way. What do you think I see when I look out there?"

"You probably think about all the places you might be."

"You've mistaken me for someone else. I am where I find myself. Let me tell you what I see." He used his hand to indicate the approximate dimensions of there. He turned his head toward me to see if I was paying attention. Then he jabbed his finger at the center of my chest. "Understand?"

I thought I had to thump him on the heart. I stared at my hand and tried to will it to move.

"You're in love."

I was indeed.

"When I first met Shiloh, he was in love, too. It didn't go so hot. When he told me he was returning to that damp shack, I figured he was going down there to die. He'd seen enough, I thought. You can imagine how surprised I was when the three of you showed up on my doorstep. It really picked up my spirits. That was something I was in need of, too.

"Things don't necessarily have to go so bad for you. For one thing, your girlfriend probably can't believe her good luck. She's been around the block. She used to be married, right? Shiloh said her ex wound up in an institution. You know what they call that? Nobility. They both had it in spades, Shiloh's ex and Alice's. Well, she's a good-looking chick, a little flat chested, but you look at her like she's the reason the sun rises."

I asked him what he meant by "nobility."

"Shiloh's ex shot himself through the heart. That's noble. That's fearless."

"He told you that?"

"I'm the one who found the body."

I was staring at his profile and trying to figure out how he could say things like this. All the while, he was doing mundane tasks, like combing his hair, folding, then unfolding the cuffs of his pants. "What brought you up here? Does it have something to do with the thing you stole?"

"You and Alice are obsessed with crime."

"Shiloh said you took something from some people."

"He must think he can trust you."

I said, "So Shiloh was in love with a boy."

"You catch on quick," said Parker.

10

Dust

Shiloh showed Alice a receipt for three rolls of yellow fiberglass insulation. The night before Parker left, I heard him and Shiloh padding above our heads, laying the batting out in the attic. Through the plaster ceiling I could hear the crinkling of the paper backing and their quiet breathing. Alice slept beside me, unaware of the bodies working above us.

Then I was in the kitchen with Shiloh. He asked me if I had a moment. The two of us went outside. He had cut a piece of plywood to cover the broken window. Working together we used tape and wooden shims to hold the board in place.

It seemed one of those rare opportunities where something genuine might be expressed and—here was the miracle—understood. I might have said this thing.

Finally Shiloh asked me how I thought the tires looked. We checked the four corners of the van. Then Shiloh hopped on the rear bumper and jumped off to see the way the van reacted. It needed new springs, he concluded.

Across the road, a red-winged blackbird made a racket.

Parker came through the front door with his little mattress on top of his head, his hands pulling the sides down to make it fit. When he was outside he let go of the sides and it sort of flopped about, balanced on his head. We opened the back of the van. The mattress rested on a platform above the wheel wells.

"Well, I'm out of here," said Parker. "Good luck and take care."

Shiloh looked a little underwhelmed by these remarks. "I'll take care of everything," he said.

"You'll be fine."

"I'm sorry you had to leave." I reached out my hand.

"Unavoidable. You've got a good thing. I wouldn't want to spoil it. Tell Alice I wish her the best."

"You didn't say good-bye to her?" This distressed me suddenly.

"It's okay. She'd come out if she wanted to."

"Let me get her."

"It's fine."

I went back inside the house. Alice was in the kitchen washing dishes.

"You have to come say good-bye to Parker."

"He's really leaving?"

"The van is loaded."

She rubbed her wet finger over a dish until it squeaked.

"Right now," I said.

She and I were coming out of the mudroom when the van went over the hill. Shiloh stood in the yard, waving. Alice and I joined him.

"You sad?" I asked him.

"Things are good."

"The fun is just beginning," said Alice.

"I know," said Shiloh. He dragged his heel across the driveway, making shapes in the dirt.

When at some point it stopped raining, we hardly noticed. The sky stayed blue and empty. From our bedroom window the meadow looked as bright as the skin of an airplane.

Alice and I practiced the rhythm method—we liked the fact that it was natural. In the middle of her period, we had sex on beds of moss in the humid heart of the forest. Afterward, contented and raw, we'd wander to the swimming hole to wash; a certain type of minnow, about an inch long, with a dark horizontal stripe, would groom us, picking off the flecks of dark blood that dotted our legs and groins. Abstinence was a chore. While she ovulated her body got so hot and insistent that we slept with our clothes on to keep from betraying ourselves.

We hardly ate. Our clothes hung off us. Shiloh punched new

holes in my belt. When Alice's breasts no longer filled the bras she had along, she stopped wearing them. She took to wearing a boy's T-shirt she'd found abandoned at the lake. The shirt fit her so tightly that it made her new, angular body look positively obscene. Between the hem of the shirt and the waist of her cutoffs, four inches of brown skin and the elastic of her underwear. Sometimes on the weekends she and I drove to town and watched Little League games from the aluminum stands. Gas was cheap.

Alice's Plymouth suffered these excursions. Three of the four hubcaps, having been jarred loose on washboard, rode in the trunk; one we never recovered. It was impossible to go anywhere without raising a cloud of dust that followed you until you stopped. Operating the windshield washer created a film of mud that the sun-baked wipers troweled like mortar.

It was all really the same day until, after a road trip that had taken us within a few miles of the Canadian border, we returned to Shiloh's inexplicable wrath.

"Where've you been?" he asked.

Alice and I tried to remember the names of the places we'd passed through.

"When was the last time you two lovebirds tended to our garden?"

Alice and I exchanged looks. We'd been there recently. A few days ago. We'd walked past it, I was sure.

Shiloh wanted us to go and take a look at it.

The soil in that part of the state was rich and glacial—stone walls that a century ago had marked the boundaries of fields had been overrun with forests. Things couldn't help but grow.

The three of us headed around the house. Shiloh led the way. Our first mistake had been in selecting this spot—the only places that overlooked it were the window in the pantry and Shiloh's room. If we'd had it to do over again, we would have picked a place that we had cause to walk past more often. But how could we have known our habits before we'd initiated them?

What confronted us was more an act of God than evidence of any misdeed on the part of Alice or me. Like I said, the rain just stopped falling. The same sad story was probably playing itself out in every other garden across the state. This fantastic soil had been baked ashen gray. Fissures showed where the soil had contracted and torn apart from itself. Staring at it, I couldn't say when I'd visited it last. The garden looked so different from the garden in my memory. Alice and I inspected the plot, shook our heads, and tried to piece together what we were seeing. Tomato plants hung on their wire gallows; all the small fruit had been carried away. Where I remembered slender corn, we found shattered stalks. Shiloh gathered the desiccated vegetation and made a neat pile. Everywhere clumps of weeds sprouted; their health, relative to what we'd planted, was instructive. We might have fared worse, but the baked earth had kept scavengers from digging anything up. Whatever had eaten the tops off the carrots hadn't bothered with excavating the roots; when I dug them out they were withered and ancient looking. A tangle of yellow vines was all that remained of the pea plants. Alice recovered three overripe eggplants while I scraped up the radishes. The onions had matured into papery bags of pungent mush.

"What do you think?" Shiloh asked. He'd assembled enough dead material for a bonfire.

Alice said, "I'm really surprised."

"Look," I said, holding up a perfect zucchini, only about two inches long.

"You're smiling like it's some sort of joke. That was our food."

"Settle down," said Alice. "There's no way Thomas and I could have known the drought would last this long. This kind of weather has to be an anomaly."

Shiloh reached into his pocket and pulled out a piece of paper. He handed it to me.

"Water Us," it read.

"I didn't write that," I said.

"I hung that on the tomatoes two weeks ago. When I came out here this morning, it was still there."

Alice sat on the cracked earth.

"How do we know you're not making that story up?"

"That's exactly my point: you don't know."

I walked up to him and shoved him backward. I felt like a stranger in my skin.

"Thomas," he said, raising his arms to ward me off. "I'm right. You and Alice aren't taking things seriously."

I shoved him again. To prove he couldn't stop me, I suppose.

"Stop!" shouted Alice. She seized my ankle.

"Why didn't *you* water it?" I asked.

"In order for societies to work, people have to behave ethically. By ignoring your responsibilities you've chosen to act unethically."

"This isn't a social experiment," argued Alice.

"Right," said Shiloh. "This was our garden. This was our food."

I went inside the house and filled the watering can. The wrinkled ground refused to drink. The water sluiced across it. I shuttled back and forth, until the pipes coughed and clanged, but no more water came.

I roared at the ceiling.

Shiloh came in. He tested the handle, but the water still didn't flow. He tried the hot water. It worked fine.

"Can you fix it?" I asked.

"Nothing's broken. We're just out of water."

I turned the hot water on again.

He told me to turn it off. What remained in the water heater was all the water we had.

I grabbed an empty bucket and carried it, along with the watering can, to our swimming hole. Hardly a trickle came off the hillside. I filled the two containers and carried them back across the yard.

Alice came out of the kitchen and intercepted me. "Shiloh says we're out of water."

"I think the well's dry."

"What does that mean?"

"It means we're out of water, at least for the time being."

"I didn't know wells could run dry."

"You know the phrase 'the well ran dry'? This is where it comes from."

"Ask Shiloh if Parker's constant showering didn't have something to do with this."

"You ask him," I said, pushing past her. I delivered the water to the dry ground.

11
Safe

Shiloh thought it would be a good idea for the two of us to initiate a plan for water conservation. A plan, he reasoned, would guarantee that everyone knew their responsibilities. Up until this point, he believed, we had left too much up to chance. Alice had taken the car out to buy groceries and get me a surprise (she said it as though it was part of our shtick—I wondered if this wasn't a remnant of her marriage that she'd wrongfully attributed to me). I thought we should wait until she got back. There was no need to include her, according to Shiloh. If I could wait one moment, he would go to his room and get a tablet of paper and a couple of pens. He jogged upstairs and got his things. "Is it hot in here?" he asked when he came back. Sure, but what choice did we have? He motioned for me to follow and he led me to the basement stairs.

He went down two stairs, motioned for me to stand on the one above him, and told me to shut the door. He didn't bother to turn on the lights.

"Are you trying to freak me out?"

"Just close the door."

I did.

"Give me your hand."

Slowly we descended. I kept my shoulder against the wall of the house until the staircase opened up and all I could lean on was a shaky handrail. His shoes made a muffled sound when they reached the unfinished dirt floor. I stuck my foot out and found that I'd reached the bottom. I couldn't see anything but the thinnest sliver of light at the top of the stairs. As promised, the air was cooler down here, but it was more complex than that. There was a particular smell in that close place that eluded me, a vaguely sulfuric scent that I thought might be traced to the molten core of the earth. He tugged my hand and I followed.

We walked far enough that I didn't see how we could still be in the basement. Then Shiloh turned me around and we zigzagged back. His intention was clearly to confuse me. I might have complained if I hadn't thought that my complicity was essential.

"We're almost there," he said.

I didn't respond for fear that my voice would betray what I knew, that we'd almost been there as soon as we'd come down the stairs, that we hadn't been following labyrinthine subterranean tunnels, but had crisscrossed the finite confines of a basement.

"Here we go."

Apparently he'd reached a wall—his hand scraped across it. A yawning sound and a swirling of the air told me a door had opened. Shiloh gave a grunt and his shoes scraped across the floor. The hand on my wrist tugged downward. My foot found the base of the wall that he was trying to pull me through. My hand measured an opening, a hole in the wall maybe two feet off the ground.

"How should I do this?"

The hand gave an insistent tug.

I crawled through head first. The floor in this new space was a few inches higher than the basement and finished with something exceedingly hard. I got to my feet. Shiloh took me by both hands and guided me to a chair. Once I sat down he went back and closed the door.

"Voilà," he said.

Such a pervasive light filled the room that my eyes clamped shut and it was only through an act of will that I opened them. Everything had been rendered glossy white: the walls, the ceiling, a narrow workbench, and the cabinets that overhung it. I think an operating room would have been more intimate than the space I found myself in. The cabinet had four doors and each door had its own hasp and padlock. Two spotlights with brushed metal shades opposed each other. An adjustable magnifying light was mounted to the workbench with a

C-clamp and a brace made from wood scraps. Shiloh took a spot on the immaculate counter; his feet swung above a concrete floor.

"Where the heck are we?"

My question pleased him immensely. He raised one eyebrow.

Peering around him, I saw that the door we'd come through was obscured by a large piece of cardboard. The room was just four or five feet deep and twice that long. I'd been cautiously stooping when I'd come in, but I saw that the ceiling was high enough to permit me to stand. Something about the construction of the ceiling and walls bothered me. I touched the near wall and knew what he'd done. He'd insulated the walls and ceiling with rolls of fiberglass insulation, taped the seams, and then painted the backing.

Four cabinets, three lights, one workbench, a chair, a toolbox, a concealed room.

It may have been cooler when we first entered, but with the two big lights going and the metabolic output of our bodies, I began to sweat. Shiloh flipped on the magnifying light and turned off the other two. A white halo shone on the work space.

"You hungry?"

He took a key from his pocket and unfastened one of the padlocks. He got two Clark bars out from the cabinet.

"Why are you locking up candy bars?"

He hesitated before replacing the padlock on the cabinet door. "They last longer if it takes deliberate action to get to them."

His ritual with the candy bars reassured me somehow.

I said, "So, all that talk of the mortar being in bad shape. What do Alice or I know? The whole time you were building this."

The walls seemed to wick away the sound. Every word we said, every noise we made, was disassembled and lost.

A wave of regret passed over Shiloh's pudding face. "Parker didn't think you needed to be involved."

"But what is it?"

"It's just a place for me to go to clear my head."

"Cool," I said.

Beneath the bench sat his red enamel toolbox. An iron spike, like one might use to anchor a circus tent, had been set into the ground near one wall. Attached to it were nearly a dozen thin, insulated wires, each a different color, which in turn ran to some of the objects in the room: all three of the lamps, the frame of the chair I sat on, another fastened to the handle of the toolbox. Half a dozen coiled wires concluding in alligator clips hung from small nails set into the workbench.

"Alice and I wouldn't have been much help building a bomb shelter," I admitted.

With his heel Shiloh pushed the toolbox farther beneath the bench. "It's really more a workroom than a bomb shelter."

"Parker must have thought you were crazy when you told him you wanted to build this."

"It wasn't my idea, Thomas."

I looked at the locked cabinets.

"What? He thought you'd need a room to get away from Alice and me?"

"If I wanted to hide from you, why would I bring you down here?"

He pulled a pen out of his pocket and set the writing tablet on his lap, signaling that he wanted to change gears.

"So he didn't build this for you."

"Doesn't seem like it."

"Then he built it for himself."

Shiloh bit the cap off the pen and wrote something on the pad. He turned it so I could see what he'd written. "Methods and Criteria for the Conservation of Limited Water Resources."

"Is the thing he stole up there?" I asked, pointing at the locked cabinets.

"Don't take it personally, Thomas. I just like to have a bit of privacy."

It made sense to me.

He seemed as if he might have been on the verge of saying something, but then he turned away. "Here's how I see it," he said. "The only essential uses for water are food preparation and personal consumption." He wrote these things and then he made a slashing line underneath them.

"What about personal hygiene?"

"Yes," he said, "yes." Then he made a frustrated sound and tore off the first page of his tablet and copied what he'd written before, leaving space to write "personal hygiene."

"What about dish washing?"

"Sure," he said, smiling. "I'm going to call that 'cleaning.' You and I will know what I'm talking about."

We looked at the list for a moment and considered whether we'd forgotten anything.

"What we've got to do," explained Shiloh, "is make a conscious effort to reduce consumption and increase conservation in these specific arenas." He tapped the pen on the pad of paper. "This is a good start. Before this is over you and I might have to boil stream water for drinking."

"Alice will love that."

"Even if we don't always see eye to eye," said Shiloh, "she gave me a place to stay when I didn't have anywhere to go. She didn't know me from Adam and she invited me into her house. I owe her a debt. What I don't know is if she's going to let me stay around to repay it."

"You belong here as much as me or Alice."

"I think you're a great kid, but that's not my point."

I tried to tell him that I liked him, too. Then I tried to tell him that, in my opinion, most people liked him. When I realized what I was saying, I just sort of let the words dry up in my mouth.

This struck him as funny. We were some type of friends.

"Are all the cabinets full of candy bars?"

"Just that one," he said, pointing to the one we'd been in.

"What's in the other ones?"

"Pop."

"Seriously?"

He shook his head. He pointed up, as in "Let's go upstairs," and when my eyes followed his fingers, he switched the bright lights on and off, blinding me. "Sorry."

I heard him toss the cardboard aside and then the hatchway

opened again. He took my wrist and helped me crawl back into the basement.

Alice discovered a contempt for me. At issue was whether I'd ignored something she'd said or forgotten it. Forgetfulness (a passive offensive, instead of the active one) seemed the lesser crime. The problem I faced was that to convince her I'd forgotten something, I needed to remember it. Alice recognized this and refused to aid me with clues. Of all her features, her mouth hated me the most.

I promised her that I had only forgotten momentarily, that it was on the tip of my tongue. I got her to sit on the edge of the bed and rubbed the back of her neck. I lifted the hem of her shirt and pulled it over her head.

"I have to teach you everything." She was one of those people who could say anything as long as she believed it.

"Yes."

"You don't even know how to fight."

"How should I fight?"

She gave me a pitying look.

Later the sun caught us in bed.

Horses clomped down the road. A man and a woman, each steadying a child in the saddle in front of them. The woman rode on a piebald, the man on a sweaty chestnut. They wore straw hats and tight western-style shirts. Something about the way they wore the clothes told us that these were really just costumes for riding; they probably had other costumes for working, or, in the children's case, for school. The family rode down to where the road ended and then they came past us again and were gone.

Across the fields, something skirted the edge of the woods. When the sun hit its coat, Alice said, "Fox." It seemed to be keeping an eye on the riders. This pleased Alice, the idea of prey tracking the hunter—not that the riders were fox hunters, but still. Even before the fox disappeared, she said she wanted to see it again.

I stared at Alice standing at the window. She had gotten so skinny. Where she used to have a little belly, now there was only a crease of skin. Her hand kept catching her underwear as it fell off her hips. And, inexplicably, I remembered the thing that Alice had accused me of ignoring.

"Come here," I said.

She wouldn't leave the window. "It's crossing the road," she said.

"But why did it cross the road?"

"They're supposed to be very intelligent," she said, turning to see why I'd called her.

"Where's my surprise?" I said.

She held up a finger, telling me to wait. I heard her open the hall closet. She shifted things inside.

"Close your eyes."

A heavy box landed on my lap. "What is it?"

Alice stood defiantly, her arms crossed beneath her breasts. She walked back to the window and took another look.

I turned the box in my hands for clues.

"You've drawn this out too long already. Just open it."

Inside, two winter boots nested among crumpled tissue paper. They had high, laced leather uppers mated to chunky rubber bottoms.

"Boots," I said.

"Boots."

A small note card was propped between them.

"Should I read this?"

"Ugh."

I couldn't really read the card right away, though, because I felt so overwhelmingly happy.

"Do you hate them?" Alice asked, sitting next to me and considering the boots.

"They're my favorite thing."

"Did you read the card?"

I shook my head.

"'Thomas,'" she read. "'With your feet warm and dry this winter, you won't have an excuse for abandoning me. Until then you can park them under my bed.'"

I said, "Thank you. Thank you. Thank you."

She took one out of the box.

Even barefoot I couldn't get my foot in. "They probably need to be broken in."

I held the boot to my foot. No amount of breaking in would be sufficient.

Alice looked upset. She'd gotten the size from my old shoes. I reminded her that the reason I'd stopped wearing those shoes was that they no longer fit.

"How can you still be growing?"

"Let me try them again." I almost wrestled a foot in. And I believe I would have succeeded, just to spare Alice.

She yelled, "Stop! You're making it worse."

Which was true. Already the seam where the leather and rubber met showed signs of extraordinary stress. My toes weren't faring much better. Maybe my mistake was trying too hard. Despite the mix-up I felt certain I was in a moment that I would recall later when I needed to feel truly loved.

The store clerk took one look at the torn seam and refused to exchange them.

Alice asked Shiloh to try them; they fit him fine.

12

High

I was pulling weeds in the driveway. The grass that grew there wasn't any sort of bother, but once I started pulling it up, I couldn't stop. It wasn't work; it was an imitation of work. I looked forward to the imitation of satisfaction I would experience when I was done. Alice sat on the porch swing, feigning an interest in what I did.

Across the road a hawk stalled and plunged, again and again. Whatever it hunted eluded it. Maybe it only pantomimed hunting.

Alice reached a foot down and set the swing rocking. I stood up and stretched my back. An engine strained just over the hill. I heard the stones pinging off the fenders.

A truck came racing toward us, fishtailing in the loose gravel, too fast. The driver locked up the brakes and the four tires carved four furrows in the soft road. The truck came to rest sticking halfway in the ditch that ran alongside the road. A cloud of dust, as fine as flour, drifted across the field.

The driver hopped out to look at the truck. He wore yellow nylon wind pants and one of those four-flapped hats like Sherlock Holmes.

Shiloh got out on the passenger side. He called out to us, "This is Dupree."

Dupree said, "That was my first attempt parking."

"I'm teaching him how to drive," said Shiloh.

"That's what it looks like," said Alice.

Dupree put his hands on the truck and rocked it back and forth. The right-rear wheel didn't touch the ground.

"We need to borrow Thomas for a couple of hours," said Shiloh.

"Me?" I asked.

"Borrow him for what?" asked Alice.

Silk-screened across Dupree's shirt: SECRET AGENT ORANGE.

"I can't say," said Shiloh.

Alice asked me what this was about.

I had no idea.

Alice sat up. "You're not planning anything illegal or dangerous?"

Shiloh put his hand over his heart. "As God is my witness."

The three of us climbed into the truck. Shiloh put it in reverse, but we didn't go anywhere. The wheel in the air was the only one turning.

Shiloh told me and Dupree to get in the bed to act as ballast. The two of us clambered in back. Dupree said, "Hi." He seemed to be either in great spirits or insane. We crouched beside the tailgate. Now the spinning wheel was on the dirt, but still the truck didn't want to back up, so Shiloh drove into the ditch instead. He didn't stop, but picked up speed and then, with a turn of the wheel, launched the truck up the embankment and onto the road. I felt my body lifting up and weightless and then I was crashing down on the metal bed.

"Oh, God," yelled Alice. She started running toward us.

Shiloh stopped the truck.

"Hot dog," I said.

I turned around to trade looks with Dupree, but he wasn't in the truck anymore. I looked up. He wasn't in the air. Then I saw, lying in the middle of the road, Dupree. I climbed down from the truck.

"He's okay," said Shiloh.

Dupree sat up compliantly. "Wow," he said.

"Sorry, pardner," said Shiloh.

Alice asked him if he was okay.

Dupree wandered off into the ditch.

"You going to be sick?" Shiloh asked.

Dupree looked up, surprised. "I'm looking for my bike."

"What's he talking about?" asked Alice.

"You fell out of the truck," explained Shiloh.

"Maybe you should rest for a while," said Alice.

Dupree sat in the ditch.

The three of us looked down at him.

"Who is he?" Alice asked finally.

"He knows Gregor," said Shiloh.

After a minute Dupree stood up. He dropped his pants. We turned away while he pissed in the high grass.

When he got back onto the road, he said, "I'm ready to travel."

"Maybe you ought to see a doctor," said Alice.

"You want to see a doctor?" asked Shiloh.

Dupree didn't seem to realize that they were talking to him. He got in the truck.

"Thomas?" said Shiloh.

I leaned toward him.

"Aren't you coming?"

Alice didn't look at me. She didn't wave as we drove away.

Dupree told Shiloh where to turn. We came into this town that was exactly where I never thought a town might be, and then, in the middle of this town, we came to a golf course. I'd only seen golf on television, but it was the same in person. Men zipped around in gasoline-powered carts.

"I didn't realize it would be so hectic here," said Shiloh.

"They're having a father-son tournament," explained Dupree.

On closer inspection, in every cart we saw an older and a younger version of the same person. Which explained why the golf pro wasn't happy to see us. He wanted us to come back later in the afternoon. He made an appeal to Dupree, but Dupree wasn't listening. Finally the four of us got onto a cart—Shiloh and me holding on back where the golf bags are supposed to ride—and the pro chauffeured us across the course. The golfers waved to the pro as we scooted past.

The pro dropped us off at a maintenance shed on the other side of the course. Outside there were rain gauges, piles of fertilizer, and a wind sock. The shed was ringed by all types of broken machinery and the most beautiful lawn I'd ever seen, which was actually their sod farm. Dupree opened a big green garage door. Inside were all manner of lawn mowers, a few battered tractors, and a white-and-peach, single-engine Piper Cub.

Shiloh put his arm over my shoulder. "That, my friend, is an airplane."

Dupree wandered around the plane, checking mechanical connections, the angles of wires, the blades of the propeller. He popped the engine cowling and tried to wiggle the spark plugs.

"You guys ready?" Dupree asked.

"Before we take off," said Shiloh, "could you tell my friend if there's any particular safety concerns he ought to be aware of?"

Dupree stopped his inspection to smile at Shiloh.

"Have you ever had to crash-land or anything like that?" Shiloh nudged me as though I'd put him up to the question.

"Not yet," said Dupree.

"Should we be wearing parachutes?" Shiloh seemed bent on portraying himself as a rational person.

"Get in already," said Dupree.

"How come you didn't know how to drive a car?" I asked him.

"I'm fifteen," said Dupree.

*   *   *

I climbed onboard through a door that folded down. There was a bench seat in back and one up front where Dupree and Shiloh sat. I had a small rectangular window all to myself.

Dupree asked me if I was comfortable.

I didn't bother replying because at the same time he fired up the engine and I couldn't hear myself speak. We rolled out of the garage, and this is why the pro had been less than thrilled to see us. The golf course and the runway were one and the same. As we taxied out the golfers scattered.

The engine noise grew until it was as essential as our heartbeats. Shiloh twisted in his seat and shot me a thumbs-up. We bumped our way down the grassy track. I felt heavy in my core. I wanted to holler "Stop." Things got very still. The ground fell away from my window. We banked above the trees. Presently, I was in the sky.

The engine noise backed down a notch. The little plane rocked like a boat. We sailed on a river of air.

Shiloh turned around to see how I felt.

"Okay?" he shouted.

I nodded a vigorous assent.

"It's just wood and canvas. It's like we're inside a living animal."

"How long do we fly around?" I yelled.

I saw water through my window, a lake or a pond. For some reason this bothered me more than anything I might have imagined. I noticed, for the first time, the tremendous amount of air pushing through the cabin. My mind wanted me to think awful things: Alice far below and me with no way to lower myself from this height.

Dupree turned around to look at me. "Happy birthday!" said Dupree.

I didn't know what he was talking about.

Shiloh turned in his seat. "I hope you don't mind that I told him."

"Happy birthday," Dupree said again.

"Thank you," I said.

"I bet you never figured you'd go up in a plane," said Shiloh.

I shook my head.

"Shiloh can be very persuasive," said Dupree.

"I have my talents," said Shiloh.

"Should I loop the loop?" asked Dupree.

I couldn't will myself to speak.

Shiloh turned around and pointed his finger at me. "He's pulling your leg," said Shiloh.

"Oh," I said.

"I'm not aerobatics certified," said Dupree.

I looked through my little peephole window at the distant world.

At some point my inner ear detected that we were starting to lose altitude. I didn't want to tell Dupree his business. Still, the treetops appeared to be getting closer. I had the unmistakable sense that the plane was sinking. I wanted greedily to gain altitude. Down, down we went. I didn't consider we might be landing until the wheels hit the ground.

We were on a dirt-and-gravel road, in a dirt-and-gravel land-scape. I didn't recognize a thing, or know how far we'd come. This might be Canada, I thought, looking out at dwarf trees and scrub. The plane rolled to a stop.

Shiloh turned around, his face green tinged, a wide, dry smile, a window to his teeth. "How was your first flight?"

"Great," I said.

"You want to trade seats?"

"No," I said.

"Do that," said Dupree. "Trade seats."

I climbed up front. There was a guy carrying two big duffel bags walking toward us. If it wasn't for him, we could have been anywhere.

The interloper threw his bags in back and squeezed past me.

"Are we in Canada?" I asked.

This was some sort of joke. The new guy laughed and Dupree laughed. Shiloh tousled my hair.

"This is nowhere," said the new guy.

"This is an Indian reservation," said Dupree.

"Indian Nation," corrected the new guy.

"Indian Nation," repeated Dupree.

"Let's split," said the new guy, who was older than any of us by twenty years. I looked at him for a moment, but Dupree gunned the engine and I wanted to see what it looked like to fly.

As soon as we were in the air, Dupree turned toward me. "I've been to Canada," he said.

"Yeah?" I shouted.

"I might go to Hudson Bay, sometime."

"What's in Hudson Bay?"

"That's why I want to go there."

Shiloh tapped me on the shoulder. He leaned forward so I could hear him. "Pretty great, huh?"

The stranger was saying something to me. I cupped my hand around my ear.

"You look like you could be an angel or something." His voice reverberated in the cockpit. He rolled a sleeve up. On his forearm there was a tattoo of a red crucifix floating between two mountains. Blood dripped off the bottom of the cross into a lake.

I gave him the thumbs-up.

He stuck his hand out and we shook.

Dupree pushed the control stick forward and dropped the nose of the plane. A feeling like itchy electricity traveled from the back of my throat down to my balls. The engine sound was replaced by the high-pitched crying of the guy wires. There was something about falling inside a plane that made it much worse than falling outside a plane. Dupree leveled us off.

We made a beeline for what, at first, appeared to be a black scar on a mountainside. We came in just above the trees. It didn't resemble a runway any more than the golf course had. Dupree set the plane down just the same.

Before I knew what was what, the passenger and his luggage had gotten out. Then the engine noise and once again we were in the sky.

Shiloh leaned forward so his mouth was just an inch from my ear. "Do you believe they let someone like me see the world from up here?" He leaned back and nodded.

I shook my head, like no, I couldn't believe it.

He tapped a finger on his chest and mouthed "My first time, too."
Dupree turned around in his seat. "You want to see your house?"
That's exactly what we wanted.

We scanned the countryside for our hidden home. All of a
sudden, Dupree set the plane on edge. The horizon turned like a
wheel. There at the still point we saw our little place. Something
about being in a plane made the general seem very grand and the
specific insignificant.

I remember the relief I felt, after surveying a county brown with
drought, to see the golfers scatter from the improbably green fairway.
I was still alive.

13
Deluge

Alice and I woke to a cool breeze rushing through our bedroom. We
heard tree limbs rattling. Outside our bedroom window, in the half-
light, small forms flitted across the empty field. This dark flock burst
in through our open window. They circled, close to the ceiling. Then
the spell was over and the leaves settled around us, on our bed, on the
floor, one, not quite escaping, perched on the windowsill.

The rain crashed into the house.

It overwhelmed the gutters (later, after collecting a dozen tiny
mice corpses in the yard, Shiloh deduced that a nesting family had
been flushed from the downspout). It ran off the roof in sheets. The
din of the drumming, the comfort of being warm and dry, these
things conspired to put us back to sleep.

It could have been five minutes later or the next day, the rain still
hammered down when I woke. I got Alice up and convinced her that
if we didn't go outside, we'd end up regretting it. She suggested that
we take this opportunity to wash our clothes; we hadn't done much of
that since the drought began. We stripped the sheets and collected
the pillowcases. Taking the squeeze bottle of dish soap, we headed
out into the weather. The rain had turned the road into a muddy
river; it plastered hair to heads, stung our bare skin. Crossing the field

we passed within twenty feet of a pair of turkey hens huddled beneath a low bush.

We heard the stream before we saw it—a grinding, industrial sound. Arcs of spray hung above the white water. Smaller, auxiliary streams formed along the flooded banks. Where it clobbered the dam, the water stood up in a frozen wave. I left the dirty clothes on the bank and waded in. Alice gave our clothes a shot of dish soap before handing them to me. I scrubbed these things in the rushing water. Pants held in the current kicked with phantom legs. A quick twist to dry, and then I tossed them back to Alice. I lost half of my only pair of dress socks. A few minutes later, a pillowcase swam away. The bedsheets were saved for last. I'd gotten pretty good about keeping my footing, and though the top sheet was many times larger than anything I'd washed before, it didn't give me that much trouble; I got it done. Next came the fitted sheet. As soon as the current took it, I knew I was in trouble. The articulated corners filled up like a sail and pulled me off my feet. What came to my mind was a kite pulling a boy into the sky. I scrambled to regain my footing. I saw Alice jump in the stream. She stood between me and the angry water at the dam. My body hit her and she stayed fast. I gave a sharp tug on the sheet and it dumped the water. I stood up.

"You idiot. We can replace sheets."

I thanked her.

She was shaking. "I had to get in the stupid water because you didn't let it go."

I wrapped the sheet around her shoulders and led her back to the bank.

"I'm sorry."

She reached up and pinched my lower lip. When she held her thumb in front of me, there was a dab of blood on it. I'd bitten my tongue.

Even after the storm, Shiloh insisted that we continue following water-conservation protocol. He spoke very expertly about aquifers and water tables. When Alice asked how long it would be before we could forget about conservation, Shiloh said, "We're on geologic time now."

Elsewhere the changes were sudden and dramatic. The rain had knocked the grass flat in the fields, but by the time Alice and I went to retrieve our clothes, not only had it rebounded, but new growth was thatched with the old. In a demonstration of hydraulics, our lightest garments rode the green shoots into the air. Despite the sun, the heat didn't return. Alice and I wore clothes again. I wound up cutting a V in the heel of my sneakers so I could cram my feet inside. (Alice observed this without comment.)

Alice and I tended our garden. The zucchini came back strong, but everything else had to be forgotten. We spaded the plot under. Before dark we drove down to the five-and-dime to see what was still worth planting. The clerk suggested Swiss chard. We bought six packets of seeds.

At the grocery store we bought bags of beans and rice, cases of canned tomatoes, peas, and tuna fish. Alice bought a demijohn of red wine. On the drive back we slowed to look at a field that was filled with pumpkins. That evening the three of us sat on the porch. Shiloh watched while Alice and I drank the wine. I got drunk for the first time in my life. They explained the four kinds of drunks: surly, morose, even-keeled, and like me. I talked too much.

Just before dusk Alice's fox trotted right down the middle of the road with a bird in its mouth. It turned to look at us as it passed.

"Maybe it was someone's pet," said Alice.

Shiloh said, "He sees we're no threat, and it's easier to walk on the road than in the hay."

"Is anyone coming to harvest that stuff?" I asked. The grass rolled in the slightest breeze.

"No," said Shiloh, "besides, it's full of brush."

"That's great stuff," I argued.

"Do foxes mate for life?" asked Alice.

"Swans do," said Shiloh.

"I'd like to make a haystack." I poured the last of the bottle into my glass.

"Let me have that." Alice stuck her hand out to me.

"You're thirsty?"

"I'm trying to save you from yourself."

I finished off the glass.

Shiloh appeared holding a sickle. "Here, champ, go make your haystack."

Alice protested in vain.

I examined the wooden dowel handle, the rusty metal crescent.

"Make a big one like in all the French paintings."

I didn't know the paintings Shiloh was talking about.

Alice announced that she was going inside.

Wading into the waist-high grass, I tried swinging the blade into the thickest patches. This didn't work well—the grass bent away. What I ended up doing was gathering a bunch in my left hand and chopping it free with my right. Being drunk infused the methodical with a certain grace. I tried to spiral out from my starting place, but determining the center became difficult. Instead of a circle I cleared a more amoebic shape. Once, stopping to stretch, I caught Alice in our window, but she moved away. Shiloh raked the cut grass with his fingers.

I didn't want to wait to see if Alice would come back. I told Shiloh I was heading in.

"You can't quit now," he said.

On impulse I threw the sickle. As soon as it was out of my hand, I imagined it curving in the air like a boomerang. I dropped to the ground.

Shiloh jogged over to see what had happened. I told him I'd lost the sickle. He grabbed me beneath my arms and tugged me to my feet.

We walked over to the haystack, really just a little hump.

I said, "I'm going to check on Alice."

Shiloh pushed me onto the haystack. I got up and pushed him down. We were laughing some. Then I lost my balance, so I lay down in the grass.

"We have to cut your hair," said Shiloh. "You almost look like a girl. Like a gangly girl."

"Everything is spinning."

"You really are drunk."

"Would you get Alice for me?"

"There's nothing she could do."

"I bet she can hear us talking."

Shiloh's head was just a shadow above me.

"You going to be sick?"

I stuck my tongue out.

Shiloh put his hand on my forehead.

I had to close my eyes.

"I don't think I'll ever drink again."

"Are you cold?"

"I guess a little bit."

"I'm going to lie down beside you."

"I love Alice."

"Thanks for that information."

Our shoulders touched. He kicked my foot in a friendly way.

"I haven't told Alice about your workroom."

"You're a good person, Thomas."

"Parker said you used to love a boy."

"Did Parker say anything else?"

"He said Alice's husband wound up in an institution because of nobility."

"A person doesn't need nobility to wind up in an institution. I'm proof of that."

"What kind of institution were you in?"

"Orphanages, juvie hall, and jail. Three institutions, off the top of my head."

Shiloh held his arms out in front of us and wiggled his fingers. An optical illusion made it seem as if we could see right through them.

"Parker said the boy killed himself because of nobility."

"This isn't something we can talk about, Thomas." His voice sounded wounded.

I wanted to tell Shiloh that I didn't have any nobility either. And

I wanted to tell him that I loved him. The more I thought about it, they both seemed like shitty things to say.

I woke up in the middle of the field. Alice and Shiloh were standing at my feet. Alice announced that she and Shiloh would be taking the car. I tried to catch her eye, but she was busy looking everywhere I wasn't. Sometimes her face defied me and was only a face.

It hurt to keep my eyes open.

"You hungover?" asked Alice.

I guessed I was.

"Who do I look like?" asked Shiloh. He had on huaraches, jeans, a blue workman's shirt, and his sunglasses.

"A semiproductive member of society," answered Alice.

"I've got them all fooled," said Shiloh.

Once the sound of Alice's car died away, I went inside the house. I experienced a brief exhilaration at finding myself alone. Immediately afterward I felt dread. In order to distract myself, I tidied Alice's and my bedroom—folded our clothes, shook out the sheets and made the bed, pushed the bed square with the wall. In the kitchen I put dishes away, wiped down counters, washed out the refrigerator, culling the unidentifiable and the rancid. When all that was done, I went outside to wait for my friends to return. A blanket of translucent clouds obscured the sun. Butterflies and grasshoppers made imprecise flights above the meadow. The haystack had turned from gold to a dull yellow. So as not to be seen as taking shortcuts, I went around back and weeded the garden. Returning to the house, the kitchen didn't seem so immaculate anymore. I washed it again, now sponging the dust off the cabinet edges, polishing the sink fixtures, wiping down the black surface of the woodstove. I climbed the ladder-steep back stairs and swept out the house from top to bottom. I swept the pantry, careful not to excite the dirt enough that it might reach the kitchen counters. I pushed all of the filth to the threshold of the front door and swept it out. Then I swept the rectangular granite block of the front step. I removed five burned-out lightbulbs from their sockets, but when I couldn't find new bulbs, I returned the dead ones to their places.

I went into the bathroom, put the stopper in the tub, and ran a bath, scrubbing the dirt off my skin with chips of soap wrapped in a washcloth. The water turned gray. By standing up and checking myself in the mirror above the sink, I could tell which spots I'd missed because the dirt stained like a bruise. I sat in the hot water, working on my feet and under my arms. I rinsed myself. Even our cleanest towels smelled earthy. I squeegeed the water off with my fingers. In front of the mirror, I shaved, using soap suds for shaving cream, the hairs came sparse and black on the sides of my mustache and under my neck. I'd used soap on my hair, too, and already it was drying, shiny and limp, in a ragged crown. The last thing I did was rinse out the tub.

It started raining again. I made a fire in the stove and boiled three hot dogs. They tasted salty and delicious. Where, I wondered, had my friends gone to? I couldn't keep myself from imagining twisting wrecks. What if Shiloh had taken Alice up in the plane? I couldn't bear it. Forcing myself to consider other things, I thought about the hideout in the basement and those shiny new locks. But I was afraid that if I went down there, I wouldn't hear their return.

I went upstairs and tried Shiloh's door. He'd hung a beach towel in front of his window. The towel moved back and forth with a subtle sway. I turned his light on and closed the door behind me. The room was practically unchanged. The upside-down flag thumbtacked to the wall; the pitcher of water—almost empty, the surface dimpled with dust—was now closer to his mattress; his hay-flecked clothes were in a pile, and beside them was another pile showing sweat-hardened socks, greasy jeans, and his few shirts; by his mattress was an English-Italian dictionary, a pocket comb, nail clippers, a pile of change. At the head of his mattress, there was a closet door. Inside the closet wire hangers waited for clothes.

A cigar box stuck out from beneath his bedsheet. It was secured with a brass hook and loop. Inside I found a collapsible Polaroid camera and a stack of photographs. The pictures were held together with rubber bands. The top picture showed a skinny boy riding on top of a train car full of coal, his arms extending across the frame to usher the viewer in. On the back of the picture, Shiloh had written "Utah." The next picture showed the boy standing in front of Mount Rushmore, but at an angle so that his head was the same size as the presidents'. Shiloh appeared in some of the pictures, in strange cities, on mountain trails, eating out of a can, pointing at the horizon. Denver, Akron, Butte, Lawrence. Men sleeping under a bridge, looking older than corpses. An indigo sky. Shiloh owning a younger face. There was a picture of someone jumping off a train trestle and another one of a man's wounded hands ("poor landing in Portland"). Every picture was focused on the same middle distance; because of this, all of the landscapes seemed related. Then I came across the pictures I'd expected to find: a hard-on laying on a palm like a trout; the top of a boy's head over what I was certain must have been Shiloh's crotch; a self-portrait where Shiloh holds the camera straight over their heads and he and the boy—naked, holding hands—look into it. It is the same boy each time. Shiloh's lover. And then, toward the bottom of the stack, the boy disappears. Instead the pictures show junkyard cars slipping into a slow river; contrails crossing at angles; half of a coyote resting on the side of a road, Shiloh's shoes just edging into the frame.

I heard the car coming down the road. I got the photos back into shape, refastened the lid, and replaced the box. I tucked the bedsheet around it. I was reaching to turn the light off when I saw the sign he'd affixed to the back of his door:

> *The breaking up of power from within by restoration of authority can be the result of isolated individual endeavors, but in a police state it would have to be discreet and well-organized.*
>
> —GIOVANNI BALDELLI

I turned off the light.

The house was dark. I didn't hear anyone come in. I went downstairs, flipped on the kitchen light, and walked onto the porch. Ribbons of night cut through the clouds. I could hear the hot engine clank and hiss as it cooled. But the car parked in the driveway wasn't Alice's.

"You alone?" a voice asked, gruffly, from inside the car.

All I could say was, "Huh?"

"Come here, guy."

I took a step off the porch.

"I need a hand." The driver's door creaked open. The car rocked each time he moved.

I was completely unnerved. "I don't know who you are," I said, my voice shaky and thin.

"That's my insurance." He stood up. The whole state was populated by giants. "Mags told me how to get here."

Mags?

"I think you've got the wrong place."

This troubled the man for a second. He looked at the house and at me. "I'm Gregor's brother."

He didn't have his brother's accent or his stilted speech. Standing beside the car he patted down his pockets. He reached and grabbed the door handle. He paused for a moment and looked at me.

"What do you want?"

"Shush," he said. He opened the back door and pulled a bundle out. It was a child wrapped in a blanket. "Let's get her in the house," he said.

"In our house?"

"Don't start hassling me."

So I led the way and the giant carried the girl in. He looked at our spindly chairs and took a seat on the floor. The nails in the boards cried. Sonya shifted in his arms and got back to sleep.

"What's going on?"

"There's sort of a situation."

I really had no idea how I could enter into this negotiation. Alice would have been able to find a solution, I felt. But she had abandoned me to this mess. And it wasn't enough to know what she'd say. I had to understand her reasoning and I needed to pit that against this man's will.

"Well," I said, "there's a situation here, too."

Like a gambler laying down a winning hand, he said, "Gregor told me you were an orphan."

"I'm not the orphan. Shiloh's the orphan."

"Who're you then?"

They hadn't told him about me.

"I live here with Alice and Shiloh."

He didn't seem to give this much thought.

"Let me explain: Gregor is having a routine problem with the government. It's a tax thing, but they like to make tax things into social-service things. Right? So, unless you want Sonya to grow up in some foster home, you need to look out for her for a couple of days."

I understood why he was looking for Shiloh.

"Why can't you take her?" I asked.

"My lifestyle isn't appropriate for minors." He set the girl on the floor.

"I don't even know what to feed a kid."

"She eats food, man." He eased himself up.

"I don't know."

"Someone'll be by Wednesday to pick her up."

"What day is today?" I asked.

"Are you serious?"

Where to begin?

"They'll be here in four days."

"Why then?"

"Because that's the plan."

I stared at the sleeping girl while he let himself out.

She stayed there, curled against the baseboard. Her dark, insect eyelashes twitched and her feet kicked inside her blanket. I was amazed that a whole person could take up such a tiny space. I didn't quite know what to do with myself. I crept about the room easing the windows down in their sashes. I rekindled the fire in the stove. With her pip nose and hair half as long as her torso, she was some type of beauty, if not entirely human.

At that precise moment I felt capable of protecting her, but just on the other side of her nap, the rest of her life waited. An arm snaked out of her blanket and she plugged her thumb into her mouth. Sooner or later she would wake up . . . and what would it mean to her, of all the faces in the world, to be confronted with mine? She wouldn't be able to protect me from the depth of her disappointment. For the moment, she was safe in sleep. Until then I would be faithful and true. And when anticipation exceeded patience, I clattered the pots on the stovetop.

When Shiloh and Alice returned, Sonya was sitting at the table—I'd put two pillows on the chair and still her chin just barely peeked above the tabletop. She'd already eaten pork and beans. Since we didn't have any desserts, I put a couple of ice cubes in a cereal bowl; this was fine with her. She'd get the ice cube in her spoon, then ladle it to her mouth. When it got too cold, she'd spit it back in the bowl. Sometimes she'd fan her mouth afterward and say, "Hot." It was a joke.

"Shiloh," I said, "you remember Sonya."

He walked over and shook her tiny hand.

"Hi, sweetie," said Alice.

They looked at me for an explanation.

"Where's the rest of the gang?" asked Shiloh.

"She's staying with us for a few days."

"You're kidding," said Alice.

"Hot," Sonya said. Waving her hand in front of her face, she accidentally catapulted the spoon out of the bowl. She burst out laughing.

I picked the spoon up and rinsed it before returning it to her.

The next time it wound up under the stove.

"You guys got her all riled up," I said.

"Wait." Alice raised her hands like she was trying to flag down a train.

Sonya slid beneath the table.

"What, exactly, is going on?" Alice looked as though she was preparing to multiply two large numbers in her head.

"She's hugging one of the table's legs," said Shiloh.

"Apparently Gregor has some sort of P-R-O-B-L-E-M with the IRS."

"*Irs?*" asked Shiloh.

"But it's not our P-R-O-B-L-E-M," said Alice. "We have to take her H-O-M-E right now."

"We can't do that," I said.

"Did you give them your word that we'd look after her?" Shiloh asked.

I said I did. "She's only going to be here for a few days," I repeated. "Gregor's brother came by to drop her off."

"Goger!" shouted Sonya, transforming the name.

Alice picked the girl up and cradled her.

"Where's your mommy?"

Sonya sucked on her pointer finger and then aimed it at Shiloh.

Alice said, "I don't believe that they take children away in tax cases."

"You're wrong," said Shiloh. "That's what the government does. They get one thing on you and then they use it to tear you apart."

"Thomas did the right thing," said Alice.

"How do you mean?" Shiloh asked—we were both surprised to hear she'd reached that conclusion.

"God only knows where she might have wound up if he'd refused to take responsibility."

The girl's head dropped onto Alice's shoulder. She was asleep.

Alice rolled her eyes. "We'll take her back in the morning."

"Wait a sec," said Shiloh.

But no amount of waiting would be sufficient for him to find an argument to counter Alice.

The three of us went upstairs. Shiloh and I laid towels out on the floor. Alice placed the girl on the makeshift bed.

We all tiptoed downstairs. What we found was a changed house. It moved all around us; breathing it in made us feel like better people. The temperature had dipped, which provided the excuse for us to crowd around the stove. Shiloh made a pot of coffee. Our spirits were high. I would never have friends like the friends I had in that room.

14

The Tale of Foolish Curiosity

In the early morning Sonya got into bed with us. As if auditioning for the role of a sleeper, the little girl took to assuming different poses, holding them for only a few seconds. It was as if she meant to demonstrate a comprehensive familiarity with sleep, or a mastery over it. She could sleep draped over our legs or sitting up, with her hands clasped in prayer or thrown wide. The performance ended when Sonya fell asleep on her stomach, her arms extended, making her as thin as a needle, like a swimmer diving into a pool.

I got up to make breakfast and discovered Shiloh camped outside our door.

"I was afraid she'd wander off and fall down the stairs," he said.

He knew the world was full of danger. People had to face that: children fell down stairs, aspirated bottle caps, mistook pills for candy. What did I think houses were full of? he wanted to know. Electricity. Water. Fire. Knives.

"You've been up all night thinking about that?"

We heard giggling inside the bedroom.

Alice came out with Sonya slung over her shoulder.

"Breakfast," said Alice.

"Breakfast!" said Sonya.

Shiloh and I did our best to please them.

Afterward, Alice and Sonya went out to play in the meadow. Some type of moth had taken up residency in the field and Alice and the girl ran about trying to catch them in their hands. When Alice finally caught one, she gently placed it on Sonya's head. This got no response from the girl, who could not see where the insect was perched and seemed to lack the capacity to imagine it. Alice placed a second moth on her own head and this caused the girl to shriek delightedly, both at the initial contradiction of an insect on a young woman's head and again when the insect ended its complicity and flew off. With a schoolteacher's fondness for repetition, Alice placed another moth on

Sonya's head; she only brushed it away, frustrated. It makes my heart sick to remember them. Their game stopped when Sonya began to braid Alice's hair, which had grown and lightened over the summer. I stood watching this and my first thought was one of regret, that it wasn't me braiding Alice's hair; that I didn't know how to braid hair struck me with real poignancy. Sonya got up and walked around Alice to admire her handiwork. Lightning quick the girl clapped her hand on the top of Alice's head. It was apparent what had happened even before the girl collapsed with laughter—Sonya had caught a moth. In her exuberance, she had killed it; the humor was the same for her. Alice's brushed the top of her scalp.

Later that day Alice made a top for Sonya out of a single handkerchief. The four of us piled into the car and drove to the lake. I bought ice cream and sodas for everyone from a guy in a truck, spending forever my last three dollars. After he served us we milled around the truck with our sodas. Alice had to lick Sonya's cone whenever it threatened to drip (if the ice cream touched her hand, she was inconsolable). The guy in the truck was maybe ten years older than Alice, wearing a base-ball cap and a cheap-looking watch. On the counter was a book he'd been reading about real estate sales. Shiloh tried to draw Sonya away from the truck, but the truck had a hole for trash painted to look like the toothy mouth of a shark and Sonya was fascinated. "Shark fish," she said. She stooped to pick up pull tabs and bottle caps and green triangles of glass just to push them through the mouth.

When she ran out of trash, Sonya threw away her cone.

The guy offered to replace it.

Alice handed me her soda and picked Sonya up with her free hand.

"Where you from?" the guy asked.

"We're on vacation," answered Shiloh.

The guy reached under his counter and got a candy ring for Sonya. "Here you go, sweetie."

Sonya looked at the candy, perplexed.

"What do you say?" prompted Alice.

"You're welcome," said the girl, taking the ring.

"You say, 'Thank you,'" the ice-cream man corrected.

Alice bounced the girl in her arms.

The ice-cream man raised his hand to show that he also wore a candy ring. "Now we're married," he said.

"What do you think of that?" asked Alice.

Sonya tried to kick her shoe into the shark's mouth.

I bent down and picked it up.

Alice thought we had better get to the beach. We thanked the ice-cream man, who kept waving like an idiot, even while Sonya refused to acknowledge him.

The four of us wound up on an exhausted-looking beach; grass sprouted up through a thin blanket of sand and everywhere there were muddy pits children had excavated. A swing set dangled pairs of chains (I suppose someone collected the seats after Labor Day). Charcoal grills dotted an otherwise empty field, like speakers at a drive-in. In the shallow water yellow perch fanned pale stones. The air didn't move. Rafts of ducks huddled together on the still water. Beyond them a central channel shimmered where the occasional sailboat or yacht passed.

The sun, in its vanity, had forced all the birds from the sky.

Alice and Sonya explored the edge of the lake.

Shiloh and I stretched out on the grass. The sun made me sweat. At some point I fell asleep. I was wearing a uniform that I wanted to get out of, but there were no buttons or zippers. It was a brown uniform and people seemed unimpressed with it. Try as I might I couldn't get it off. It was a very straightforward dream. Then I was hiding in my closet back at my parents' house. I couldn't say whether they were one dream or two. I woke up feeling sick.

Shiloh leaned over me, so his head shaded mine from the sun.

"You up for a swim?" he asked.

I sat up.

Alice and Sonya hadn't disappeared anywhere obvious. It bothered me that Alice would choose to abandon me on consecutive days. Then it bothered me that it bothered me.

"Come on," said Shiloh. He'd waded out to a spot where he could stand still, lean his head back, and just the high points of his face poked above the surface. He looked like a grotesque water lily, his pale arms floating out from his shoulders.

I called to him, but his ears were underwater.

On top of my shirt, I laid my flip-flops and my cutoffs. I just had on Jockey shorts when I went in.

I waded over to Shiloh. The water only reached my Adam's apple.

"It's nice. Isn't it?" He maintained his posture; one arm floated out and brushed against me.

"I'm going to try and swim across."

He pirouetted to take a look across the water. "I think it's too far."

I had no idea how to judge distances. The opposite shore seemed a long way off, but not too far, not unreachable.

"It's fine."

I made a dozen crawl strokes, but that thrashing wore me out. I switched to the breast stroke and Shiloh came up along my side.

"What's the farthest you've ever swum before?" he asked.

"This will be a new record."

"Great," he said, "for me, too."

We kept at it for a while, our chins prowing through the water. The important thing was to stay relaxed. As long as I breathed deeply, there was no way I could sink. I looked at Shiloh to see how he was doing and I saw him check me out. The hard thing was allowing my body to find a natural attitude in the water—my feet wanted to sink into the colder depths, where they felt vulnerable and separate. My body seemed aware of the lake bed retreating. There were two rhythms: stroke and breath. The ducks, noticing our approach, squawked and paddled away.

Shiloh tapped me on the shoulder; I hadn't noticed him getting so close.

"If you get tired swim on your back awhile."

I spit water at him.

We'd reached a point where the lake opened up, showing where we'd come from as a sort of promontory; Alice and Sonya weren't on the shore waving frantically for us to return. If we hadn't reached the halfway point, then we'd at least come to a place where retreat was as miserable as going on.

My arms grew heavy. I swam sidestroke for a while. Shiloh stayed close to me, still breaststroking, his eyes looking a little disengaged. There was nothing to look at out there. The sun glared into your eyes.

"How many people have swum across Lake Champlain?" I asked him.

He didn't answer right away and I saw that we'd drifted apart.

"How many?" he asked.

The next time I checked on our progress it seemed unlikely that a person could swim to either shore. This, I convinced myself, was only an optical illusion—what I thought of as the shore was probably a point far inland.

"Swim on your back awhile," Shiloh instructed me. "I'll keep us pointed in the right direction."

I allowed myself to roll onto my back, conducting myself along with great sweeps of my arms. From time to time Shiloh would come up beside me and get me back in line. Swimming ceased being an activity that my mind took any interest in; my body was fully in charge of the project. My mind was free to return to the problems it had encountered in my dreams. A powerboat roared past; I didn't connect the boat to its sound until its wake washed over us.

"Here," said Shiloh.

I followed his voice. Stroke and breath.

I was relieved when something came between my eyes and the sun and more relieved to see it was a tree. I turned onto my stomach. Shiloh stood up.

A dozen feet short of him, I tried to do the same and went over my head. I had to summon all my energy to fight back to the air.

"Welcome to New York state," he said.

Whether because we were out of the sun or the water had turned colder, maybe just because the swim had exhausted us, we both shivered.

"You're not a very strong swimmer," he said.

"I made it here."

"Halfway."

I pushed off the silty bottom and pointed myself toward the far shore.

I hadn't been in trouble, just sidestroking, checking my progress when I remembered to, correcting my course. My body didn't feel tired, just distant and inattentive. Nothing in the world felt threatening. I could consider lying on the bottom without it causing a corresponding anxiety. The bottom seemed a beautifully remote place carpeted with cold algae, impenetrable to light and sound. I could imagine the white bellies of fish and the way the stones would taste if you sucked on them. So when Shiloh touched me, I didn't care whether he wrestled me to the bottom or towed me along. My back brushed against his chest and I could feel the warmth coming off his body.

"I got you," he whispered in my ear.

My feet trolled beneath us.

"You want to go to shore under your own power?" he asked; it could have been a hypothetical question, because he knew we would never stand on land again.

"I'll swim."

He released me.

It wasn't far, a hundred yards. We swam side by side, like we'd started. The point of the exercise seemed to be patience. No amount of effort made us move any faster. I closed my eyes and held my breath and took a few strokes and the next time I checked, I was in the same place. Once my body forgot when to breathe and I sucked in a bit of water, but by then I'd already reached the shore's gentle apron. I crawled out of the water like some dumb animal. My heart was pounding and my arms twitched like they were still pulling me along. There were rust-colored stains on my hands from the cheap sand that covered the beach.

Shiloh lay on his back and laughed. "The next time I get a case of gloom I've got to remember to try a stunt like that. That was misery."

I said, "A lake would make an awful bed."

"You're not even an average swimmer," said Shiloh, lifting his head enough to look at me. "You're a liability." He dropped his head in the sand.

I apologized.

"That's okay. If I'd known, then we never would have tried it."

"Did you ever swim in the Ohio?"

"About a million times. Never across it, though."

I closed my eyes to keep the sun out. Water running down my scalp formed little pools in my ears. I felt a responsibility to remain perfectly still and preserve them. It might have been the first week in September. I wasn't just a runaway anymore. I was a dropout, too. The difference was that running away required decisive action, while dropping out didn't require anything at all.

"Something's happened to Sonya," said Shiloh.

A soft breeze carried these words, "You idiots!"

I turned on my side.

Alice was jogging toward us, shaking her fists in the air.

Our little houseguest was nowhere.

"Where were you?" asked Alice.

"We swam across the lake," I said.

"Of course," said Alice. "And in the meantime Sonya got stung by a bee and her leg has swollen up like you wouldn't believe. I think we have to take her somewhere."

Shiloh and I stood on our unsteady legs and ran after Alice, back toward the car. She kept turning to berate us for our slowness. Every step on the still burning asphalt was jarring since our bodies were too tired to run right. We came upon Sonya sprawled out in the grass in front of the car. For an instant I thought Alice was lying, that she'd accidentally run over the girl. Sonya's right calf looked as though it had been replaced with the extremity of some squat monster—it was discolored and shiny. Her arms were crossed over her eyes and a trail of red drool ran from the corner of her mouth and down her neck.

"It's horrible," Alice wailed.

Even all splayed out, this was a catastrophe in miniature. Looking down at the girl created the illusion that her body was still far away. I couldn't figure out what had happened to her leg. Seen beside its twin they weren't recognizable as the same family of thing. I looked at Shiloh; he seemed just as puzzled. We stood right above her and Sonya didn't even look at us. Her resilient heart made her chest thump and her stomach twitched like someone stifling a hard cry. Nobody made a sound.

Shiloh reached down and his probing finger pushed through her calf.

"Fooled you!" screamed Sonya.

I sat in the grass.

"It's clay," Sonya shouted. "It's clay."

I tried to remove a sliver of glass that had lodged in the ball of my foot.

The little girl danced around, taunting us for our gullibility.

"What's that horrible red liquid?" Shiloh asked.

"That's just the candy ring," said Alice. "Look at her leg. Isn't that cool?"

My feet were full of glass.

Sonya kicked me with her clay leg.

I groaned.

"Did you kick Thomas?" asked Alice.

Sonya kicked me again. Then she kicked Shiloh.

"Be nice," said Alice.

Sonya kissed Shiloh's face.

"Thank you, sweetie," he said.

Alice knelt down to look at my feet. "You really swam across the lake?"

I nodded my head.

"Did he put you up to it?"

"He just followed along to look out for me. It was my idea."

"Serves you right," she said.

Grateful fools that we were, Shiloh and I felt vindicated that the only people hurt were us. And later we did drive to the pharmacy because Sonya developed such a bad sunburn on the points of her shoulders. As we drove back to the house Sonya fell asleep on my lap, and I would have told Alice and Shiloh about it, only Shiloh had fallen asleep and, in an instant, so had I.

15
Our Lovely Faces

Having the girl in the house gave us the illusion of a purpose. There was this wonderful feeling you got if she asked for a glass of water or a cracker or something. She was very easy to satisfy. After the disaster with the garden, it was nice to see something flourish under our care.

On the third perfect day, Shiloh found me alone in the kitchen.

"We need to rethink this arrangement," he said.

Whatever he was referring to, it was clear he'd been turning the matter over in his head for some time. As far as he was concerned, the rethinking had been done.

Then it dawned on me. "You're talking about Sonya."

"I'm talking about her alleged parents." Shiloh had his arms crossed and his chin held up proudly.

We'd had an unspoken agreement not to discuss our guest's departure.

"They'll be here tomorrow."

"What do you think I'm talking about? I know when they're coming. We have to consider a response."

I could only look at him and wonder. "You want to charge them a fee or something?"

"I don't need anything from them. I want to save her, Thomas."

"From what?"

Alice came in carrying Sonya piggyback.

"Are you girls fighting?" Alice asked us.

Sonya grabbed fistfuls of Alice's hair. "Girls!" she shouted.

"Very funny," Shiloh said in a droll voice.

Alice attempted to lift her passenger over her head. "Let go of my hair, honey."

"Girls!" Sonya repeated, yanking on the makeshift reins.

Tears ran down Alice's cheeks. "Help get her off me."

"Serves *you* right," said Shiloh.

Sonya tried to spur her mount with her heels.

Alice dumped her rider onto the kitchen table.

"You really love her, huh?" said Shiloh.

Alice grabbed the girl's ankle and spun her like a top.

"He thinks we should K-I-D-N-A-P her," I said.

"That's not what I said," said Shiloh.

"I won't entertain these ideas," said Alice.

"That's what I told him."

"What I'm talking about," said Shiloh, "is looking out for someone's welfare."

Sonya took Alice's hand and pulled her upstairs.

On the fourth day we let Sonya sleep in while the three adults moped around the kitchen getting in each other's way. Finally Sonya came down.

In our hearts we did not believe we were lucky people.

"Should we tell her?" Shiloh asked.

Alice shook her head.

Sonya stomped her feet. "Tell her."

"We were sad you slept in," said Shiloh, "because today is a very special day for you."

"Birthday?"

"Better," said Shiloh. "Today is Sonya Day."

The girl clapped her hands ecstatically. She hopped around on one foot. Then, as though she'd suddenly remembered her manners, she curtsied to each of us.

Sonya Day began. While Shiloh worked on breakfast, Alice took our guest out for a bath. I volunteered for the most difficult job; I went through the house making sure that there would be no signs of her left in the place. I dismantled her blanket nest, collected the few items of clothing she'd arrived with (we'd found extra undershirts and underpants stuffed in her blanket with her) and piled them together with some things Alice had bought for her, a toothbrush, a hairbrush, Flintstone vitamins.

My job done, I joined Shiloh in the kitchen. He'd made a triangular hat out of newspaper and set it at Sonya's place on the table. I stopped to admire it.

"We might take her farther upstate," said Shiloh.

"I don't think we can."

"Want me to tell you how? Because I've already figured it out."

He measured love by what you'd do for someone—Sonya's family had hidden her to keep her safe, but he was proposing that we destroy the life we made for ourselves just to protect the girl.

"You just want her to know that she's wanted. Is that it?" I asked.

"I know what it's like to be raised without love, Thomas. They left their kid with strangers."

"And you were the one who defended them. Remember? Alice would have had us return her that same night or take her to the police or something."

"Do you think I'd make a good father?" asked Shiloh.

The question seemed directed at the surface of the table.

The two of us stared out on the field. We didn't see them anywhere. I asked him if he'd heard any cars. No, he said. Of all the things we might have done, we waited.

"You really care about her," I said.

"I don't even know her," said Shiloh. "But she's a kid and someone ought to be thinking about her."

I went upstairs to find one of the girl's tiny socks, where I knew it would be, where I'd left it.

Alice and Sonya came in, damp hair twisted in towel turbans, faces pink, their clothes sticking to them.

I said, "We were afraid we'd lost you."

Alice glared. She rubbed her hands up and down Sonya's arms.

"I hope everyone's clean," said Shiloh. He looked resigned to serving the cold food. Maybe he'd pictured the girl complimenting him, but at her age selfishness is biological.

Sonya began an excited monologue about a fort in the meadow above the house. It wasn't really clear if this was something that she wanted to build or if she was telling us a story about the ancient past. You had to listen carefully because kids always test you to make sure that you are one of those adults who actually listen to them.

I nodded my head while she talked about pillows and walls and ramps. The more she talked about it, the less certain I was that we were really talking about a fort at all. It seemed to me that this was some entirely unfamiliar category of structure. The problem, it seemed, was that no matter what she built, it was bound to disappoint her in some fashion. On the other hand, maybe her imagination would allow her to superimpose her hopes for this place over the place itself.

"Is she talking about a fort?" I whispered.

Alice shook her head.

"That's what I thought," said Shiloh. "Because of the walls and the tower. But it's beginning to sound like something else."

"All you two can think about are forts," said Alice.

Sonya started talking about horses, how they were going to be tied up outside this unnamed structure.

"Maybe a tent?" I asked.

"A tent. Exactly!" Shiloh clapped his hands together. He got up and patted Alice on her back—a gesture that she didn't seem to appreciate.

"Let her finish her story," said Alice.

In Shiloh's defense, Sonya was hardly telling a story.

"I've got a better idea," said Shiloh. He crouched down so that his face was just inches from Sonya's. "Instead of talking about it, honey, Thomas and I will help you to build your tent."

Sonya's head snapped sideways. She gave me such a look. I didn't know what I'd done to betray her. "Alice makes it!" she roared.

Shiloh brought me up to his bedroom to show me a junker bicycle he'd rescued from the dump. I don't know what he hoped to make of it. But he said if we could fix it, it might be a nice gift for Sonya. He'd managed to correct a bend in the frame simply by standing on it, and maybe he hoped the rest of the repairs would come as easily. We attacked the bike with a few wrenches, a can of solvent, and a hammer. The oak floorboards accepted errant hammer blows. Black crumbs fell from the tires. Rubbing solvent into the rust-welded chain, I broke it in two places. Shiloh refused to recognize the hopelessness of our situation. "A bike's about the best thing a kid can have," he said. "It's their first taste of freedom."

There was a knock on the door. Alice came in with a particular windmill focus. She didn't even acknowledge us. She grabbed two pillows before blowing out.

Shiloh said, "What does your girlfriend know about tents?"

"You don't think she could screw it up. Do you?"

"I've made tents. I've made them with carpet scraps and garbage bags and things most people wouldn't even touch."

"If they need to make it more disgusting, I'm sure they'll ask you."

He turned and smiled at me. "I forgot you can be funny sometimes."

I could feel myself blush.

We returned our attention to the bike.

"There's no way for us to fix this," I said.

"I don't have the right tools."

Even then.

"Do you suppose anyone's ever taken her picture before?" Shiloh asked.

My mind wandered to Pawpaw, who used to cut paper profiles of the veterans at the old soldiers' home. Once he'd made a cutout seven feet long of a circus parade, complete with elephants marching trunk to tail and acrobats doing handsprings, lions pacing in wheeled cages, the huge shoes of the clowns, and up front the top-hatted ring master, and, before him, leading the parade, a single boy beating a bass drum. I wanted to tell Shiloh that the boy was me.

After retrieving his camera from the cigar box, we went downstairs. In the kitchen Alice assembled cucumber sandwiches.

"We're going to take her picture," announced Shiloh.

Alice looked up from her task. "You got film for that thing?"

Shiloh and I shared a look.

By draping a sheet over three intersecting clotheslines, Alice had created a child-scale space. Breezes pulled ripples across the walls of the tent. At the entrance a burgundy runner extended like a tongue. Shiloh got down on his knees and crawled in. Inside, the light filtering through the sheets made the rug look as dark as blood. Sonya had taken her turban off and draped it over a bank of pillows where she reclined. Her posture suggested royal casualness. She'd placed eight white flowers in the eight creases between her toes. I didn't crawl inside; there was no room for me. I know what he saw because it was preserved in the picture. Shiloh backed out of the tent and flapped the sheet of milky emulsion in front of me. What emerged first was a composition of dark and light—the bright slash of the girl suspended over a pit that would become the rug, a single slim shadow indicating the vertical on the radiant scrim walls. When the film finished developing, there was something wrong with it. The only color on her face was dots of pink, no bigger than thumbprints, right beneath her eyes. Her body wasn't draped over the pillows as much as pitched over them, with her bony knees, hard belly, and its knot of navel. We looked at her pinched nose, at the shadows in her eyes. The photo made clear that what we'd mistaken for beauty was a fleeting prettiness. It showed that her eyes weren't totally under her control. Her sadness was too close to her skin, and she had a crooked smile. Even at four Sonya seemed aware of these shortcomings. Her gaze was all boudoir, as if she believed that she would be forced to gift those minor fortunes of youth and prettiness to hungry, inexpressive men, for them to squander.

Shiloh and I passed the picture back and forth, not knowing what to do with it.

"Give it back," the girl yelled inside the tent. "It's Sonya's!"

If Alice hadn't come along when she did, I think we would have destroyed the picture, as if a person might be freed from fate if they only had other people around them who cared enough to try and change it.

I'd like to see that picture once again. Sonya isn't the only one pre-served in the frame. That vertical shadow on the wall was the proof that I had been standing behind the sheet. What became of the pic-ture? I can't say. I don't know what happened to Sonya, either. True to our fears, she left later in the day. She and Alice were napping in the tent when a car came down the hill. Gregor's brother parked in the driveway and blew his horn.

We left the tent standing, to bleach and billow and snap. When it rained Shiloh brought in the rug and the pillows. A storm carried the sheet down toward the ravine where it trailed off the top of a black maple like a veil or the escape route of an eloping tree-house bride.

In our bed I tried every trick to separate Alice's body from her mind. Her skin drove me crazy. Everything was surface about her, everything was outside. She wouldn't uncross her legs or open her lips or unclench her fists. I wanted to tear her to pieces. I dragged my teeth beneath her jaw. She breathed in snorting huffs. I bit her nipples. The corners of her eyes brimmed with water. I sucked on her hard shoulders.

We were two irreconcilable wills. I was destruction and she was preservation. I kept flinging myself at her. I tried to wedge pillows beneath her. The smells rising from her body seemed to demand all this effort. A slick perspiration grew from the exertion of my attacks and her parries. I wrenched her fingers open. I hooked my thumbs inside her lips and pried her mouth open. She was like some horrible fish. When finally I unknotted her legs, I pushed my mouth against her. She tried to crack my skull with her thighs. We made incursions into the narrow territory where violence borders love. She bucked against me when she came.

I said, "There's no fun like you."

"Say it again."

I said, "There's no fun like Alice Lowe."

"Tell me you feel the same after I say the thing I'm about to say. You have to call your parents."

I'd been intending to write them a letter, from the moment I left.

What had prevented that letter was a question that I didn't know how to answer. How to explain that Alice and Shiloh and a car had been enough to lure me away from the home my parents had kept for me? The letter that excluded this issue would hardly be a letter at all. I tried to explain this to Alice, the problem of starting the letter and then the problem of finishing the letter, the problem of the letter's essential shortcomings.

"That's why you're going to call them," said Alice. "You make them tell you what they need to know."

And wasn't it true that Alice and Shiloh were only half as brave as me? They hadn't left anything behind, while I had left people who loved me, and all because of the way it felt to hold someone's hand and the magic of watching her sleep, and that, for me, turning away from those things would have been a betrayal of myself. What if I had died swimming across that lake? Wouldn't that have been far superior to dying some other way, like not swimming across that lake? Then again, what if my parents had used the same justification for similar actions? What if Mary had run off in order to see some stupid sculptures she remembered from Berlin, or if Fran had quit that job at the plant he couldn't have enjoyed too much? Or if Pawpaw had gotten into one of his blue spells and just laid down and died?

Alice walked across the room, her legs slicing the yellow light. She lifted her hair above her head and let it sail down.

"What?" she said.

We put on our filthy clothes. Eight miles down the mountainside.

At the corner of the grocery-store parking lot, beneath an oversize sign that had been colonized by swallows, we found a phone booth. Alice showed me a fistful of change. She put the tips of her fingers in my front pocket, tilting her hand so the coins cascaded in. The birds swarmed above us. I stepped inside the booth and pulled the door shut. There was a recess in the ceiling where a light fixture had either been scavenged or never installed. I fed the phone my money. There was a moment, after I'd dialed, while the machine ratcheted away, when my bravado evaporated. And the only question they could ask I still didn't have an answer for.

Mary answered with only mundane expectation. "Hello?"

"It's me," I said. "This is Thomas."

"Thomas?"

The sound of water muttered behind her voice.

"Are you standing by the sink?"

"Yes. The water's on. One second. No one's here. Your father's off at work and your pawpaw, he could be anywhere."

The voice that came through the line was filtered and changed. It was her voice and something else. I didn't know if this new voice was the voice that Fran heard in their bedroom or if it was reserved for me.

"Do you have a cold?" I asked.

"I had a cold a couple of weeks ago, but I recovered. Do I sound ill?"

"I haven't heard your voice in a while, I guess."

"Where are you, Thomas?"

"I'm in a parking lot."

"Great. A parking lot." It sounded like she was squeezing all her words out of a single breath that she'd taken before answering the phone. "I wish your father was here. It's too bad, I know he would like to speak with you. He thought the two of you had an understanding. All the time you spent together last summer."

Maybe she meant that it was a shame for me that Fran wasn't home. Fran would be easy. Fran would be a cinch. Instead I had Mary and her hard questions and her intelligence and her implacable patience.

"I'm sorry for not calling sooner."

"I can't understand it, Thomas. I mean, I can understand it and I can't. Listen to me prattling on. You must have something to say."

Alice was checking her face in the rearview mirror. I watched her put her teeth on edge for a type of exaggerated smile.

"I didn't mean to hurt anyone."

"Your father and I know we didn't raise a spiteful person. You're a young man and you want to make some decisions on your own."

"That's it. I wasn't even thinking, really."

"Your father talked with one of the detectives in town. He suggested we try Chicago. They didn't have any luck, obviously, though your father was nearly mugged. Your grandfather managed to interrupt things with the car. At least that's the story they told me. Those people who seemed like they were interested in helping find you were interested in something else instead. That was their experience. 'Throwing good money after bad' was how your father characterized it."

"I never was in Chicago."

"They believed they were very close to finding you. Sometimes they were told that they'd missed you by just a matter of minutes."

"It wasn't me."

"Are you with that Shiloh character, or is it just a coincidence that he ran off at the same time?"

"He's not the reason I left."

"Are you with him?"

"He's here."

"Thomas!" Her voice drilled into my ear. "Tell me you're not in California. You're not way out there, are you?"

"I'm in Vermont."

"You're kidding. There's nothing in Vermont. We assumed you'd head to a city."

"I was in New York for about a day."

"You're not making any sense . . ."

The line cut out and I had to feed more coins to restore the connection.

"Are you still there?" asked Mary.

I explained that I was at a pay phone.

"Your voice sounds very flat, Thomas. Are you on something?"

"No I'm not *on* anything. I'm the same person you know. I'm just tired, if anything."

"Well, do you have a job?"

"We're sort of outside the economy."

"Oh," said Mary.

"I mean we're not really buying anything."

"You keep saying 'we.' That's you and Shiloh?"

"There's a girl here, too."

"This was the other theory."

"We're going together."

"Did she run away, too?"

"She couldn't really do that."

"I don't understand."

"She's twenty-five."

"Let me tell you, buster, you've painted quite a picture. I see the three of you sitting around together—my son, his unreliable friend, and this strange woman. Three months have gone by and in all that time you call once to tell me you're okay. You didn't call on Father's Day. You didn't call to wish your father and me a happy anniversary. Yesterday was your pawpaw's eighty-first birthday and you haven't mentioned that yet. I'm not quite sure what I'm supposed to say. You're standing beside a pay phone in Vermont; at some point you're going to run out of money and we're going to be disconnected."

Everything Mary said was true, of course. I opened the door of the booth.

I said, "I'm happy here."

"And that's what your father and I want, too, but it's not all we want. You know your pawpaw has heard some disturbing rumors about that friend of yours."

"I don't think most people know much about him."

"He wasn't abandoned like some Moses, floating down the river or whatever he says. His mother put him up for adoption. She used to waitress at the Koffee Klub. Now, your mother doesn't like to cast aspersions on someone's character, but apparently she had a reputation for being friendly with her regular customers. And that hokum about his father, well, I think it's just a sad story concocted by a nobody wanting to be a somebody. I know you can understand that."

"He's still a friend of mine."

"Well, the police want to speak with your friend. Remember the car that got smashed into the floodwall? It was hot-wired! Can you believe that?"

"And they think Shiloh did that?"

"The detective told your father that if he found out where Shiloh was, to let them know because they already had a judge's order to pick him up."

I told her that Shiloh had been blamed for lots of things he had nothing to do with.

"I just pray you look out for yourself."

She started saying something else, but got cut off. I put in the rest of my change.

I told her the situation with the phone. That the next time we got separated would be it.

"Your father is going to be really sorry he didn't get a chance to speak with you."

"Tell Pawpaw happy birthday for me. I'm sorry I forgot."

All around me there were acres of immaculate asphalt, but between my feet little green plants were springing among the dead leaves and litter. Pushing the leaves around with my toes, I uncovered a dime. I left it there.

"You can call us collect, whenever you want."

"It's not too easy for me to get to a phone. We're sort of in the middle of nowhere up here."

"Do you want to tell me anything more than the name of the state? You know your father is going to have a look at a map. That's just the way he is."

"We're not really too near anything you'd find on a map. We're sort of on a mountain, but I'm not sure if there's a name for it."

"Of course they have a name for it, if it's really a mountain."

I told her I'd try to find out.

"Tell me what the weather's like."

"It's warm. It's nice. It's not so humid."

Alice had gotten out of the car. She was walking around with her hands on her hipbones.

"What are you doing about school?"

"I've learned more in the last four months than I ever learned in school."

I could hear Mary turn the water back on.

"Oh my Lord, you're seeing that exhausted-looking teacher. What was her name?"

Alice looked at me through the windshield. She'd put on Shiloh's mirrored shades.

"I can't believe you. Your pawpaw circled her name on your report card. Two As. You only earned two As in your whole life. She ought to be arrested."

I said it in a soft voice. I'd never betrayed Mary like this before. And I knew by saying it I would have to live with it for the rest of my life. I said, "We're in love."

"Ha," said Mary. She hung up.

Eight miles back.

I wasn't talking.

Alice kept winging me with sidelong glances. Finally she said, "There's no food in the house."

I said, "You're always hungry."

That shut her up.

When we pulled into the drive, Shiloh kneeled in the front yard, concentrating on some small mystery, no doubt. Beside him, a metal bowl caught the sunlight. Alice marched inside.

"Get over here, Mahey."

I had one foot on the porch.

Shiloh turned toward me. Dark smears angled across his cheeks. There were more slashes on his arms. His hands were caked with gore.

He tossed a bloody rag toward me. When it landed it unrolled itself into a map of an animal. Mucus and strings of blood laced over the white skin.

"I'm teaching myself how to set snares." He lifted a pink haunch out of the bowl.

"What was it?"

"Turn the skin over."

Gray-and-white heather: a rabbit. I petted the fur. "What are you going to do with it?"

"I could make a drum head, earmuffs, a rabbit hat. I could

make slippers or, if I catch enough, I might make a blanket or a coat."

"Do the rabbits feel anything?" The animal's experience was suddenly important to me.

"Depends—either the snare breaks their necks or they asphyxiate."

"What happened to this one?"

"It died."

The animal's legs and two strips of loin bathed in pink water. Shiloh cradled the other parts of the animal in his hands. He'd left the skin on the head. It looked like a cross between a mammal and a fish. With its eyes closed, mouth slightly open, it might just have been asleep. Shiloh instructed me to bring the meat into the kitchen while he disposed of the body.

I got a fire going in the stove. I drained the water from the bowl and rinsed the meat. I coated the pieces with fried onions from a canister. When the stove got good and hot, I put a large skillet on with some oil in it. I dropped the loins in. The meat spit and sizzled.

When the onions started to blacken, I turned the meat.

Alice came downstairs. "Is someone actually cooking?" She pushed past me to stand beside the stove.

I removed the loins to a plate and fit the shoulders and haunches into the frying pan. The skillet was really hot now and the rendered fat gave off a rich, oily smell.

"A miracle," Alice exclaimed. "Where did our friend get this? This?"

I told her Shiloh had snared a rabbit.

Once I'd seared both sides, I opened the oven and slid the whole thing in to cook through.

Alice picked at the loins and licked her fingers. "Do we have to wait for him before we can eat?"

"Probably a good idea."

She lowered herself to the table and stared at the food.

Shiloh had stopped by the swimming hole to clean himself up. He came in looking scrubbed and pleased with himself. He had a shirt on and it was wet where it touched him, at his shoulders and belly.

"You devious mountain man," said Alice.

I took the food out of the oven and placed it on the table.

We moaned and sighed and groaned. There was very little, actually, hardly enough for one, so the more we ate, the more demonstrative we became. We narrated every bite. It was theater and Shiloh enjoyed it so much that he gave his portion to us just so that the praise could continue. When everything that could be consumed had been consumed, after the knuckles had been gnawed and the bones broken and the marrow sucked, Shiloh placed the skillet in the sink. Alice and I fell asleep with our heads in the nests our arms made on the table.

A few days later Alice introduced me to charades. We did *All Quiet on the Western Front*, *The Wizard of Oz*, Gordon Lightfoot, and Kareem Abdul-Jabbar. We managed to enlist Shiloh, only to frustrate him when neither Alice nor I knew who Emma Goldman was. A hero of his, evidently. It was probably a little after eight when Alice and I decided to get ready for bed. She and I stood shoulder to shoulder as we brushed our teeth in the bathroom sink.

"Close your eyes," she said.

I heard her spit and then sip a handful of water.

"Okay," she said.

She went to our room while I finished up.

She was standing in the gabled alcove when I came in. Outside, in the moonlight, the field looked like it was made of ash. Deep inside the haystack the straw moldered and the heat from this caused wispy curls of vapor to rise. She pointed her finger. The fox paused as it crossed through the high grass. Maybe Shiloh was out on the porch swing. A moment later it darted off and was gone.

"They're good luck," said Alice.

The temperature had started to drop at night. I decided to pull another blanket out of the closet—it was one of the ones we'd used to make Sonya's bed. Absently I put it to my nose. I didn't know what the right thing to do was, but I carried it to Alice. "Smell."

"Our little girl. Our little ragamuffin." Without getting up she shook it out and let it settle over us.

And the odor also settled over us; we breathed it, held it inside. After the smell dissipated we found that by kicking our feet we could conjure up the little girl, but each time it was more fleeting.

We were too worked up to sleep.

"What do you think of my face?" asked Alice.

I traced the whole landscape with my fingertips.

"It's like my face," I said.

"Shut up," she said.

I said, "I mean your face—it's as familiar as my face."

"Familiar," she said. "Ugh."

"Your nose is smaller than mine."

"Obviously."

I kissed her. "Your lips are softer."

"My lips are thin," she said.

"I like thin."

"You'd better."

"What kind of face do I have?" I asked.

"Unblemished."

If anyone wonders what I looked like that fall when I was seventeen, I say I had an unblemished face. And something else: I have not maintained it.

16
What's Wrong with My Face

Later I would spend a winter on the Gulf Coast of Florida, working as a landscaper. The couple who owned the company practically adopted me; they found me an apartment overlooking a canal where, night and day, kids yanked bullheads from the quiet water. One night I watched an alligator and a golden retriever locked in a struggle— the alligator had the dog by the neck, but for the longest time they stayed like this, as if the dog wasn't being eaten, but tamed. Then the dog's owner came down with a pistol and dispatched both animals, still in their strange embrace. I worked with three guys who were amateur bodybuilders and two women who were in love. The six of us drove around in a panel truck. We'd pull into your driveway and the bodybuilders, on principle, refused to use ramps to unload the machinery. They wore spandex shorts before the rest of us knew what the stuff was. I knew the women were in love because they had owned a flower shop in Missouri and left that to work outside together. They kept a houseboat on another canal system. One time someone broke into my room and stole three thousand dollars that I'd secreted in a Tupperware container in my freezer. Still later the police broke in to charge me (charges that, contingent on my leaving the state, were dropped) with the distribution of child pornography, which, they told me, was where my employers buttered their bread.

I drifted north to Baltimore. My arrival corresponded with the Iranian hostage crisis. Which I mention because my next job was with a Pakistani family who owned two used-car lots. For no reason but ignorance, windshields were smashed, people urinated into gas tanks—the police arrested a forty-two-year-old housewife who urinated into the filler, one of those behind the license plate setups, on a Cadillac; she became a minor and not so reluctant celebrity. I was hired to pose as part owner and, by my presence, Americanize the place.

A cocktail waitress who worked at a bar across the street helped me soften up prospective buyers. I'd order rum and Cokes and she'd serve me Tabs. After work I'd drive her back to her place, a damp-smelling row house. It looked awful from the outside, but it was furnished with all this elegant salon furniture she'd inherited from grandparents, prairie royalty from Terre Haute. At work she wore her hair in bilious piles, and short skirts with purple tights, but the hair was a wig; she had a hereditary condition that caused her hair to grow in clumps—she kept it razored tight to her head so that her skull felt like a strange globe with smooth lakes and oceans and fuzzy, forested continents. When we got to her place, she invariably changed into print dresses with lace collars. Everything was on the up-and-up. I don't think she ever figured out why I liked her, nor did I tell her enough about myself that she might have formed an opinion about me. Her parents were Episcopalian; we'd drink coffee and talk about that. If we had an understanding, it was that we were both lonely.

A young couple with three kids came in to buy a station wagon and I'd nearly sold them an Oldsmobile convertible when my waitress barged in, crying. She waved her hand in front of me as if it had been crippled in an accident.

"I'm engaged," she said. "I'm engaged."

She came around my desk and threw herself across me. She'd decided to return to Indiana and marry an old beau, a pharmacist. She'd planned to take the bus back home, but I used all my skills and part of my savings to sell her a Renault coupe at a loss.

I loaned her money for a moving truck so all that wonderful furniture could get back where it belonged (she'd considered selling it); I was crazy for that furniture, but it's probably much worse now from children and such.

On the day she was to leave, I went to see her off.

"You're so sweet," she said, going crazy, running in and out of the place.

I asked a favor.

Anything, she promised.

Could her pharmacist prescribe a cure for a broken heart?

Overcome with emotions neither of us could have named, she slapped me across the face. Before the shock wore off, she hugged me, rubbed her hands up and down my spine, and, the only time, kissed me. (And yes, where was Alice? And how had I lost her?) There were tears on her cheeks when she drove away. I never saw the money I loaned her.

Reagan took office. The hostages came home and my figurehead proprietorship ended. The family sold both lots to a third party and moved to California.

After relying on it for five years, I totaled a Chevy Cavalier in Tulsa. A trauma surgeon—a reputable specialist, but, I believe, no genius—closed the forehead I'd opened on the plastic steering wheel. I spent two months living with a physician's assistant, loving her on a twin bed half-filled with stuffed animals and beneath a framed illustration of a kitten in a nurse's uniform (a gift from her father—a hard case himself—whose ugliness surely primed her for me). She was six years my junior; we'd go out with her friends—all optimists—and I couldn't take it. Finally I suspect she started seeing a good-looking security guard, a well-mannered kid who did two seasons in the CFL as a wide receiver. She asked me to move out. I rubbed a weal into my forehead with a piece of 600 grit sandpaper (at that time I worked as the manager of a hardware store, even though I knew less than most of my employees and all of my customers—Tulsa was full of oil jobs at the time, but I never roughnecked) in the hopes she might take me back. I was also aware that eventually I'd bore through the hard shell and get to the nut of my problem. Her name was Shaylanna.

When the oil boom died, the hardware store closed its doors. I called her to say I was leaving town and would she meet me for coffee, but she wasn't home or wasn't answering.

17

Trapline

Shiloh Tanager had no people. It was a common phrase. In most instances it was a qualitative remark masquerading as a quantitative one. In Shiloh's case it was a statement of fact.

"I am the prodigal son," said Shiloh. "Left on the courthouse steps. My birth announcement ran on the front page. 'Boy Abandoned' was the headline. Sixteen months old. Ripe for adoption."

The two of us were walking through the woods above the house. Shiloh had offered to give me a tour of his trapline.

"The room with yellow walls. That's my first memory. I have no idea where that room was. I've known plenty of rooms. For the first three years, I lived with the Jacobs. I don't remember too much. I was admitted to the hospital for shingles and, upon my discharge, I wound up with a different family. Uncle Gil and Aunt Gert had a nice in-ground pool with a little plastic mountain at one end that caused a hose's worth of water to splash into the pool. No other siblings. A quiet place. They never seemed to know what I was doing in their house. I think they were using me as a dry run on the idea of having children. Twice I was admitted to the emergency room for the ingestion of household cleaning products. Gil decided to change careers, and they packed up and moved to Alaska. I got two letters from them when I first moved in with the Murrays. The Murrays were very active in the Pentecostal church. They were petitioning for sainthood—trying to raise fourteen of us in a great big shell of a house. We all went to church as a group on Saturdays and Sundays. After services the congregation made meals for us and generally treated us like stray dogs, with kindness and nourishment and a healthy dose of suspicion. After the meal they all went back to their ordinary lives and we went back to our place, what the Murrays called Willow Grove and the older kids called Pussy Patch. They had actually adopted a couple of kids—a crippled Japanese girl and a blind kid who swore continually. The older kids would suspend you by your ankles from the top bunk and ask if you wanted to be adopted. The Murrays had it all down to a science with their picnic tables in the dining room and chore schedules and wood-paneled bunk rooms crowded with foot lockers. You were assigned to an older sibling whose duty it was to look out for you and show you the ropes. Claude Wopanski was my big brother; a real gentle kid with a dent in his skull that he combed his black hair over. Whenever anyone got on his case, he'd fidget with his hair to make sure the hole was concealed. If we were supposed to clean the bathroom, he'd pass the whole time checking his face in the mirror. He carried his head at an angle like one of those classroom globes.

"As much as the Murrays believed the spirit was in us, they didn't account for hormones, bad judgment, experimentation, and youth. The younger boys were coerced into circle jerks, violating vacuum cleaners. At night you could hear the squeaking of the mattress springs, like peeper frogs singing all around. And we were expected to interact normally with the regular community. The high school principal used to come over at the beginning of the year and give everyone a big pep talk about how, in his eyes, we were just like everyone else. But he wasn't fooling anyone. He got back in his car, returned to his office, and told his secretary what a bunch of savages we were.

"Claude left for a junior college in Illinois, where he was killed crossing the street and just because he was so vain about his stupid melon head. The driver who hit him said Claude walked right into traffic. I was inconsolable, and then the Murrays took in a sullen, reed-thin kid with wavy black hair and too close eyes, and they promoted me to older boy. The new kid's name was Field. I tormented him out of basic psychology.

"I ran away at thirteen, fourteen. Each time, they caught me and sent me back. I made up names. I was Steve the Swede. I was Button Yurlip. Tanto Tanto. Charlie Tuna. I hitched. I road trains. I tramped and squatted. I spent six weeks in a mansion outside Scottsdale, Arizona—me and this other kid, we watched TV, drank Chivas Regal, and at night we took this brand-new Pontiac out of the garage and drove through the desert outside town. And then we got it in our heads to pawn all these trophies, but the pawnshop owner, of all people, had a conscience. I spent three months in a work camp and then I saw a chance to light out and that's what I did. Yard bulls caught me in Joliet, beat me up, and locked me in a train bound for Tijuana and I probably would have been dead long before I got there, but in Missouri we got diverted for a military train and a real, genuine guardian angel saved my life."

"Who was the guardian angel?"

"Just some person who saved my life and didn't ask for anything afterward."

When we came across a snare, it was usually triggered and empty. Shiloh'd get down on his knees and carefully reset them. He carried a bunch of our withered carrots to use as bait.

"Why did you ever return to our town?"

"They say birds figure the first thing they see is their mother, doesn't matter if it's a cat or a bicycle. That's how it is for me. It's hard-wired in my brain. I smell that water and I just want to curl up and go to sleep. Tell me it's different for you."

I didn't want to talk about what I'd walked away from. And wasn't it true that if you knew a place well enough, you could take it with you anywhere?

"I was just a kid. I expected the fuzz to come by any day and round me up. Children's services or what have you. People assume that you can hide from people by living on the periphery, but my experience has been just the opposite. If you ever want to disappear somewhere, get a job, show up and punch your card every day. I've been ignored, but I've never been invisible. I'm not knocking it. I had a place of my own. I knew where to get my food. I was there fifteen years. I might never have left, but in the middle of the night, some abject motherfuckers tried to burn me out."

"Fran said you beat up five guys."

Shiloh stopped in his tracks. We were on some twisting game trail. It was the middle of the day, but the sun stuck close to the horizon. "Does that sound like something I could do?"

"He said you used an ax handle."

"Then tell me why I left. If I had just beat up five guys, why did I light out?"

"Maybe you thought they'd retaliate."

"I wasn't alone when those guys came by, Thomas. It wasn't me who hurt them."

"Then why did you leave?"

"Because the person I was with told me I had to."

"It still doesn't explain why you left."

Shiloh reached his hands up and pulled his hair back from his face. With his low forehead and his cue-ball chin he wasn't conventionally attractive, but he seemed comfortable in his skin. That was worth something. "He was a cop."

"Oh," I said.

"You understand?"

"But is he the one you were in love with?"

"He was just there."

"I want to know about the one you were in love with."

"I don't know how to tell a love story. I've been locked up for vagrancy, sodomy, drunkenness, having no clothes, and having the wrong clothes. My whole life I caught one break. I won't march it out like some trained bear, just to entertain you."

I felt embarrassed for us both.

I said, "Mary thinks you're the one who crashed the police car against the floodwall. She said the police are looking for you."

"I'll let you in on a secret—that car crashed into the wall of its own accord."

I thought he was trying to make me laugh, but he kept a hard set to his face.

We'd come to one of the snares. A little figure-4 he'd carved out of wood scraps was supposed to act as the trigger mechanism. He poked the trigger with a stick, but nothing happened.

"My ideology is less forgiving than yours," said Shiloh.

"What's ideology?"

"Ideology is how you live your life."

"Why is yours less forgiving?"

"Because if I had knocked a hole in the wall, it wouldn't have mattered to me if the whole town drowned."

"You don't mean that."

"Who are you to tell me what I mean?"

The trigger's precarious geometry undid itself. The stick jumped at the end of the wire.

*Lonely Landscape Stretching Beyond
the Isolated Traveler*

TWO MEN

*I*n Zaire they had spoken with a boy who claimed he'd been swallowed whole by a hippopotamus and returned to the world unmarked. They interviewed an expatriate Welshman in the later stages of cirrhosis who, so his neighbors claimed, had the ability—though rarely the inclination—to cure nodding disease with his touch. And they determined that a nun who had impressed her superiors by undertaking to write down all the names of the people in heaven was actually in the process of reproducing a copy of the London telephone directory. Finally, there had been an afternoon wasted when the men had traveled many hours into the bush to listen to a very depressed man tell them that his donkey possessed the spirit of his late wife.

The younger man had noticed that the reporting of miracles followed some larger geopolitical fabric. There had been a rash of miracles in India, for instance, just as the British got out. If a person could imagine a map, then miracles tended to occur along the boundary between the Church and what was not the Church. And, no doubt, this helped to promulgate the incursion of faith. Which was not to say that there could be no faith without the Church, the younger man didn't mean to imply that. But without the promise of salvation, faith was like a string without a kite.

The older man had a bath towel wrapped over his shoulders while he drank a glass of sherry. The hotel was so new that the air-conditioning still worked. It felt about fifty degrees inside the room. Down on the street, in what passed for traffic, a child led ivory-furred cattle past the hotel's entrance.

"Have you tried the television?" asked the younger man.

"It would not work for me," said the older man.

"I thought the same thing, so I spoke with the manager this morning. He told me a funny story. It seems the nearest television broadcast is more than a thousand miles away. The builders were quite aware of this, yet when it came time to appoint the rooms, each and every one was equipped with a television."

"I suppose people find them comforting," said the older man.

"Yes. I think that was the reasoning. One of the hotel's first guests happened to be the minister of the interior. Because the hotel often hosts state visitors and investors, he was embarrassed by these blank television screens. So now they are in the process of converting one of the rooms into a television studio. When construction is complete a local official will come in each morning to read the newspaper on camera. The rest of the day they intend to broadcast movies."

"That's very inventive," said the older man.

"I thought you might appreciate it."

The phone rang and the older man walked over and answered it. After a moment he returned the receiver to the cradle. He said, "Shame can be a great motivating force." After a pause he added, "Our car is here."

The younger man walked to the window and looked down at the street. A black limousine waited at the curb.

The route the driver took paralleled a broad river. Shanty houses lined the banks. The road was newly paved. On a couple of occasions, their driver seemed to veer toward oncoming bicyclists until the riders made for the curb. Soon there were small houses, then small houses with yards. Finally, stone or brick walls, just the tops of trees visible on the other side.

The younger man and the older man exchanged a look.

The driver put on a cap. He turned his head around quickly. "Very close. Very close."

Up ahead a number of vehicles had been parked along the side of the street, delivery vans, mopeds. A group of men played cards on a handkerchief that was spread on the hood of a Mercedes sedan. There was a break in the wall where a wrought-iron gate had been left open. The driver took them up the cobbled drive. As the path wove through a topiary garden, now and then the two men caught glimpses of a large white edifice. It was a tremendous house, poised on a bluff above the river. Their driver stopped the car beside a splashing fountain. He sprinted around the car and opened the door for the two men. "Sorry," he said. "Sorry." In the next moment he was back in the car and driving off.

A valet came out of the foyer of the house. He wore an ivory suit, oxblood English boots, and an exaggerated smile. "Pleasure to meet you. Pleasure to meet you. Welcome. I wish I could give you a tour, but the cardinal and his guests are repasting." He exhibited a pained look. "May I show you to the library?"

"That will be fine," said the older man.

The three of them entered the house. The hallways were as wide as an airport concourse. In some unseen corner of the house, a string quartet played.

"How many guests are there?" asked the younger man.

The valet explained that they were forty-three. By occupation, more than three-quarters of the guests were local clergy, but there were also a few ambassadors, some members of the business community, some representatives of the government, and two poets.

"Two poets?" asked the older man.

"A local poet and with him a Scottish woman preoccupied with translating his work."

They entered a large chamber. From the center of its high plaster ceiling, a silver-and-crystal chandelier hung like a glass parachute. The walls were covered with the spines of books. Polished wooden ladders ran on tracks. Rows of chairs had been set before a study table.

"Your audience should file in shortly. Once the cardinal has taken his seat, you may begin." After making a crisp bow, the valet left the room.

The older man set a leather valise on the table.

"I think it suits you," said the younger man.

The older man looked up at his colleague. "There was nothing wrong with the briefcase it replaces. My father gave me that case when I received my first appointment."

"Quite a generous gift, I'd expect."

"Replacing the old with the new serves no purpose but to please time."

The younger man had been turning toward the wall to see if he might make a cursory inspection of the books, but his colleague's comment had the effect of interrupting his plans. "How do you mean that?" he asked.

At that moment a pair of oak doors at the side of the room swung open. The two men were unable to continue their conversation. Their audience had arrived.

The older man took a seat facing the assembly and the younger man followed suit.

While the Church had successfully made inroads into Africa, a quick glance at the audience confirmed that Africa had yet to make inroads into the Church.

A gaunt man in an immaculate white cassock made his way into the room with the assistance of the valet. When the gaunt man had taken a seat, the valet gave the men a quick nod before taking his seat.

The older man took a sip from a glass of water before beginning.

"It is my pleasure, this evening, to have been invited to discourse on the subject of the forensic investigation of matters of faith. This is a subject with which I have been closely and passionately involved for well on forty years. I will dispense with the formalities that so many rely on to confer authority upon their opinions. In my case that is quite unnecessary as I will not be judged by time or man, but by God."

On that note, a cross between an invocation and an appeal, the older man paused to allow his audience to get comfortable.

"Our gracious host has asked me to extemporize on the relative criteria for the resolution of an investigation. It is as follows: there must be no explanation short of the direct and intentional intervention of the Lord our Creator."

The older man looked at his associate.

"Do you wish to add anything?" he asked the younger man.

"I don't suppose I could," said the younger man.

The audience shifted, collectively, in their seats. The cardinal's valet stood up, brushing his shirtfront with his palms. "Could you, perhaps, entertain us with an instance in which the presence of the divine was without doubt?"

"The most perfect example," said the older man, "would be the original miracle, that is, creation itself. One can't imagine a more profound or far-reaching miracle. Everything else is just ripples on a pond."

Many in the audience turned to their neighbors so that they could be seen nodding.

"I don't suppose there is anyone here who would count themselves unmoved by Genesis," said the valet. "However, we had hoped you might be able to share news of more recent events."

The audience tittered.

"There was a boy," began the younger man, "who developed a tumor at the base of his cerebellum. His reporting symptoms included blurred vision, acute headaches, and a loss of appetite. There's no surprise there at all. Due to the location of the growth, his doctors deemed his condition inoperable. His health deteriorated in a manner consistent with models. He lost the sight in one eye and, a week later, lost the sight in the other. In order to counteract the headaches, he was prescribed a number of painkillers. The boy's decline was rapid and complete. And then one day the boy started speaking. This was noteworthy because verbal communication had been limited after the onset of the headaches. But what was more remarkable was the language that he spoke. A boy of eleven . . . did I mention this happened in Spain? This happened near La Coruña. This eleven-year-old started speaking in perfect Latin. The subject of his communications was the throne of God."

The younger man had not expected that he would speak to the crowd and, in the same spirit, he had not foreseen the moment he would finish speaking. He stared at their upturned faces.

"So what happened?" Posing this question was the man they supposed to be the poet—beside him a long-faced woman scribbled notes into a binder.

"The boy died," said the younger man.

The additional information seemed to depress the crowd.

"One has to wonder," said the poet, "at least from the boy's perspective, might it not have been a mixed blessing? Surely he would have preferred to have been healed?"

"And what is healing?" asked the older man.

"I suppose it would be the removal of symptoms," answered the poet, gamely.

"I would submit to you that those 'symptoms' are not indicators of disease, but, rather, signs of mortal life. In all my scholarship I've never come across an instance of a person who had any success clinging to mortal life."

"There was a priest in China who had built a small church in the mountains." Again the younger man surprised himself by speaking. "The provincial authorities decided to make an example of him. After shackling the priest inside, they doused the building with kerosene. While the building burned the front door yawned open. Witnesses described the priest, sheathed in pale blue light, at the center of the conflagration. Yet when the fire ceased, no trace of the priest's body could be found."

"What, if I may ask"—the poet turned to his host and made an ambivalent gesture with his shoulders—"is the Church's interest in gathering these phenomena? Is it curiosity? Or are you trying to do what the Greeks did? Are you trying to find your God in the stars?"

The younger man was embarrassed that he'd allowed himself to get drawn into this debate. Handing out wonders like so many glass beads had never been his intention.

"This is an interesting question," began the older man. "If I understand, you seem to suggest that by identifying the light in the darkness we make an error of extrapolation. To expand upon your analogy, we are using crude instruments—witnesses, hearsay, and legend—in order to prove the existence of God. However, God's existence is in no need of proof. No, we are studying the palimpsest. We are finding God's handwriting. At its core, faith may be reduced to wonder. I would suppose that you know this, but it is only because you and I call this wonder by a different name that you are chafing. Consider an insect trapped in amber. What a humble wonder that is, but one must not forget to consider the tree that produced the sap and the roots that drew the water up and the sun that fed the leaves and that the insect came along and, this too, you must consider your eyes, considering the glassy lump. Please don't tell me that I am just seeing points of scattered light."

The cardinal was helped to his feet. "I think now is a good time for us to take a break from this serious stuff, that we might return to talking of cricket and other concerns that occupy the mortal mind."

At once servants wheeled in carts laden with cakes and cookies. A coffee service was set up at the back of the room.

The older man leaned across to his colleague and put a hand upon his shoulder. "You handled yourself very well," he said.

Before the younger man had a chance to reply, they were surrounded by members of the audience, the poet included, who seemed, all in all, to be good-natured men. And the younger man watched the guests crowd around the older man, who had now perched himself on the edge of the table, clutching his valise to his chest like a refugee.

I

Admitted

Alice and I were fast asleep when the house jumped. We sat bolt upright in our bed.

"Forget it," she said, falling back. "It was only a bad dream."

Did she mean we'd had the same dream?

She tried to soothe me with a searching hand, but despite her insistence that there was nothing to understand, I didn't feel reassured.

"Bad dream," Alice repeated.

The creaking floorboards announced that Shiloh was coming up from the basement. I went downstairs hoping he would help me understand what I'd heard.

He wasn't waiting for me in the hall or sitting in the living room. I went into the kitchen. The chairs held our places at the table. I poked my head into the pantry—a bunch of things no one cared to eat. There was no sign of him on the porch. Back in the hall I peered down the black hole that led to the basement. A sharp, sulfurous odor leaked up. I wrenched the front door open. The moon's reflection perched on the Plymouth's roof. It seemed that I hadn't woken from a dream, but into one. Then I heard him sigh in the living room. When I went to investigate, I discovered a monster had overwhelmed the sofa's steel springs, settling within the pine walls of the frame. Familiar eyes found me from behind a grotesque, moon-shaped mask. It was Shiloh. It was my friend.

"Get me to a hospital," he said. His voice sounded as if it was trapped inside his head.

The mask looked like a cross between a catcher's mitt and his mask. There were two recessed eye holes and a beakish point, but no mouth. Sweat-damp hair almost hid the strap and buckle that held the mask in place. Lifting it off revealed Shiloh's damaged face. Vessels had hemorrhaged in both his eyes. His face was in the process of swelling and it made his skin appear newborn and wrinkle free. Blood flowed out his nose, over his lips, and stained his teeth. His tongue pushed at his lips as if it considered leaving its damp burrow.

He let out a labored hissing sound.

"Man, I think you're blind."

"Are you okay?" he asked. "And Alice?"

"Shiloh, what happened to you?"

He reached a hand up and held it before his eyes. I didn't believe he could see.

The hand was seized with tremors. I replaced it on his chest.

The other arm was pinned behind his body. Struggling to free it I discovered why he'd settled so low in the sofa. An X-ray smock was draped from his shoulders to his knees.

He picked up his free hand and studied it again.

I moved my face in front of his. "Why are you dressed like this?"

"See if any blood's coming out of my ears," he said.

Everywhere I looked I saw blood.

I said, "I can't tell." I tried to lift the lead blanket off his chest. Ties at the waist and neck held it in its place. I got a knife from the kitchen, sliced the cords. His strange costume felt like a casualty in my arms; I laid it on the floor.

Shiloh turned his head ever so slightly in my direction. "Where's my other hand?"

I tracked his arm from the shoulder to where it disappeared behind his body. There didn't seem any way to get a look without having him shift his position. "I'm going to have to get Alice."

"Thomas, this is the stupidest thing I've ever done." He kept talking to me as I ran up the stairs.

I burst into our room. Alice recoiled. Maybe, like me, she only wanted to be sure that this wasn't the opening to a frustrating and confusing dream. She had no choice but to follow; I hustled back to the living room.

Shiloh's hand fluttered above the crotch of his pants. "I think I peed."

He had. The urine puddled on the floor.

Alice came down the stairs one at a time, unwilling or unable to commit to our drama. She walked over and stared down at us.

"I'm so sorry, Alice." He could see.

Together she and I rolled him toward us and I followed my hand down past his elbow and lifted his arm.

"Your hand is fine." It wasn't exactly true. His index finger bent behind the other fingers at a strange angle. And something about his wrist . . .

"I still have my hands." He was crying.

Alice sat back on her heels and quit both of us. I mean she ceased being a participant and became a spectator. "What do we do?" she asked.

"I'm taking him to a hospital. You ready to go?" I asked Shiloh.

It wasn't really a question.

"How are we supposed to get him to the car?" Alice wanted to know.

I slid my arms beneath Shiloh and pulled him to my chest.

"You can't carry me," he said.

But I stood up with him in my arms.

"Okay," he said.

To avoid the tremendous front step, I had to carry him through the kitchen and out onto the porch. I stumbled across the yard. Alice trailed after us, like a hostess relieved to see her final guests departing. I leaned Shiloh against the car and opened the door for him. When I got in on the driver's side, Alice still stood by the open passenger door.

"You have to hold him up," I said.

After a look back at the house—the lights still burning inside—she got in. With all the potholes and washboard, we crept along until we reached pavement.

Alice flipped on the car's dome light. It felt like we had God's eye upon us. "What did you do to yourself?"

Shiloh reached up and dabbed at his smashed nose. He touched his rubbery lips.

"I don't think he can hear," I said.

"Shiloh?" said Alice. "Shiloh!" she screamed.

Everywhere we looked, dark cars docked beside dark houses. We were the only three people left on earth.

"You have no clue where you're going." Alice sounded like a person talking to a television.

"Just make sure he's comfortable," I said.

"Did he try to kill himself?" Alice asked.

I didn't know the answer.

Shiloh reached his mangled hand out and set it beside mine on the steering wheel.

"He smells awful," said Alice.

"You're going to be just fine," I said.

"I feel like catastrophe's bride," said Alice. A moment later, "Again."

Shiloh watched me, through the waning slits of his eyes. "It's my fault. Promise you'll just leave me there."

I shook my head.

"You don't know the answers to the questions they're going to ask," said Shiloh.

He tried to clear his throat. He spit blood against the inside of the windshield. "Mercy," he said.

"Thomas, I think he's right. We have to drop him off and get out of there." Alice was leaning forward so she could look at me.

"I can't see," said Shiloh.

I waved my arm in front of him.

"I think his eyes have swollen shut," Alice said.

I was praying the road might fork, because that was the way I remembered it. I had only the foggiest idea how to get us to the hospital.

Each time Shiloh breathed we heard a percolating, liquid sound.

Alice rolled her window down and stuck her head outside the car.

I reached a hand over and patted Shiloh's leg.

"I'll be back in no time, Thomas. Don't worry."

We came into a little town. A string of streetlights were flashing against the car like a strobe. Damp sewer grates nestled in the road. I listened to Shiloh's wheezing breath.

And then, unmistakably, on the side of a building, a red cross. I slid the car into a carport. A nurse, two orderlies, and a doctor waited in a peculiar white light. They looked disappointed to see us. They stood on a platform about four feet above us, like a rampart. They watched me pull Shiloh out of the car. I didn't see any stairs to get where they were so I lifted him and set him at their feet. They stubbed their cigarettes on the brick wall.

"This is the loading dock," said the nurse. A cornflower blue cardigan hung over her shoulders.

The doctor stooped and took a passing interest in Shiloh's face. He talked in that confident, pandering voice that doctors have. Shiloh was shivering and chattering his teeth.

"Were you in the accident?" the nurse asked me.

Was *I* in the accident?

"Do you know today's date?" she asked.

Her questions were incredible. "Were you in the accident?" I asked a little hotly, vaulting onto the loading dock.

"What happened to your friend?" asked one of the orderlies, a grisly old-timer.

"He's not our friend," said Alice, blinking up at us. "We just came across him."

"In your skivvies?" asked the nurse. I was in a T-shirt and underwear. Alice wore shorts and a ratty sleeveless shirt.

"Looks like a hit-and-run," said the other orderly, a stocky guy with a thin red mustache.

The doctor gave me an appraising look. He saw a wild-haired kid who'd been shocked from sleep. "So you don't know then if he's on any drugs."

The old-timer was having a one-sided conversation with our friend.

—You okay, pal?

—Tell me where it hurts.

—What's the other guy look like?

Meanwhile, mustache went inside.

The doctor had on a yellow paisley tie that ducked between the third and fourth buttons of his shirt. He looked Alice up and down. He wore a wide gold wedding band.

"Is he going to be okay?" I asked.

"We'll patch him up. He's going to be in a fair amount of pain, though. I can't give him any meds until I know if he's on substances."

"We have no idea," said Alice.

The doctor nodded. "A shame."

Mustache came back with a wheelchair.

"He say what his name is?" asked the nurse.

No, we didn't know his name.

The orderlies sat Shiloh in the wheelchair. They placed his feet on the little fold-down stirrups, then rolled him through the swinging doors.

That left the doctor, Alice, and me in the incriminating light.

Alice opened the passenger door. "Come on," she said. "Let's get out of here."

The doctor tamped a cigarette on the back of his hand.

I jumped down to the car.

The dirt roads looked as white as bone. It felt important that I get us home before morning had ushered night to bed. Alice cranked up the car's heater. She had her arms wrapped around her knees.

"Where were you when it happened?" Alice asked.

"I was next to you."

"Right. That's what I thought. So you don't know anything about it."

Was it possible that there might be a connection between the conversation Shiloh and I had walking his trapline and whatever had shot us into the night? What was I supposed to make of Shiloh's catastrophic youth? Was he trying to tell me something about my parents' dry little house or Mary's pork chop or Pawpaw's wheezing snores? What did he think of Fran looking down at him from his office window, or from his yellow car? All Shiloh's talk of ideology had sailed over my head. Another person might have been able to console him, but I hadn't known the perfect thing to say. Maybe he had some fantasy about exiting this world in order to join his dead lover in the next. And maybe he wanted to take us along for the ride.

That talk about not caring if everyone had drowned—you were supposed to pay attention when someone said something like that. People give out warning signs. He might as well have said, "Duck!" I should have asked him to explain his point. It must have been a burden to watch Alice and me with our joy.

Then again, maybe it wasn't about us at all, maybe all his hope and effort had proved insufficient to mend his crippled heart. And what about that mask? Maybe he just wanted to save his stupid face. I couldn't believe Shiloh was in some hospital.

Alice pressed her face against my shoulder. "It's okay," she said. "You did exactly as he asked."

When we pulled into the drive, Alice's fox was sniffing at the open door. We sat there holding hands. In the early morning light, he was the most beautiful animal either of us had ever seen. For all I knew, we could have been dead already. If I could have built my own heaven, it would have contained that house and Alice and our faithful beating hearts. The fox kept its dagger-shaped head pointed at us as it trotted away.

2

Unpacking

The light switch by the basement stairs had no effect at all. Alice retrieved a flashlight from the glove compartment of her car. "Come on," she said, "come on." There were little spots of blood on the dusty treads. We might have been descending into an animal's lair. Alice made a quick inventory of the basement: the wheelbarrow lying on its back; sheets of plywood, neatly stacked; a shovel and a broom; a pile of lumber scraps; a galvanized pail; a laundry tub; a gallon can of paint. Aiming the flashlight beam at the unfinished ceiling, we saw how someone had removed the bulbs from the fixtures. In her dogged way, Alice was trying to come up with the equation that when solved would give her the missing information. She turned round again and spotted the same innocuous things.

The basement stairs mirrored the stairs above so that at the bottom we faced the south side of the foundation, approximately beneath the front door. I took the flashlight from Alice's hand and walked over to examine the mortared wall. In some places the cement ran down the wall like candle wax; they'd just slopped it on. Unlike the round stones of the fireplaces, the foundation stone was sharp and angular. Halfway up the east wall, a stone rib stuck out, maybe three feet square, the support for the entrance-hall fireplace. The north wall, like the south wall, was unremarkable. The west wall, on the other hand, had a different character. For one thing, there weren't half as many stones sticking out. And though the living-room fireplace was somewhere overhead, there was no rib to support the weight. What caught Alice's attention was this: six dark polka dots in the dirt and, a few feet above that, a rectangular section of the wall had detached and swung in.

She got down on her knees and pushed the door open with a finger.

We both jumped backward. A voice whispered to us from the hole, then piano playing.

Alice swept the beam inside. Everywhere we looked: broken glass.

"It's his workroom," I explained.

She painted my face with the light. "You knew about this." Not a question.

"He showed it to me once."

She reached through the entranceway and brushed clear a spot where she could stand. She wiggled her way inside. The radio clicked off.

"He had you down here?" her disembodied voice asked.

When I didn't answer she stuck her face out the hole and pinned me with the light. "Huh?"

"Maybe a month ago."

I heard her sweep the glass around. After a minute this stopped. She told me to be careful coming in. "And where was I?"

She wasn't interested in my answer; she was busily trying to decipher this secret room. But where she saw things as they were, I was looking for the room I remembered. There were no things, just parts of things. While I recognized objects—his desk, the cabinets, the light fixtures—everything had undergone a transformation. Part of the magnifying lamp lay twisted in a corner of the room. The desk's glossy white paint had been replaced with a dark scorch mark. The walls above the desk featured dark organic shapes, smoky tendrils resembling the shadows of some tropical jungles. Only one cabinet remained latched. We saw half a dozen aluminum containers marked "Red-Dot Smokeless Powder"; a screw-top mason jar filled with fabric squares; mismatched batteries scattered to one side.

"I don't even want to know what he has in that one," she said, indicating the locked cabinet.

"It's just candy bars in there."

She studied my face.

"Seriously," I said.

Under the desk she spotted his toolbox. "That thing was in my apartment."

I lifted the toolbox onto the table. Inside were the normal sorts of odds and ends. Transistors. Vacuum tubes. All grouped by color or size. Wire strippers and crimping tools. The shelves lifted out and he had set screws and bolts and fasteners. In the bottom of it, in the sort of heart of the thing, he had a hacksaw and a soldering iron. A bunch of surgical steel hemostats and a chrome C-clamp. All these bright, blameless objects.

"Remember when you couldn't find Parker?" Alice asked. "He must have been sleeping in here."

"That occurred to me."

"You mean it occurred to you now, or when he had you down here?" Her voice sounded strangled.

"Parker wanted to build it. That's what Shiloh told me. It's like a getaway, I guess."

"Getaway from what?"

I shrugged my shoulders. I didn't have an answer. "Shiloh was using it as a workroom."

Alice had her arms folded across her chest. She was interrogating everything with her eyes.

I needed fresh air and sunshine. I bent down to use the hatchway.

"Wait," she said, "look at this."

I stood back up. Behind where he must have been working, frozen on the wall, was a picture of Shiloh at the moment of his accident. In the instant of ignition, as the hot gases expanded, and the shock wave pushed him against the wall, there, with only his body to shield it, those gases had burned the paint on the paper. What was left was a portrait of our friend in negative. His white arms flung wide, owl head and rectangular torso, all surrounded by thunderclouds of encroaching malevolence, a dark halo.

"He was building a bomb," said Alice.

While low clouds raked the land with mist, I cleaned the living room and the car. Alice decided the time had come to unpack those things that remained in the fiberglass trailer. Maybe she wanted to see if Shiloh had any more secrets.

Alice didn't know what to think about Shiloh. Previously she'd considered his excitement about anarchism just some empty talk. His accident forced her to confront the possibility that she didn't know him at all. And that I'd known about his secret room made me his accomplice.

And maybe she was right. Maybe I shared some blame. Did my careless talk about nobility put some harmful ideas in his head? Maybe he was trying to send me a message about the sort of person he could be.

Alice and I were both afraid of seeing that person in the hospital.

We donned yellow slickers and propped the mudroom door open. Making our way around the house, we scared up a pair of partridges. The birds exploded into the air with buzzing wings, almost causing us to go into cardiac arrest.

The white trailer stuck out of the high grass like a suppurating wound. Alice fit the key and popped the lock. Usually the thing would yawn open, but all that sun had conspired to weld shut the rubber seal. I latched my fingers around the lip and pulled. The gasket came apart with a crack. Here, I thought, was air that we'd brought with us all the way from our distant home. But while I wanted the Ohio, that familiar rankness, constant sunlight had refined a petroleum smell from the plastic.

It was hard to get too worked up about the things we found inside. Woolen blankets. An army-surplus sleeping bag. Clothes I'd forgotten I owned: a few pairs of jeans that made my legs look spindly, a ski sweater, a crocheted hat, gloves, and a pair of mittens. My suit—my only suit—a pinstriped number with a gray vest, balled up in the acetate bag it came in. (I'd brought it along only because I had no real understanding of where I was off to and because, had I left it behind, it might have made things worse for my father—he'd bought it for me on the occasion of his mother's funeral.) Now the thing was curled up like a cat in a bag. It depressed me completely. I held it in front of Alice, who recognized what was going on inside my eyes, without knowing what caused it.

"It's a suit," I said.

"As soon as we get the stuff stored away, you're going to put that on for me."

I ferried things inside, an armload at a time. I set Shiloh's things—some shirts and pants—on his bed. I told myself that I couldn't wait to see his face again. But having Alice in the house was enough for me.

Alice wanted to build a fire, so she sent me out to see what I could salvage from that wreckage in the yard. We believed it had been a silo, once upon a time. We liked to imagine the upright silo and the neat little home in a time before us, in a time of industry.

We tore up grocery bags to get the fire started. The wood I found produced more smoke than heat. Even after the kitchen warmed up, the upstairs rooms still felt like meat lockers. I climbed the stairs to change.

I unzipped the garment bag. Coat, vest, pants, a shirt with collar points that curled like an elf's shoes, the belt was as thin as the strap on a woman's purse. Everything gave off the same chemical smell. The creases that used to define the shins were replaced, or maybe overwhelmed, by new folds in the fabric; one that traversed the jacket diagonally made it appear as though I leaned against an invisible wire. By opening the medicine cabinet and standing on the rim of the tub, I managed to get a look at myself. Barefoot, the pants ended a few inches above my anklebones (a fact that the suit tried to conceal by falling off my hips—there was enough room around the waist for me to stick both hands down the front); no amount of tugging or adjustments to my posture would allow the shirt cuffs to cover both wrists simultaneously. I looked at my image in the mirror. I wasn't a kid playing grown-up, but a grown-up aping a child.

I called to Alice. She came up carrying a stack of towels. "That can't be yours," she said, setting her things down on the sink and moving around me. I was seeing myself through her eyes. The muscles of her mouth started to riot. It was one of those smiles that only show up in candid photos. "You look like . . . I don't know. Why is the vest a different color from the suit?" She hid her face behind her hands.

I opened the jacket to display the vest to its best advantage. She squeezed tears out of the corners of her eyes.

She made me take it off so she could try it on. I made her wear just the suit without the shirt, only one button holding the vest together and the swell of her breasts. I ran a bath.

The hot water released a smell that you only get from well water, a smell like frying mud. The windows fogged up. Alice hung my suit from the shower curtain rod. The steam would take the wrinkles out, she promised. (This prediction didn't pan out, but, for whatever reason, the suit stayed there, over the tub until our final hour. Many times the surprise of that dark silhouette gave me access to my most veiled fears.) Alice and I lowered our bodies into the water and watched our skin turn pink. I'd never had sex in a tub before.

We returned to the kitchen and the whispering fire. The meager outside light faded right away. The only color in the kitchen was the orange light from the cracks in the stove. While she made hot cocoa, I shook out the sleeping bag. We both fit inside.

On the pine floor, there in an empty husk of a house, beside a road that at one end led into the sky and at the other drowned in a lake, Alice Lowe and I. Her hair retained that earthy smell from the water. This on a forgotten day in October. Surely the partridge came back and nestled beside the foundation. The mist sizzled on the tin hat of the stove pipe.

3
Moonface

A week passed. Alice and I sat on the porch swing. My head was in her lap. We hadn't seen a cloud all day. The sun was like a photograph of a sun. We'd shared a box of animal crackers for lunch.

It might have been three or four. Alice clapped a hand over my mouth. I struggled to sit up. I watched Shiloh come over the top of the hill on a bicycle. Inexplicably, it was a girl's bike—a sissy bar was clamped behind the banana seat; a white wicker basket decorated with bright plastic flowers hung between the handlebars. He wore a green poncho that flapped as he descended. He dragged his feet in the gravel, as the pedals egg-beat. He coasted into the driveway and dumped the bike onto its side.

I ran out to greet him.

He raised his hands to ward me off. A plaster cast covered his left wrist. He tugged on the poncho, first one side, then the other. He didn't seem to be able to lift his arms above his head.

"He needs some help," said Alice.

Instead of answering, he struggled some more.

"Maybe you should have stayed there a little longer," I said.

Bruises hugged the bones of his face. He blinked slowly. He seemed to be reconciling the place with his memory and this seemed to take an inordinately long time. What he did was walk over to us. "Grab the hood," he said.

He backed out from under the poncho, leaving me holding it.

A stenographer's pad dangled from a string necklace. He took a spot beside Alice on the swing. Perspiration bloomed at his hairline and rolled into his bloody eyes.

"I stole the bike."

This, of course, didn't even scratch the surface.

"I'm not hearing things very well."

"I'm sorry," said Alice.

"Am I shouting?" Shiloh asked.

His voice hardly reached me. I shook my head.

"I'm out of breath. Of course that I'm here at all is a miracle. I'm going to try to live my life with a constant awareness of that."

I went inside and got a glass of water and brought it out for him. He thanked me and drank it down. He said "fine" and "smell" and "horse." Maybe he forgot that he was talking; the words dribbled out of his mouth.

"All further communications must be conducted on the paper I've provided. Unfortunately, in the process of cycling, I lost my pen. If you don't mind, I'm going to retire. Tomorrow, I will outline a few plans for our future. I only trust you haven't let the garden go to shit. Comrades. Statues. You silent fools. Delinquent mimes."

I followed him inside. He poked around the kitchen and pantry. I watched him peer out toward our garden. Turning around he almost bumped into me. "Don't mind me, my head's scrambled." He walked past the basement door and patted the frame with his cast. In the living room he studied the sofa where I'd found him. We'd gotten the blood off the floor, but the upholstery hadn't given it up so easily. I followed him up the stairs. "It's probably real quiet right now." All I could hear was his breathing. I followed him into his room. He leaned against me as he kicked off his shoes. There was a scab in the crook of his arm where an IV must have been. I helped him into bed. I pulled the blankets up to his chin. His eyes were already closed and for a moment I was taken with the efficiency with which he'd made the passage from consciousness to sleep. "If I'm not up in the morning, come check on me." He didn't look to see my response. I flipped the lights off and backed out of the room.

In the kitchen I told Alice that it was a miracle he got here, how he barely made it up the stairs.

"He's probably on all sorts of medication," said Alice.

"What do we do now?"

"We watch him like a hawk."

I banked the fire. I put my palms on the cold metal and waited for the heat.

The next morning Shiloh paused outside our door. "I'm going downstairs to make breakfast."

I considered going to help him with the stairs, but underneath our blankets, Alice and I were naked. Her body began saying the nicest things to mine.

We listened as he scuffed his butt down the stairs, one at a time.

"Blessed mercy," he said. "Whore's sons. Cocksucking gravity."

It occurred to Alice that he might burn the house down around us. We dressed and went downstairs. He turned when we came into the kitchen. Somewhere he'd found enough wood to get the stove started up. Eggs and American cheese bubbled in the skillet. The thin envelope of heat made us huddle close. He had his mouth half open and he whistled while he breathed. He pivoted toward us and shared a wry smile.

"Did you sleep all right?" Alice asked.

Instead of answering, Shiloh ducked his head under the sink's faucet and wet down his hair.

Alice took a spot at the kitchen table. "Looks like you did some damage," she said.

"Breakfast is ready," said Shiloh, carrying the skillet to the table. I got the utensils and napkins and plates. He pulled the string necklace with the pad of paper out from beneath his shirt. He tore some sheets out and shoved them in front of Alice.

After Alice finished with the papers, she passed them to me.

The top sheet was a nice, open cursive:

Can u read this? Good. U had an accident. Do u remember? That's okay. Don't be upset. The doctor will be down to see u. Mansard. It often returns in a few weeks. Maybe sooner. Often. Because I'm a physical therapist. Gwen. Thank u. We're having some trouble locating family. U weren't carrying any identifica-

tion. Do u think u live here? Because of your accent. Sometimes traumatic events esp. brain can bring on accents, but it makes us suspicious. Plus the trouble we're having finding any records. Sorry. These things will come back to u. I guarantee. I can come back later. Rest.

In tiny block print:

feel like talking Dr. Mansard how are you how's the pain <u>normal</u> remember anything fine broken left radius a few ribs nose dislocated ring finger left hand 1st & 2nd degree burns on both palms minor laceration on right cornea multiple extensive contusions concussion overall could have been worse something blew up in your face a propane stove that's my theory right you hear it now sometimes that will go away usually we have to wait and see point taken 4th of July I saw six people from propane stoves they should be illegal Everyone hates something I'm like Don Quixote tilting windmills any problems you let me know hang in there.

A new hand:

You were screaming.

The cursive again:

Give me a telephone number. Off the top of your head. Say the first thing that comes to mind. Thnxs.

That's the # for dialing time. Don't be upset. Maybe you're an operator.

Almost indecipherable script:

I got to give you a sponge bath. I'm an old pro. Don't worry— nobody's drowned yet. It's a joke.

Gwen, again:

Hearing <u>anything</u>? Other than that? These things take time. Are u comfortable? It's possible insurance would pay for a private room. That's why we need to find some contact people. Usually *people call looking for u. Maybe you're a tourist? If we put everyone who screamed in a private room, then this wing would be empty. Embarrassed? U shouldn't be. Do u remember who dropped u off? A young man and woman? Remember a green car? I <u>don't</u> think you're lying. We're just not finding any information. There are databases but we can't find anything. Remember what I said about accents? Don't get upset. The ringing will stop. I promise. I got an idea. Close your eyes and sign your name. Pretend you're signing a check. X_____*

I didn't mean to get you agitated. The most important thing is that u get some rest. U have to heal. Maybe in a week. The doctor wants to make sure your hands heal right. Burns can be tricky.

Dr. Mansard:

hows my grilling enthusiast you look good you been spotted moseying around I can't stand being laid up either—wanderlust eyes are going to clear up shortly maybe we take pictures of the ribs in 6 weeks same time we take the cast off the arm neat little trick saw cuts plaster but not flesh sounds awful though sorry yes well months from now you wake up birds singing sprinklers ratcheting lawn mowers the whole wonderful din but we have to wait a bit longer before we run any tests I'll come by before they discharge you & remember charcoal imparts a smoky flavor and won't try to kill you.

Filling an entire page:

This happen in Vietnam?

Gwen:

That look isn't for me is it? U stopped talking. Let's make up. Dr. Mansard says you're making good progress. But we can't very well release u if u don't know where to go. If it's just a matter of recognizing things I might be able to get one of the police officers to drive u around. I don't think you're nuts. To be honest u got us stumped. I think you're better off staying here. I do.

A new print:

My name is Officer Gorman Gwen Atkins asked me to pay a visit. I'm with the State Police. ~~The problem with your case is~~ I should say difficulty is that Missing People really focuses on finding missing individuals or parties, but the thing about your case is that we found you, but the people who should be looking for you are missing. You see my point. It's not as simple as running the protocols in reverse either. If you could maybe describe the people who should be looking for you we might be able to pretend they were missing and then we'd be back at square one, but at least we'd know how to proceed. There are procedures. Can you meet us halfway here? If you think of anything ask for me. Keep your chin up.

Gwen:

I've got a surprise. U thought I forgot. I called the papers and the TV station and they're going to send some people over tomorrow. Get some rest. Big day tomorrow.

Alice nibbled on some dry toast and stared out the window. I put the pages back in order.

I reached my hand across and patted Shiloh's purple fingers where they stuck out of his cast.

"Ask him what he was doing down there in the first place," said Alice.

"Just like that? Now?"

"Write it down," said Shiloh.

"You heard him," said Alice.

I wrote, *You've never told us about your accident.*

"Just going to keep bird-dogging me," he said.

Alice shook her head.

"We were worried about you," I said.

His face showed no recognition. I wrote it down.

"I wanted to make sure we were safe. You won't believe me, but that was what was on my mind." He tore the last sheet of paper off and stuffed it in his pocket.

"Useless," said Alice.

4
Fortitude

What woke me was Alice stripping the covers from the bed. The frosty air leaped onto me. It was either very early, or else about to rain. "Chop-chop," she said. "If you want to soar with the eagles, you have to be ready to run with the hounds." She took the buckle of my belt and branded me with the cold metal. "Get a move on," she said.

I followed her down the stairs.

Shiloh's pink bicycle stood on the kitchen table.

"Voilà!" said Shiloh.

Alice asked me what I thought of it.

It was part of my nature that I couldn't think well if roused from sleep. What use did I have for a little girl's bike? I said, "It's very nice. Thank you."

Alice swatted me across my chest.

Shiloh had a knack for interpreting gestures. "For Sonya."

I endeared myself to them by pointing out a strand of cobweb beneath the seat.

Alice gave Shiloh the high sign and he picked it up and cradled it in his arms.

Was I coming? she asked.

The three of us crowded in the front seat while the bike rode in back.

"We should get a bow," Shiloh suggested.

The five-and-dime was stocked for Halloween. Boxes and boxes of paper masks with thin elastic bands and painted faces. The anonymous latex faces of murderers and maniacs. Instead of ribbons Shiloh selected orange crepe-paper streamers.

Back in the parking lot, Alice wove the paper through the spokes and then strung it back and forth from the sissy bar to the handle-bars. We were lighthearted and smiling.

It started to rain, big, fat, greasy drops.

We put the bike back in the car. Alice told me to drive.

Shiloh said, "I'm sorry I might have hurt you. You are my best friends."

Alice said, "I'm writing that we forgive him."

"Good," I said. "I think he's a bit fragile right now."

Across the lake a narrow band of trees hugging the New York shore burned yellow and red, but everywhere else you looked you saw brown. Probably something to do with the long drought.

Most of the trees had already lost their leaves. Peering past the bare branches I glimpsed the secret symmetry of the land. It struck me that around us were hidden valleys and brown meadows that hadn't been visible to us before now. The grass lay down in the ditches. Leaves choked puddles. All at once we were at the Sound of Music Commune. There were no cars in the lot. No smoke trailed from the chimneys. Where were the picnic tables? The oil-drum grills?

I laid on the horn. Nothing happened. We got out.

"They must be working," said Alice.

Shiloh walked over to the nearest house and peeked inside. But I knew he wouldn't see so much as a table, knew it because I noticed other changes. The wood that they'd stacked between the cedars had been removed. Under the eaves of the A-frame, a row of naked nails showed where someone had taken down all that painted gingerbread. Alice asked if I remembered flower boxes on the porch rails. The place looked destitute. Looking through the windows Shiloh saw that everything had been cleaned out. No sleeping bags. No bead curtains. There was no sign of their furniture or those futuristic stoves.

I pointed out to Shiloh where the gingerbread used to be.

"That's a crime," he said.

Alice went from house to house. Not one had been spared.

She yelled, "Do we even know which house she lived in?"

In all the emptiness we only missed the little girl.

I carried the bike over to Gregor and Magdalena's place and

propped it under the eaves to keep it dry. The idea of wet crepe paper depressed me.

We loitered beside the car while the raindrops whistled down. Alice asked Shiloh where he thought they'd gone.

Shiloh nodded his head gravely. "Well, they wouldn't have any trouble slipping into Canada. There must be a hundred logging roads that cross the border without so much as a sign. It's not necessary to leave the country. Lots of folks head to California to see what that's about. From what I've seen, too many people are trying to impress each other out there, but once you've made the trip, it's just a short shot to Mexico. Farther south things just get weird. The Rockefellers own a whole forest in Central America; whenever one of their family gives birth to a bastard, they send them down there to oversee their coffee plantation. But there's plenty of space left in this country. If you want to find yourself, you head to Montana, or Alaska even. If you want to get lost, you don't have to move more than a block or two. If you go underground, not even your shadow can find you."

Underground. I thought of the earthy smell in our basement.

Now mixed in with the rain, granules of white pinged down: snow.

"Let's get out of here," Alice said, returning to the car and its heater.

I tapped Shiloh on the shoulder, nodded my head at the car.

He jogged back up onto the porch and picked up the bicycle. In the next instant he'd thrown it through the sliding glass door. It was madness. He stepped inside the empty house.

When he came out he couldn't conceal the look of triumph on his face. Cradled in his arms were four cardboard tubes—the blueprint plans.

5

Idyll

Shiloh announced he was feeling well enough to check his snares. And after what he'd been through, he deserved some recreation. If the snares didn't work out, then he'd try the beaver ponds. He'd picked up a telescoping rod and reel somewhere. We waved him off. "Good luck," we said. "Good luck." We thought of fresh meat on the stove.

In preparation for his catch, Alice and I resolved to come up with something that might burn. A run of frosty mornings had depleted our stack of aviation magazines. We'd already looted the few loose beams from the wreckage in the yard, but thick steel hoops held the bulk intact. Armed with claw hammers and some wire cutters, we approached. However, this closer examination revealed that most of the wood was in no shape to burn. It crumbled in your fingers. When a nail punched through the sole of Alice's shoe and threaded the keyhole space between her big toe and its neighbor, we decided to give up our effort. The prospect of visiting the emergency room again took the wind out of our sails.

We decided to make one last visit to the swimming hole. We stared into that clear water, at the piled rocks and the leaf boats rushing over the top of the dam.

We undressed. The cold ground made our feet tingle. We jogged in place, gave little shouts, all in an attempt to work ourselves into a condition to get in the water. Alice grabbed my hand and we rushed in together. The cold water scalded us. It stole our breath and our grace. We flopped around. When we couldn't stand it another second, we thrashed our way to shore. And then, for a moment, the air felt positively tropical. We dashed back into the water to feel that way again.

The next time we came out, our hands were numb and cramped.

"So clean," Alice said, meaning, I've never felt so clean in my whole life.

"Thank you," I said. "Thank you." Meaning: I am in love completely; the argument for all of this is you; tomorrow I will try to pull you back into the water, and the day after.

It took a long time to get back into our clothes. We shuffled across the meadow.

At the top of the road, Shiloh was coming toward us. He had the duffel bag in front of his chest; the tip of the fishing pole whipped back and forth in front of him. From his other hand dangled the long, puffy tail of Alice's fox.

Alice stormed inside—I thought so as to be spared seeing the animal reduced to a pennant. He probably wanted to tie it to the car's antenna. Seeing me, he waved his prize. "I caught the thief."

Alice came back out holding the mantel clock over her head. It was, Shiloh liked to point out, the only beautiful thing he'd ever owned. The clock was about three feet high. Counterweights shaped like pine cones pendulumed at the end of tarnished chains.

In his silent world Shiloh didn't understand the transformation Alice had undergone. But he saw her intention. She searched the yard for something.

He was screaming, "Please, no! Not my clock!" The words piled on each other to form a single awful sound.

What Alice was searching for was something hard. She trotted over to the flagstone and flung the clock down. The effect was irreversible.

Shiloh sat down in the grass.

I gathered the clock pieces together in a paper bag. There was no way that I found everything. Some of the parts had been under tension; when the cabinet came apart, so did they.

"Will you talk to me?" Shiloh asked. "I don't know why she hates me."

I pulled the notebook from around his neck. I wrote, *She's mad about the fox.*

He gave me a look of incredulity. His hand brought the tail before us—there was blood on the fur at the base of the tail—and pointed at it as if to say, This fox?

I nodded.

"Alice," he yelled at our bedroom window. "You broke my clock because of a stupid animal. Who's crazy, Alice? You're the crazy one."

I wrote, *And we're both concerned that we could have been blown up.*

"No," he said. "Never."

I wrote, *Did you think there was any chance of blowing yourself up?*

He rubbed his fingertips around his eyes.

"I'm sorry," he called to Alice, "for the fox, but especially for my accident."

I wrote, *I think it's better that she doesn't see the tail or the carcass. Or the skin.*

"It doesn't seem right to let it go to waste."

Please.

"I've got trout." One by one, he pulled fifteen fish out of his duffel bag. Pieces of dead grass stuck to their flesh. But their colors, their vibrancy, gun-metal backs fading into cream-colored bellies, vertical stripes of red and purple, they looked as if they'd been skewered by rods of light. The scales came off in his hands, like dust off a butterfly's wing.

We got them in the sink. Guilt went hand in hand with wonder.

Shiloh stuck the knife's blade in their vent and slipped it up until it split their lower jaws. Their organs, a cornucopia of miniature fruits, sacs of color. Shiloh separated four egg yolks, coated the fish in the eggs, rolled them in cornmeal, and dropped them in the skillet with half a stick of butter. From the back of the fridge, he produced a plastic lemon. He turned the fish over, sprayed the juice over them. He put five on a plate and asked me to deliver them, with his apologies, to Alice.

She couldn't forgive him. But she accepted the fish. The pink flesh was sweet, and with the smallest ones we ate the bones.

6

The Knight of the Wood

Alice and I were running errands when she spotted a flier put up by someone who dealt in firewood. I called from a pay phone. A man answered. I said we needed to buy some firewood. Did we want rounds, split, quartered? Loose or stacked? For a woodstove or fireplace? Aged or green wood? And how many cords were we looking for?

I gave Alice a look; we'd found the guy for our firewood problem.

There was a pause during which he expected me to tell him what I wanted.

"I'm willing to trust your judgment as far as what's best," I said.

This loosened him up some. So he put me through a questionnaire. We planned to heat with wood alone. We needed to burn the stuff this season. We didn't own a sledgehammer or a maul, so we'd need it quartered. I told him I'd seen a hatchet somewhere; he congratulated me. We could stack it on our own. He taught me the basics: a cord was equal to one hundred and twenty-eight cubic feet of wood, or, as it was commonly described, a pile four feet by four feet by eight feet. He recommended we buy six cords. If we were older, he said he might suggest eight cords. Older people just enjoyed watching wood burn, he explained. Where did we want this stuff delivered? To our home. Right; and where could he find this domicile?

I told him where we lived.

Here was the deal: certain larger economic forces had caused a run on firewood in the north country. His boss was trying to take care of his regulars before he started supplying new customers, but our guy just happened to have six cords of aged hardwood, quartered and cut in lengths between seventeen and twenty inches, loaded in the back of his truck—he'd taken this out of their woodlot this very morning. If we wanted it stacked, that was a two-person job, which meant including his boss (not a very sympathetic character the way he painted him), but since we could take it loose, then he could just dump it in the driveway and we'd be done. How did that sound?

My enthusiasm must have been apparent. I was goosing Alice, who spun around within reach of me so it became a game we were playing. "Fantastic," I said. "You've made this very easy."

He said, "In Burlington they're getting a hundred per cord."

"What about around here?"

"Seventy-five."

"Four hundred and fifty dollars?" I asked.

Alice got a panicked look on her face. She shook her head and mouthed, No.

"You there?" he asked.

"That seems like an awful lot," I said.

"Wood may grow on trees, but it doesn't fall down, cut itself into equal lengths, peel apart like an orange, and then jump into my truck." Then he hung up the phone.

Alice chewed on her thumbnail. She wanted to know what her four hundred and fifty dollars would get her. I described to her six piles of aged hardwood, measuring four feet by four feet by eight feet. And was I certain that this was enough wood? I felt very confident.

I called the guy back.

"Listen," he said, "I'll make a deal with you. The hydraulic lift isn't working right. If you and your friends unload the truck, I'll knock fifty off the total. I'm no bank—I don't take checks."

When the truck came rumbling over the hill, all I could think about was the promise of heat. Downshifting about ten times, our guy stopped the truck just past the driveway. He backed it in.

There was a ratcheting creak, probably the emergency brake, and then the driver hopped out of the cab with a piece of wood. A sample, I thought. He dropped it and kicked it beneath the front wheel. He wore a shirt with coconut buttons and slashes of brown and red like a scene from the end of the world.

"I'm Clovis," he said. "Tell me it's not just the two of you."

I shrugged.

"My only rule is that you don't bang up the paint outside the bed. So when you're throwing stuff out, you got to be sure to throw it clear. You got it?" He pulled a pair of work gloves out from the driver-side door. He handed them to Alice. "You're going to get splinters otherwise."

I watched her put on the filthy gloves.

"How do we know when we've unloaded six cords?" I asked.

"When you're down to sheet metal, you're done."

Alice and I had planned to stack the wood in a single row alongside the kitchen wall, beneath the windows, but the mountain of wood in the back of the truck was a little overwhelming.

I climbed into the truck's bed and reached down to give Alice a hand up.

The sun burned right above the trees in New York.

Clovis swung himself back into the cab and turned the radio on.

The music confirmed that we were doing something beautiful. A man sang to his love that he had to get on a boat and sail away. The lyrics were what he wanted to say and the secret of the song was that he had already left.

There had to be more than a thousand pieces of wood in the back of that truck.

Once the sun finished turning the lowest clouds pink, a blue twilight filled the valley. I hoped the man might give us a hand, but neither he nor Alice seemed to notice or care how long this operation was going to take. I needed gloves. I could feel the insides of my fingers forming tender spots that would bloom into blisters.

Shiloh came down the road. I can't say what the accident did to his head, but there was a new quality to the attention he paid things. I think he saw the growing pile of wood before he noticed the truck, though they weren't ten feet apart.

"Look here," he said, as if he'd discovered it.

I lobbed a stick close to where he stood.

"My head," he said, cowering and dancing off. "Look at that truck. Thomas."

Alice and I waved to him.

"I'm going to go inside and clean these fish." He unzipped his duffel bag to give us a look.

I couldn't see anything.

Clovis said, "Buddy, why don't you help your friends first."

Shiloh may have looked into the cab, but I don't think he saw Clovis sitting there.

The man got out of the truck and climbed the side rail, like a cowboy clinging to the side of a bull ring. "Strange cat."

"He's deaf," said Alice.

"I'm sorry," said Clovis. "Why don't you take a break and I'll pitch in for a while."

"I don't think we can afford your help."

"Maybe I can donate my labor?"

There's no question they flirted.

"That's okay," said Alice, "we wouldn't feel right about that."

"It works in my favor, too. The sooner the truck is empty, the sooner I can get out of here."

Alice kept finding the perfect log and tossing it out.

Clovis swung his leg over the rail.

"Stop," said Alice. "You can't rush us."

This perplexed the man; he'd never been told to stay out of his own truck.

"What's all this wood really worth?" Alice asked. "Two-fifty, three?"

"It's worth every cent of four hundred."

"I thought it was worth four and a half, but you were giving us a deal."

This caught him off guard.

"It is a deal." He snatched up a piece and dropped it on the lawn.

"I suspect you're taking advantage of us, just a little bit. If you would have taken four and a half, and you'll drop it down to four, just so we feel like we've got a good deal, then I'd bet your regular customer wouldn't pay you more that two-fifty. Am I right?"

"It's pretty clear you folks don't know what you're talking about."

"But am I right about two-fifty?"

"You're forgetting the oil embargo. That changes the rules."

We weren't forgetting the oil embargo; we'd never heard of it.

"We'll give you two seventy-five. That way you won't feel like you're cheating us and we won't feel like we've been cheated."

Clovis sucked on his lower lip. "Your friend here agreed to four hundred."

"Yes, but it's not his money, for one, and—being more trusting than I am—he took you at your word."

I think, had it been lighter out, if he'd seen me smile when Alice baited him, he could have stonewalled us and he would have ended up getting the price he'd set. But just so there'd be no hard feelings, Clovis agreed on two seventy-five and even helped us unload the truck. After we'd transferred the mountain of wood to our yard, the two of them settled up by the light of his headlights. He wound up driving away with two-eighty because he didn't carry any change.

Inside, Shiloh had the trout ready. We banked a fire in the living room. The heat pushing through the house made the timbers creak.

Shiloh called to us from his room, "I'm sweating," he said, delight in his voice. "All the poisons are coming out of my system."

It felt like the third summer of the year.

7
Snug

I had the bright idea to stack the wood in the living room. Alice put some newspaper down and I stacked the wood nice and neat. When Shiloh saw what I'd done, he said, "Try that in a modern house. The wood would have dropped straight into the basement."

As a reward Shiloh decided to cook a genuine hobo stew, a recipe entrusted to him by a dying man, a gypsy who traced the recipe's history back as far as the Caucasus Mountains. Shiloh promised this would be a rare treat—the secret was saltpeter. It made the meat soft. This old gypsy used to carry a tin snuff box full of the stuff, but saltpeter had other uses and Shiloh happened to have a small supply down in the basement.

Alice and I went upstairs to clean up. We confessed to each other that every moment, we expected the floor to collapse in the living room. After Shiloh mentioned the possibility, it only seemed a matter of time before it happened. The big question was whether the whole house would collapse in on itself, folding itself into the basement as neatly as one of those camper trailers with the cloth walls.

So when Shiloh called us down for dinner, we stopped in the living room to unburden the floor of a few measly logs. Here was the other reason people didn't stack wood in their living rooms: millipedes, centipedes, earwigs, daddy longlegs, pill bugs. I got the broom and started sweeping them out the door. Some of the bugs startled Alice by flying.

Alice actually said, "I knew this was going to happen." At which point I handed her the broom and went to see Shiloh.

Our friend stirred a blue enamel stockpot. I looked in the trash to see what he'd put in there. Stewed tomatoes. A can of white potatoes. Kidney beans. Pinto beans.

He motioned for me to look in the pot.

I rubbed my stomach.

"After you eat this"—he pointed at his crotch and let his hand dangle from his wrist—"the navy used to feed the stuff to sailors, for morale."

I wiped my hand over my forehead. Whew, like, what a burden erections were to me.

"It'll be like a snake on a cold rock. The real trick is what this stuff does to the meat. Mark my word, you can't even tell it's the same animal."

"They're vanquished," Alice announced, coming in.

Shiloh ladled stew into bowls, filled glasses with water. He pulled a pan of corn bread out of the oven. We rubbed his arms to thank him. Alice fetched his notebook so we could tell him how much we were going to like the stew.

"I have an announcement to make," Shiloh said, nodding along with his words. "My birthday is next week, in five days, actually. I would very much like it if either of you made me a yellow cake with chocolate frosting. I think this is reasonable."

But no matter how much I loved him right then, for asking for what he wanted, for his sad, bruised face and poached hands, the problem with Shiloh Tanager was that he didn't want to be one hundred percent reliable. He didn't want to be one hundred percent anything. He wanted to be coy, clever, dangerous. He liked to think that he knew what was best for people. He thought of himself as a person of vision. And the worst of it was that he thought he had either the intelligence or the charisma to make people see only what he wanted them to see. What else could have goaded him into serving Alice a stew made from her good-luck fox.

One taste of the meat and all his talk about the transformative powers of saltpeter evaporated for me. It wasn't beef, and the cubes were too large to come out of any of the rabbits he'd caught.

I pulled the stockpot off the edge of the stove. It hit the floor, bounced once, splashed over my pants. The lid rattled while the contents seeped across the floor. Alice shot up, probably intending to salvage some of the stew, so I swept my shoe through it.

The thud of the pot hitting the floor must have sent a tremor into Shiloh's legs, because he looked from the mess to me—I shot him a hateful look. He left the table and went upstairs.

Alice hadn't quit on the food. While she considered how we might recover it, I took the three bowls and rinsed them in the sink.

"Thomas, what's gotten into you?"

"Eat your dinner. I'll clean this up." I grabbed her beneath her arm and stood her up.

"But you've taken my dinner away."

I slid the corn bread in front of her. She picked at it.

"Poor Shiloh. He's probably crying. I've never had hobo stew. A shovel, Thomas? What are you doing? Don't scratch the floor. And I was so hungry. I love potatoes. You have to apologize to him."

"I'll apologize to Shiloh. Why don't you go to town and get us a pizza?"

"Baby, we can't afford to buy pizzas."

"Just buy one."

"Tell him it was an accident."

I rushed her out of the house.

Upstairs Shiloh had locked his door. I pounded on it until it rattled on its hinges. I was building myself up to kick it down, but then I heard him shuffle over and unbolt the lock.

Shiloh retreated to his bed, where he had stacked the Polaroids. He straightened them out and put them back in the box.

"I don't want to hear your apology," he said. "God knows why you and Alice make it your business to destroy anything that I show interest in."

I reached out like I meant to fix the collar of his shirt. He looked down to see what it might be. I grabbed his nose and bent it sideways a few inches.

"Oh God," he said, "you're going to kill me. I'm innocent." Blood flowed out of the left nostril, dripped off his chin. The drops dotted his bedsheet.

I found his little notebook. *That,* I wrote, *is for the fox.*

He wiped the tears off his cheeks. "Why did she have to ruin that clock? What else do I care about? There were little bells inside it that would have played songs if the time was right. Imagine for a moment that you are me. And now my nose is going to swell up again. She must hate me."

I told him she didn't know.

"Remember when she and I left you here? That was the day Sonya got dropped off. She offered to buy me a bus ticket anywhere I wanted to go. Why? Because I was getting to you. She didn't like that we'd become friends. Remember Parker? She doesn't want anyone else coming near you. She left her first husband. Did she tell you? She just walked away."

I told him I didn't want him talking about her.

Shiloh shook his head. "She'll leave you, too, Thomas. Who's going to look out for you then?"

So I wrote it down on his little pad. *Who is going to look after me?*

He didn't have a thing to say.

Not you, I wrote. I was thinking of Alice, on those silent nights at her old apartment, moving through that scarlet light. And just past the door, Shiloh stretched out on her sofa. Had he chosen us or had we chosen him?

Why didn't you take the bus ticket?

"I'm not done here, Thomas."

How could he know?

Craggy Mountains

TWO MEN

*T*he glass-walled bedroom overlooked a small coastal city. The older man tried to make himself comfortable in a chair made of canvas slings. He was having very little success. His sister, who was in the bed, seemed disappointed in him.

"It is a very expensive chair," she explained.

"I don't think that's the problem," said the older man.

His sister reached for a glass that sat on her bedside table. She took a small sip.

"Do you remember that white pitcher that Mother used to cherish?"

"With the tulip-shaped handle."

"I should like to see that again."

"Have you any idea where it is?"

"Lost," said the sister. "I used to love it when Mother washed my hair with that pitcher. She had a little step stool and I'd hold my head above the basin. But she wouldn't let me use her precious cellulose combs."

"No. She did use the combs, though sometimes your hair broke the teeth."

"I had very strong hair. All the men I've known have cherished my hair. Young women these days have terrible hair and then they wonder why they aren't happy."

The older man got up and drew the curtain a few inches so that it kept the sunlight off his sister's face.

"Thank you," she said, taking another sip from her glass. "So you and your protégé were in Africa again; tell me how that was."

The older man stood looking out at the jumble of houses. Laundry hung on lines between the buildings. "The problem with Africa is that it renders the rest of the world superfluous. Of course one can't actually say that."

"I suppose those fossils are part of the problem," said his sister. "I expect that whole continent must be littered with bones. At the rate these scientists are leapfrogging into the past, it's only a matter of time before they find records of man that predate their little squirming fishes. What will they do then, I wonder."

The older man watched a girl in the street below. She wore a green tartan skirt and a white blouse. Her hair was in pigtails. She smiled at him. She reminded the older man of a girl he had seen walking through a park during a shower sixty years before. He had been a boy waiting inside a gazebo for the rain to let up when that first girl had come along. She had smiled at him, too. The boy didn't know why the girl had smiled at him, but it dawned on him now— she was barefoot! A barefoot girl in a park during a storm sixty years ago. The older man waved to the girl on the street, who was not barefoot but had on blockish black shoes. She waved back to him.

"Do you think we were happy as children?" asked the older man.

"I may have been happy for a child," said the sister, "but I wasn't happy as a child."

"I don't remember," said the older man.

"Do you remember when you had spotted fever? I prayed for you to die, you know."

"You asked me to absolve you once, as I recall."

"Well, did you?"

"I did," said the older man.

"I suppose you were required."

"They permit me some discretion."

"Would you please sit down? You don't show any sensitivity to my situation."

The older man returned to the chair. "That is exactly how Mother spoke," said the older man. "Do you remember that young surgeon she kept having to usurp?"

"Young! He's head of the academy. He built an enormous house up the coast, in that place where people used to go to be indiscreet. You and he would get along famously, I imagine."

"What makes you say that?"

"He has no time for patients anymore. He's transcended them. He only cares about disease."

The older man extricated himself from the chair and returned to his place at the window.

"My decline hasn't been so unpleasant," said the sister, "with the exception of that frightening episode that prompted my letter."

"I was thinking you seem rather well."

"I'm not."

"Maybe you are only a bit depleted. Perhaps you shall recover."

"No. Death could come at any time. The girl who takes care of me, she and I do this delicate operation to change the linens and I always think what an indecorous opportunity that would be. It shall be a relief to forfeit my vanity. Anyway, I'm resigned to it."

"Do you take comfort in that?" asked the older man.

The woman gave her brother a hard look. "Do you?"

"I can imagine two models for heaven. In one we are permitted our memories, while in the other we forfeit them."

"We carry our memories with us," said the sister.

"What makes you certain?"

"Heartbreak."

"Go on," said the older man.

"It is impossible to imagine experiencing heartbreak in heaven, yet without the memory of heartbreak, heaven would have no purpose."

"I trust in the wisdom of His grace," said the older man.

Someone walked across a tiled floor. They heard the ringing footsteps.

The sister reached out and took another sip of water. "He may come up to see me if he likes."

The older man excused himself. He returned a moment later with the younger man in tow.

"I trust you could muddle through my directions," said the sister. "Though, with the way you hop around, it's a wonder you can remember where you are from one moment to the next."

"The directions were very helpful," said the younger man.

"Did you find the cathedral inspiring?" asked the sister.

"Absolutely."

"Was there a correspondence waiting for us?" asked the older man.

The younger man held up an envelope that was secured with a dark red seal.

"Why don't you open it."

The younger man was apprehensive, but did as he was told. He ironed the crease out of the letter with the flat of his hand. After reading the letter he passed it to the older man.

"What does it say?" asked the sister.

Her brother walked over to the window. "We must go to New York."

"And I thought they only posted you to the hinterlands."

"It only seems so," said the younger man.

"Can you divulge the nature of your visit to New York?"

The older man looked to the younger man.

"Inquiries on behalf of the Holy See," said the younger man.

"What are you chasing now?" asked the sister.

The older man returned to the uncomfortable chair. "We don't chase. We witness." He looked out upon the town, which had been his boyhood home.

"It can feel like chasing," said the younger man.

"I expect this will be our last meeting," said the sister.

"You seem better today," said the younger man.

"And it has put her in quite a mood," said the older man.

"Keep insulting me," said the sister. "One day soon you'll be mortified."

I
Then

Alice came back. She didn't have a pizza. In explanation she led me out into the yard. The valley below us was lost to fog. As we watched, it climbed out of the ravine and advanced on our home.

When the fog rolled in the two of us went to our bedroom to be above it. I felt the same awe I'd known standing beside the rising Ohio. The fog kept heaping up. It drowned the windows. It probably crested the roof. The last part of the house to be overwhelmed would be the smoking chimney.

In the morning the room was infused with such a pervasive light. It came in beneath our door and through the green blanket we'd hung over the curtain rod. I believe it came through the walls.

When Alice moved the curtain aside, I swear the light came through her. "Oh my, baby, come see the yard." She wasn't wearing anything and the fantastic light that pained my eyes originated from between her legs.

"Tell me about it."

"It's like we live inside a sugar egg. I can see the individual barbs on the barbed wire. Yes. And the grass in the field, it looks . . . you have to see this. Everything is more mathematical." She turned to me.

"What are you looking at?" she asked, shifting her hips.

"Paradise."

"It's too bad you didn't eat some of that stew." She returned to the window. Her enthusiasm could barely match the cold that had seeped into the room. The fires must have burned out. Her legs stretched to rub each other.

"If you don't come back to bed, I'm going to call you Cricket."

"I wonder how cold it is. It looks like it must be about a hundred below zero."

"Let's hope not."

"We're safe, so long as Dr. Damage doesn't blow us sky high."

Something in her voice set me off. "Don't call him that."

"What he can't hear won't hurt him." Her bangs had grown out and now she was tucking them behind her ears. Sometimes I would whisper into one ear, telling that ear to keep a secret from the other ear. Sometimes we were playful. "How about Professor *Oops*?"

"He told me you asked him to leave."

With a snap she yanked the curtain off its rod.

"You were drunk and he had you out there dedicating a ridiculous haystack to me."

Past her I saw a haze on the horizon, as if all the crashing light had excited itself to a higher state of energy.

"You're the one who bought the wine."

"He was trying to play you against me. I told him I wouldn't permit a contest for your loyalty. I also told him that if you were the only reason he was sticking around, then he might want to move on. He gave me that hurt look of his. He told me I'd probably be happier if he got on board a bus. So I said I was willing to test his hypothesis."

She had turned her back to me.

"Did it occur to you that that might have made him feel isolated?"

"Where did you develop this habit of appropriating people's sadness?"

"Do you think that maybe, in some way, you might have contributed to his playing with explosives in the basement? Has that crossed your mind?"

"It was an argument, Thomas. We were trying to hurt each other's feelings. Remember the way he chewed us out about the garden? He needs to be right about everything." She folded her arms and defied me. "I won't accept the blame for his accident."

"What reason did he give for staying here?"

"He said somebody had to look out for us."

"And what did you say to that?"

"I said he might be right."

When she got under the sheets, she was as cold as stone.

Wish

I went downstairs to investigate a knocking sound and found Shiloh in the pantry. He was nodding his forehead against a wall stud. He'd forgotten that things which made no noise for him weren't always silent. What he was doing was trying to find the antidote to the ringing in his head. He knew that radio waves could cancel one another out if their frequencies were perfectly reversed. Another jolt, he reasoned, might quiet the ringing in his head. As evidence of the technique's viability, he cited a particular quality of stillness that accompanied each blow.

He wanted to know what type of friend I was. How would I respond if he asked me to strike him? For the time being he was only speaking hypothetically. Complicating matters, he knew that his mind might be leading him toward a too permanent solution. He had come to regard his head as an exquisite liability.

His cake came out of the oven looking like a yellow brownie. It's hard to believe that elevation could have been a factor. Instead, in my effort to do a good job, I probably overmixed the batter. Alice decorated the frosting with those jelly candies that look like slices of lemon, lime, and orange.

We didn't have birthday candles, so instead she inserted safety matches in a ring around the edges. "Go get the birthday boy," she told me.

I checked the living room and his bedroom. It was easy to lose track of him. I couldn't find the flashlight. As it turned out, I didn't need it. When I reached the bottom of the basement stairs, I saw light coming out of the square hatchway. Probably I'd surprise him doing something delicate and that would be the end of both of us. When I got close to the hole, I knelt and peered in. The doorway provided a view of his hands, what I'd come to think of as the unreliable part of him. His fingers drummed on the desk. This gave me the confidence to crawl in.

When he saw me his face tried to apologize, like a person who has just been accused of pettiness and can offer no defense. The metal C-clamp was fastened around his skull. I saw it and he recognized my look and he reached up and started to loosen it. He took it off and passed it to me.

I moved his hair about until I found two perfect circular depressions.

"I was thinking."

"Jesus, Shiloh, you weren't thinking very well."

He, of course, didn't hear this. I looked around the place. He'd cleaned up the loose glass and fixed the two spotlights. The magnifying lamp, still out of commission, was on the floor. I'd forgotten what brought me down there while he'd forgotten that I'd just arrived.

I noticed something for the first time. This little room was bounded on the north and west by the house's original foundation, his masonry comprised the eastern wall, and the support column for the living room fireplace marked the room's southern extremity. But the fireplace was in the middle of that wall, while Shiloh's facade continued all the way over to the other side of the house. His little compartment had a twin. Even as Shiloh was letting me in on his secrets, he was keeping me out.

He reached a hand out and I returned the clamp. He laid it on his desk. I pointed a thumb upstairs and gestured for him to follow me. I had wiggled halfway through the trapdoor when he yelled, "Boom!" I made a spastic leap to escape and fell down on the floor. Shiloh laughed and laughed.

The cake was on its second crop of matches by the time we reached the kitchen. The charred remains of the first group stuck out of the frosting like some wasted forest.

Shiloh blew the matches out as Alice and I cycled through signs we'd made:

Happy
Birthday
To You

Happy
Birthday
To You
Happy
Birthday
Dear
Shiloh
Happy
Birthday
To You

Alice's idea: Happy and Birthday were on opposite sides of the same piece of paper; To You was alone; and Dear and Shiloh shared a card. He got all choked up. Nothing could get him to wipe the tears off his face—they got hung up in his sideburns, they lined up on his quivering jaw.

Make a wish, I wrote on the back of To You.

"I wish that I had friends like you a long time ago. I wish that this ringing goes away."

You can't say what you wish for, added Alice.

"I didn't mean to say that out loud," Shiloh said, looking truly heartbroken.

I cut the cake. Crying had left Shiloh's mouth so dry that he had to drink water with each bite to get it down.

He thanked us both continuously.

Would he like his present now?

There was no way for him to get the words out. His meaty lips struggled to hold his face together. "But you already got me a cake."

Alice produced the package from the pantry, just a paper bag rolled over at the top.

He squeezed it, weighed it in his hands, bent it carefully. "I have no idea."

We pointed to the message written on the bag. It said, *Thanks for keeping an eye out for us.*

"Okay," Shiloh said, opening the bag. It was a white terry-cloth hat with "LIFEGUARD" embroidered around the crown. Alice had picked it up on clearance at the five-and-dime. He balanced it on his head like a book.

3
Apology

The first snowstorm of the year began in the middle of the night. We woke up to pine boughs unburdening themselves in chain reactions. Snow melting in the crotches of beech trees turned the bark a more steely shade of gray. Sodden red birches appeared as frayed as lengths of rope. Sticky snowflakes pinwheeled down.

Alice and I ran outside to throw snowballs at each other. Shiloh stood on the front step and watched. He was afraid to participate. What about his mask? I asked. He went down to the basement and got it. He adjusted the cotton batting so that it didn't bother his nose.

"Beware of Owlface!" Alice shrieked.

Shiloh sent a snowball over my head. He lifted the mask off so he could speak. "No ice balls."

I hit him in the stomach with a loosely packed projectile.

"Got me!" he shouted. He lobbed a snowball at Alice.

The mask made him look very sad, just the two eye holes and the suggestion of a beak. He didn't dodge or duck, but stood stock still. He had to face us for fear of taking a shot to the back of his head.

Ignoring me, Alice focused her battery on Shiloh.

He may have assumed he was giving as good as he was getting, but his throws, hindered by his tender ribs, were usually weak and off the mark.

Alice kept pounding him.

When he threw one my way, I intentionally moved into it. His eyes lit up when it caught me. "Argh," I said.

Alice made a lucky throw that burrowed into one of the eye holes.

"Time out," I distinctly heard him say, almost cheerily.

She got him again, after he'd lifted the mask off. She caught him on the chin. Certainly he was startled. I have heard that stress and injuries, even fatigue, can magnify involuntary reactions. I preface this because of what happened the moment she hit him—he relieved himself. He looked down, disappointed with his body's failure. "Oh Christ," he said. Alice was covering her mouth when a fastball caught the side of her head. I threw it. Yes.

Shiloh scoured the damp spot with a handful of snow.

"Don't blame me," Alice cried. She ran over to Shiloh. "Shiloh. Shy. Look at me. You're being such a baby. Here." She grabbed his jaw and tried to aim his face at her.

"Stop!" he said.

We stood in the middle of acres of diamonds.

Alice let go of him. "Fine," she said. She pleaded her case to me. "How was I to know?"

"You heard him call 'Time out.'"

"He was laughing. How long has it been since he's laughed about anything?"

I told her I didn't know, not as an answer, but to say I was washing my hands of this. What need did I have for excuses?

"You SOB, Thomas. So he pissed himself. He thought his head was going to fall off. What are you doing? Look at me."

I had decided to go inside. I wanted to do something for my feet. "I don't understand why you won't apologize."

"What's come over you people? I can't live like this. Tell me, Thomas, why are you sad?"

"Because you're lying."

I didn't think that she would try to leave and I didn't think her car would start and I didn't think it would make it up the slippery hill, but I was wrong three times.

I took a bath. With my ears underwater I thought I heard sounds from miles away, tractor trailers and railcars, vehicles approaching and pulling away. The whole world kept on moving while I passed time in a bathtub. My legs were bent double, my bony heels touched my bony ass. I'd gotten that tall.

Finally Shiloh knocked on the bathroom door. I climbed out of the tub. He wanted to pick up my spirits.

Making firecrackers, he explained, was not unlike making a cigarette. A piece of oak tag was trimmed to size and, with a bit of fuse protruding from one end, it was rolled up. To ensure a good seal, tape closed off one end and then wound in an overlapping manner to the business end and snugly around the fuse. He lit a safety candle in the fireplace and set it on the table before us. When he showed the fuse to the flame, it hissed and sparked. With a flip of his wrist, he tossed the firecracker into the wood pile. A sharp clap and bits of cardboard and bark rained down around us.

Shiloh made another and threw it into the fire. Ash and embers jumped out.

I got his notebook and asked him if he could hear these explosions. He shrugged.

Shiloh made a teeny little firecracker, about as big as a housefly, by putting a pinch of powder in the center of a piece of tape and twisting it up. He lit it and then placed it on top of his hat. I brushed it off. It went *pop!* somewhere inside the sofa. I told him not to do that.

I looked outside, at the failing light.

"Don't think about her," Shiloh said.

I don't know how long we waited. Sometime in the middle of the night, headlights came over the hill. Shiloh went to bed. Alice came in and climbed onto my lap. "This is my apology," is what she said.

4
Work

Clovis stopped by the house. It was out of the blue, entirely. Alice and I heard him coming over the hill. "Shit," she said. We both expected there was some problem with the money we'd given him. Maybe his boss had found out, or some other business. I didn't see why we had to answer the door, but Alice gave me a shove. The reason he stopped by was to see if I was interested in some short-term work. Was I in or out? he wanted to know. I made a snap decision. "Good," he said. "You'll need a hat and gloves." The next thing, I was in his truck.

He had his heater cranked over to bake. Most of the roads were just single lanes. He drove for half an hour. Apparently we'd gained some altitude because there was more snow here. He checked the side mirror, then turned the headlights off. "Now we're under the radar," he said. The truck rolled to a stop. Beyond a small rise I could see a farmhouse set far back from the road. Clovis handed me a folding saw. Christmas-tree season. What he wanted was trees from five to eight feet high. I should drag them down near the road and he'd be back in a few hours to help me pick them up. Where was he going to be? Well, he wasn't going to be sitting around with his thumb up his ass. That wasn't quite what I'd meant. Did I have any food? He passed me a pack of Twinkies. The trees he wanted me to go after were just above the road. If I did a good job, he'd pay me a dollar a tree. I jumped out and he drove off.

I went over the rise. Row after row of trees stretched before me. I realized what was going on. On the one hand, I might have just walked home. But where exactly was my home? Some of the trees had ribbons on them, and since they were about the right height, those were the ones I started on. The saw was a right triangle with a blade for a hypotenuse. The frame was old, but the blade was new and the teeth bit into the soft wood. Once the blade had passed completely through the trunks, the trees didn't fall so much as swoon, a sort of loss of balance where they pirouetted and then, overwhelmed, collapsed on the snow. (I thought of the deer we'd seen lashed to car hoods, their legs failing under them, that same crumbling, only to wind up mounted on plaques on the walls of rec rooms or smoky corners of bars, and now these trees cut down and lashed and mounted in the same rooms.) A car drove up to the farmhouse. A couple got out. Someone went inside; someone stayed on the porch and smoked a pipe. Lights went on and off throughout the house. I stood stock still. The figure knocked the pipe to clear the bowl before going in. I crouched on one of the felled trees and ate the Twinkies. The moon rose. The lights went out in the farmhouse.

Two at a time I dragged the felled trees over close to the road. There was no sign of Clovis so I went back and cut some more trees, a few shorter ones—they sort of hopped off their stumps and fell, as stiff as tin soldiers. I'd knocked down maybe fifteen of the smaller ones when I heard the truck pull up. I peeked over the embankment and Clovis motioned for me to toss the trees down to him. There wasn't much growing on the hillside. They just sledded down. He tossed them in the back of the truck. We took care of all the big ones and I went back to grab the shorts. I grabbed four and dragged them to the truck, let them roll down to him. Going back to grab the others, I stopped about twenty yards shy of where I'd dropped the last tree. A shadow moved up the hill a ways, hugging tight to the tallest row of pines. The folding saw was where I'd used it last. I trotted over to pick it up, and when I got to it, I saw a figure running toward me. He had something in his hands that could have been a baseball bat or a gun, but couldn't have been, say, a telescope. We had a moment where we hoped we hadn't seen each other and then we were in a footrace. The last thing that registered as I turned to flee was that either he had the biggest pair of boots I'd ever seen or he was wearing snowshoes.

When I got to the top of the embankment, I started hollering that we had to GO! I didn't dare yell earlier because I thought that since Clovis already had the trees, he might not be inclined to wait for me, and, another thing, since my pursuer didn't know I had a partner, he might have been holding his fire figuring to catch me before I could get a car started. The guy behind me made all sorts of awful curses and oaths. Also he seemed to take two steps to my one. I leaped down the embankment, the saw held high overhead. Clovis was hanging out by the tailgate, probably wondering what I was yelling about, but when he saw the way I was moving, he raced to the driver's door and got inside. I tossed the saw in the bed and went up front. He had the passenger door open and the truck was already rolling away. I threw myself inside. For a moment it looked like a clean escape; I checked the side mirror and there was no one back there. But Clovis couldn't find first gear, so the truck wasn't under power, just sort of rolling along with gravity. The guy came bounding down the little hill. He fixated on me. Things got real slow. I saw that it was an ax he carried, a single-bitted one. It was obvious that Clovis had no intention of stopping. With a jab the stranger pushed the ax through my passenger-side window, just as simple as could be. The glass hung in the air for a second and then it was all these noises at once. The radio played the last song I would ever hear. The guy at my window had to be about forty; he was breathing so hard, it was the same as being yelled at. He'd stuck the ax through the window with the blade pointing away from me, but neat as could be, he switched it around so the blade sat under my chin.

"Stop the truck," he said.

Clovis struggled to mate the gearshift with the transmission.

My pursuer took a hand off the ax handle to reach through the exploded window and lift the door-lock button. Clovis found a gear and my throat jumped toward the blade. The man turned the ax sideways so the metal only brushed against my cheek as it retreated through the window, and we rumbled off. I saw the man wind up to deliver the ax head into the rear tire, which, because it was spinning, wrenched the tool from his hands. Luckily Clovis's truck had a dualie rear end; the rear axle still had three good tires turning. The ax made a few loud orbits around the wheel well before it was ejected. My pursuer stood in the road, hands on his hips.

I reported what the man had done to the tire.

Clovis didn't turn the headlights on right away. A guy like that obviously didn't know when to quit.

"Sorry about your truck," I said.

I could hear the tire disintegrating behind us. Great black chunks of rubber flew off and littered the road. The night air came in through the smashed window.

"People don't show any sense," said Clovis. "He might have killed you, and over some trees. See if you can't plug up that hole with your jacket. I catch colds easy."

We went over hill and dale, through towns that I could never find again. Finally we pulled over beneath a highway underpass. The two of us got out to survey the damage. The outside tire had torn itself apart; only the two flapping sidewalls remained on the rim. And the window, which he checked, proved uncompromisingly broken, gone forever and always. Clovis said something about this eating into his profits. I counted the white circles of the tree stumps piled in back. There were fifty trees back there, thirty-one of which were mine. With thirty-one dollars I could buy two weeks' worth of food. But that maniac had ruined it for me. A panel truck drove up and parked tail to tail with us.

Clovis told me to wait for him inside the cab. A guy got out of the other truck and the two of them had a conversation. The guy in the other truck wore a great big ski jacket about two sizes too large for him. It almost covered his knees. Then they transferred the trees from our truck to the other one. The panel truck rumbled off and Clovis got back in.

He handed me a fifty.

I said thirty was okay, since that's what I'd agreed on and since his truck had taken a beating, not me. It wasn't coming out of his pocket, Clovis explained. I should take the fifty and that was that. I'd convinced myself I'd never see home again, but when he went around a corner I knew where we were.

It wasn't until I'd gone inside—when Alice screamed—that I noticed the thin red stripe along my jawbone where the blade had passed. She cleaned me up and bridged the cut with a series of bandages that pulled my face off center. It didn't hurt until the edges stiffened up overnight, and then it ached so that I tried not to talk or chew. The black hairs of my beard got confused coming back in and formed red eruptions that I couldn't keep my fingers off. When he saw me touching the scab, Shiloh reminded me, unless I wanted it to scar, I should leave it alone. I picked at it; a scar didn't seem entirely undesirable.

5
Weather

What seemed at first like an unremarkable storm hunkered down and refused to leave. For a while we listened to an AM station on Shiloh's portable, but once the battery died, that was that. We stoked fires in the living room and the entrance hall, but the heat wasn't adequate to fill the place. We didn't have storm windows, but the shutters actually worked, so Shiloh and I played rock-paper-scissors to see who had to go outside. I lost. I latched the shutters that latched and nailed shut the ones that didn't. Alice took a wooden ruler she'd found in the kitchen and used it to stuff rags in the chinks between the window frames and beneath the door.

We compartmentalized the house, shutting and plugging the doors to the basement, the pantry, the mudroom. We closed closets and improvised blinds with sheets and blankets. Like that, with everything as snug as a drum and the fires blazing, things weren't so bad. The floors stayed cold, along with the walls, but the air itself cheered us. The hot-water tank didn't have the capacity to warm the pipes, but if someone wanted a bath—it was the only way to flush the chill out of your bones—we'd set the stockpot on the stove.

Outside, chickadees and nuthatches huddled on the barbed wire. Drifting snow rose in peaks beside the fence posts, but the wind carved perfect, symmetrical gullies beneath the wire. Two days passed before a plow showed up.

As Alice pointed out it was only December, yet three feet of snow had piled up outside. We had to be self-sufficient if we planned to live out in the middle of nowhere. We decided to take our remaining cash and sock away a larder.

I dug the car out. Somehow in my exertion—and because the cold sapped the elasticity from my skin—the cut split open again. When the car refused to start, Shiloh brought the battery inside to warm it by the fire. Per his instructions I carried a tin bucket of hot ashes outside and spread them beneath the oil pan.

After we returned the battery to the car, Shiloh put a few drops of rubbing alcohol on the air filter. The car roared to life. We waited inside while the engine warmed up. When everything looked hunky-dory, the three of us got in. The upholstery was like sheet metal. Alice fishtailed up the hill, the front wheels clawing and the rear tires just sort of getting dragged along. The snow had transformed everything into soft humps, really a desert landscape with trees poking through. This wasn't civilization; civilization was something buried. The wind caused steady streams of snow to drift across the road, every icy particle playing leapfrog. Even the road echoed as if it was hollow, as ponds can freeze and then the water beneath trickle out, so a thin skin of ice arcs over emptiness.

We loaded up on things like potatoes, rice, and onions. They almost couldn't go bad. We grabbed a few pounds of butter to stash in the freezer. We grabbed chili mixes and tomato paste. Alice and Shiloh went nuts in the canned aisle, from kidney beans to mandarin oranges (a treat we planned to save for the darkest days). Shiloh grabbed another box of matches. Alice picked up a bar of beauty soap.

We filled two shopping carts. Twenty pounds of white rice. Evaporated milk. Two pounds of salt (this I think was for tanning the rabbit hides). A case of potted meat—for the protein. Three canned hams. Enough orange juice concentrate to fill a kiddie pool. Four dozen eggs—to be eaten before the potted meat. A flour sack as big as a pillow. Shiloh had the butcher put extra wrapping around ten pounds of hamburger, ten pounds of chicken thighs, and ten pounds of flank steak, figuring we could bury the whole cache in a snowbank. Peanut butter in a plastic pail. A bucket of shortening. Shiloh insisted on a five-pound bag of frozen smelt. Spaghetti. Ricotta cheese. Cottage cheese. American cheese. Cheddar from up the lake in Shelbourne. Did Alice know how to make pies? We got pumpkin filling, mincemeat, cans of blueberries, all kinds of apples, but especially red delicious, especially winesap. Cool Whip, Shiloh happened to know, could be stored indefinitely. Sweet peas. Green beans. Pinto beans. Creamed corn. Peanuts. Raisins. Toilet paper in gigantic "institution-size" twenty-four packs. Dried apricots. Cinnamon. Breakfast sausage. Sunflower seeds. Animal crackers. I craved Twinkies. More Clark bars. Ritz crackers. Nilla wafers. Cheese spread. Jiffy Pop. Little paper muffin cups. A canister of cloves. Orange marmalade. French's mustard. Or Gulden's? Four loaves of Wonder bread.

The cashier, a glass-haired woman, flirted with the bag boy who slumped at the end of that river of commerce. He made no attempt to impose any order on the bags. When a bag of cans came apart in his hands, he gave us a contemptuous look.

Shiloh tried to ease the kid's burden, told him not to worry about the bread, the eggs, the apples. As things came down the conveyor, Shiloh talked about how unimportant they were.

The initial total exceeded our resources by about thirty-six dollars. To help us out the cashier got a flier and started plugging in coupons for everything she remembered us buying, but we were still twenty over. Alice and I gave up our sweets, the ricotta, the cloves, the Ritz. Eleven dollars. We gave up the marmalade and the premade pie crusts. The smelt had to go, which depressed Shiloh. Alice and I reviewed the receipt, dumped the canned beets.

Finally we gave all our money and the kid released our food to us.

Shiloh pronounced himself rehabilitated and, using tin snips, removed his cast. He made no mention of the fact that his hearing still hadn't come back in any measurable fashion. The injured wrist looked slightly jaundiced, about what you would expect from something that had been hidden from the light for six weeks. He put it to his nose and sniffed it. He forced Alice and me to sniff it. What kind of smell was that? he wanted to know. We agreed, it was familiar, but there was something nauseating about it. Cloying, said Alice. The particulars of this stink had a hold on Shiloh. Why couldn't he remember where he'd smelled this smell before? He wouldn't wash the arm—it was evidence. He searched the fridge and pantry for the source, the all important original smell that his arm was derived from.

"He's off his fucking rocker this time," Alice said. "Who gets infatuated with their own stink? He has to let this thing go. If he shoves that arm beneath my nose one more time, I'll chop it off."

Narrowed things down, yet? I wrote on his notebook (he carried the notebook around again).

"Animal, vegetable, or mineral," he said.

You think you might be taking this a bit far?

"Odors are often considered a bastard nation of science, viewed as characteristics of matter rather than matter itself. It is possible that as a result of my accident, my olfactory sense has compensated for the damage to my auditory center. This is just a theory, but I have smelled something just like this arm." He presented the arm between us, although not so close that I might smell it casually. "This sort of identification, I recognize, is extraordinary. The arm is only the first step—I have to train myself to harness these new powers."

Due to the exponential growth of this neglected sense, Shiloh requested that Alice and I cut back on seasonings. He thanked us for our cooperation. Since smell comprised such a large component of taste, even a dash of pepper became an almost unbearably complex experience. Had someone left an onion uncovered? Yes. See, the onion molecules had stuck to the butter molecules and this made his French toast (no cinnamon, just eggs and bread) unappetizing. It's going to snow a little later, he'd say. And either it did or else a high front would come in (smelling of dear old Kentucky) to nudge the snow off to our north.

"It's not mineral," he told me, after inhaling the intoxicating pale skin of his forearm. "If you can imagine, mineral smells are *heavy*."

"Is there something, maybe you can detect it, Alice, cedary about this?" He presented the arm to us one more time.

She said, "If there was I'd put it in my closet."

Shiloh sniffed it again. "No."

Alice asked him if he'd smelled his bellybutton recently.

Shiloh lifted his shirt and picked at the moist hole. He put the finger to his nose.

Familiar?

"I can't believe it," he protested. "Why would my arm and my bellybutton smell the same? It doesn't make any sense. Look here." He showed her a section of his notebook. "I recognize over two hundred unique odors, but my arm ends up smelling like my bellybutton and I can't make the connection. It was right before me. I can't think with all these impossible smells. It's like my nose is farsighted. How can I eat when I'm smelling the kitchen, the miserable bathroom? A cold front is on its way here from the Arctic—I smell all of goddamn Canada, for Christ's sake—and I'm trying to differentiate my belly-button from my arm. And you know what? You want to hear my prediction? I'll tell you this: it's only going to get worse."

6
The Room Inside Is Immaterial

Shiloh came into our bedroom and woke me. He led me to the kitchen. Outside, the snow looked indigo. He opened up the faucet. I couldn't believe we'd run out of water.

"No," he said. "It's frozen."

This, he explained, was an emergency. Either we thawed the pipes before a hard freeze set in or else we said good-bye to indoor plumbing. Shiloh showed me how the pipes ran along the baseboard before they poked through the floor. If the pipes burst down below, then the well would empty right into the basement. But the basement floor was dry.

He sent me to restring blankets over the windows while he tended to the stove. We stoked fires in both fireplaces.

We ladled warm water on the pipes. After half an hour he'd coaxed a trickle of the coldest water into the sink.

I asked him where he'd learned to do this.

"In a tiny town called Improvisation," said Shiloh.

There were new angles on his face. His clothes sort of floated around him.

When I returned upstairs the place was sauna hot. Alice had kicked the sheets away. She was laid out on the platter of our bed like a Christmas goose.

7
Return to Improvisation

As resident expert it fell to me to find a tree for the house. I bundled up, tucked the hatchet in my pocket, and went out. The wind had made steep-sided wells around the trunks of trees and, in some cases, I could see all the way down to the shivering grass.

Unlike the symmetrical wonders at the tree farm, the hillside above our house was crowded with lopsided and dog-legged pygmies. I settled on a specimen that had, from one angle, a reasonable profile. I knelt down and started with the hatchet. I pulped the base until it was as white and hairy as a green onion. Once it fell I kicked the resilient fibers apart. I felt every bit a murderer.

Back at the house some trick of the wind caught the smoke rising out of the chimney and pushed it down across the field. It left the faintest stain on the empty snow. The patchwork of blankets hanging inside the windows made me want to return to that warm and filthy air.

I tugged the tree inside. The two of them had passed the time making ornaments. There were paper stars and paper birds. A garland of stick figures linking arms. Alice pointed to the ornaments she had made and by contrast I knew which belonged to Shiloh. He'd made a rocketship out of a couple of Sunkist cans. Alice pretended not to notice while I admired it. It was amazing what he could do with his hands. It had fins and a bullet-shaped top and there was a little gangplank that folded out, so you didn't know if it had just landed or was about to take off.

Whenever I kissed Alice's cold-scarred face, I'd find frizzled hairs she'd singed feeding wood to the fire. The palms of her hands were tough and dry. Her breasts filled her bras the way nutmeat filled shells. In bed we were a collision of bones. The horns of our pelvises rasped during sex. I'd tell her how much I loved her. I'd say how wonderful I felt. Your nose, I'd say, this smell, your fucking eyes. You're fire. She could have such fickle moods. She made the peace sign in front of her face, the tips of her fingers before her eyes, and then she stretched the arm in my direction, gesturing wires that connected our eyes.

"What? I see you."

But she didn't have anything else to say so we just looked at each other as the light left the room, a quarter past four. Was I sleeping? she wanted to know. No. Could she tell me something? About herself or about me? Herself. Sure. Sometimes a voice in her head told her to hate me.

Another morning, Alice and I entangled, trying to subdue each other, inflict points toward some colossal argument. Shiloh began banging pots. Alice and I dressed in the humid clothes we found trapped at the foot of the bed. We took the back stairs into the kitchen.

He'd gone nuts. A pile of scrambled eggs, something like blueberry Danishes, steaming sausages, and a pitcher of orange juice. He wore a red union suit with a white plastic belt and a red wool sock tugged over his head. He'd covered his sideburns, with something (flour?) so they appeared white.

"Ho, ho, ho," he said.

He grabbed Alice by the waist and pulled her onto his lap. "Have you been naughty or nice, little girl?"

She kicked and struggled, but while she was full of hostility, he had given himself over to the Christmas spirit and this made him invincible. He couldn't hear her threaten to box his ears. I sternly warned her not to.

She beat at Shiloh's arms, but he wouldn't release her.

"And what do you want for Christmas?" Shiloh asked.

"Let go of me, you idiot. You boob. You deaf catastrophe."

I pulled Shiloh's hands from around her.

"And what about you, little boy?" He let Alice go and pulled me onto his lap, "What do you want for Christmas?"

I petted his head. He flinched at first, but I was gentle, rubbing circles over his scalp. I touched his sideburns.

"Taste," he said.

It was powdered sugar.

Santa said, "All the good children get breakfast. After the food is gone, we can exchange presents."

We were always hungry, but we never really ate anymore—it was too much of a bother. I wrote a thank-you on his notepad. Merry Christmas. I didn't know what to do about Alice's outburst. I felt as though my most human parts were hibernating, just like the green earth, like

Alice's softness, those parts of Shiloh that had become insensate. All day we breathed that scalded air. That empty brightness outside couldn't reach us. We lived in a vacuum. Heat and sound didn't communicate the way they used to. We were left with degrees of friction. We rattled off one another like billiard balls. We rang like crystal. Nothing could change until those frozen rivulets on the windowpanes ran as meltwater.

Alice left the room—as a protest, I thought. When she came back she had a message for me. "Enjoy it while you can, because he really got us presents and when he sees we didn't do anything for him, he's going to hate us."

I pushed my food in front of her. After her announcement the piles of eggs, those glutinous Danishes, the fat that sweat through the sausages, all of it seemed a monument to our failures. Whatever could he have gotten for us? What did I want? What did I need? This secret would be revealed to me. I could offer nothing in return.

Shiloh made contented noises, clapping his lips and snorting.

"I ought to christen him with the rolling pin," said Alice.

Something about her tone made me feel that her complaints were as much with me as with him. Could these times be the ones I would pine for? And was her fury nothing more than a reflection of the strength of her character? And why couldn't I summon up a force capable of neutralizing it? Why couldn't I have rescued us from that house? And later I would drive into a hurricane to see a woman who refused to take my phone calls. And later I would lie about my age, my earning potential, the countries I'd visited, but never about my first love, never about Alice.

Shiloh reached out and patted my hand.

"Ignore her," I told him. "She's a flower that produces meanness instead of color."

"Don't talk to him," said Alice. "It's like people who talk to their dogs; it robs them of dignity."

"Ho, ho, ho," said Santa. He pushed himself up and headed toward the living room.

"How can you eat so much?" I asked Alice.

"Because I'm hungry, Thomas." With a sausage staked to her fork, she brought her thumb back to hook her hair over her ear. She chewed with her lips pouted to try and gross me out.

I lay my head in my arms and listened to her fork scrape across the plates. In the other room Shiloh threw wood on the fire.

Alice walked over to the pantry.

"You can't still be hungry?"

"And yet I am. What do you suppose might cause that?"

She stood facing me, defying me.

"Just the idea of this conversation exhausts me, Thomas."

I knew exactly what she meant. Sometimes I felt completely brittle inside. I said, "What do I care if you're tired?"

She put a cold hand under my jaw and tilted back my head. "I'm pregnant."

We had an impromptu staring contest. The longer I looked at her, the easier it became to convince myself that she was a stranger.

"Who are you?" I asked.

"I have to leave," said Alice. She leaned over and planted a kiss on my forehead.

"I couldn't wait any longer," Shiloh announced as he came into the room. He carried two packages wrapped in paper grocery bags. He handed one to each of us.

We received the packages without joy.

"Open them," said Shiloh.

Out of the rabbit fur he'd stitched a hat for Alice and a pair of mittens for me.

Alice held the hat to her nose.

"What does it smell like?" I asked her.

She pushed it in my face. It smelled like blood.

"I can't wear this," she said. She handed it back to Shiloh.

He didn't understand. He pushed it back to her. "Try it on."

Alice started crying. She tugged the hat over her head.

Shiloh looked to me for an explanation.

I took his notebook. Shiloh watched me write *She's pregnant.*

He leaned over Alice, shielding her body with his. "Thomas," he said, "come here."

I joined my arms with his and we crowded her, as if we feared she would float away.

Alice and Shiloh lost themselves in a storm of tears. When that passed Alice sat on my lap while Shiloh poured pancake batter directly on the stovetop.

"I bet I'm crushing you," said Alice.

"Crush me, please."

She bounced on my lap. She laughed.

I stood up, holding her in my arms. She was too light. Shiloh said, "Be careful with her." He pushed the chairs out of the way so I wouldn't trip over anything.

"Put me down," Alice said.

I carried her into the pantry.

"I won't," I said.

"I'll get dizzy."

"Merry Christmas!" shouted Shiloh.

I carried her into the living room and around the tree. Then I wanted to see Shiloh again and I carried her back to the kitchen. She wanted me to put her down, but I refused. I was trying to prove something to her about what I was capable of.

"I give up," said Alice.

I made her kiss me before I returned her to the ground.

Shiloh said, "I think I have enough rabbit left to make booties."

I tried to pick Alice up again. She pushed me away.

Shiloh insisted Alice eat half a stack of buckwheat flapjacks.

She didn't feel well. She cursed me for getting her agitated. Her upper lip got dewy. I escorted her outside and watched her be sick off the porch. I kissed her wet forehead. I looked at the mess on the snow. A tremendous waste of food.

8
Anything for Alice

After finishing the eggs she moved to the flank steak.

With all the meat she took in, her body produced a new oily

sheen and a particular rankness that startled me beneath the close sheets. Her moods improved. She wasn't nauseous again. Her breasts returned and then her butt and belly, too. Heat poured from her body. I liked the feeling of one of her legs over my abdomen. I looked forward to her being huge. I wanted her conspicuous.

If the baby was a boy? Solomon, said Alice; Earlie, suggested Shiloh (after his first friend); Lake, I said, Lake Lowe. Lake Mahey, said Alice. What about the middle name? Lowe, regardless. Lake Lowe Mahey. And a girl? June, suggested Shiloh, for the month we'd arrived. Rain, said Alice. What about Brook? I asked. Alice thought it should be Shiloh's choice. He'd need to think about it. Would it be June? Would it be Rain? Brook had been my suggestion; it wouldn't be Brook, he concluded, since then I would have named both the boy and the girl.

Our baby would never wear shoes in the summer, never wear clothes, swim like an otter, grow as brown as a bean. I would take a job down in the valley. Any job. It wouldn't matter. Even though all the green life had receded around us, it hadn't disappeared, but only traveled inward. If, in a snow-choked valley, a hothouse could produce rows of perfect poinsettias, couldn't Alice's body contain a slow uncurling?

And did it anticipate us as much as we anticipated it? Here we were coming into January and thinking about a date in August. This was good for Alice. She'd never been more vibrant. She could crush me in her arms.

And who would we be? Alice and Tom. Shiloh would be Uncle Shy—what a gift for an orphan, a nephew, a niece, family. "She'll be Rain," declared Shiloh. "In August you always need rain." Rain Lowe Mahey.

On New Year's we stood in the snowy pasture and measured ourselves against the stars. When the hour came we heard the distant report of shotguns celebrating. Something about the spaces between people made you want to be heard. Those faint popping sounds were our connection to the world. Shiloh asked if we heard them. Did *he*? No, but he'd expected them. From his pocket he produced a firecracker he'd fashioned for the occasion out of two tin cans and Alice's sisal rope. Would Alice mind? Just this once. He buried it in the soft hummock of the haystack. From the top of the meadow, we watched the spitting fuse burrow into the mound and then a yellow-orange blast. A ring of snow jumped. The shock registered in our chests as the hay drifted across the pristine field.

We stamped our feet. Down in the valley, in some silent town, sparkling arcs launched into the sky, blue, green, white. Ropes of colored light sent up to lasso what? To us they described feathers or ferns. Shiloh explained the chemistry of colors: sulfur, copper, magnesium. What must have been the grand finale presented pinwheels like bouquets of flowers, silent reports that expanded and contracted in the same instant, a flurry of mortared shells that lit the valley. 1974.

As the two of us cuddled on the living-room sofa, Alice asked if I'd considered our never-ending supply of firewood. Had I compared the rate of consumption to the progress of time? Her point: in a little more than a month, we'd burned more than a third of our stores. We'd put in three rows of wood. We had two left. That and a scattering of bark, spiders' eggs, and dust. If the weather didn't get any worse, the next row might take us to the end of January, the final row to March. Wasn't that something? I asked. She named that thing: insufficient.

When the fire died I swept the floor and poured the dustpan over the coals—sparks as small as stars shot up the chimney. Our Christmas tree left the house the same way.

Shiloh got my attention. He signaled me to follow him into the basement. What I'd been doing was rubbing Alice as she sprawled on the sofa. I tugged socks over her feet and tucked them beneath the covers. Kissing her sticky chin I tasted canned peaches.

The opening to Shiloh's crawl space glowed like a furnace door. I poked my head in. He had half his hand crammed in his mouth. His toolbox was open on the table.

I scrambled in. Luckily his lamps put some heat in the air. A sort of hazy smoke spun off them where dust smoldered. I held my hands up near the bulbs to let the heat infuse my blood, but my twining shadows only served to annoy him.

I reached up and grabbed the back of the aluminum reflectors. As soon as I touched it, I knew I had burned myself. Shiloh took his hand out of his mouth. "See?" he said. "Now you burned yourself."

I found instant relief placing my hand on the cool metal of the toolbox.

"You have to touch everything?"

We stared at each other for a moment. He pointed at a spot on the table.

It was a tooth, a bicuspid, I believe. A bit of flesh clung to it the way fruit will stick to a pit. I pointed from it to his mouth.

He yawned to show me its old home.

What's this about? I asked him.

"It just came out," he said.

No, my chin argued.

He picked the tooth up and pushed it back in place. Maybe it would take root? He couldn't let it rest. He balanced it on his tongue.

Bite something hard?

This was why he'd invited me down, he had some theories and some countertheories. What had started the whole thing was this overwhelming sensation of looseness. His body was feeling sort of arbitrary, kind of accidental. He thought it might be related to his accident. I wanted him to stay with the tangible, with this tooth he'd lost. He asked me, Did my teeth feel pliant? Did they have some give? It was with a real sense of apprehension that I checked. Everything seemed basically rooted. That was the way he understood it, that the roots sort of anchored them to the jaw.

But, see, we, the two of us, we're eating all these soft foods now. There wasn't any sort of pressure keeping the teeth *in line*. (Every so often he picked the tooth up and reinserted it.) Was he suggesting that our diet had caused this? This was the heart of his problem; he couldn't be sure. He'd sort of gone around conducting an inspection, but it was hard for him to know how much of the wiggle he had felt was just a product of that more general looseness. And how loose, I wanted to know, was the tooth that had fallen out? That was the thing, it was the first tooth he'd noticed and he'd just kept working on it until it came out, but some of the other teeth, he couldn't be sure—he was missing what you call clinical data—they seemed looser. Which one bothered him? For instance? Sure. His main teeth. The front ones? For instance. And which other ones? All of the other ones.

I wiped my hands on my pants legs and he scuffed his teeth dry with his shirt sleeve. They seemed solid to me. I tried putting opposing forces on the pair, but they didn't want to move.

A-okay, I reported. He checked for himself. Was I sure? Positive. This didn't reassure him at all; if anything it made him more uncomfortable. *One bad tooth is all,* I wrote. What if it was a good tooth and he'd just refused to leave it alone? I reasoned that if it really was perfectly healthy, then he'd never have been able to get it out. It took a long time, he explained. I opened my hands. What's a long time? The thing had kept him from sleeping. Not knowing had driven him crazy. Not knowing? Whether it was loose or not. He'd had to tap it before it finally came out. Tap it? Right. With your finger? At first. Then? With a wooden spoon. Was that it? No. No? With a screwdriver; with a screwdriver and a hammer. I was adamant; he had to stop this. What should he do? Maybe he could put it back? He was afraid he would swallow it. I told him he had to stop fucking with his teeth. Did it, he wanted to know, mar his smile? He showed me every smile he knew. His smile was intact, I promised. The ringing, he told me, was part of the problem. Does the tooth hole hurt? I asked. Terribly. Maybe it would keep his mind off his ears. It possibly might.

Where I had touched the lamp shade, I now had a little white blister.

"And the other thing," said Shiloh, "it refuses to stop bleeding."

9
Idyll

Sometime the previous summer, one of those days where the warm air sat close to the earth and the only way to enjoy it was in a car, Alice and I found ourselves in the middle of a broad valley. It must have been a remnant of a prehistoric ocean or a once great river. We'd reached a place behind all the old familiar mountains where shallow ponds were strung together and didn't flow into anything, just gathered the rain and gave it back to the clouds. And the ponds were so shallow, they could be tens of acres and yet we saw people standing in the middle who weren't past their waists. What disappointed us was that there were people everywhere. Everywhere we saw temporary communities, teepees and yurts and circus tents. Tire tracks knifed into the soggy ground where someone had left the road and headed for some farther corner of the remote. Those people seemed so irresponsible to us, no home, no rooms. (By now they surely have retreated—Baja, the Keys, the coast of Texas, farther south.) We decided they weren't like us. They were nomads, while we were pioneers. They were unattached, where we were rooted. They were careless.

We came across a car accident—it was hardly that, but what else to call it? It looked as though the driver had wandered onto the soft shoulder. The black earth swallowed the van's wheel and now the vehicle was on its side. We were the first people on the scene. The place smelled fantastic because the van had crushed a lot of spearmint before coming to a rest. The stuff grew everywhere alongside the road. Two guys with bushy mustaches and high, dull hair stood imagining that the van was back upright, but without any idea of how they might achieve this. Sitting on the road was a girl with cascading ringlets of red hair and strings of blood coming out of her mouth. She didn't seem to be in any pain. The blood was like cobwebs.

Maybe we expected the guys to come running to us. They paid us no mind, but remained on the far side of the van supposing how it might get back on the road. Alice asked the girl if she was okay. She'd bitten off the tiniest piece of her tongue, but this wasn't a pressing issue for her. When enough blood welled up in her mouth, she sort of blew it out between her teeth. One of the guys came around. "She's fine," he said. Was anyone else hurt? (Something about the lack of symmetry—two guys, one girl—I anticipated a body pinned beneath the van.) They were all fine; she was just bleeding a little. Could we take them somewhere? Call them a tow truck? "People are coming," the guy said. The girl got up and wandered out through the spearmint. We could see for miles in every direction. Whoever they were waiting for was still a long way off. After getting back in the car, we waited to see that they didn't change their minds.

A few hours later, returning home, we came back through the valley. The van was still overturned but the people were gone. As we drove past I saw two dark trails where the girl had dragged her bloody hands over the furry leaves and purple flowers of the spearmint.

10
Grow!

Alice unbuttoned her pants so Shiloh could put his ear down at the base of her belly. But he's stone-deaf, I argued. He can feel vibrations, said Alice. Yes, I said, and he has a hypersensitive sense of smell.

Shiloh made sure to listen each and every day. He was keeping a vigil, not over Alice, but over the baby. He'd palpate her and nod his head, as though being sworn to a fantastic secret.

"How big would it be right now?" Shiloh wanted to know.

Alice took his pen and drew the letter *o* on her belly, as it might appear on a Bible page.

She couldn't get enough heat. I moved the sofa forward until it sat just off the hearth. She liked to lie with her back to the fire and let the flames bake her. When the underwires in her bras started to cut into her skin, she had Shiloh remove them. Lying on her side, she was forced to clutch her boobs.

Her face became buttery. Where before she had cheekbones, now there were cheeks.

She sat up and adjusted the pillow that she used to keep her feet above her womb—to give the baby the heavy blood.

I asked her if she would let her ex know.

She couldn't tell him. He would be too happy to let the news kill him. The guy had wound up in the hospital for loving her. I felt ashamed; he had all that tragedy to recommend him.

A few inches beneath her bellybutton, Alice drew an *o* the size of a honeybee. Could it be that big? That big. How big would it be when the snow melted? A fist.

Dark Night
When Strange Sounds Are Heard
and Ominous or Lovely Visions
Are Conjured Up

TWO MEN

One thing led to another and by the time they reached New York, it was already the second week in January. They scheduled a meeting for early the next morning. That night the two men stayed at a monastery in Brooklyn Heights. The brothers operated a soup kitchen, oversaw after-school programs, and hosted a free health clinic. They patrolled the streets in their robes and sneakers. Tough-looking youths lined up to high-five the monks. The younger man was quite impressed with the brothers. To him they seemed like God's firemen, the way they were always rushing out to attend to some emergency.

The two men took their dinner alone.

"It is very tangible here," said the older man.

"I thought the same thing," said the younger man. "It would be a rewarding place to work."

They sat at a square table that had four mismatched chairs. The floor was painted cement.

"I expect you might miss the travel," said the older man.

"Are we talking about me?"

"It would be a mistake, I think."

"Do you imagine I would be reluctant to work so hard?" asked the younger man.

"It is not that. I think the allure of the tangible would evaporate. Faith is a tool to allow human beings to contemplate the divine. It is wasted if it is only used to consider other human beings."

The younger man turned his colleague's words around in his head. "The implication, clearly, is that your choice is somehow more right than theirs."

"And what is the significance of that?"

The younger man did not know.

In the morning they took a train across the river. When they arrived at the rectory, a police officer stood out front drinking coffee from a paper cup. He watched the two men let themselves in.

They found the archbishop sitting outside his office reading a newspaper. He wore a coat over his cassock and rubber overshoes.

"It's too dim to read in my office," the archbishop explained. He folded the paper and stood up. Then he escorted them in. There were two leather club chairs for the men to sit in. The archbishop took his place behind a wide, cluttered desk.

Indeed it was a dim space. Walnut paneling absorbed any light that squeezed through the three narrow windows. A rather large painting hung behind the archbishop. In the painting's foreground Dutch colonists shook hands with painted savages. The background was idealized nature, deer peeking through the bushes, birds roosting on every branch. Seeing the younger man notice the painting, the archbishop swiveled in his chair. "My father. He called it *Faithful Commerce*."

"Of course," said the older man.

"A very brash man was my father. See, he signed his name in red."

They considered the painting some more, longer, indeed, than the younger man thought it warranted.

The archbishop began. "For the past six months, I have heard some disturbing rumors. I had intended to get to the bottom of the matter myself, but I've run into an impasse. This is why I asked to see you. We are all aware of that narrow bridge between the known world and the world of faith. In my sermons I have often relied on a crude analogy, that of walking on a rope bridge where each step draws into question the integrity of the surface upon which one stands. It seems I have reached a point where I am no longer certain whether I stand on the side of faith or heresy."

"I doubt you are a heretic," said the older man. "Heretics usually have conviction on their side and this is not something you present with."

The archbishop folded his hands across his chest. "It is my understanding that in order to be considered for canonization the blessed must have led an exemplary Christian life. They must, in short, have, in their person and deeds, represented that which we consider most holy. In addition, they must either have died for their faith, by their faith, or with their faith. Is this all true?"

The younger man responded. "These are some of the conditions, yes."

"I am losing control of my flock," said the archbishop.

The older man leaned forward in his chair. It seemed, at first, that he had something to say, but then, reaching out his right hand, he picked something off the carpet. He held it out. It was a sewing needle.

The archbishop set the needle on the leather blotter in the center of his desk.

"And how is it that you have come to lose them?" the younger man asked.

"They think God's ear is deaf to them, and so they have turned instead to other means. They direct their prayers to a dead boy."

"A dead boy," repeated the older man.

"Somewhere in that newly minted blight outside these doors, they insist, is secreted away a corpse, the body of a boy," said the archbishop. "They are reluctant to speak of him with me. I hear whisperings at confession. They are concerned that the Church will try to cover this up. He was homosexual, this boy. A drug user, most likely.

It's as though they've constructed God in their image instead of the other way around. Tell me, can one who lived a life blind to God's will find himself privileged to His graces?"

"So your flock has faith, but no virtue," said the older man.

"There is more false virtue than virtue, more false faith than faith. Yet this dead boy galvanizes them."

"When did you first hear about this boy?" asked the younger man.

The archbishop put his hand to his head. "Last spring I heard a story about a young woman who overdosed. Her companions just watched her fade away. One of them knew of the dead boy. I guess in their state it made some sense, the symmetry of it. They had a dead boy stowed away and now this dead girl on the filthy floor. They brought the boy out and laid him by her side. It was, I understand, meant as some type of macabre joke. Yet when they set the boy down, the girl began to breathe."

"These witnesses had been high, of course," said the younger man.

The older man turned toward his colleague and gave him a puzzled look.

"Influenced by the intoxicants."

"Heroin," said the archbishop.

"Was that the only miracle they have spoken of?" asked the older man.

"This summer there was a fire in a tenement house just a few blocks from here. Somehow three adults clawed their way through a brick wall in order to escape. I saw the hole they made. The brick came apart like gingerbread, but just in that one spot. It certainly saved their lives. Of course they claimed the dead boy gave them the power to get out. Now they pray to him when buying scratch-off tickets at the store. Every five-dollar winner is a testament to his powers."

"And what of the losing tickets?" asked the younger man.

The older man reached across to clap his colleague on the arm. "Even true believers don't expect that every wish can be fulfilled. He's not a genie in a lamp after all."

"Yes," said the archbishop, "but they covet him in the same way."

"I would like to see this boy," said the younger man.

"As would I," said the archbishop. "That's the problem. Apparently no one has seen him in months. We've had two break-ins at the church. In the first incident somebody got into the basement by taking a door off its hinges. They poked through a few closets and made off with a case of the wine we use for the sacrament. We thought the wine might have been the aim. A week later one of the priests intercepted a man who was in the process of breaking into this rectory. We learned that a rumor had circulated that we were in possession of the boy. I addressed the congregation directly, but rather than mollify them, it only heightened their anxiety. They've lost their center, so to speak."

"Hence the police officer we passed out front," said the older man.

"Yes. A courtesy from the mayor. But let me continue. About three months ago I was hearing confessions when a man approached me to inquire if I might be interested in the boy."

"How do you mean 'interested'?" asked the younger man.

The archbishop lifted the sewing needle from his blotter and placed it inside his desk drawer. "This individual wanted to know if the Church would want to take possession of the dead boy."

"And what did you say?" asked the older man.

"I never forgot that we were talking about a human being. At the least he deserved to be accorded the right of burial. I told this man that we'd accept the body. I planned to turn it over to the authorities and let them proceed. Maybe they could determine if there had been foul play. However, I had misunderstood this person's intentions. He wasn't offering to give me the boy. What he proposed was that the Church buy the body."

The younger man leaned forward. "Did he have a figure in mind?"

"He asked for fifty thousand dollars."

The two men were silent for a moment.

"And this was when you contacted us?" asked the older man.

"I spoke with the cardinal, who spoke with Rome."

"Is there some way that you can put us in touch with this man?"

"I have no means of contacting him. He shows up out of the blue. Since our initial conversation he has been by twice, the last time about a week ago. He seemed quite disturbed. He believes he's in some danger. I don't doubt he's correct. There are people who would like very much to find him. I again offered to take the boy. He said he was getting frustrated with the Church. His exact words were: 'I can't believe the fucking Roman Catholic Church, after chasing charlatans and frauds for two thousand years, can't get their shit together to conduct a simple transaction when they have a chance to get their hands on the genuine article.' Then he told me the price had gone up to a hundred thousand." The archbishop trained his face into a tragic little smile.

The older man reached up and stroked his thinning hair. "When you see him next, please tell him he will have his ransom."

"That is your solution?" the archbishop asked, shaking his head. "How ironic. I had been concerned about the congregation's faith and yet you will have me tithe them to satisfy an immoral character."

"It would be immoral of us," said the older man, "to leave a person in bondage when we have the power to free him."

"Bondage," said the archbishop. "I suppose. I am reluctant to consider the corpse a slave."

The younger man pressed his hands on the arms of his chair. "Would it be possible for my colleague and I to have a few words alone?"

"Of course," the archbishop said, standing up. "I will wait outside, just let me know if you need anything."

The two men stood while the archbishop let himself out.

The older man walked over to get a better look at the painting hanging behind the desk. "You want to preach caution, perhaps."

"It is not this."

The older man turned around. "If you did, I would not think less of you." He set his hands on the archbishop's chair. The leather sighed. He grimaced.

"When you brought up the idea of bondage, you weren't talking about the dead boy, but about the ransomer."

"And you have a question about that."

The younger man sat back down and put his head in his hands.

"My question touches only the periphery of the matters we've discussed this morning."

The older man looked down. There, beneath the archbishop's desk, two rubber overshoes waited side by side. "You want to know the process by which the living are plighted to the dead."

The younger man extended a finger toward the ceiling of the room. "I think you are mistaken when you discuss the merits of the tangible. There is no great difficulty in pledging oneself to the dead or to God. Rather, it is where the living give themselves to the living that the world turns."

"What do you see as our purpose?" asked the older man.

"We seem to serve at the whim of frauds and fakers. We hope to chart God's mystery and instead we find ourselves exploring human passions."

"Are you making a renunciation?"

"I have nothing to renounce," said the younger man. "I have never seen a miracle. Nor do I expect I ever will."

"What about the boy who spoke Latin?"

"You remember his physician? He had compassion for the child's family. He could not save their son; perhaps he discovered a way to give them a measure of retribution."

"And your priest in China?"

"Maybe he had a friend in the army who concealed him. Or, more likely, one of his former parishioners coveted his bones."

"Whom do miracles serve?" asked the older man. "Who is their beneficiary?"

"You wish to lead me in a circle," said the younger man.

"Is it the prospect of a dead boy that upsets you?" asked the older man.

"I don't see how I can answer that question."

The older man raised his eyebrows. "Why is that your answer?"

"Because should the dead boy prove a dead boy, what joy is there? And should the dead boy prove a saint, he would not cease being a dead boy."

There was a light knock on the door. The older man stepped

from behind the desk. He brushed his trousers with his hands. The younger man opened the door. The archbishop took a step inside his office. In his hands he held a crumpled brown paper bag.

"There is one other thing," said the archbishop. "When the gentleman came to see me last, he gave me something. I don't know if it will be of interest to you."

The older man unrolled the neck of the bag.

"And did he explain the point of this?" asked the older man.

"He said it belonged to the boy."

The older man reached in and pulled the object out. It was a calf-length white athletic sock.

I

Alice Ate Rabbit

Alice ate rabbit. Alice ate butter beans. Shiloh and I made a thin soup from the bones. Sniffing his hands Shiloh recalled the smelt that he had returned for the sake of the budget. We craved sugar and beets and rhubarb pie. And we had forty-one rolls of bathroom tissue.

At night Alice and I retired under a strata of blankets. Falling asleep required conquering the fear of being buried alive, an instinct that might be traced back to our earliest cave-dwelling ancestors. Just as we dropped off, gravity would hiccup and our feet would kick and claw beneath us. One time Alice scared me to the edge of death when, returning to our bed, she sat squarely on my chest. I tried to complain, but her weight pushed a whistle out—searching for my face she stuck her fingers in my mouth.

Many times the floorboards' creaking recorded trespassers who entered the room and curled beneath the bed. And in the loneliest hours I know I heard men stomping about on the roof. I could hear the scrape of hobnailed boots. If they came down off the ridgepole to stand by the dormers, only the blankets would have prevented them from watching us sleep. I expected to wake to breaking glass and their dark bodies rushing in.

*   *   *

The three of us sat in the living room. It was warmer after Shiloh and I discovered that the entrance-hall fireplace had a damper. That we only learned of it at this late date was the saddest story any of us knew. Closing the damper was a simple matter of shaking a lever until two metal doors swung down. The organ-pipe hum that, for months, we'd thought of as part of the house, stopped. Just how much wood we'd wasted was the only question worth considering.

"The damper," Shiloh said. "That is something everyone knows about."

Alice remembered hearing something about how there were supposed to be chains one could look at to determine whether the damper was in the open position.

"Some are like that," said Shiloh, "but this system was different."

We had started on the final row of wood.

2

Visitors

Alice and I were sitting in front of the living-room fireplace when something came down the chimney. It made a racket, scraping soot and creosote on its way. A black cloud pushed into the room. Alice vaulted the sofa and stopped halfway up the stairs. Did I get a good look? Did she? I sneaked back into the room, my fists held in a boxer's guard. In a pinch my will would cave. I edged to the woodpile and chose a club. I saw nothing unusual in the fireplace. I examined all sides of the sofa. I looked behind the window curtains. The room was empty.

I told Alice that whatever it was, it must have rolled under the sofa. Since I couldn't simultaneously lift the sofa and look under it, I asked her to be my eyes. She came down the stairs. I bent over to lift it up and Alice stopped me. Did I have to stick my fingers underneath? Couldn't I lift it up by the arm? This seemed like sound advice. I hoisted my end up off the floor. Well? There was nothing there. Was she sure?

"Behind you," she said.

I dropped the sofa and danced away. A crow perched on the corner of the woodpile.

"Open the door and I'll shoo it out," I told Alice.

"I think it's probably hurt. It landed in the fire."

It looked perfectly normal, except that it had fallen out of the clean world and into ours.

"Do crows carry rabies?" Alice asked.

"No," I said—though I had no idea then and still don't.

"I think we ought to examine it."

It seemed perfectly reasonable coming out of her mouth. I unhooked the curtain and shook it out.

"Are you scared?" Alice asked.

I found it a bit unnerving when the animal cocked its head. I tried to toss the blanket on top of him, to sort of float it down. With one flap of his wings, he escaped my trap.

Alice recognized its plan. She yelled, "No!"

It probably thought it was in the clear until it struck the glass.

It was still shuddering when I reached it. One wing was tucked beside the body and the other stuck out, how an elegant man in a cape might take a bow. Some of the feathers had been singed. The eyes were only halfway closed.

"Is it dead?" Alice asked the only question.

"It's alive," I said. Who could tell?

Alice carried it upstairs in the cradle of her arm.

In the middle of the night, Shiloh took a spill on the stairs; my ears perceived shock troops coming up. I expected the door to be shivered in. Alice forced me wide awake. We found him in the kitchen, dabbing the back of his head with our only sponge.

He said, "I was heading down to the basement and I thought I heard someone talking. When I turned around, my feet skated out from under me."

Alice found a goose egg above his ear. Otherwise he didn't look so beat up.

I scratched a note, *Just your head?*

"Talk to me," he said, his voice sputtering.

"Can you hear, Shiloh?"

Alice wrapped some ice in a dishtowel and showed his hand how to hold it in place.

He turned to Alice. His eyes were wild. "The voice said, 'Alexander Stephen Mills,' which is my given name. Who do you think it could have been? Alexander Stephen Mills. I'd give anything to see the people who know him."

I asked Alice for her diagnosis.

She believed he was in a dream when he came down the stairs. She thought he needed a night of rest. The isolation had him conjuring up long-lost friends. She said she wouldn't be the least bit surprised if he remembered none of this in the morning.

I wanted him to return to his bed so I could return to mine.

"Shiloh is a massacre and Tanager is the name of my favorite bird. This describes perfectly how I felt at eighteen." He stood up and tossed the dishtowel in the sink. "I'd like to thank you both for coming out." He took the stairs one at a time. "I'll probably start hearing as soon as one of you says something interesting."

When the crow came back to life, Alice named it Phoenix, after the Egyptian bird that lived for five hundred years above the desert, then fell in fire, only to rise again. These were things she knew just from living.

It was the fire stoker's job to collect grubs and spiders. Sometimes when I peeled back the bark, I found the worms they call red wigglers. Shiloh said it was a shame how the weather was outside. When the ground thawed we could use his electric prod to collect nightcrawlers. We speculated that a crow fed such a diet might grow bigger than an eagle. I can't explain what that meant to us, the idea of a giant black bird to do our bidding.

We endured a series of disparate storms. Gray, dark clouds that brought an early dusk and a slanted salting of snow. Another time the air turned white and snow came down in fluffy clumps. Finally a swirling wind tried to pull the clapboards off the house—the air was so agitated that the snow still drifted down a day later under a clear blue sky.

I was shoveling the porch when the plow truck came down the hill. The driver raised his hand as he went past. I shuffled out across the yard to stand beside the road. At the bottom of the hill, he turned around. The plow pushed a dense wave of snow above my knees before he came to a stop.

Leaning across the cab the driver cranked his window down. He wore a scruffy leather cap that sort of matched his face—he had windburned cheeks and acne scars. Maybe he was forty. The front seat was littered with newspapers, pull-top cans of soda pop, an empty box of doughnuts. A fresh mound of red sand, a shovel, and Styrofoam coffee cups were all that was in the bed. On the radio Johnny Paycheck sang "She's All I Got."

"Something wrong?" he asked. A CB radio sat wedged on the dash. I introduced myself. I said, "I always see you driving by."

His name was Bill Legg. He said, "It's called a job, Thomas."

It seemed that there was a slight embedded in his words.

"I was just digging us out," I said.

"How many of you living there?"

"All of us," I said, trying to redeem myself with a joke. He wore these big wool mittens and he rubbed one beneath his nose. "There's three of us."

He looked at the house. "I believe it's owned by a bank in Montpelier."

That was that, I figured. We'd been found out. And where could we go next? Jail?

"I don't imagine they'll give you any trouble. There's hundreds of places just like this scattered across the county. It used to belong to a Dutch family who ran a dairy farm, but they were what you might call trendsetters; they got out of the business."

This was exciting and worthless news.

"At one time they owned the whole hill, I believe."

"What was their name?"

"I'm useless with names." He pointed a mitten at Alice's car. "Does that thing run?" The Plymouth was buried up to the fenders.

"Sure," I said. In what I hoped would be a reassuring gesture, I waved my arm toward town.

"You and your friends have a phone?"

I tried to explain how we were doing a back-to-the-basics thing.

"You got to have someone check up on you from time to time," said Bill Legg.

"We get along fine." I really believed it.

"Suit yourself, I guess." He shifted his attention back to the road, forgetting us.

I said, "Thanks for plowing, Mr. Legg."

"You're welcome, Thomas."

He took a mitten off so we could shake hands. Then he rolled up the window. I was standing there, waving. He motioned for me to move. He raised the plow, drove into the driveway, and dropped the blade about an inch behind the bumper of Alice's car. Backing up he dragged the snow into the road. Then he reset the blade and pushed it up the hill.

Alice and Shiloh waited for me in the kitchen. They wanted to know what had possessed me to flag down a complete stranger. It didn't seem any more reckless than hiding behind the shades. It was a relief to see a new face.

Shiloh apprenticed himself to the cross-country skis. He taught himself how to walk up slopes with his toes pushed apart. Pointing himself down the field, he would glide toward the ravine's edge. If he tried to change direction, the equipment came apart. He said if not for the ravine, he'd never stop. He said the person who could thread his way between the trees would live in harmony with winter. I watched him from the dormer windows. Sometimes he would scream and shout in pure exhilaration.

I had an enormous headache. Every now and again I launched into a violent coughing fit, as though some part of me had come loose inside my chest. Alice asked me not to talk, as it only seemed to exacerbate my condition. Something about my cough drove her to distraction. Alice would stroke the back of her faithful pet and sigh if she sensed I might start up again. When I complained that the temperature in the room seemed to dip and soar from one moment to the next, she accused me of gross exaggeration. Phoenix refused to caw, but liked to stretch its mouth into a yawn, which is what it did from its roost on the headboard as I stole from the room.

Several hours later Alice found me huddled in her car. She led me back inside. What was wrong with me? she wanted to know. The bird whispered in her ear.

"You have a fever, silly goose. Didn't you notice how you weren't yourself? This is what you deserve for getting so run-down. I expect the bug was a gift from your snowplow friend and I assume it will make its rounds."

She kept me in bed, brought me fruit cocktail with oatmeal, took over the fire-stoking chores. She put Phoenix in the closet and removed the curtain so the light came in. Nothing was expected of me. I drifted on the verge of sleep and ate when I was fed.

From our bed I watched Alice perform the daily miracles of arching her back, twisting her hair. My chest ached from laughing when she danced for me.

It took a few days, but slowly my energy returned. To mark my recovery we had sex. It had been a couple of weeks since the last time and we were both self-conscious. Our happiness embarrassed us. How can I recapture that humility? Nobody has that anymore. People get nude, but where is the nakedness? Everyone's just so proud of themselves. I slept straight through the night. In the morning I was cured, but Alice had my fever.

"I don't like this," I said.

"I suppose we all have to pay the price for your civility."

"I mean because of your condition."

"I know," said Alice. "I guess I'll drink lots of water."

"Can a baby get a fever?"

"What do I know?"

"We should probably have a book or something."

"That is exactly the kind of father I always expected you to be."

I wanted to ask her if she meant that.

She told me to fetch Phoenix out of the closet. I said what if she had caught the fever from the bird? How dare I blame the bird.

My second duty was going downstairs to feed the fire.

There might have been a hundred logs left. The same quantity hadn't lasted a week in early December, but now it might bring us to the cusp of March. I tried to remember what March was like.

I went upstairs to look for Shiloh. He was in his room engrossed in the skis. We admired them for a while. He gave all his attention to the way the boot mated with the binding. He'd shake his head, pull them apart, and then refit them. "You tend the fire?" he asked.

I showed him the match I planned to use. I hadn't noticed before, but half of one wall was covered in a different wallpaper; bright floral vines contrasted with the burnished gold on the other walls. Something like that would have driven Alice mad. I pointed to the mismatched wallpaper.

I should say, even though we were indoors, we wore hats and scarves and winter coats. That's the way it was.

He winked at me, which I thought was strange, since it was just the two of us. But then he winked again and I thought that maybe there was something wrong with his eye.

I was still holding the match out. I returned it to my pocket. We were probably fifteen minutes closer to summer. I started to cough, dry explosions.

"Are you laughing at me?" Shiloh asked.

I stumbled down to the kitchen to get a glass of water. I saw how, in the kitchen sink, a thin icicle had formed at the faucet. In the living room, I struck the match, applied it to the wood. Once again, heat beat cold in the battle for the plumbing's heart.

Food healed Alice. Her plump cheeks wounded me. Wrapping my arms around her, I could just barely contain her. This was different. She stopped buttoning her pants and the copper zipper yawned. She was magnificent. Dimples formed at the small of her back. Beneath our blanket tent, sweat gathered on the points of her breasts and painted my chest. I found myself a spectator to our pleasure. When she came to me, I didn't have the strength to stop her.

On a clear day, when the sun was just a nickel in the sky, Bill Legg came over the hill. He pulled in the driveway, honked, and rolled his window down. He left the engine running, the tailpipe puffing a trail of vapor. I waved from the porch and made my way to the driver's-side door.

"Business been slow?" I said. There hadn't been any snow in more than a week. I was concerned that he'd come out of his way.

"This isn't a full-time gig. I just subcontract for the county, Thomas. I'm not the kind of person who can sit at home watching the snow fall." He pointed across the seat at some unidentifiable gear. "Diving is my number one passion. I teach snorkel and scuba classes at the Burlington Y." A recent shave only made the pockmarks more pronounced.

"Oh," I said, remembering how to have a conversation, how to let someone talk.

"Yeah," he said. "I'll do anything underwater. Property recovery. Geological surveys. People think the Caribbean is the only place worth diving, but there's plenty to see around here. I saved a girl's life once."

"Really?" I said.

"She was ice skating when she broke through. The skates just dragged her to the bottom. I didn't get there until almost twenty minutes later. When I brought her to the surface, she was blue but they got her to the hospital and forced the life back into her."

"Wow," I said.

"She won't take baths anymore—isn't that something? She's been to the other side and back. Her mother claims she saw a golden merry-go-round inside the gates of heaven. The mystery of the human mind."

"So she wasn't really dead."

"She was dead when I had her in my arms." Bill gave a wave toward the house. "One of your friends?"

I turned around. Shiloh was staring out one of the kitchen windows. He turned and walked off.

"He's paranoid."

"What about?"

I didn't know what to say.

Bill raised his hand, to show he didn't need an explanation. "It's none of my business."

It was no problem, I told him.

He wanted to ask one more question.

Shoot.

"I have to ask a favor of you." He twisted around in his seat and started to overturn the supplies he had in back. He found a sheet of paper and passed it to me.

There was a grainy reproduction of a sketch of a girl's face. The words "Missing" and "Reward" were in the largest type. According to the poster her name was Joanna-Marie; she was five foot four and she weighed a hundred and fifty pounds. "Help us find our daughter," it said. "We love you very much. Ran away 4/72." There was a number to call.

"That's my baby girl," said Bill Legg.

I tried to pass the poster back to him. "I haven't seen her."

"Her mother and I didn't do anything but love her."

The poster was less than useless. The sketch looked like every girl. Why didn't they have a picture to reproduce? I said, "I'm sure she wasn't running away from you."

"Why do you say that?"

I didn't really know.

"Your parents know where you are?"

"They know I'm fine."

"I love my daughter, Thomas."

I said, "I'm sure she loves you, too."

"I apologize," said Bill. "I didn't come by with the intention of giving you the third degree. It can make you crazy, driving around. I probably don't have the disposition for it." He leaned over, reaching down where a passenger's feet would go. He lifted a grocery bag onto his lap. "I picked some things up at the store." He peeked into the bag. "It's real basic stuff. I'm no gourmet. Instant potatoes. Gravy. There're some cans of stew, pancake mix and a little bottle of maple syrup—that just seemed appropriate. Consider it a housewarming present." He hefted the bag onto the windowsill.

I saw the plump profiles of the cans through the paper. "I don't know what to say."

"I'm not one to make empty gestures. Take the food, Thomas. I don't expect anything in return. If appearances can be trusted, it's been a while since you've had a decent meal."

"It's really not that bad."

He held the bag out the window. "Take it."

I wrapped my arms around his gift. I thanked him.

"You can't hide it," he said. "Someone raised you."

He lifted a hand off the steering wheel, a casual good-bye. Then he backed out the driveway and drove over the hill.

No one was in the kitchen. I washed my face in the frigid water from the sink before carrying the bag upstairs.

She was feeding Phoenix cashews! The bird looked plump and shiny.

I dumped the bag's contents onto the bed. "Compliments of the infectious Mr. Legg."

She sorted the food, counted the cans, examined the box of pancake mix, read the label on the syrup. "This everything?" she asked.

No matter where she turned, Alice saw insufficient things. Her eyes came to rest on me.

"What?" I asked.

"Nothing." She reached out to touch my filthy hair.

We prepared two cans of stew, adding boiled dumplings to make it more substantial. Carrots and corn bubbled in the caramel-colored juice. The smell drew Shiloh from his room. He crept down the back stairs looking as though he couldn't remember how he'd come into the house. He took his usual spot at the table, tucked a dingy napkin in the neck hole of his shirt, waited.

"Valentine's Day?" Shiloh asked.

Alice thrust her thumb over her shoulder, Ask Thomas. The sour sea of my stomach threatened to back up into my throat. We each got a bowl and we sipped the stew from teaspoons. There was enough left for me to give Alice a second serving. Then I filled the pot partway with water to loosen whatever clung to the sides. While I waited for this to boil down to a gruel, I put a kettle on the stove to make hot water for the dishes. When the stew was done, I poured half into my bowl. Shiloh refused the other half.

"I'm not that hungry," he said.

Impossible. I tried to serve him regardless, but he took his bowl and delivered it to the sink. He folded his hands over his empty gut.

"Maybe he's got a secret stash," said Alice, pausing from blowing on her stew. "I wouldn't put it past him."

There could be no truth to what she said. Shiloh enjoyed sacrifice too much. All his heroes were martyrs or pariahs. He preferred suffering publicly to everything else. This might have been the core of his character. He had that kind of recklessness that marks boys who, for whatever reason, feel most themselves while being dismantled by bullies.

There was a scrap of paper in Shiloh's hand. Before he saw my intention, I snatched it away. Alice had written: *Thomas begged his friend for this.*

Shiloh wanted to explain the indignity of begging. But I wasn't interested in his argument. I tossed the note back to Alice.

She wouldn't look at me. After a moment she stood and went upstairs.

I wrote, *She lied to you. It was a gift.*

I finished my food and relieved Shiloh of his station at the sink, washed the dishes and returned everything to its proper place. I arranged the cans in pairs, to show Shiloh how we could eat like this for six more days.

He looked unmoved. "You two can share that stuff."

I tapped the pencil on the note, underlined *a gift*.

"She's just protecting the baby, Thomas. It's biological." Absently he pulled the hem of his shirt up. Where his skin went over his ribs, there were greenish bruises.

Remember, I wrote, *we rely on you.*

"Good." He turned to walk toward the living room. When his shoulder hit the doorjamb, it spun him around.

3
Appetite

On sunny days, when we remembered, we opened the curtains to let in the light. At night, or when the sky was overcast, the curtains remained closed. Days passed unobserved. With our wool blankets and shuffling feet, magnificent blue sparks leaped from us whenever we passed too close to wall outlets or plumbing fixtures. Alice learned to flinch every time I bent to kiss her.

I told her about the men on the roof. To her mind the sound of a window rattling in its frame denoted a master thief removing the pane with a suction cup. Where these specters came from I can't say, but there were shadows that retreated from me even as I walked through that dark house. My empty suit turned its back to me each time I entered the bathroom.

Alice taught Phoenix a trick where he flew to her shoulder from across the room. It was a strange ritual, Alice separating herself from this thing she loved in order to experience the wonder of its return. When the bird got bored, abandoned on some chair back or a volunteer's wrist, Alice's face cracked with tics. Then the bird might do something that endeared it to Shiloh and me, pluck a button from a shirt or bend over to study the ground between its feet.

Shiloh gave Alice a leash for the bird. There was a knotted handle for Alice. At the other end, the leash concluded with a loop which could be cinched around the bird's foot by tugging on some beads. It was a very thoughtful gift. Phoenix picked it up and flew it to the top of the closet door. The leash hung from the bird's beak like the plundered body of a snake.

"Last night," Alice started, "I caught Shiloh coming up from the basement. He stood there like a statue, like he was invisible or something."

I asked, "What were you doing downstairs?" It never dawned on me that she might be moving around at night, that she might be doing things.

"I was getting a snack when he came up the stairs."

Shiloh and I had taken to stirring baking soda into tap water to settle our stomachs. He could make my eyes glassy by whispering a word like "oranges." "What sort of snack?" I asked.

"Do you have any idea what he does down there?"

"I really don't think he's going down there anymore."

"Are you listening to me? I said he was down there. You have to listen to what I'm saying." Her bird was combing her hair with its beak.

"Maybe he was sleepwalking."

"If I find out he's doing anything stupid, I'll kill him."

The bird flew at me with its cloaking wings. I threw my arms up to protect myself. It lighted on my forearm.

"Don't do that," Alice said to one of us.

Shiloh called me into his room. He directed me to sit on the corner of his bed. He handed me the photographs. This was why we'd come to Vermont, he told me. He wanted me to see what he was talking about. But most of the pictures weren't from here. They showed brick-colored mesas, salt flats, city streets, a bowl of noodles. The intimate ones were missing. And I tried to remember what I'd seen in the pictures the first time I'd looked at them. The boy. He was in just two of the pictures I was being shown. In one he sat with his back to the camera, his face caught in profile. In the other picture Shiloh and the boy were peering into a skillet.

I pointed at the boy.

"We met outside the train station in Burlington," said Shiloh.

"He could juggle any three things. A quarter, an iron spike, and a handkerchief. That sort of grace leaves its mark on a person. He had an arrangement with gravity."

"What's his name?"

Shiloh wasn't paying attention to me. I bent down so my face was before him. I repeated my question, slowly shaping the words What. Is. His. Name?

"Alexander Stephen Mills."

I shook my head and touched my finger to his chest. "You are Alexander Stephen Mills."

"When I think of his face I don't know what to do. It's murder missing someone like I miss him. Can you believe someone that beautiful was in love with me?" From his shirt pocket he pulled out another picture. He handed it to me. Shiloh and the boy stood on the edge of a train trestle. In the world of the photograph, they were reduced to dashes of pale skin, knobby knees. Their toes curled over the edge of a wide steel beam. Shiloh looked at the picture taker while his friend looked down at the abyss beneath them.

Shiloh pulled the picture back. His fingernail traced over the emulsion. I expected him to say something. He licked his finger and cleaned up the picture.

I wrote this in his little pad: *What's in the basement?*

"I know you poked around while I was in the hospital."

That's not what I mean.

"Say it, Thomas."

The other side of the chimney.

He directed my attention to the picture. "The real tragedy isn't how people we love become invisible to us, or that we lose track of them, or that we ask them to wait for us but never return. The real tragedy is that before those things happen, you can't let them know how sorry you are."

This was the sort of thing Shiloh was capable of.

Alice was yelling in a place so distant that at first I thought it was a particularly insistent memory. I went out in the hall. The sound reached me from so many directions at once that I knew she'd gone outside. I went into our bedroom and pulled aside the window shade. Out in the driveway, between the wreck of the silo and her snowbound Plymouth, Alice was engaged in a tug of war with the crow. The bird strained at its leash, like a balloon on a string. The events leading up to this were easily reconstructed. Alice had gone out to promenade the bird and the bird had seen an opportunity. Their struggle now came down to wills: did the bird have the strength to snap the leash, and would Alice risk injuring the bird just to retain it?

I pulled Shiloh to the window.

"Poor bird," he said.

Alice stood on tiptoe. She couldn't imagine Phoenix wanted to be free of her and so she was stretching to see if she and it might reach an altitude that suited them both. The struggle loosed feathers that, after they'd escaped the flurry of the bird, floated slowly down.

"She's never going to let go of that thing," said Shiloh. "That would kill her."

All at once the bird stopped fighting. The leash went slack, arced, as the bird fell from the sky. It plunged into the snow.

"It had a heart attack," Shiloh said. "That little muscle just gave up and quit."

I shut the shade and the two of us went downstairs to mourn. I expected that Alice would require sublime attentions. She came in with the bird cupped in both hands. Its beak was opened in a manner recognizable as panting.

"Phoenix just went crazy," Alice explained.

Shiloh got real close and smelled the animal. "I hear it shrieking," he announced, but the bird was silent.

I felt the gathering weight of snow piling on the roof. Alice was a soft mountain in our bed. I wrapped myself in a blanket and wandered down to the living room determined to do something decisive. I built a fire, stacking the wood almost to the flue. I had had enough of conservation. I wanted to explore the viability of consumption. Getting by wasn't working for us. We needed another solution.

The greedy fire chewed up the logs. Fingers of flame reached outward, toward the mantel. I stripped down to my underwear. The fire was like a beautiful television.

I woke up with Shiloh throwing water on the sofa and me. The upholstery had begun to smolder. If his implausibly sensitive nose hadn't alerted him to the danger . . . he didn't want to guess what would have happened. The bracing water returned the edges to the room.

"You sabotaged my authority," said Shiloh, pointing at the paltry stack of wood I'd left.

Now we'd discover what would happen after the firewood ran out.

"Tell me," said Shiloh. "Who's the anarchist now?"

4

We Have Needs Innumerable

In bed I huddled against Alice's voluptuous back, against her summery skin. She stayed fast asleep, even when she spoke. I lost track of where we were. The boundaries between sleep and conversations were indistinguishable, and I lost interest in charting them. My mind was playing all sorts of tricks. I was sure people were entering and exiting the room. I didn't quite believe in them, but they were as real as me.

Bill Legg's truck came over the hill. It was dusk and the sparks that spit off the plow blade skipped along the frozen ground. I found my way to the road.

Bill had to bash around at the bottom of the hill to give the truck room to turn around. He drove past where I stood, slowed the truck to a stop, raised the plow, and let gravity tug him back. He unlocked the door and I moved to climb inside. My foot slipped from the running board and I almost fell on my face.

"You ever been in a truck before?"

"I've been in trucks."

"How come I don't see smoke coming out of the chimney?" He pointed at the two cold stacks of bricks.

"It's not so bad."

He handed a tissue over to me and had me blow my nose. My attempt at hygiene didn't satisfy him. "Hold still," he said. He reached over with another tissue and pinched my nose. "Good."

I felt embarrassed and dropped my chin. There were some weight belts and other scuba stuff on the seat, but that was it. "What's your daughter's name, again?"

"Joanna-Marie."

I thought, In this world a pretty name is no charm at all. And, at this rate, my baby is going to be bigger than me.

"You guys are all right in there?"

"We're okay."

He looked around the inside of the truck. There was all kinds of recent trash. "I didn't think to get you anything."

"No matter." I opened the door and lowered myself from the seat.

"Are they looking for you?"

I didn't know.

"You want to call them? Do you want me to call them?"

He wrote the number on a slip of paper he picked up off the floor. I loitered by the window. "What are you going to say?"

"What do you want me to say?"

"I'm not a jerk. I don't want them worrying."

"Is that your message?"

"You can say whatever you want, just don't tell them where I am."

"Right-oh," said Bill Legg.

Shiloh told me to bring the hatchet to his room. When I did he slid the drawers from his dresser, showed me how the joints were joined, told me which was maple and which yellow pine. I noticed one wall was now covered with an older wallpaper, antique-looking stuff with lilacs and bluebirds. I walked over to see just what was happening. Vertical scoring marked the plaster. A thin strip was already missing from the adjacent wall.

I tapped my finger on the wall.

He took out a Barlow knife and opened the short blade, held it up to where the wallpaper met the ceiling, and carefully pulled it down.

Next he eased the blade between the top layer of paper and the one beneath and, in one piece, removed the top layer from the wall. He examined the backing, showed it to me (what was I looking for?), then dipped it into a basin of water. It left a cloudy residue. He took the paper out and indicated I was to lick it. I wouldn't.

He draped the damp paper over his hand, inside out, and then scraped his teeth across it. A sticky goo built up, which his tongue cleared away. I rubbed a nail over the paper and sucked my finger. There was a sweetness—it tasted doughy, or like silt.

"Wheat paste," said Shiloh. "There was half a bag of the stuff left in the basement."

All of this, an entire wall so far, he'd been eating this stuff? Either to prove this wasn't a stunt, or because he was hungry, he scraped some more of this reconstituted glue. I made a disgusted face.

"It's the same stuff you ate in kindergarten. I'd rather it was corn or cucumbers. I'd be eating bugs if someone wasn't saving them for a bird. What we have here is a situation where our resources are limited. I'm just stretching our stores."

He went back to the dresser and hefted out a drawer. He punched the bottom out and collapsed the empty rectangle. I carried the pieces to the living room while he took the hatchet to the frame.

We burned the pantry shelves and the coat hooks from the mudroom. I unscrewed the porcelain pulls from the kitchen cabinets, collected them, and took the doors off their hinges. Both the dressers, the coffee table, a beautiful birch hat rack, Alice's chunky wooden beads, the three-legged stool, we converted everything to smoke.

"It's a fire sale," Shiloh said.

Alice hunched beneath the dormer-window curtain, like a photographer beneath a shroud. I joined her in the tight little space. It was the middle of the day. I felt the sunlight on my skin. Alice had her eyes shut. Looking out toward the field, I willed something to pass before me, something I might share with her. A few clouds sailed past, but none resembled anything. She breathed twin plumes of condensation on the pane. Now her eyes were open.

"Thank goodness," she said. "For a second I thought you were the mumbler."

She lifted the window an inch and let the cold air flood our feet.

"You can't be mean to him anymore."

The cold air came in like water. It reached our knees.

"So, the student reprimands the teacher." She pulled the window shut. "The other day he came in here to measure the bed for the chimney."

"He's doing what he thinks is best."

"Don't let him burn the bed."

She didn't seem to appreciate the spot we were in. I explained that Shiloh had reduced himself to eating glue.

"Tell me why he's doing that," said Alice. "You don't believe he's sticking around just to make sure we scrape by."

"I still love you, Alice."

With our faces so close to the glass, it was as if we were holding a conversation with our own ghostly reflections.

"Why did you say it that way?"

"How did I say it?"

"It's like you're accusing me of something."

"You have no appreciation for the things Shiloh and I have done."

"Shut your nasty mouth."

I walked straight away. I was too mad to speak.

Her voice reached me in the darkened room. "I love you more than I love myself," she said.

A Volkswagen Beetle came putt-putting over the hill and parked in the driveway. The driver honked the horn. Bill Legg had hung his truck up on a stone wall. This was his wife's car. I asked if he'd been hurt. Right there. On the ass? On his wallet. He'd busted the axle, snapped a ball joint, punctured the radiator, plus smashed up the grill and all the lights. This was why he had insurance. What happened? He'd swerved to avoid a herd of rabbits. A herd of rabbits? That's what he'd told Mrs. Legg; he'd actually fallen asleep. He was glad to see we had a fire going again. I counted two grocery bags on the backseats.

"I called your parents." He slid his hands over the steering wheel, pretending to take a sharp turn.

"You talked to them?"

He pulled the sun visor down. "What if I told you your father is in the hospital. Heart problem."

I said, "Oh, man. Jesus. Fran." The car was shrinking. I couldn't get any air.

Bill reached across and rolled down the window.

"Is he okay? Did you talk to my mother?"

"Yeah," Bill said. "She was upset."

"I'm wondering if it's my dad or my pawpaw. You have to take me to a phone."

"You worried?" Bill asked. He'd sort of turned his body toward me. "I mean, how does it feel?"

I was trying to get the words out, but tears were rocketing from my eyes. I fell apart, my hands shaking, my mouth just hanging open, so my teeth got dry.

Bill clapped me on the shoulder, craned my neck back with his thumb. "You got lucky," which even at the time seemed an inappropriate introduction to bad news. "Everyone's fine. I made the hospital bit up."

My fingers fumbled with the handle and I fell out of the car. I got my feet under me and slammed the door. As it bounced back I kicked it shut. I was in no shape to be jerked around. I sat up to my armpits in the snow.

Bill got out, too, but stayed on his side of the car.

"You needed to know what regret feels like." With his mittens he swept the snow off the car's roof. "Your parents have had all this time to question how they raised you, feeling like they're the bad guys. Yours is a generation of runaways. You got to know what it feels like when you're the asshole."

"Don't tell me who I am. Tell me what happened to your daughter. Tell me something you know!"

Leaning inside the car he took out the bags. He set them on the snowbank.

"We don't want that stuff," I said.

He got in the car and put it in gear. "Spare me, Thomas."

The mudroom door creaked. Alice shuffled out onto the porch. Bill raised a hand to her.

I went over to the passenger-side window. "I put a dent in the door."

"Remember, it's not my car. Watch yourself," he said, putting his arm over the passenger seat, as if he meant to back out. "Your mother begged me to tell her where you were."

"You didn't tell them anything?"

"I gave you my word."

I thanked him.

He shushed me. "I wasn't doing you any favors." He revved the engine and started up the hill.

Alice watched me gather the food. She held the door for me as I carried it inside. "Should we get the glue eater?" she asked. I felt too empty to eat. It was all for her. She fell on it, a wolf.

5
Idyll

I'd found a can of yams behind the stove. With fork and knife I cut them into pieces so small that I could have impaled one on each of the four tines of the fork and they wouldn't have touched.

"I want to let Phoenix go," Alice said.

That couldn't have been what she meant. That bird's antics were her only entertainment. Instead, she had to have anticipated that we might experience something like joy, watching the bird take to the air. It couldn't have been an easy decision for her to reach, this sacrifice.

But when I saw the bird, I knew that it wasn't generosity that guided her. From just beneath its chin, the whole breast was just the palest skin. The bird had preened itself bare. She didn't want to free it as much as she wanted to be free of the guilt of watching this pitiful animal.

Alice bit her lower lip. It appeared the bird was shivering.

"You can't let go of him like that," I said. "He won't make it."

Alice was crying.

I went looking for Shiloh. A strip of red cloth, the tie from a bathrobe, spanned the doorway to the basement. The treads from the stairs were stacked beside the fireplace.

I found him in his room, writing in his notebook. I told him I needed his help with a delicate situation.

He had Alice spread the crow's wings while he studied the bird. He cut a crude bib for the bird out of shirt cloth. He traced the bib onto a piece of possum fur. He cut this out and tried it on the bird. There were further fittings, fine-tuning. When he had everything the way he liked it, he sewed the ties together so they couldn't come undone, a crow in an apron. Did he think it would work? He knew it would work.

The hour was late. Alice thought we should wait until the morning before we released Phoenix.

Shiloh shook his head. "Right now."

I pointed at a dark window.

"The moon will be along. Besides, this is when they travel."

I asked Alice what she thought.

She didn't like the idea.

"It has to be now," said Shiloh, and, for some reason, I joined his camp.

Alice went upstairs to retrieve the leash.

Shiloh put his lips to my ear. "Tell me how a bird pulls feathers from under its own chin." His answer didn't come until my love was heading down the stairs. I heard her footsteps, but still I leaned closer. "She's gathering tragedies."

Alice fastened the loop around the bird's foot. "I can't wait all night for the moon to rise."

She didn't have to. A pale wash of light burnished the countryside. The moon was a gleaming sickle.

Alice buttoned the bird inside her coat. We went outside. The three of us cursing the sharp night air, the bird making its silent yawns, swiveling its head. The thinnest shadows undulated across the lumpy snow. Alice set the bird on her shoulder.

In that part of the country, you could see forever. We should have gone outside more often. But it was always colder than we could bear.

I clapped my hands to force the blood through them. The wind pushed through the bones of the trees.

"Take the leash off," said Shiloh.

Alice tried to do this one-handed, but experienced some difficulty. The crow, growing anxious, picked at its foot. She cawed to soothe the bird.

Alice was using both hands to free the crow when it leaned over and nipped her on the nose. She gave a startled shout as the bird unfolded its wings and took flight. I pulled Alice's hands away from her face. It got her right on the septum, a little snip. Droplets of blood fell from her upper lip and drilled into the snow.

"Why'd it do that?" Shiloh asked.

Alice bent down and made a snowball; she daubed at her nose. In no time the bleeding stopped.

The crow had landed on top of a bush across the road, the leash draping over the woody branches. I made to go after it, but Alice said the bird trusted her. She tried cawing and snapping her fingers, but it didn't return. "Shit," she said, throwing the bloody snowball down. She crossed the road, straddled the barbed-wire fence, and closed in on the bird. "Momma forgives you." She had almost reached the bird when it took off again, heading down the field. It flapped its wings a lot, but didn't gain much altitude, just sort of followed the slope of the ground. The end of the leash hung over the valley like a noose.

At first I was sure it would turn back before it reached the wall of trees at the top of the ravine. It couldn't make it over them. But it flew right into their midst, pumping its wings. I expected a branch to thread the dangling loop, for the flight to come to a vicious halt.

We watched the bird until it was beyond the trees, a black spot passing over snow.

Shiloh took the hatchet outside and knocked every other slat off the porch swing, leaving it a skeleton of its skeletal self. The gray wood burned hot and white, so we unhooked the chains, brought the rest in, an hour's warmth.

After moving the mattress and box spring to the floor, Shiloh and I broke apart the sleigh bed. It didn't come apart easily; the joints were mortise and tenon. Finally it succumbed to violence. What I did to the bed was one of the crimes for which Alice would never forgive me. She waited until it had gone up the chimney before calling me names. Thief. Impostor. Murderer. "Where has my Thomas gone, my boy?" she asked, cocking her head as if addressing her fretful bird, but the bird was gone.

Shiloh and I wandered from room to room, collecting everything extraneous and combustible. Our search kept leading back to the main staircase, the banisters, the newel post. Where would it stop? And when? He thought if we took our time, we could make it look all right. Saw everything flush. It would look modern. We demasted the stairs. It looked precarious. Alice asked that we dispatch her in her sleep before we continued disemboweling the house. Also, she wanted to know, was anything sacred? Yes, I replied, Shiloh was sacred. I was sacred. She was sacred.

6
Empty

I stumbled upon something odd in the entrance hall: Shiloh's legs in the abandoned fireplace. I thought it was a trick. I touched my toe to his trouser leg. He danced to the other side. Then he crouched down and peeked out. Arrows of soot streaked his face. "Go to bed, Thomas." He stood back up in the chimney. When I touched him on the back of his knee, his hand appeared, giving me an annoyed wave. I walked over to the narrow window adjacent to the front door and stepped behind the curtain. The stars were pinpricks. In the middle of the field, three thin deer, like animated sawhorses, gnawed at trembling shrubs. I heard Shiloh extract himself from the fireplace. He ducked inside the curtain. Our faces and hands floated around invisible bodies. That's just the kind of light it was—alpenglow, Alice called it. In the condensation I wrote *What's Parker got in the basement?* He reached up and jammed a finger in my eye. I bent over and covered my face. He towed me by my elbow into the kitchen.

He'd meant to grab my hair, he explained. He soaked our sponge and dabbed it at my face. The eye wasn't so bad, he told me. A little red. It looked as though I was crying, only just on one side of my face. He apologized until I accepted. He found his notebook and a pen. What did I know about the basement? I told him how it had occurred to me that his secret room must have a twin. That, I assumed, was why Parker had refused to leave before; either he hadn't finished setting it up, or else there was work he needed to do in there.

Shiloh said, "Don't tell Parker you know about that space."

What was he doing down there? I wrote.

Shiloh shook his head.

Do you know?

"It's why he left New York." All the while Shiloh made these imprecise adjustments, shifts and bobs, as if he were being buffeted by a swirling wind. "It's too easy to get caught up in these questions."

Which questions?

"That's what I am talking about, questions chasing questions."

We'd been stripped of everything. Maybe that's why he was reluctant to forfeit the last thing he'd held on to. *Bad things?* I wrote.

It was, he promised, beyond my imagination.

He sucked on his lip.

Explosives? Guns?

"It's beyond your imagination."

Drugs?

"It might be the most spectacular thing."

Is it money?

"Are you sure Alice is asleep?"

Are we going to go downstairs?

"Nothing's downstairs anymore." He gave me a long, appraising look. "Close your eyes," he said.

Shiloh left me alone in the room. I watched my hands on the kitchen table.

"Do you smell anything?" he asked when he came back. "What'd I say? Close your eyes."

I could see all the tiny mouths where the wood breathed.

"For God's sake, close your eyes. Use your hands if you have to. Now what do you smell?"

Smoke. Damp wool. That close human stain each of us trailed. Burned oil. Roses, maybe. Looking through my palms the world seemed pink. Roses.

He pulled my hands away from my eyes.

There on the table was a package furled in green canvas. The fabric was marked with soot—he must have been storing it inside the chimney. My first thought was guns, four or five of them wrapped up inside. And I decided they were long guns, Civil War–era rifles, bundled up like sticks. I almost didn't need to see them.

Shiloh walked over to the back stairs and checked to see if Alice was watching. He didn't just glance up, but stood there for a moment and waited. He turned to me. "Careful."

One corner was safety-pinned. Once I undid that I began to unroll the bundle. The more cloth I unwound, the more details came through. It was like shucking corn. At first the ears feel perfectly cylindrical, but as you go down through the layers, you discover the taper, the elasticity, at last the ordered rows of kernels, like perfect teeth. As I unrolled the cloth, I began to see the dimensions of things. It wasn't a collection of firearms. At the widest place, no wider than a clothes hanger, I found a pair of hips. And folded arms across a chest. Slightly bent legs, pointing toes. Yes, at the opposite end, a hard, smooth skull.

I turned around. Shiloh had his hands clasped together, a thumb vised between his teeth. He was bound with anticipation, like a person who has given an extravagant gift and is uncertain whether it will be appreciated. What? I asked him. The air was full of roses. He urged me to go on.

But I couldn't go on. So Shiloh pulled away the last wrap of canvas. Here was the boy from Shiloh's photographs. His jaw was a bit offset and his hair, which at one time might have been in a bowl cut, stuck up in some places and was plastered down in others. A fine nose came in a straight line off his brow. His eyebrows were full and dark and he had long eyelashes. Because of the way his jaw was fixed, his lips made a thin, crooked line; if the arrangement could be said to convey an expression, it would have been a cross between a smirk and a pout. He was not sleeping. There was a dead boy on our kitchen table. I put my hand on a cold wrist just to make sure. His skin showed a sort of olive cast. He probably had green eyes, I thought. It was hard to tell how tall he might have been, maybe five-six or five-seven. He had a slender, pale neck. A few dark hairs showed above the collar of a bleached, green shirt. The jeans he wore were a faded blue and as soft as flannel, with leather fringe sewn at the seams. One foot was in a white gym sock and the other was bare, as pale as the flesh of a radish. I couldn't take my eyes off him. I was thinking that someone must have been missing him.

"I told you he was beautiful," said Shiloh.

I was afraid Shiloh might peel open the boy's dead eyes. I felt that old fear, that death breeds death, that this boy drew me a little nearer the edge. But if it was an edge, how had this boy stayed so preserved after he had stepped across? I looked at Shiloh, at his battered hands and yellow teeth, his crooked nose with its knuckle hump. Living was the force that broke us down. And nothing was deader than the dead boy.

I kept my hands at my sides. Maybe I only imagined it, but I thought the boy looked something like me.

"He used to love me," said Shiloh, stroking his hand over the boy's leg.

"Parker did this?" I asked. But I might as well have been speaking to the boy.

Still the roses, faint, but pleasant, as fresh as rain. I couldn't be sure if the smell came from the shroud or the boy. My finger found a burned spot on the center of the boy's shirt. It looked as if he had walked into the lit end of a cigar.

"It isn't easy, the way I grew up, to trust a human soul. Remember what I told you, walking in the woods?" Shiloh adjusted the boy's shirt so that the hole in the cloth lined up with the hole in the boy, a puckered, black mouth. Tears made dark spots on the shroud. "He wanted me to admit that I needed him, but I refused. I told him I needed space to be. I grabbed my shit and left. I knew it was a mistake just as soon as I was out the door, but pride kept me from turning back. If I stayed away long enough, I thought, he'd forget what I had said. I camped out a couple of blocks away."

I watched Shiloh's trembling hands.

"The counterargument he came up with was irrefutable." Shiloh reached down and cupped the boy's naked foot. "It was just some gun someone had around for potting rats. He pulled the trigger with his toe. It should have been me who found him, but Parker came along. It wouldn't have been any good to have cops poking around the place. So Parker stuffed him in a seaman's bag and dumped him in an alley—problem solved. When I found out I made him take me to the spot. A mountain of garbage had piled up. I dug through it with my hands. I wanted something to say good-bye to. This is what we found. You know what you call that?"

I shook my head.

"You call it wonder." Shiloh walked over to the sink and filled two glasses with water. He handed one to me. I felt relief when I was certain that the second glass was for himself and not the boy.

We sipped the water and looked at the dead boy on the table. Even a person who was perfectly ordinary while alive becomes spectacular when dead. The dead are one of the few things society sees the magic in. There is no stronger taboo than a dead body. Our greatest crime: making a dead body. Here was a boy who had transformed himself into a body. And what an extraordinary body he was.

I didn't know where to begin.

Shiloh touched the dead boy on the lips. Then he turned toward me, saying, "That's my explanation." He started to wrap the boy back up. There was great solemnity to the operation. The rough cloth knew how to hold the boy.

I touched the back of Shiloh's hand. When he gave me his attention, I asked him the obvious question: Why was he here?

"Parker and I hid the body in a dumbwaiter shaft. I returned to my river home, because I thought he would be safe. But Parker couldn't leave things alone. It didn't dawn on him that where he saw a curiosity, some folks would see a proof of God. Those sorts of people can't be deterred."

Did I believe Shiloh? Was there something other than coincidence that caused us to arrive in New York when we had?

Your accident in the basement?

"I was building a trap for Parker."

Shiloh carried the boy into the entrance hall. I doubt he weighed fifty pounds. He propped the boy up in the empty fireplace. Then he stooped inside and hefted the boy up to a little ledge. How alone was Shiloh? How alone the boy? After extracting himself, Shiloh closed the damper.

Shiloh said, "The ringing in my head isn't just some empty noise. He's calling my name."

Did he mean the boy spoke to him, or that his mind kept the boy's voice alive? How could you tell a person the nature of the sounds in his head? I would never forget the sound of Alice calling me from another room.

Alice's body was conspiring against her. There was an itching inside her. She only knew one cure. Hers wasn't really a request. She slid beneath the sheets to work me up. I thought about the role of biology in history, men like me, my predecessors, a line connecting me all the way to the beginning of civilization. Creation, humiliation, and failure. She emerged smiling, covered me with her body. Can you feel it? she asked. I had a dream in which I might have been in a black boat on a black ocean. Beneath the surface the water teemed with silver fishes. Crazy, she said. Her elbows bowed my clavicles. I tried to lift my hips. She patted my cheeks with her fingers.

The fog of her breath. I stroked her back, felt the wet skin chill. I pulled the bedsheets above her shoulders.

The next morning I heard her crying. I didn't know whether to seek her in my unfurnished dreams or in my unfurnished home.

She lay on her back with her hands crossed over her chest. Her eyes were squeezed closed, but tears gathered in the wrinkled corners and followed trails into her hair. Tiny muscles jerked under her cheeks. Whatever it was, I promised to fix it. My voice triggered a real snorting fit. And why shouldn't she have been crying, imprisoned in the house, starved, her deaf antagonist and me. The constant cold exhausted us; it made our skin thick, obdurate. I made a point of avoiding the bathroom mirror because of the person I saw there: red gums, shovel-size teeth, blunt hair, and dumb eyes. (That vaguely handsome me whom Alice had recognized, tapped, chosen, where had he gone?) Poor Alice.

I promised her we would leave that day. As soon as she was ready, we would get in the car and drive. In two days we'd be in Florida, thawing in the Gulf. A straight shot, I didn't need sleep. We would travel there, she and I. Mangrove swamps and coconuts, alligators, DisneyWorld, pink grapefruit, mosquitoes. That healing water was just going to waste without us. We couldn't forget that we were free.

I told her I understood. She'd come up here to escape her ex-husband, to find a new life, to find her happy face. Well, she'd already accomplished those things. There'd be no dishonor in leaving. All I needed was for her to say the word. The word was "Go." I'd get her there, I promised.

Her body continued its convulsions. She swiped at her runny nose, knocked the scab off. Finally, though she continued crying, the tears stopped.

I thought her storm was passing.

Spring, I reminded her, was almost here. I lied and said I'd seen a cardinal skimming over the meadow.

She began to hyperventilate.

We kept a mug on the back of the toilet. I was going to dash in there to fill it. I swung my legs off the side of the mattress. My groin, my stomach, the tops of my thighs were speckled with flakes of dried blood. I studied the markings. She'd started menstruating.

What followed was an interval of silence. I didn't have the compassion to weigh her hurt above mine. We maintained a space between our bodies, a sagging of the sheets, perfect for a child. I searched for the word capable of containing our misery.

"Enough," Alice said.

I wrapped my arms around her shoulders. She put my wrist in her mouth and clamped down, not to hurt me, but so I couldn't let go. "Cry," I said, and she did. It wasn't a miscarriage. There'd been no unease, no discomfort. Instead, what we'd mistaken for fertility was the opposite—her cycle in suspension. This illuminated a paradox: had she not told me her situation, if Shiloh and I hadn't watched to see that she ate, then the illusion would have remained intact; she could have carried this ghost child, a child's negative, a conception of hunger, indefinitely (she would have continued to shrink as the months added up, six, nine, twelve). There had never been a child inside Alice, but now we had to mourn the children each of us had imagined who would never be resolved in flesh. And because my imagination is not strong, the girl I mourned looked a lot like Sonya.

Finally Shiloh knocked on the door frame, a series of taps signaling that he was coming in. Alice and I had been in the room for a few hours, days.

I waved him out of the room thinking that he would set Alice off.

He slouched in the doorway, his sideburns sticking out on one side and creased on the other. He looked like someone you'd meet beneath a highway underpass.

"I haven't seen you," he said. "I got lonely."

Alice had patience again. She shook her head. She gestured that she had to write him a note. He fetched pad and pen. She brought her knees up and wrote on this. I pushed my lips against her arm, not caring to see the words she chose.

"I'm very sorry, for both of you," Shiloh said. Surely he'd already heard a small voice calling him Uncle, and this was another silence for him to categorize.

I petted Alice's hair.

"Alice," he said, "I don't want you to change the way you're eating. We're fine like this. A few weeks and we'll have ferns and mushrooms. Trout and rabbit, too. You could be pregnant tomorrow. Right?

My beautiful friends." He looked at the two of us on the thin mattress (we'd smashed the box spring for its wooden frame). "I'm so sorry about the bed."

Shiloh took up the floorboards in his room, reducing the day to a cadence of hatchet blows. The square-headed nails whined as they were pulled from the floor joists. Beneath the floorboards you saw the dark lathing that had been tacked to the joists to support the plaster ceiling of the living room. You could see the history in the wood, the marks of the original tools. The planks were not pine, but oak, eighteen inches wide and the color of tobacco juice.

If a person was to go back now they wouldn't find ten houses in the state that still have first-growth oak. In the 1980s, when everyone was flush with cash, cabinet and furniture makers offered small fortunes for boards like those. They made them into highboys, wardrobes, captains' chairs, into dining tables and lustrous bars for ostentatious restaurants. That whole state was ransacked for the authentic, the historic. Wrought-iron door latches were shipped to prairie mansions in Ohio and Illinois. Antique glass was collected from the windows. On the oldest shacks there was a type of window that had a round glob of glass in the center of the pane, like the bottom of a bottle, and these were auctioned off to speculative Texans who, rich from oil, collected them in warehouses. Hotshot architects straight out of graduate school, kids who had designed houses without a curve or without a plumb wall or without a door, they were commissioned to incorporate this antique glass into definitive modern homes. Those panes became shower stalls; they bored through interior walls; they hung like snowflakes in the middle of huge, uncurling staircases. That whole world was slated for destruction; I still regret my part in it.

Sometimes snow came down, sometimes rain. To make time pass I engaged in random fasting, deciding some mornings to allow myself only water, or a single pancake. I had no appetite for what remained in the pantry, the hodgepodge of ingredients stacked across the floor. Alice feasted on brimming bowls of oatmeal and plates of buttered potatoes. She ate slowly, setting things on the floor beside the bed for long pauses, resuming meals hours later, even after the oatmeal had turned cold and rubbery, the butter congealed.

Down in the valley, tractors spread silage across the frozen fields. Clouds of crows gave protest. Their inflamed voices echoed across the valley. Alice, on the porch, cawed half the day. The birds corkscrewed thermals, disappeared into the atmosphere.

Shiloh took his skis out again, but the snow had changed in some unknowable way and now they refused to glide. Even coming down the hill exhausted him. He left them in the yard. In a few days they sank beneath the surface; the whiteness subjugated everything. If we left the door open, it would swallow the house. What could prevent it?

I returned to Alice and our empty bedroom. She chewed on knots of bread. Her hair had turned a dark auburn. Her patience evaporated. She pinched me in her sleep.

All I could think about was the ramrod stiff boy, propped inside the chimney. It occurred to me that everything that we'd come to think of as bad luck might be traced back to the entombment of the boy. Hadn't Alice been happier, Shiloh less serious? Wasn't the world warmer then, plus fertile? Didn't the air smell better? And weren't the partitions between our days and dreams more definite? Weren't there fewer terrors? Weren't we less guilty of smallness, of failures of character? Hadn't our faults seemed forgivable, less damning?

But in that bedroom Alice had yet to slip away from me; we still agreed to recognize each other. I put my body beside hers. "Never go away. Never leave me. Stay here forever," those old prayers. "Don't talk that way," she said. She might have meant that the time for pleading had passed.

"We'll have a baby," I said. More likely she'd give birth to a locust's husk or a walnut shell, something dry and empty. "I'm counting days," I told her. But when I looked she'd left the room.

On a warm day that set the snow melting, I wandered outside the house. A ring of green appeared where the dripping eaves cut through the drifts. Alice and Shiloh came out to see it with me.

"Do you smell skunk cabbage?" asked Shiloh.

"I think I smell roses sometimes," said Alice.

"What did she say?" asked Shiloh.

Nothing, I signaled. We smelled nothing.

At some point a horse had come over the hill—we only saw the trail of hoof prints in the thawing road. At the bottom of the hill, an irregular pyramid of droppings. A flock of small birds occupied the tangles of a shrub, and an owl hooted from the pines above the house. Pairs of squirrels chased each other, chattering, through the naked branches of the trees.

Over the empty field the ice crystals rose in spinning towers. I listened to the trees creak and the wind moan as it scraped over the roof. The animals had returned to their hiding places. Alice found me sitting in our bedroom closet. I may have crawled in to be near the boy, or to collect the black feathers that from time to time still trickled out.

"I can't get warm in bed," said Alice. A thin scab ran in dots and dashes across her cheek. I couldn't remember what had happened to her. Something had reached for her, a door hinge or a nail. The wound angled toward her mouth.

"How long have I been here?" I asked her.

She reached out and pinched my arm. "Did you hear me?"

I got up quickly, as if I had somewhere to be. I took a step forward but she blocked my body with her forearm.

She helped me unbutton my shirt. She helped me with my pants. She led me to the cold mattress and covered me.

"What," I said. "What?"

She inched her way down my body, kissing my shoulder, chest, and stomach. She pulled her pants off before she returned to me.

"Please," she said.

I imagined her body as a boat I might row away. I only wanted to move her. I was sweating for the first time in months. All my hair hurt. The mattress scuffed against the wall. Alice coughed into her fist. I reached my moment without drama.

Alice held my face to see how I wore humility. "It's okay," she said.

I kissed my girl's hands. "Of course," I said.

She stroked the seam of my chest.

Here was the moment we might have healed each other, if either of us knew the thing to say. It needed to be concise and beautiful. It had to offer a clue as to how we should live the rest of our lives. I still believed in such things. What could those words have been? Would they have sounded like a trumpet's blast or a trickle of water inside a cave? If you moved to Vermont in 1973, this didn't seem too much to ask for, one insight. All around us people were unlocking the secrets to themselves and they had luminous faces and long, wild hair. They were us. If we found this one thing, then we could go anywhere, even home.

For a few months we had lived among green flowers, between blue sky and bluer water. But now across the valley a black rift tore the lake in two and instead of blue water I saw a patch of starless space, a gaping mouth. The sky looked ancient, bled of vibrancy; the birds fled from it, puffed their feathers, waited on branches, sang three-note dirges, songs that echoed in the cathedral chambers of the earth. We'd become so low and dusty, so defeated, so poor. What had become of our graces? Where were the simple pleasures? We lived in a world of unadorned things. My hand moved over Alice's shoulder and slid beneath the blankets. And to touch her with the same hand that had touched the dead boy. I asked a pledge of her heart, that it continue its clenching. Yes, we are souls and spirits, but never more than a body—there is nothing else. Our most personal memories die with us, so what lives on is not us, but the person who carries it. In that way Shiloh is the dead boy and Alice, my most beautiful girl, is Sonya, and her crow is more human for her. And so I carry my sweet Alice with me. These many years later I can see her in the way I pour milk; when I whisper to a friend, I pretend their breath could be her breath. And sometimes still, in the shower, I hide my face in the crook of my arm and her fingers run over my ribs. No she would not recognize her boy; days and nights have changed my face. I've driven twenty hours to visit my pawpaw on his deathbed and once I have found him crying in the garage and once I have found him on a stainless-steel cooling board. And I have buried my mother on a cold day in May when yellow-throated violets hid in the green, green grass. And wandering about I have placed my favorite faces in crowds that could not hold them, just to suffer the disappointment.

I retrieved my clothes and dressed. I thought I might try to escape the house, if only for an hour. There seemed to be a toxic gas building up inside. It displaced the oxygen in your blood. I asked Alice if she was interested in going out. She thought it best that she remain still for a while. She clasped her pink knees to her chest.

I was afraid that if I took a swab and stuck it inside her, all I'd find would be dust and feathers, as though instead of impregnating her, I'd stuffed her like you would a pillow.

7
Hope

I walked past Shiloh's open door, and took the main stairs down. The light filtering into the living room told me we were suffering another bright and empty day.

Parker leaned back on one of the kitchen chairs with the heels of his boots resting on the edge of the table. A tinfoil boat of takeout food balanced on his lap.

"Hello, horndog," he said.

Parker wore his hair brushed apart, like two sheaves of black wheat. His mustache drooped over the corners of his lips. A bone necklace, like a string of babies' fingers, ringed his neck. Beneath his deep-set eyes, blue-green circles.

He set the food on the table and stood up. "What do they put in the water up here? I bet you've grown four inches since I saw you last." He clapped his hands on my shoulders. It seemed he was only measuring how much of me there was to bully.

A real raccoon coat draped over his shoulders, like the carcass of a dog.

How, I wondered, would I protect Alice and Shiloh and the dead boy? "You're not welcome here."

He peeked into the pantry. "This is some desperate living. Don't tell me you ate those other folks." He seemed to be in high spirits.

"They just left."

He studied my face. When he saw that I was serious, something like pity flowed between us.

"When?"

"I think it was October. They just took their things and left. Supposedly they had tax problems."

He went to look out the window. "She just gave you the car?"

I thought he'd been talking about the Sound of Music Commune. What I'd seen in his face was a type of awed respect for that person who, he thought, had accomplished all those exhausting tasks that together constitute survival. That he could think I was so capable and then having to correct him.

"I misunderstood."

Parker looked relieved. "Who had the tax problems?"

"DWG."

He resumed picking at his food. He did everything as though it were perfectly reasonable. His lips made a soft humming noise, like a machine at idle, just before or after it does the one task it was designed for.

"So what's the story with the cabinet doors?"

"We burned them."

"I got to hand it to you, you out hell's-kitchened Hell's Kitchen." Parker balled the tinfoil up. Walking over to the sink, he opened the faucet. He turned to me to show me that the water wasn't coming. He shook his head, as if he was ashamed.

All I wanted was to return to Alice in our bed.

"You shouldn't be here, you know."

Parker walked over to the back stairs. He opened the door an inch. "How's your little Alice?"

"Thomas," Alice cried, "who are you talking to?"

"Don't come down here," I answered, but I heard her getting up.

"Reunions," said Parker, returning to his chair.

He couldn't be allowed to stay. I knew what I had to do.

Alice flew down the main stairs. She had transformed from incubator into Fury. She was magnificent. She pushed past me and into the kitchen. "Get out of my house, you son of a bitch!"

"At least someone's been eating," said Parker. And then, "You're a cow!"

She turned around and marched out.

Parker dared me to deny it.

She came back clutching the fire poker.

Parker covered his head with his hands. With a furious swing Alice knocked a leg off his chair, dropping him to the floor.

"I had that coming," said Parker. "Never insult a woman's waistline. Lesson learned."

I told Alice to get Shiloh.

"It sure don't take much to rile you folks up." Parker stood up and brushed himself off. "I just have to pick something up, then I'll be on my way. Pardon me," he said, stepping past me.

The quilts over the windows, the empty spaces left by furniture we'd burned, the half-charred sofa and the sooty mouths of the fireplaces, this was a different place than he'd left. If he noticed that, he might have deduced that we were different people. At the top of the basement stairs, he yanked the red bathrobe tie from the doorway.

He found the light switch and flipped it up and down.

He stared into the dark.

"You burned the stairs." He shook his head. "You burned them. What about firewood? What about, I don't know, logs? I can't believe you people." With both his hands gripping the door frame, he lowered a foot in search of something that might support his weight.

"There's nothing down there."

Parker reached a hand out and shoved me away from him. "Just back up." He dipped the foot lower.

"He's not down there. The dead boy's not down there anymore."

He forgot about the basement for a second. Using his fingernail Parker scraped the plaque off a canine tooth. "Don't worry about that anymore. I'm here to take him off your hands."

Alice called down to me, "Shiloh's not in his room."

I told her to wait in our bedroom. I don't think I'd ever told her what to do before, but, just the same, she did as I asked.

"You must really pluck her strings," said Parker.

It didn't matter if the dead boy was just a dead boy. It didn't matter if he wasn't an argument for God. Shiloh loved him. I could not permit Parker to strip Shiloh of his most cherished thing. I would not witness my friend's humiliation. I told Parker, "I can't let you take the boy."

Parker stuck his lower lip over his mustache and sucked on the hair. "Sacrifice is overrated, kid."

We'd lived with stillness for so long that we never expected to move again, just as we never expected to find warmth or to escape hunger. Each of us had consigned ourselves to the house. We had forgotten that we might leave—a theory often employed to explain the origins of ghosts.

Parker seized me by my neck and pinned me to the wall. It happened in an instant and all my strength bled away. He lifted me off the ground. My heels drummed the plaster and my spine received this rhythm like a radio in an empty room. Neither of us knew how to improvise beyond that moment. If Shiloh hadn't appeared, Parker might have held me there even after I was able to imagine it.

"Stop!" Shiloh yelled, his awful, wounded voice.

Alice appeared on the landing above us. I watched her watching me. I hated her to see me subdued like that.

"Let go of him!" Alice screamed.

Parker released me. "Don't make me take the place apart," he said.

Shiloh began to recite an eclectic list of things: "All our money, a little girl, my hearing, Alice's fox, the clock, my tooth, the crow, their baby." It was an accounting of everything we'd lost.

"Take a look at yourselves," said Parker. He thought his will was immutable, but that house twisted everything.

All of our frustration with the house and the cold, all of our disappointments with ourselves and each other, these things found in Parker a target for their annihilation.

What must it have been like for Shiloh, in his silent world, to see us stepping forward? No, we had never given him his due, we had never thanked him for looking out for us, we had never been able to let him into our hearts, to love him, to accept that our fate and his were tied. But he had chosen the right people after all. In this moment we became his vengeful family. I knew what I was capable of.

It broke my heart when Parker hit me. His fist caught me on my forehead and drove me to my knees. The sum of my anger and determination didn't amount to anything. I watched Parker draw his black boot back.

But Shiloh decided to capitulate. He stepped in front of me. Parker could take the dead boy and drive away. And who knew what would happen then, when it was just the three of us and the ruined house, after Alice had seen me defeated, and I had seen her will quit, and after Shiloh had surrendered the last thing he cared for? How bankrupt we would be in that next moment! Slowly Shiloh raised his palms, in a recognizable gesture.

"I didn't ask for this," said Parker. He pointed a finger at me. "You brought it on yourselves, all of you. I've been a reasonable man my whole life."

Shiloh looked at his hands as though they, on their own, had come up with a compelling argument that he needed to consider. Then, no harder than you might push a child on a swing, Shiloh gave Parker a shove, high on the other man's chest. Instinctively, Parker took a step back to catch his balance, but there was nothing there to catch him. A quivering sound escaped his lips. Through the doorway it was a ten-foot drop to the basement floor. We heard a sharp crash followed by a whispery sound, like wind through leaves.

The three of us crowded in the doorway.

I stared into the dim space. Parker had come to rest on his stomach, but his face twisted back toward us. A few inches of water covered the basement floor. His hair radiated out across the water like rays of black light. The sound we heard was wafers of ice jostling to reknit.

"What have you done?" asked Alice.

"The pipes have burst," said Shiloh. "The house is no good for anyone."

8
Packing Up

With a screwdriver and pliers, Shiloh started Parker's van. The two batteries were linked with jumper cables. The sleeping engine woke. With new snow muting the sounds, the vehicles purred like giant cats.

Alice went upstairs while I wrestled the trailer from the frozen ground. I turned it upside down and towed it like a sled, out into the road.

Shiloh shuttled his things—the theme-park plans, the cigar box of photographs, the red toolbox, the bag containing the pieces of the mantel clock—out to Parker's van. I went to help him carry his green parcel across the snow-bright yard.

The plywood patch still covered the window I'd broken out. The mattress waited, a feather pillow in a crisp white case, blue flannel sheets turned neatly back. Red shag covered the ceiling and walls. A velvet curtain stretched between two brass rods, separating the sleeping area from the front. Something about the richness of the carpeting made the van appear noble or grand. I picked up a corner of the sheet so Shiloh might tuck the boy in. But that was not where he meant the boy to go.

Shiloh pointed with the toe of his boot at the platform the mattress rested upon. At the top I found a clasp. When I unfastened it the end of the platform swung down on a piano hinge. Maybe ten inches high, it served to raise the mattress above the humps of the wheel wells. The storage space contained the spare tire and a jack, a combination tire iron/lug-nut wrench, tent stakes, a raincoat stuffed in its own pouch, a baseball bat, an orange thermos, and, after we were through, the dead boy. Exhaust fumes hung in the air.

Alice opened our bedroom window and dumped our clothes into the yard. I gathered them all up. Everything went in the car. Dirty and clean, hers and mine, entanglements were preserved. I had an un-examined hope that we would never have to differentiate. I don't think one of us had a clue as to what we'd do next. But we'd follow this path as far as it took us and we'd make another decision when the time came.

The air, the trees, the birds, everything remained still.

Alice came out carrying my mangled suit.

What about the dishes and the pots and pans? What about the shovel and the trowel? "Do we just leave everything?" I asked.

She stabbed me with her eyes.

For some reason it fell upon me to give the place its final inspection.

Heading toward the house I noticed something, maybe a chim-ney's slight deviation from plumb. It appeared to me that the door had been forced open rather than swung, the way in forest cemeteries tree roots will unlock sealed crypts.

I would have liked to have seen a mouse, something fast and quick, a darting shape. The next person to come inside would infer that we had less than no respect for history or architecture, for that sanctity due every home. I could hear the distant sounds of the en-gines trying to blow themselves apart. It was rotten to be inside. Why do I forge my strongest bonds with objects? When my pawpaw died I was free of grief until I learned the fate of those clever silver shears he used to cut portrait silhouettes from black paper. Mary had given them to the man who shared his hospital suite, a machinist wasted by emphysema. It galled me to think of the stranger idly trimming his chin hairs with those fine scissors.

I couldn't bear to climb the stairs alone. I didn't want to see the ransacked bedrooms. Even worse, I didn't want to look outside to see my friends waiting by the cars. I wanted to see the green pasture and the hunting fox and I wanted to turn from those things to Alice in our fantastic bed.

On a whim—if it is a whim when there is no lightness—I ducked into the fireplace. I found that faint ocean sound that survives in seashells. My nose detected the perfume in the close air. When my back scraped the wall, I thought the fragrance grew. Had it permeated the soot and stone? Above, the only thing that I could see was a perfect square of gray, one perspective on the infinite. A few snowflakes drifted down, heavy with light.

9
Escape

The Plymouth's transmission refused to slot in reverse. Every time Alice eased off the clutch, it produced a metallic gurgling.

Misdiagnosing the problem, Shiloh positioned himself in the road and beckoned with his arms, as though she were backing up a tractor trailer or bringing a plane out of a hangar.

I put my shoulder to the bumper and, though my feet kept skating out from beneath me, I got the car moving. At the end of the driveway, I watched Shiloh reach inside the open window and help Alice cut the wheel. I wasn't paying attention to the task at hand. When she tapped the brakes, it caught me by surprise. I flipped over the hood like a stunt man. Then Alice was out of the car and running toward me.

"You boob!" Shiloh yelled.

In her rush to attend to me, Alice forgot to set the parking brake. Watching the car pick up speed, we consigned it to the bottom of the ravine. This is when it hit the trailer. The tow bar became wedged beneath the car and things came to a gentle halt. The clouds issuing from our mouths dispersed.

Shiloh brushed the snow from his clothes, then he walked over and kicked the trailer hard enough to make it shiver.

"Why do you always root for me to fail?" Alice asked.

I wrapped my arms around her waist and picked her off the ground. She kicked and clawed me as I stumbled beneath her weight. My face pressed against her spine. I was privy to her warmth and smell. (How much better to love her than a dead boy.) She screamed for me to put her down. (Complicity is the grace of a dead boy.) My hat slipped below my eyes, or I didn't want to see. I held her aloft despite her threats. My arms circumscribed my happiness. Still she defied me.

"This!" I said—I have no idea what I meant. I tried to toss her higher, to get an arm beneath her legs. My feet hit the snowbank and I fell forward. We dove beneath the snow. I had to let go of her to breathe.

Shiloh walked around the van, sweeping the bumpers clean. "Tear each other apart," he said.

Alice got in her car and drove a few feet up the hill, so we had room to connect the trailer and its hitch. I fixed the cotter pin and safety chain. Shiloh reached inside the trunk and spliced the brake lights from the trailer to the brake lights for the car.

I raised my arms to say, What else do we do?

There was something desperate in Shiloh's eyes. He leaned inside the van and lifted something out.

It was a grasshopper pie, seven-eighths intact. Parker must have been saving it for dessert. Shiloh passed three pieces out. I inhaled the sweet gas of crème de menthe. The mint like some perfect compromise of ice and spring. We ate the dead man's food with pinches of snow and crumb. Our mouths hung open. We bared our shiny teeth. Shiloh brushed his mustache absently before serving up the rest. I couldn't remember the last time I'd tasted something sweet.

Shiloh ran behind the house. Neither Alice nor I moved.

I wondered how much longer it would take before winter broke, how long before the deep snow coursed through the ravine as melt-water. How long could the house shelter its icy heart?

When Shiloh returned he carried two coiled lengths of garden hose. "You're going to have to siphon gas," he said.

There were all sorts of things we would need to do to continue to survive.

"We'll get money," said Alice. Her complexion was like flour. "I'll call my sister."

I was worried about myself, about where I'd go next. When I looked up, Shiloh said, "We're on different paths, partner."

My head disagreed.

Shiloh stood, resolute. "Alice, if someone asks you what happened, what are you going to say?"

She didn't answer him.

"It was an accident," I said. "Parker just fell."

Shiloh kept his eyes fixed on Alice.

"You pushed him," said Alice. "He pushed him."

10

Shiloh

Shiloh sat on the van's bumper, his head resting in his hands.

"He probably saved our lives," I said.

Alice reached out a hand and stroked Shiloh's back.

"I'll look you up sometime, Mahey," said Shiloh, but I've never seen him since.

He stood up and wrapped us in his arms.

I was searching for the perfect thing to say as he climbed into the van.

As soon as he'd shut the door, the wheels began to turn. Where could he go in this world?

"We have to follow him," I said.

Alice and I got in her car.

Patches of gray ice glinted on the road. Twice the wheels began to spin, we lost our speed, and the house pulled us back, but on the third try, we made it out.

In the light snow we followed the only set of tracks. Shiloh kept to secondary roads. A few times he veered toward one side of the road or the other. It seemed he might be driving very fast, or eating. All of a sudden we were in that empty valley where Alice and I had come upon the overturned van and the girl who'd bitten her tongue. A steady wind scoured the snow from the road. On an otherwise frozen pond, a flock of geese crowded into a section of open water. Across the valley Alice and I thought we saw something moving. If it was Shiloh, then that was the last time we saw him. Then we were back in the foothills where the trees could tame the wind. A few inches of snow covered the road, but there were no tracks before us.

11

Alice

The Western Union office was located in a grocery store. It shared its desk with the customer services counter. Alice called her sister. It's the nature of such calls that you can ask for anything so long as you show contrition. Alice told her sister that she'd just come through "a disaster." I stood beside her in my jerry-rigged shoes, shaking my head. For two hours we sat on these hard plastic seats, looking at all that food we didn't have the money to pay for. People walked around sharing their bored faces with each other. Alice fell asleep beside me. She snored softly, her head resting on her shoulder. If Shiloh had driven past, I would have gone with him. It would have been a sacrifice, but I could live with it. The manager came over. "What happened?" he asked, pointing at his own forehead. I said, "I got punched." He nodded toward Alice. "I'm not supposed to let people sleep in here." But he didn't ask me to wake her.

The money came. We tried our best to spend it, but everything we wanted totaled under seven dollars. We ate in the car in the parking lot. It was cold, but Alice left the engine off. The world was a noisier place than we remembered and we couldn't bear to hear anything, not even our own voices. And I wanted to make love to her, but I didn't know how to tell her. How sad is that? I leaned over and kissed her fat face. She started the car.

By the time I took my turn behind the wheel, it was the middle of the night. My perception was cloaked by pure exhaustion. At some point I decided Alice and I were back in our old bed. The glow of the headlights was, in my mind, moonlight. I was grateful to be able to return there. I was only dimly aware of our velocity and the concrete things we passed.

An air horn returned me to my situation. Just like that, the bed went up the chimney again.

There was a silence in the car, as though one of us had just screamed. Alice sat there, her eyes wide open, stretching the muscles in her jaw.

"Why are you squinting?" she asked.

"Can you read all the road signs?"

"Do you need glasses?"

"I might."

"If you do, get contacts—you have such a fine face."

I said, "Do you think you could be pregnant?"

"Let's not talk about this."

I reached over to hold her hand.

"There'll never be a baby."

"But you don't really know."

She yawned.

The road stretched before us in taillights.

"Maybe Parker loved him," she said. "Why else would he come back?"

I didn't tell her about the boy.

"You don't even know why you're mad at me."

I kept my thoughts to myself.

"Did you expect that the three of us were just going to start all over again?"

"Do you know where he'll go?"

"He'll find someplace, I don't doubt it."

What would that place look like?

All these quiet houses slipping by in the night. The world reduced to cones of light and the things they passed over. "Where am I driving to?"

She didn't answer me.

"It was an accident with Parker," I said. "He didn't mean to hurt him."

"I saw what I saw."

"Can I ask you one more question?"

"You don't have to say it like that."

I looked at her beautiful fucking face.

And then she did scream.

But we lived.

*   *   *

I picked oranges. I took a job in a bakery, but didn't last a week. For a while I lived with a girl in a giant house on an island—her father patented a way to grow lettuce hydroponically. She and I would make a pitcher of margaritas and take a pontoon boat out onto the lake. We had many inconsequential accidents. Halley pioneered ways to help disabled kids communicate with horses. I met her at a poolside concession I managed outside Phoenix, Arizona. When it came to cursing, I've never met her equal. We make choices and then we make other choices. That's what I'd like to tell you, Alice. And it's warm everywhere I go. Tina and I slept on a green air mattress, like a square lily pad, in the midst of a garden of yellow flowers. There were these seedpods that looked lighted from inside and burst all of a sudden, triggering other seedpods. In the morning we hosed off on a wooden pallet to keep the grass from getting muddy. Alice, I missed you always.

We reached the Ohio in a misting rain. A raft of dark barges hugged the near shore. The bridge rose before us like a photograph of a dream. Seagulls perched in the ironwork to spread their soggy wings. Sodium floodlights in the guy wires seemed to manufacture the bridge as much as illuminate it, a yellow, caustic light. The tires made a humming sound. Alice's car shimmied over expansion joints that looked like enmeshed steel teeth. On the dash the radio's station-indicator light sparked from time to time. The roadway still angled up. We drove through the ceiling of the clouds and entered a silent world of rhythmic light. Before and behind were indistinguishable. We flew above the river. My heart leapt in the moment after we began to fall, before the bridge caught us.

Acknowledgments

For their support during the writing of this book, I would like to thank the Iowa Writers' Workshop, the Fine Arts Work Center in Provincetown, and the Michener/Copernicus Society of America. Thanks are also due to Bill Clegg, Tom Griffiths, Terry Karten, Ted Lasala, Salvatore Scibona, Zach Tussing, and, most significantly, Sarah Braunstein.

About the Author

Justin Tussing's short fiction has appeared in several publications, including the *New Yorker*, *TriQuarterly*, and *Third Coast*. A graduate of the Iowa Writers' Workshop, where he was also a Teaching/Writing Fellow, he has received fellowships from the James A. Michener/Copernicus Society of America (in support of this novel) and the Fine Arts Work Center at Provincetown, Massachusetts. He is a former director of the Iowa Young Writers' Studio and, from 2001 to 2004, he was Writing Coordinator at the Fine Arts Work Center. Justin Tussing lives in Portland, Oregon. This is his first novel.

TUS   Tussing, Justin.

             The best people in
             the world.

$24.95

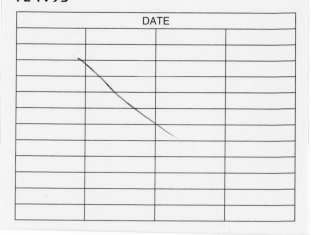